John Hervey Bristol

Diary, with extracts from his Book of Expenses, 1688 to 1742

With appendices and notes

John Hervey Bristol

Diary, with extracts from his Book of Expenses, 1688 to 1742
With appendices and notes

ISBN/EAN: 9783337118488

Printed in Europe, USA, Canada, Australia, Japan

Cover: Foto ©Andreas Hilbeck / pixelio.de

More available books at **www.hansebooks.com**

THE DIARY

OF

JOHN HERVEY,

FIRST EARL OF BRISTOL.

WITH EXTRACTS FROM HIS BOOK OF EXPENSES,

1688 TO 1742.

WITH APPENDICES AND NOTES.

WITH FIVE ILLUSTRATIONS.

———•———

Wells:
ERNEST JACKSON, 5, HIGH STREET.

1894.

PREFACE.

THE Manuscript Volume at Ickworth containing the Diary and Expenses of John Hervey, first Earl of Bristol, is a folio, 17 inches by 10½, of 231 leaves, bound in limp boards covered with brown vellum. On the outside is written, By Book of Expenses and Disbursements beginning the 1st November, 1688, and ending at Lady Day, 1742. As the book lies open, the Diary is on the left hand side, the Expenses on the right. The Diary being a very skimpy one, that page is often not half filled, while the right hand page is filled as close as it can be. The whole of it is in the large, clear writing of Lord Bristol, and shows him to have been a thorough man of business, methodical, orderly, and industrious. I have put all I know about him into the Preface to his Letters, and will not repeat it here. I have printed the Diary verbatim, but have only given extracts from the Expenses, putting them under 14 heads.

There only remains to express my thanks to Lord Bristol for allowing me to have the book in my charge for so long a time ; also to those who have helped me to draw up the list of portraits in Appendix No. 16 ; also to Mrs. George H. W. Hervey for two excellent sketches, as elsewhere explained.

S. H. A. H.

Wedmore Vicarage,
    Somerset,
  August, 1894.

ILLUSTRATIONS.

CONTENTS.

JOHN HERVEY'S DIARY.

1 6 8 8 .

NOV. 2.—A proclamation to suppress ye Prince of Orange's declaration.

NOV. 3.—Ye Dutch fleet discovered between Dover and Calais.

NOV. 4.—Ye Prince of Orange birthday.

NOV. 5.—He landed his army.

NOV. 6.—King James puts out a declaration.

NOV. 16.—Ye Bishop of Exeter was translated to ye See of York for leaving Exeter upon ye approach of ye Prince of Orange.   *(Note* 1.*)*

NOV. 17.—Was published an account of ye Dutch forces.

NOV. 22.—King James put out a proclamation of pardon at Salisbury.

NOV. 28.—King James ordered writs for ye setting of a Parliament on Jan. 15 following.

NOV. 29.—Prince George came to ye Prince of Orange at Sherbourn Castle.

DEC. 8.—Lord Hallifax, Nottingham and Godolphin sent proposals to ye Prince of Orange from King James.

DEC. 9.—Ye Prince of Orange answered them.

DEC. 11.—King James went from London towards Gravesend in a little boat.   Same day ye Lords spiritual and temporal made a declaration at Guildhall.

B

DEC. 13.—On Thursday morning about 2 of ye clock there was an alarm that ye disbanded Irish in a desperate rage were approaching London burning houses and putting men women and children to ye sword as they came along.

DEC. 15.—Ye Prince of Orange entered Windsor Castle, erecting his standard there. The same day King James removed to Rochester, in order to return to London, and the next day being Sunday ye 16th he returned to Whitehall about five afternoon.

DEC. 16.—Lord Feversham carrying a letter from King James to ye Prince of Orange was committed to the Castle of Windsor. Ye same day a proclamation against ye mobbs plundering of houses.

DEC. 18.—King James went down again to Rochester, and ye same day ye Prince of Orange came to St. James's about three in ye afternoon a very rainy day : King James continued at Rochester till ye 23th, and about 2 in ye morning withdrew himself, taking only Mr. Ralph Sheldon and Mr. Delabady, went to Dover and embarqued for France.

DEC. 22.—Ye Lords spiritual and temporal assembled at Westminster, and ye 25th sign'd an address to ye Prince of Orange, desiring him to take ye administration of publick affairs civil and military untill ye meeting of ye Convention to be on ye 22th day of January next, in order to which they signd an other address ye same day, that he would cause his letters to be written to ye severall Counties that they would chuse Representatives to be present at Westminster on ye foresaid day.

DEC. 26.—All Commoners who had serv'd in any of ye Parliaments of Charles ye 2d were desired to attend ye Parliament, and about 160 coming to St. James's to him, and he acquainting them with ye state of things, desir'd them to repair to ye Commons house at Westminster, where they chose Powle their Speaker, then sending to know what the Peers had done, concurred with them in their two addresses.

1 6 8 9 .

JAN, 8.—A declaration against quartering soldiers in private houses by ye Prince of Orange. The Treasury had (as was said) but £40000 in it, wherupon ye Prince of Orange desir'd ye City of London to advance a a summe of money for his present occasions, and ye 10th of January they agreed to lend an £100000, but it being raised by way of subscription amounted to above £150000,

JAN. 22.—Ye two Houses mett, ye upper house (there being no Lord Chancellor) chose Marquiss Hallifax their Chairman, and ye Commons Hen : Powle their Speaker.

JAN. 28.—Ye Commons passd a vote that King James ye 2d having endeavour'd to subvert the constitution of this Kingdom by breaking ye original contract between King and people, and by ye advice of Jesuits and other wicked persons having *violated* ye fundamental laws, and having withdrawn himself out of this kingdom, have *abdicated* ye Government, and that ye Throne is therby become vacant.

FEB. 6.—Ye Lords concurr'd with ye vote ut supra, but on ye 29th of January ye question was put in ye house of Peers whether a Regency with ye administration of regal power under ye name and stile of King James ye 2d, during ye said King's life, be the best and safest way to preserve ye Protestant religion and ye laws of ye kingdom ; upon which ye House divided, (Contents 48, Non-Contents 51.)

FEB. 12.—Both houses fully agreed all things in dispute between them, and that day put out a declaration wherin they declar'd that William and Mary Prince and Princess of Orange are and that they should be declar'd King and Queen of England, France and Ireland, and that the sole and full exercize of ye regal power be only in him ye said Prince. The same day her Royal Highness arrived in ye Thames.

FEB. 13.—Lords and Commons order'd them to be proclaim'd King & Queen.

APRIL 11.—Was ye Coronation day of King William & Queen Mary.

MAY 1.—His Majesty gave ye royall assent to an act for raising money by a Poll and otherwise, towards ye reducing of Ireland. Also an Act for preventing doubts and questions concerning ye collecting the publick revenue. Also an Act to enable younger Cook Esq. to sell lands to pay his debts, and provide for his younger children.

MAY 3. Ye great Seal of England was found at ye bottom of ye Thames by a fisher-man in a red bag between Lambeth and Vauxhall, and presented to King William : dropt by Queen Mary King James's Consort as she was crossing ye river to goe to France with ye Prince of Wales.

MAY 8.—Was our hearing before ye House of Lords upon our appeal from 2 Decrees obtained in Chancery by Lord Holles, and ye 9th they made an order reversing Lord Jefferys.

MAY 9.—A Proclamation requiring all Papists to remove 10 miles from London.

MAY 13.—A Proclamation for preventing of false Musters.

MAY 14.—I went to Aswarby in Lincolnshire.

MAY 24.—His Majesty gave ye royal assent to an Act for exempting their majesties Protestant subjects dissenting from ye Church of England from ye penalties of certain laws. Also an Act for anulling and making void ye attainder of Alicia Lisle widow. Also an Act for ye sale or leasing ye capital Mesuage late Henry Coventrys Esq. in Piccadilly.

APRIL 26.—Ye Commons presented an address to ye King that he would please to prohibitt all commerce with France, and assuring him that when he thought fitt to declare warr with that King, they would give him such assistance as should enable to goe through with the same.

APRIL 25.—A Declaration by ye King and Queen encouraging French Protestants to transport themselves into this kingdom. Same day a

Proclamation prohibiting ye importation of any manufactures or commodities of ye growth or manufacture of France.

JAN. 16.—Paid Lady Carr in full for ye 3 black Coach horses and all due to her at ye same time from my wife, her debt being forty eight pounds, 5 shillings, and mine thirty pounds, in all seventy eight pounds and a crown.

JUNE 17.—Sister Porter died. *(Note 2.)*

AUG. 12.—Pope Innocentius ye 11th died, aged 78 years, he held ye Pontificate 12 years, 10 months and 22 days.

SEPT. 5.—Ye Mayor, Commonalty etc of Londonderry presented an Address to their majesties.

SEPT. 11.—Mentz was surrender'd by ye French to ye Duke of Lorraine, General of that part of ye Confederates forces.

SEPT. 26.—A Proclamation by ye King for ye setting of ye Parliament on ye 19th of October next.

OCT. 3.—My dearest wife was brought to bed of a daughter, being Thursday, about three quarters after noon-day.

OCT. 6.—Peter Ottoboni a Venetian, aged 79 years and 5 months old, was chosen Pope, taking ye name of Alexander the 8th. The same day and year ye Corporation of Bury St. Edmonds in Suffolk presented an address to ye King William at Newmarkett by Lord Cornwallis then Lord Lieutenant of that County.

OCT. 12.—Bonne was surrenderd upon Articles by ye French to ye Duke of Brandenburg, General of that part of ye Confederates Army.

OCT. 13.—Ye Pope was crowned.

OCT. 31.—On Thursday my daughter was christened and named Isabella Carr Hervey; answer'd for by my Father Sir Thomas Hervey, Lady Carr, and my sister Elwes, Baptized in ye King Street house by Mr. Thomas.

NOV. 14.—A Proclamation by the King for ye apprehending Coll :
Edm : Ludlow, ye reward promisd £200.

DEC. 16.—His Majesty gave ye royal assent to an Act granting to
their Majesties an aid of two shillings in ye pound for one year. Also an
Act declaring ye rights of ye subject and settling ye succession of ye
Crown. Also an Act for naturalizing William Watts an infant. Also an
Act declaring John Rogerson to be a natural born subject of this Realm.

DEC. 23.—His Majesty gave ye royal assent to an Act to prevent all
doubts and questions concerning ye collection of ye publick Revenue.
Also an Act for punishing officers and soldiers who shall mutiny or desert
their Majesties Service ; and for punishing false musters. Also an Act to
enable ye Lord Viscount Hereford to make a Joynture upon his marriage
with Mrs. Elizabeth Norbourne notwithstanding his minority.

1690.

JAN. 16.—His Majesty gave ye royal assent to an Act for a grant to
their Majesties of an additional aid of twelve pence in ye pound for one
whole year. Also an Act for ye charging and collecting ye duties upon
Coffee, Tea and Chocolate at ye Custom house. Also an Act for setling a
maintenance on ye children of Sidney Wortly, alias Mountague, Esq. in
case his wife survived him.

JAN. 27.—His Majesty gave ye royal assent to an Act for ye review of
ye Poll bill, and for an additional Poll. Also an Act to prevent vexatious
suits against such as acted in order to their bringing in their Majesties,
or for their service. An Act for ye better security and relief of ye Irish
Protestants. An Act to discharge ye Duke of Norfolk upon payment of
certain summs of mony to ye Lady Eliz: Teresa Russell, wife of
Bartholomew Russell Esq. An Act to enable ye Earle of Radnor to make
a joynture to his wife, and to raise a sum of mony out of divers lands and
tenements in Cornwall. An Act to enable Thomas Edon Esq. to sell lands

to pay his debts and to make provision for his wife, and for his children in case he shall have any. Also an Act to enable William Batson Esq. to sell lands in ye County of Oxon, and to purchase and settle an estate in ye County of Suffolk to ye same uses. His Majesty first made a speech to both Houses of Parliament, and then prorogued them to ye 2d day of Aprill following.

FEB. 5.—Mrs. Tyrell married Mr. Auchmouty. *(Note 3.)*

FEB. 6—A Proclamation for dissolving the Parliament and declaring ye speedy calling a new one.

FEB ?—A Proclamation for a general fast to be observ'd thro out England on the third Wedensday in every month during the Warr in Ireland etc.

FEB. 27.—A Proclamation requiring all seamen to render themselves to their Majesties Service.

MARCH 1.—An order of Council to ye Lords Commissioners of ye Treasury (Monmouth, De la mere, Godolphin, Sir Henry Capell, Richard Hampden) and to ye officers of ye Customs in Ireland, that Corn and Meal be permitted to be imported into that Kingdom from Scotland duty free till further order.

MARCH 20.—The Parliament mett att Westminster.

MARCH 31.—John Wadkins died 11 at night at London.

APRILL 1.—Dear wife and self went to Bury.

APRILL 9.—Return'd from Bury.

APRILL 18.—Ye Duke of Lorraine died at a Convent about five miles from Lintz in the road to Vienna.

APRILL 20.—My uncle Reynolds died at St. Edmond's Bury in Suffolk, and was buried at Bumsted in Essex. *(Note 4.)*

APRILL 23.—His Majesty gave ye royal assent to an Act for granting to their Majesties for their lives and ye life of ye survivor of them, certain impositions upon beer, ale and other liquors. Also an Act for raising money by a Poll, and otherwise, towards ye reducing of Ireland, and prosecuting ye war against France. Also an Act to supply a defect in a former Act of ye last Parliament, for ye sale or leasing of a house, late Henry Coventry's Esq. in Piccadilly. Also an Act to illegitimate any child or children which Jane, ye wife of John Lewkner Esq., hath had or shall have during her elopement from him. Also an Act to enable John Wolstenholme Esq. to sell lands for payment of his debts.

MAY 2.—My dear wife and self went to Bury, and that day his Majesty gave ye royal assent to an Act for granting to their Majesties a subsidy of Tunnage and poundage, and other summs of mony payable upon merchandises exported and imported. Also an Act enabling ye sale of Goods distrain'd for rent, in case ye rent be not paid in a reasonable time. Also an Act to enable Algernoon Earle of Essex to make a wife a joynture, and for raising of monys for payment of £6000, borrow'd to make up ye Lady Morpeth's portion, and to make a settlement of his estate on his marriage. Also an Act for ye making some provision for ye daughters and younger sons of Anthony Earle of Shaftsbury. Also an Act for ye sale of ye capital messuage or mansion house of Harleford and Mannor of Great Marlow, and other lands in ye County of Bucks. Also an Act to enable Sir Robert Fenwick to sell lands for payment of his debts. Also an Act for confirming a settlement made by Sir Hugh Middleton Bartt. for a separate maintenance for Dame Dorothea his wife, and for other trusts, and for ye better enabling Trustees to sell part of his estate for payment of his debts. Also an Act whereby ye freehold and inheritance of ye Mannor of Loleworth and the advowson of ye Church in ye County of Cambridge, and divers other lands and hereditaments in Lollworth aforesaid, and in Long-Stanton in ye said County, are vested in Altham Smith of Grays Inn in ye County of Middlesex Esq. and William Gore of London Merchant and their heirs in fee-simple in possession to the use of them and their heirs in trust for John Edwards of Debdon Hall in ye County of Essex Esq. and his heirs, to ye intent ye same may be sold. Also an Act to enable Sir Humphry Forster to settle and dispose lands. Also an Act to enable Thomas Berenger Esq. to sell lands for payment of his debts. Also an Act to vest the estate of Cadwallador Wynne Esq. in Trustees for ye payment of his debts. Also an Act for ye naturalizing David le Grand and others.

MAY 14.—Return'd from Bury. On Wedensday May 14 Charlemont surrender'd upon Articles to King William & Queen Mary.

MAY 20.—His Majesty gave ye royal assent to an Act for ye exercise of ye Government by her Majesty during his Majestys absence. Also an Act for reversing the judgment in a Quo Warranto against ye City of London, and for restoring ye City of London to its antient rights and priviledges. Also an Act to declare ye right and freedom of election of Members to serve in Parliament for ye Cinque Ports. Also an Act for ye discouraging the importation of thrown silk. Also an Act for confirming to ye Governor and Company trading to Hudsons Bay their priviledges & trade. Also an Act for ye encouraging and better establishing ye manufacture of white-paper in this Kingdom; and two private Acts.

MAY 23.—Ye King pass'd ye Act of Grace for a general and free pardon, and that day the Parliament adjourn'd to ye 7th of July following; and on ye same day there was seen off the Lizard a great whale, judged to be about an 100 foot in length, with an other fish following him, supposd to be ye sword fish; they were so near ye shore that several guns were fired at them.

MAY 30.—A Proclamation requiring Tildesley, Mollineux, Tempest, Townley, and other disaffected persons to ye present Gavernment forthwith

C

to render themselves to some of their Majesties Justices of the Peace etc An order of King and Council regulating ye musters and cloathing of ye soldiery.

MAY 31.—An address from ye flag officers, Captains etc. of ye Fleet in the Downs renouncing King James and his adherents, and assuring their Majesties of their fidelity and zeal to their service.

JUNE 2.—Sir Thomas Pilkington being elected Lord Mayor of London for ye remaining part of this year and ye year ensuing, in pursuance of ye late Act of Parliament, was sworn before ye Barons of ye Exchequer at Westminster this day. And that afternoon ye Mayor, Aldermen, Recorder, and Sheriffs went to Kensington to take leave of ye King.

JUNE 3.—Trevor, Rawlinson and Hutchins were sworn Commissioners of ye great Seal of England. Prince George sett forward to Ireland. Ye same day Sir Charles Porter as Administrator to Prettyman had a tryall against Mr. Thimbleby, and ye Jury brought in £1150 damages for Sir Charles Porter at ye Exchequer Barr.

JUNE 4.—The King began his journey towards Ireland, dined this day at Tring with Mr. Guy, and is to lye this night at Northampton, next night at Litchfield.

JUNE 9.—Munday, my brown stone horse went to Newmarkett.

JUNE 11.—Wednesday, ye King embarked at Highlake about noon for Ireland.

JUNE 14.—Saturday, ye King went ashore at Carrickfergus in Ireland about 3 of ye clock.

JUNE 17.—A Proclamation commanding all Papists and reputed Papists forthwith to depart London and ten miles round ; ye same day an other to confine all Popish Recusants within five miles of their respective dwellings.

JUNE 15—Sunday, the first day we discovered little Binny had a tooth cutt. (*Note 5*.)

JUNE 20.—Friday, ye French fleet consisting of 80 men of warr and 30 fire ships were seen off of Plymouth Harbour standing to ye Eastward.

JNNE 21—Saturday, ye Dutch army commanded by Prince Waldeck and ye French army commanded by ye Duke of Luxemburgh fought a battle in ye plain of Flerus.

JUNE 30.—Monday, ye English and Dutch engag'd ye French fleet about 9 in ye morning off of Beachy, ye French were 82 men of warr. And on ye same day King William going to view a Pass upon ye River Boyne near Drogheda was hitt on ye right shoulder by a six pound shott from a Feauconneau.

JULY 1.—Tuesday, King William routed ye whole army of King James in taking ye Pass near Drogheda, in which action Duke Schomberg was killed.

JULY 5.—An address from ye Tinners of Cornwall.

JULY 7.—Ye Parliament mett, and was prorogued to ye 28th of this present July. Ye same day ye King put out a declaration in Ireland promising pardon to all who would lay down their arms and live peacably.

JULY 10.—Earle of Torrington sent to ye Tower.

JULY 12.—An address from ye Deputy Lieutenants and militiæ of Middlesex to their Majesties.

JULY 24.—Waterford surrender'd upon Articles to King William.

JULY 28.—Ye Parliament mett, and was farther prorogued to ye 18th day of August next.

AUG. 2.—being Saturday, Lady Carr, Dear Wife, Child, and self went to Tunbridg from London.

SEPT. 5.—The King after having rais'd ye siege of Limrick, in order to return for England, embarked at Duncannon for on ye 5th of September in ye afternoon ; and on ye 6th arrived towards evening in King-road ; and being come on shoar lay that night at Kings Weston, ye next night at Badminton, Duke of Beaufort, on Munday at ye Duke of Somersetts at Marleborough, next night at Windsor, and on Wedensday ye 10th about 4 afternoon his majesty arrived at Kinginston.

SEPT. 12.—Friday, Return'd from Tunbridg, and that day came out a Proclamation requiring ye attendance of ye members of both houses of Parliament on ye second day of October next.

SEPT. 19.—Fryday, Dear wife and self went to Bury.

SEPT. 28.—Cork in Ireland was surrender'd to King William, the old fort that evening, and ye rest of ye town next day. On ye 28th of September ye Duke of Grafton receiv'd a wound in his back by a muskett shott before Cork in Ireland, and died of it 9th October following.

OCT. 1, New style.—died ye Venetian Captain General Cornaro anno ætatis 59, Mocenigo succeeds him.

OCT. 2.—Ye parliament mett at Westminster. On Oct. 2 King William's forces under command of ye Earle of Marlburrough possest themselves of ye town of Kingsale, and ye next day took ye old fort by storm, and on ye 16th of this same month ye new fort at Kingsale was surrendered also.

OCT. 8.—Belgrade was taken by ye Turks upon a Bombs falling in to ye magazine of ye Castle. Orsowa, Nissa and Widen were also taken this month.

OCT 12.—Ye Breda, a 3d rate frigate, blew up in Cork harbour.

OCT. 19.—Was observ'd as a day of public thanksgiving for ye success of their Majesties arms in Ireland.

OCT. 31.—We sett out from Bury, and arrived att London next day ye 1st November, being our wedding day, my dear wife was then very ill.

NOV. 15.—A Proclamation for ye apprehending of Mr. James Campbell, Archibald Montgomery and Sir John Johnston, designing to ravish one Mrs. Wharton ; and against her will to marry ye said Campbell ; for which Sir John Johnston was hanged.

NOV. 18.—His Majesty gave ye royal assent to an Act concerning ye Commissioners of ye Admiralty ; an Act prohibiting ye covering of houses with Thatch or straw in ye town of Marlborough in Wilts ; an Act to vest divers lands and messuages (ye estate of David Biggs Esq.) in Trustees to be sold and ye money laid out in other land more to his convenience, to be settled to ye same uses ;   An Act to vest ye manors and lands (late of George Vilet Esq.) in Trustees to be sold, for raising portions for his daughters.

NOV. 28.—I sold my grey Somersett, Strawberry Obrian, and Boney to the King for two hundred pounds,

DEC. 8.—Munday, my brother arrived at London when he came out of Ireland.

DEC. 14.—Saturday, My Father came to London from Bury.

1 6 9 1.

JAN. 5.—The Parliament adjourn'd to ye 31th of March following.

JAN. 6.—Tuesday, The King parted from London in order to embarque at Margett in Kent for Holland about 11 morning. Lord Clarendon sent to ye Tower.

JAN. 9.—Friday, The King return'd from Margett (ye wind being contrary) to London,

JAN. 16.—Friday, the King sett out again from London in order to embark for Holland.

JAN. 17.—Saturday, Richard Grimes Lord Preston was tryed att ye old Bayly upon an Indictment of high-treason, and thereof convicted.

JAN. 19.—Munday, My Brother and self went to Bury.

JAN. 22.—In ye evening Pope Alexander ye 8th died att Rome, anno ætatis 81, having held ye Popedom about sixteen months.

JAN. 28.—Wedensday, I returned from Bury ; on which day Mr. John Ashton was hang'd for High Treason att Tyburn.

FEB. 5.—A Proclamation for discovering and apprehending of ye late Bishop of Ely (Francis Turner), William Penn, and James Grahme.

FEB, 9.—A Proclamation requiring all seamen to render themselves to their Majesties service.

MARCH 20.—Friday, My Father, dear wife and self went to Bury.

MARCH 31.—Ye Parliament mett, and adjourn'd to ye 28 Aprill following.

APRIL 8.—The town of Mons surrender'd to ye French ; ye garrison marchd out ye 10th ; ye French horse began to invest it on ye 15th of March.

APRIL 9.—A fire happened at White-hall which burnt most of ye buildings on ye south side of ye privy garden.

APRIL 13.—The King arrived at London from Holland in ye evening.

APRIL 22.—I won ye Newmarkett Gold Tumbler with my horse called Davers, riding him myself at 12 stone weight.

APRIL 28.—Ye Parliament mett, and adjourn'd to ye 26th of May following.

APRIL 29.—My Father, dear wife, and self return'n to London.

MAY 1,—Ye King parted from London towards Harwich in order to embarque again for Holland.

MAY 7.—I went to Newmarkett.

MAY 10.—Return'd from Newmarkett.

MAY 20.—Wednesday, about noon, Sir John Chickley died.

MAY 23.—My father had a hearing in Chancery concerning those things which remain'd undetermined in ye Master's hands between Aunt Hervey and himself.

MAY 26.—Ye Parliament mett and was prorogued to ye 30th of June following.

MAY 29.—(New stile) died Admirall Trump, Dutch Commander.

On Friday, May 29, Lady Carr, Mrs. Baron, dear wife, and self went to lye at Doily (my Lord Ossulstones) in our way to Burford, ye next night at Oxford, ye day after we reach'd Burford, and lay that night at Mr. Barons of Westcot, Com : Gloucest : Return'd from thence ye 9th June, arrived at London ye 10th.

JUNE 22.—Sultan Solyman died at Adrianople of a dropsy. Achmett his brother succeeds him.

JUNE 30.—Ye Parliament mett, and was farther prorogued to ye 3d of August following. Tuesday June 30 ye town of Athlone (In Ireland) was taken by storm about 4 in ye afternoone by King Williams forces.

JULY 4.—Saturday, a commotion happened in ye City, occasion'd by ye walling up of certain doors out of white-fryars into ye Temple; one of White-fryars men was kill'd, 2 others wounded by ye Sheriffs power, the Guards were sent for, a Party of Horse and a detachment of foot came which dispersed them.

JULY 12.—Sunday, ye two armies in Ireland came to a battle near Aghrim, King Williams forces gave an entire defeat to King James', taking their cannon, Baggage, etc.

JULY 12.—(New style) At a scrutiny in ye Conclave, of 61 voices, 53 were given for Antonio Pignatelli, a Neapolitan, Archbishop of Naples, aged 76 years, 4 months ; was created Cardinal in 1681 by Innocentius XI, in consideration whereof he hath taken ye name of Innocent ye 12th.

JULY 16, New style.—Mr. de Louvois (Chief Minister of State to Louis ye 14th of France) dyed of an Apoplexy. His son Mr. Le Marquis de Barbesieux succeeds him in the place of Secretary of State.

JULY 25, N. S.—Was ye first time ye Dauphin was admitted into ye Council.

JULY 26.—Galloway in Ireland was actually surrender'd to King William. Henry Cavendish Duke of Newcastle died at Wellbeck in Nottinghamshire.

AUG. 3.—Ye Parliament mett, and was again prorogued by Commission to ye 5th October next.

AUG 19. N.S.—Prince Louis of Baden gave ye Turks battle between Salankement and Peter-waradin (in Sclavonia to ye South of ye Danube), where he entirely routed them, making himself master of their Camp and 158 canon, taking 12 horse-tails, 90 standards, of which one was ye Sultans present to the grand Visier, and killing near 15000 upon ye place ; ye Imperialists lost 3161, and had 4135 wounded.

SEPT. 17.—Thursday, My dearest wife was brought to bed of a son, about 3 quarters of an hour after 5 of ye clock in ye morning ; and was christen'd by Dr. Tenison on Munday ye 21st of September following ; his Godfathers were Lord Ossulstone and Sir Algernoone May, and Mrs. ffox his Godmother.

SEPT. 24.—A Proclamation requiring ye attendance of ye Members of both Houses of Parliament att Westminster on Thursday ye 22th of October following.

I lay very ill of a feaver from 21 Sept. to 1st of October following.

OCT. 3.—Limerick in Ireland was surrender'd to King William.

OCT. 5.—Ye Parliament mett and was farther prorogued to ye 22th of ye same month.

OCT. 8, N.S.—Ye French garrison of Carmagniola in Piedmont capitulated, and march'd out ye 9th, when ye Duke of Savoys forces took possession of it.

OCT. 19.—King William arrived at Kensington from Holland about 12 of ye clock at night. He landed at Margate in Kent ye 19th about 9 in ye morning: embarked Sunday ye 18th upon ye Mary yacht in ye Maese. Sir Clovesly Shovel Rear Admiral of ye Blue commanded ye Squadron which convoyd him.

OCT. 20.—I went by my self into Suffolke, and return'd from Bury in one day on ye 27th, being sent for to my dear wife who was then ill.

OCT. 22.—Ye Parliament mett at Westminster. A Proclamation for a publick Thanksgiving to be kept the 26th of November next.

NOV. 14.—About 1 clock Saturday morn my cousen Jenny Duncomb died.

1 6 9 2.

FEB. 17.—Our cause with ye Hetleys came to be heard in ye House of Lords. They affirm'd Lord Nottinghams decree for us of 9th March 1676, from which they appeald, and left them to law for their remedy.

FEB. 24.—Ye King adjourn'd ye Parliament to 12 Aprill following after having passed over 40 bills public & private, and among ye last were Sir Dudly Cullums, Kebles of Stowmarkett, Major Sheltons, Mr Halsteds, ye young Duke of Graftons, etc. He refused ye Bill for ye ascertaining ye Judges Comissions & Salaries, which was ye first he ere rejected. Charles Earle of Dorset & Middlesex was install'd in St Georges Chappel at Windsor.

MARCH 4.—Friday, ye King went from Kensington, arriv'd that night at Harwich, and sett sail for Holland next day at 10 clock in ye morning.

D

MARCH 12.—Thursday, my dear wife & self with Mr Porter sett out from London to Bury, & arrived there next day.

APRIL 20.—Return'd to London in 2 daies arriving Aprill 20.

APRIL 29.—Ye tryall between Baughes and his two aunts was heard at ye Kings Bench Barr, ye aunts were non-suited.

MAY 17.—Tuesday, I went to Burford, won ye Town Plate there on Friday ye 20th with my little nagg calld ball-mannors riding him my self, and returnd to London next day.

MAY 19.—Thursday, ye English & Dutch ffleets engag'd ye ffrench near Cape Barfleur and beat them, burning above 20 of their capital ships, & dispersing all ye rest.

MAY 24.—Ye Parliament mett at Westminster & was prorogued by Commission to ye 14th of June.

MAY 31.—Tuesday, our whole ffamily together with my ffather & brother sett out from London to Aswarby, and arriv'd there on ye Thursday following being ye 2d of June.

JUNE 7.—Tuesday, I sett out from Aswarby to London and arrived there ye next day.

JUNE 14.—Ye Parliament mett & was prorogued by Commission to 11th July following.

JUNE 21.—Tuesday, I return'd from London to Aswarby and arrived there ye 22th.

JUNE 30, N.S.—The Castle of Namur capitulated, and ye garrison march'd out next day when ye ffrench took possession of it.

JULY 1.—Friday, my dear wife and self sett out from Aswarby to London, and arrived there ye next day.

JULY 11.—Ye Parliament mett & was farther prorogued by Commission to 22 August following.

JULY 15.—Friday, we return'd from London to Aswarby, & arrived there ye day following.

AUG. 22.—Ye Parliament mett and was farther prorogued to ye 4th of November next.

SEPT. 8.—An earthquake was felt in most parts of England which lasted about 2 minutes.

SEPT. 28.—Wednesday, our whole ffamily parted from Aswarby and arrived at London ye first of October following.

OCT. 15.—Saturday, I went to Bury, and return'd to London on ye 30th following.

OCT. 18.—Tuesday, King William landed at Yarmouth (from Holland) about 3 in ye afternoon, and arriv'd ye 20th at London.

NOV. 4.—ffriday, ye Parliament mett at Westminster.

DEC. 27.—Tuesday, Mr. Thomas Jermyn going to play in a Liter which ley upon ye river behind Beaufort House, ye mast fell down upon him (they being about to lower it) and beat out his brains.

1 6 9 3.

FEB. 20.—My daughter Bell had ye first fitt of a Tertian Ague which she missed after 5 fitts.

MARCH 7.—My most dear and entirely beloved wife, Mrs Isabella Hervey, ye most excellent of her sex, died ye very moment she was deliver'd of my daughter Elizabeth (Benona I called her, Genesis 35, 18) between 5 & 6 in ye morning.

Tuque, O Sanctissima Conjux,
Felix morte tua neque in hunc servata dolorem.

O fatall Day! Lett a cloud dwell on thee; lett darkness cover thee; may'st thou not come into ye number of ye months; be thou not joynd to ye daies of ye year.

> That fatal day in which she died
> My death as well as hers contrived.

Ille dies utramque duxit ruinam.—*Horace.*

O! Quis te tantis solvet curis miseranda Dies!
Ille Dies primus Lethi, primusque malorum causa fuit.—*Virgil.*

Occidit, occidit spes omnis, et Fortuna nostri nominis Isabella interrempta. Tecum cecedi, summusque dies Isabellæ, idem Johanni fuit. O decus atque dolor! In te vivebam, in te interii. Utrumque nostrum incredibili modo consentit astrum. O mea nullis æquanda malis fortuna! Semper nobis metuenda dies. Quem dies vidit veniens felicissimum, hunc dies vidit fugiens miserrimum.

> Siccine fida cadis conjux?   Nec nostra tenent te
>   Vota. dolor, gemitus, immaculatus'amor:
> Sancta morare Anima; en propero (charissima) tecum
>   Vivere cum nequeam, te moriente. mori.
> Turpe mori post te solo non posse dolore.
> Pro quabis patiar mori; si parcunt animæ fata superstiti.
> Tres fuerant Charites, sed dum mea Lesbia vixit
>   Quatuor; ut periit tres numerantur idem.
> All offices of Heaven so well she knew
> Before she dyed, that nothing there was new.
> For she was so familiarly receiv'd
> As one returning, not as one arriv'd.
> ———— And could there be
> A copy near th' original, twas she,
> She like my soul is gone, and I here stay,
> Not her live friend, but th' other half of clay.
> To say she's now an Angel, is no more
> Praise than she had, for she was one before.
>
> ———————— O you her kindred angels,
> Since she was form'd, and lov'd, and pray'd like you,
> She should alass! have been immortal too.

Nihil mihi profuit ultimos hausisse anhelitus, nihil flatus in os inspirassemorienti ; putabam enim quod aut tuam mortem ipse susciperem, aut meam vitam in te trans-funderem.—*St. Ambrose.*

1 6 9 4 .

MAY 27.—(being Whitsunday) my best and dearest Friend, as well as Father, Sir Thomas Hervey dyed in ye 69th year of his age.

> Fatigatum magnis adversis, oppressit me hæc extrema infelicitas.
>
> Heu, genitorem, omnis curæ casusque levamen,
> Amitto Anchisen. Hic Me, Pater optime, fessum
> Deseris, heu ! ———— Hic labor extremus ————
> Nec tibi sæcla parem pietate priora tulerunt
>   Nec tibi sæcla parem posteriora ferent.
> Heu pietas ! Heu prisca fides !
> Ille dies ———— quem semper acerbum
> Semper honoratum (sic Di voluistis) habebo.
> ———————— nec te tua plurima Pantheu,
> Labentem pietas nec Apollinis insula texit.

Et ille quidem plenus annis abiit, plenus honoribus, illis etiam quos recusavit. (*Plin* : Ep : Lib : 2 Ep : 1)

Nobis tamen quærendus ac desiderandus est, ut exemplar ævi prioris ; mihi vero præcipue, qui illum non solum publice, sed etiam privatim quantum admirabar, tantum diligebam. (*Of Virginius Rufus.*)

NOV. 17.—Saturday, I fell sick of ye small pox. Gloria Deo.

NOV. 22.—Dr John Tillotson (Archbishop of Canterbury) died.

DEC. 25.—Mareschall D. Luxemburgh died.

DEC. 28.—Friday, our most gracious Sovereign Queen Mary of ever blessed memory, ye most excellent of her sex (except only my peerless Isabella) dyed at Kensington of ye small pox (after — daies sickness) about one in ye morning, in ye 32th year of her age.

On ye same day my daughter Isabella Carr Hervey fell sick of ye small pox.   God be prais'd for her recovery.

1 6 9 5.

JAN. 1.—Tuesday, my daughter Betty (alias poor Benona) dyed about 4 in ye morning.

JAN. 12.—Saturday, Lord Sunderland paid me £4525 .. 17 .. 6 in full of principal and interest.   I assigned Sir Edw: Ayscoghs mortgage to Sir Edward Ward (Attorney General) receiving £2052.   I paid Mr & Mrs Fox all ye purchase money for their interests in ye estate late Sir Robert Carrs : ye whole summe for principal & interest was £12948..18.:2.   *(Note 6.)*

JAN. 23.—Wednesday, Mr William Crofts of Saxham dyed.

FEB. 4.—Munday, ye advertisement in ye Gazette for Sir Robert Carrs creditors to prove their debts.

FEB. 11.—Munday, John, Lord Ossulstone departed this life.

MARCH 5.—Tuesday, Queen Mary was buried in Henry ye 7ths Chappell at Westminster. '

MARCH 16.—Saturday, ye Commons of England expelled Sir John Trevor their Speaker) ye House for taking 1000 guineys upon ye passage of ye Orphans Bill.

MARCH 26.—Tuesday, they expelled Mr Hungerford for taking 20 guineas in ye same.

APRIL 18.—Thursday, Antony ffisher sold me his 2 blank ticketts in ye million lottery for £14.   I exchangd and registerd ye benefitted ticketts in ye million lottery.

APRIL 23.—Tuesday, Sir Thomas Cooke examin'd by a Comittee of Lords and Commons.

APRIL 27.—Saturday, ye Commons impeachd Thomas Duke of Leeds. My cousen Robert Reynolds saw my Aunt Hervey at Utreicht.   *(Note 7.)*

MAY 1.—Lady Carr had a tryall at Barr with ye Hetleys.

MAY 3.—Friday, ye King prorogued ye Parliament to 18 June following.

MAY 8.—Wednesday, I went from London to Bury in a day.

MAY 11.—Saturday, to Boxted.

MAY 14.—Tuesday, again to Boxted from Bury. Tuesday ye 21 again.

MAY 23.—To London.

MAY 13.—Munday, ye King went for Holland.

JUNE 16.—Sunday, Sir G. Elwes went first to propose ye match with Mrs Felton to Mr Felton.

JUNE 18.—Tuesday, ye Parliament farther prorogued to ye 30 July following, by Commission Duke of Bedford.

JUNE 28.—Friday, Sir G. Elwes & my self went to Mr Felton, & ye portion agreed on.

JULY 2.—Tuesday, from London to Bury.

JULY 5.—Friday, Sir Henry North dyed.

JULY 11.—Thursday, from Bury to London.

JULY 13.—Saturday, from London to Boxted.

JULY 20.—Saturday, from Boxted to London.

JULY 23.—Tuesday, from London to Boxted.

JULY 25.—Thursday, I was married to Mrs Elizabeth Felton, by her uncle Dr Henry Felton, att Boxted about 8 aclock at night.

JULY 29.—Munday, I carried her from Boxted to Bury, where she was mett at ye Guildhall by ye Corporation in their gowns etc.

AUG. 6.—Tuesday, we went from Bury to Aswarby in 2 daies by Huntington.

SEPT. 26.—Thursday, we returnd to Bury from Aswarby in 3 daies by Cambridg etc.

OCT. 15.—Tuesday, we went from Bury to Norwich with Dr Felton to ye Bishop etc.

NOV. 1.—Friday, I was elected Burgess for Bury ye 2d time. Ye free-men chose me as well as ye Corporation, who gave me all their votes, viz. ye whole 37 again.

NOV. 4.—Munday, ye County Election for Suffolk. Sir G. Elwes & Sir Samuel Barnardiston.

NOV. 13.—Wednesday, we went from Bury to London, to Lady Carrs.

NOV. 22.—Friday, ye new Parliament mett at Westminster. Paul Foley speaker again.

DEC. 29.—Sunday, my dear brother Mr Thomas Hervey died at Bury in Suffolke about midnight of an apoplecticall ffitt, and on Friday ye 3d January he was buried at Ickworth.

> Nunquam ego te vita, frater amabilior,
> Aspiciam posthac ; at certe semper amabo.

DEC. 31.—Tuesday, my dear wife & self went down from London to Bury to my said brothers funerall, and returnd to London ye Saturday following.

1 6 9 6.

MARCH 25.—Dear wife & self went to Bury in 2 daies.

APRIL 13.—Returnd to London, arriv'd ye 14.

APRIL 24.—Sir Adam, Mr Felton & self went from London to Newmarkett.

APRIL 26.—Sunday, to Bury to see sister Elwes.

APRIL 29.—Returnd to dear wife.

JULY 3.—I took out letters of administration to my dear and blessed saint Mrs Isabella Hervey.

JULY 4.—Sir Ger: Elwes & Sir Stephen Fox (Sir Robert Carrs trustees) executed ye conveyances of his estate to me ; (Sir William Yorke, ye other surviving trustee, having first released his interest in ye premises to ye said Sir Ger : Elwes & Sir Stephen Fox, being sick at this time in the country :) and ye Lady Carr joyn'd also in ye conveyances to me as executrix to Sir R. Carr, ye interests & estates of ye Lease-hold lands being (as such) vested in her.

JULY 20.—Munday, my dear wife & self went to Bury from London, and arriv'd ye next day.·

AUG. 3.—Munday, Lady Carr departed this life, 8 at night.

AUG. 6.—Thursday, dear wife & self sett out from Bury to London, & arriv'd ye next day.

OCT. 14.—Wednesday, that wise & excellent woman my dear sister Isabella Elwes chang'd this life for a better, about midnight. And in ye same hour my wife fell into labour, bringing forth a son, between 3 & 4 aclock in ye afternoone ye next day, being Thursday ye 15 October ; which said son of mine was Christened by Dr Wake in my Jermyn Street House on Sunday ye 25 October, and named John, ye Dutchess of Lawderdale, my Father in law Mr Felton, & my uncle Mr Baptist May answering for him.

OCT. 20.—Tuesday, ye Parliament mett.

NOV. 10.—My cousin Isabella Reynolds was married to Mr John Hatley.

DEC. 24.—I went from London to Bury.

1 6 9 7 .

JAN. 1.—I returned to London my dear wife being sick.

E

JAN. 28.—Sir John ffenwick was beheaded.

FEB. 9.—Tuesday, Sir Adam ffelton dyed. And on ye same day Mrs. Bennet was married to Lord Burleigh.

FEB. 27.—Saturday, dear wife and self went from London to Bury.

MARCH 2.—Tuesday, my uncle Mr. Baptist May dyed. Buried at Windsor.

MARCH 15.—Munday, Sir Thomas ffelton, dear wife and self returnd to London from Newmarkett in a day.

*JAN. 28.—Sir John Fenwicke was beheaded on Tower Hill.

*FEB. 9.—Tuesday, Sir Adam Felton died 8 ye morning : and on ye same day Mrs. Bennett was married to Lord Burleigh.

APRILL 7.—Wednesday, Sir Thomas ffelton and self went from London to Newmarkett.

APRILL 13.—Tuesday, we returnd to London.

APRIL 16.—Friday, ye Parliament prorogued to 13 May following.

APRILL 24.—Saturday, ye King went for Holland.

APRILL 30.—Friday, ye Duke of Devon, Lord Wharton, Sir Thomas ffelton and self went from London to Newmarkett.

MAY 5.—Wednesday, I returnd from Newmarkett to London.

MAY 13.—Parliament prorogued to 17 June following.
    Parliament farther prorogued to 22 July.
    Parliament farther prorogued to 26 August.

JUNE 24.—I paid £650 being ye purchase mony of Shaws ffarm at Chevington.

JULY 3.—Dear wife and self went from London to Bury.

---

* These two entries are made twice over. S.II.A.II.

AUG. 12.—Dear wife and I went from Bury to Aswarby, lay at Cambridg, ye next night at Stilton, and arrived there ye 14th.

AUG. 26.—Parliament prorogued to 30 Sept.

SEPT. 2.—Thursday, dear wife and I went to Spilsby from Aswarby, and returnd ye Saturday following.

SEPT. 18.—Saturday, dear wife and I went from Aswarby to Bury; arrivd ye 20th.

NOV. 2.—Tuesday, dear wife and I sett out from Newmarkett to London.

NOV. 14.—Sunday, ye King landed at Margetts in Kent XI morning, lay that night at Canterbury, ye next at Greenwich, and ye 16th made his publick entry thro' London.

DEC. 9.—Thursday, dear wife was brought to bed of Betty, XI at night.

DEC. 23.—Thursday, my said daughter was christened by Dr Wake; my cousin Mr William Duncombe, ye Countess of Suffolke, and Lady Howard of Effingham answered for her.

1 6 9 8 .

JAN. 4.—White-Hall was burnt.

JAN. 5.—Lady Elwes dyed.

MARCH 16.—Wednesday, I was heard in my place by ye House of Commons to my Aunt Hervey's petition; whereupon it was again rejected *nemine contradicente.*

APRILL 3.—Sir Thomas ffelton and I went from London to Newmarket in a day.

APRILL 7.—Hautboy was beaten by Quainton, 8 stone each, 5 mile, I lost 200.

APRILL 9.—Stiff Dick beat Careless 9 stone to a feather; I made this match with Boucher and wonn 1170 guineys upon it.

APRILL 12.—My Lobcock beat Looby 8 mile, 8 stone 12 lb each. I won of this 325 guineys. Ye same day Yellow Jack paid ye forfeit to my Hogg, 250 guineys.

APRILL 13.—Colchester was matched by me against Lord Roos (?) Darius. I won 155 guineys. Presently after they run again, and I lost 105.

APRILL 15.—Bully was beaten by Darius. I lost 117 guineys.

APRILL 16.—I returnd from Newmarkett to London.

APRILL 20.—I went to Sir Cecil Bishops at —— in Sussex; and bought Cobler and Windgalls.

APRILL 29.—Friday, Charles Lord Cornwallis dyed, 1 in ye morning.

MAY 3.—Dear wife, Mrs Dursley, Berkeley and I went to Newmarkett.

MAY 4.—Spaniard was matched by me against Darius, at 2 pound under nine stone. I wonn 116 guineys.

MAY 7.—I returnd from Bury to London.

JULY 4.—Parliament prorogued to 2d Aug. following.

JULY 7.—Ye Parliament dissolvd by Proclamation.

JULY 16.—Dear wife and self went to Bury and arrivd next day.

JULY 19.—Ye King went from Kensington to Margett, and embarkd for Holland next day at 10 in ye morning.

JULY 28.—Ye Corporation of Bury choosed me again for their Burgess to Parliament with Sir R. Davers.

AUG. 10.—Wednesday, Lord D'ysert and Sir Samuel Barnardiston were chosen Knights for Suffolke against Sir Thomas ffelton and Sir Gervase Elwes.

AUG. 16.—Tuesday, Mr. Le Roy dyed at London, a good man.

AUG. 18.—Thursday, Mr Thomas Macro jun. chosen Alderman for ye ensuing year. Ye Duke of Grafton, Lord Chief Baron Ward, ye Grand Jurys, Justices and Council dined with us at ye Guildhall.

AUG. 22.—Munday, dear wife and I went from Bury to Newmarkett; ye 24th from thence to Huntington, arrivd next day at Aswarby.

SEPT. 13.—Tuesday, dear wife and self went from Aswarby to Stilton, next day to Newmarkett, and ye 15th to Bury.

OCT. 4.—I signd Mr James Davies presentation to ye Rectory of Tuddenham.

OCT. 6.—Thursday, I escapd a very great danger at Newmarkett by a restive horse called Cobler, who in starting for ye King's Plate there, run away with me, and in passing thro ye ditch took a leap over a pitt with me of nineteen foot six inches long then measurd ; and would have run down ye town with me to ye stables ; but I stopt him against ye wall of ye rubbing house, within 2 foot of ye door. Gloria Deo! in Deo confido.—*J.H.* (*Note* 8).

On ye same day Mr Thomas Coell of Bury dyed, and left ye two exauctorated Bishops of Ely and Norwich his executors. Ye latter surviv'd.

NOV. 9.—Friday, I left Bury.

NOV. 12.—My Hogg beat Headpiece. I won 450 guineys.

NOV. 14.—We went towards London in a deep snow, arrivd next day.

DEC. 22.—Thursday, dear wife with ye whole family removd from Jermyn Street to my house in St James Square. (*Note* 9.)

DEC. 26.—Munday, at night Mrs Bond dyed at Bury. (*Note* 10).

DEC. 29.—Thursday, my good friend Collonel Thomas Holland dyed there.

1 6 9 9.

JAN. 20.—Friday, my dear son Tom was born near 12 at night, (ye same day of ye year my first dear excellent wife was born) was christened by Dr Wake, ye Earle of Jersey (who was represented by ye Earle of Orkney, Lord Jersey being then our Embassadour in ffrance), my cousin Hanmer and Lady Poley answerd for him.

FEB. 20.—Munday, Dr Henry ffelton was married to Lady Isabella May by Dr Sherlock, Dean of St Pauls, in that Cathedral.

APRILL 2.—Dear wife and I went from London to Newmarkett.

APRILL 22.—Saturday, we returnd to London.

JULY 24.—Munday, dear wife and self sett out for St Albans and saw Lord Marleburgh's house there, and lay that night at Dunstable, next day we dined at Battlesden with cousin Duncombe; went from thence to Wooburn Abbey (ye Duke of Bedfords) and lodged that night at Bedford; ye next day I went to Thurleigh in ye same County (ye place from whence our ffamily originally came to Ickworth in Suffolke) to see my cousin Major John Hervey (a very honest, ingenious Gentleman); lay that night at Cambridg; and next day being Thursday arrivd at my Center Bury. (*Note* 11).

AUG. 5.—Saturday, I gave ye Corporation of Bury five hundred pounds to pay their debts, contracted by ye taxes on their ffoefment lands.

AUG. 21.—Munday, dear wife and self went from Bury to Newmarkett, next night lay at Stilton, and arrivd ye 23 at Aswarby.

SEPT. 13.—A great eclipse of ye sun.

SEPT. 18.—Munday, dear wife and self went from Aswarby to Stilton, next day to Cambridg, where we mett ye Duke and Dutchess of St Albans, and next day went for Bury ffair together.

OCT. 16.—Munday, dear wife and self went from Newmarkett to London, arrivd next day.

OCT. 22.—We returnd to Newmarkett.

NOV. 12.—We went from Bury to Newmarkett; ye 16th from thence towards London, arrivd next day.

On CHRISTMAS DAY, being Munday, half an hour after two in ye morning dear wife was brought to bed of Will, after having been above 13 hours in labour. *Gloria Deo.*

1 7 0 0.

JAN. 13.—Saturday, Dr Wake christend him, ye Duke of Somersett, Duke of St Albans and Aunt Felton answerd for him.

FEB. 10.—Saturday, Sir Thomas Felton was most unjustly voted not to be a Burgess duely elected for Orford in Suffolke: ye Division 172 and 171; whereby ye right of election was transferr'd from ye select number to ye ffree-men.

FEB. 20.—Sir Bartholomew Shower signed his award between Aunt Hervey and me. (*Note* 12.)

MARCH 1.—I paid Dame Elizabeth Hervey £4650 pursuant to that award.

MARCH 27.—Wednesday, dear wife, Sir Thomas ffelton and self with all ye ffamily (except ye children who went ye day before) sett out from London to Newmarkett, next day to Bury.

APRILL 25.—Dear wife and I went from Newmarkett, lay at Hockril, went next day by Joyses ffarm (near Rumford on Havering Plaine in Essex) to London.

APRILL 27.—Lord Jersey went to take ye great Seale from Lord Somers.

MAY 4.—I went to see my estate at Darenth near Dartford in Kent.

MAY 27.—I wrote to ye Earle of Montague about Aunt Herveys

paternal estate in Kent etc. ; and ye 5th of June he sent me his answer by Mr Dummer of ye Middle Temple.

JUNE 14.—I granted Mrs Peart a Rent-charge of £80 per annum for her pictures. (*Note* 13).

JULY 3.—I insurd my house and stables in St James Square for 7 years, and paid £75 for £5000 value, at their office in ye Rainbow Coffee house—Entry in ffleet Street.

JULY 8.—Mrs Ramsey, dear wife and I lay at Newport, went next day to Bury.

JULY 15.—Dear wife and I went to Cherry Marham, lay that night at Lynn, ye 16 we went to Dersingham, from thence to Langham, and lay that night at Alesham ; ye 17th to Hoboys alias Hobbes parva, thence to Scotto, and lodged at Yarmouth ; ye 18th to Thirne Ashby and Oweby where I saw all those estates also, and lodged that night at Norwich, where we rested ye 19th, to treat with ye Bishop about ye renewal of these lease-hold estates, and returnd to Bury ye 20th dineing at Euston in our way.

JULY 30.—Tuesday, ye Duke of Gloucester dyed of a Feaver, 1 morn.

AUG. 5.—Munday, dear wife, Sir T. ffelton and I went from Bury to Newmarket, next day to Huntingdon (from whence Sir Thomas went to Althrop) and we arrivd next day at Aswarby.

AUG. 16.—Friday, dear wife, Mrs Hopes and I went to Mr Jays at Fleet in Lincolnshire, and saw ye marshes at Moulton by ye way, then took a view of all my lands in ffleet, lay that night at Spalding, next day saw all my estates at Pinchbeck and Surfleet in my way home to Aswarby.

AUG. 25.—I signed an order on Chambers & Company for £295..0..9 payable to Mr Thomas Bond being his moytie of ye £590..1..6 payable to him by Mr Duncombe and my self (as Trustees) by ye Act of Parliament for settling Lady Bond's will.

SEPT. 20.—Friday, dear wife, Mrs Hopes and I sett out from Aswarby, lay that night at Wisbich, arrivd next day at Bury.

SEPT. 27, (N.S.)—Dyed Pope Innocent ye 12th, Pignatelli, aged 86, created Cardinal 1681, and Pope 1691.

OCT. 21.—My ffriend Mr Cullum had an apoplectical fitt.

OCT. 22.—Sir R. Davers, Mr Gage and several others viewd ye Sheeps-Course between Westley and Horningshearth, and fixd ye limits thereof.

OCT. 31.—My horse Glisterpipe wonn Swaffam Plate for me.

NOV. 1. (N.S.)—Ye King of Spain dyed.

NOV. 2.—Dear wife, Mrs Hopes and I went from Newmarkett to London.

NOV. 9.—I paid Mrs Sulyard ye £500 legacy my good Uncle Hervey left her in his will if she survivd Aunt Hervey six months.

NOV. 15.—I paid my cousin Mr Robert Reynolds ye £1000 legacy left him by my said Uncle Hervey's will if he survivd his wife my Aunt Hervey six months also. (*Note* 7).

NOV. 26.—Mrs Mary Smith my house-keeper dyed about 3 morning.

DEC. 4 —My niece Elwess came to live with me. (*Note* 14). All Smith's goods etc. were delivered to her brother Jackson.

DEC. 22.—Sunday, my good friend and old acquaintance Mr Thomas Cullum dyed of a second apoplectical ffitt. (*Note* 15).

1 7 0 1.

JAN. 5.—Sunday, between 7 and 8 in ye morning dear wife was delivered of a boy born with a cawle round his head.

JAN. 8.—Wednesday, ye Corporation of Bury elected me unanimously in my absence (being then at London) to represent them in ye ensuing Parliament to be holden 6 ffeb following with Sir R. Davers.

F

JAN. 14.—I signed ye other order (which Mr Duncombe had first signed) on Mr Chambers, to pay Mrs Gage £295..0..9, being her moytie of ye £590..1..6 mentioned in ye said Act of Parliament.

JAN. 19.—Sunday, Sir John Holland dyed, near 100 years old.

FEB. 6.—Thursday, my said son was christend by Dr Wake and named Henry ; ye Duke of Bedford, Lord Godolphin and ye Countess of Marleburrough answerd for him.

MARCH 7.—I was chosen into ye Vestry at St James's, and took my place ye 13th.

MARCH 27.—We had a verdict at Lincoln Assizes against ye Town of Bicker for little Hale Common to ye double Twelves.

MARCH 31.—Dear wife, niece Elwes and self went from London to Newmarkett.

APRIL 9.—We returnd to London.

APRIL 13.—Roger Webster dyed of a ffall from his horse at Marham.

APRIL 15.—Lynsey Levell Bill rejected again by ye House of Peers.

APRIL 22.—Dear wife and I went to Newmarket from London.

APRIL 23.—Doctor ffelton dyed at Bury. Niece Elwes's and their servants went from my house to Stoke.

APRIL 30.—We returnd to London and arrivd on May day.

JUNE 12.—King William gave ye Royal assent to ye bill for settling ye crown on ye Princess Sophia and her heirs being Protestants etc.

JULY 10.—Dear wife and I went from London to Witham in Essex, to see Mr ffrancis Hervey's Tomb (one of ye younger sons of John Hervey of Ickworth) and by him erected in ye Chancel there anno 1592. We lay at Stoke ye XIth, and went next day to Bury. (*Note* 16).

JULY 30.—Wednesday, dear wife and I went from Bury to Marham, lay that night at Swaffam, ye 31st at Lynn, and arriv'd next day at Aswarby.

AUG. 6.—Wednesday, dear wife and I went to Nottingham to see ye Plates run for. Sir William Lowthers grey Mustard won ye Gentlemens at 12 stone that day; and ye next Lord Roos' Grashopper won ye Town plate at 10 stone weight, and on ffriday we dined with Lord How at Langar Castle in our way to Aswarby.

AUG. 12.—Tuesday, we went from Aswarby to Stamford; I saw Lord Nottinghams Burleigh in ye Hill, & Ketton stone Pitts by ye way; ye 13th we lay at Bickleswayde, making ye Bishop of Lincoln a visitt at his palace at Bugden by ye way, & arriv'd at London ye 14th.

AUG. 16.—Saturday, dear wife, niece Elwes & self went from London to Reading, lay ye 17th at Marlburgh, arriv'd ye 18th at Bath very late at night, breaking ye axle-tree.

AUG. 29.—Friday, dear wife miscarried of twins there.

SEPT. 1.—Munday, I dined at Long-Leate with Lord Weymouth.

SEPT. 3.—I dined at Badmington with ye Dutchess of Beaufort, and saw Mr. Blathwayts house (Dirham) by ye way.

SEPT. 6.—Saturday, dear wife miscarried of a third child.

SEPT. 10.—Wednesday, I went to Bristol.

SEPT. 25.—Friday, we sett out from Bath, lay that night at Cirencester, went next day to Oxford, saw Winchinton (Lord Whartons house) by ye way to Wooburn, where we lay ye 28th, & arriv'd on Michaelmass day at Newmarket.

NOV. 29.—Saturday, ye Corporation of Bury elected me unanimously to serve them in Parliament, together with Sir Thomas ffelton who had 25 votes; & Sir Robert Davers ye 3rd Candidate had but 9 votes.

DEC. 10.—Mr. Joseph Alexander agreed with me to take £50 per annum of me for all ye Tythes of Ickworth Parish, so long as he continues Rector thereof.   Ye first payment to begin at Lammas day next.

DEC. 16.—My niece Elwes's came to London with their two servants.

DEC. 18.—Dear wife & self went from Bury to Newmarket, lay ye next night at Hockeril (where I was seiz'd with a dangerous fitt of ye cholick in my stomach), arriv'd ye 20th at London, where I had 2 or 3 returns of my chollick.

1 7 0 2 .

MARCH 8.—Sunday, King William ye 3d of glorious memory dyed at Kensington about 8 in ye morning.

> Rex erat Æneas nobis, quo justior alter
> Nec pietate fuit, nec bello major et armis.
> Dum numerat palmas, credidit esse senem.

MARCH 28.—Dear wife, Sir T. ffelton and self went from London to Newmarket in 2 daies.

APRIL 6.—Starer was beaten by Lord Godolphins Buskins.

APRIL 14.—Ye first night dear wife and I lay at Ickworth.   *(Note 17.)*

Linquenda tellus et domus et placens | Te præter invisas cupressos
Uxor ; neque harum, quas colis, arborum | Ulla brevem dominum sequetur.

APRIL 18.—We returnd from Ickworth to London, arrivd ye 19th.

MAY 1.—Bell, Carr, Jack, Betty and I went from London to Ickworth, lay at Newport, and arriv'd there next day.

MAY 12.—I returnd from Ickworth to London in a day to see dear wife ye sooner.

MAY 23.—My niece Elwes's went from my house at London to live at Stoke.

JUNE 1.—Dear wife and self from London to Ickworth, lay at Hockeril, next day home.

ICKWORTH CHURCH, SHEWING THE FOUNDATION MARKS OF THE OLD MANOR HOUSE.

JULY 21.—Tuesday, I appeared at Bury Sessions to give security upon ye writt of supplicavit Sir Richard Gipps sued out of Chancery against me (dated ye 10th instant). Mr Macro and Mr Grove were my sureties in £500 each, my self in £1000. Sir R. Davers moved I might give double those sums.

JULY 27.—Munday, ye Corporation of Bury elected me again unanimously to serve them in Parliament, together with my ffather in law Sir Thomas ffelton, who had all their votes except four, who voted for Sir Robert Davers ye 3d candidate.

AUG. 3.—Munday, dear wife and self went from Ickworth to Playford, I saw Bocking by ye way; Tuesday we went to Ipswich, Wednesday was ye County Election; Lord Dysert and Sir Dudley Cullum were chosen, Thursday I went to see my marshes at Sudburn, ffriday returned home.

AUG. 11.—Tuesday, dear wife, niece Elwes and self went from Ickworth towards Aswarby. I called at Marham in Norfolke to see my running horses by ye way, lay at Wisbich, and arrivd next day.

SEPT. 15.—Tuesday, we returnd from Aswarby to Newmarkett, lay at a new Inn at Stilton.

OCT. 12.—Munday, we either burnt, sunk, or brought away all ye ffrench and Spanish shipping lying within ye Port of Vigo, consisting of 15 ffrench men of warr, 2 ffrigats, 1 fireship, 3 advice boats, and 17 Spanish Galleons, with most of their loading.

OCT. 29.—Thursday, we left Ickworth with our whole ffamily, lay that night at Newmarket, ye next at Hockeril, and arrivd ye 31st at London.

DEC. 2.—Niece Elweses with their man and maid servant came to live with us at London.

1703.

FEB. 18.—My Council mov'd Lord Keeper Wright to take off my

security given upon, and to discharge ye writt of supplicavit, which Sir Richard Gipps had prayd against me, but Sir Richard making fresh affidavit of his ffear, Lord Keeper continued us bound.

FEB. 28.—Sir T. ffelton and I went from London to Newmarket.

MARCH 6.—I returned from Newmarket to London to see dear wife.

MARCH 23.—My Patent bears date for creating me and my heirs male a Baron of England. My motto is, je n'oublieray jamais.

MARCH 30.—I went from London to Newmarket with ye Duke of Bolton, Lord Hartington & Jacob Tonson.

APRIL 3.—Returnd to London to see dear wife.

APRIL 5.—Munday, my dear wife was brought to bed of a daughter first, and afterwards of a son, both born between 9 and 10 at night.

APRIL 18.—Sunday, they were both christened by Dr. Wake. Ye girle was named Henrietta ; Lady Harriet Godolphin, Lady Fitzharding & Earle of Sunderland answering for her. Ye boy was named Charles, ye Dutchess of St. Albans, Duke of Bolton & Marquiss of Hartington answering for him.

APRIL 20.—Tuesday, Sir Thomas ffelton & I sett out from London about 4 afternoon towards Newmarket, lay that night at Bishop Stafford, & arrivd next day ; came back to dear wife ye Saturday after in a day with Lord Treasurer to London.

MAY 16.—Sunday, dear wife was at ye height of her illness from a rheumatick pain & swelling, which fell upon her left side down to her foot ; which had continued so long upon her as to reduce her to a very low & weak condition ; but by ye great goodness & mercy of Almighty God (which I shall never forget (by his grace) to thank and praise him for) this day provd ye happy crisis of her distemper, for she found herself strangely refreshd by a sweet sleep she took in ye day time, & mended sensibly & daily from that time; & on Thursday ye 27th instant she found herself recoverd enough to venture abroad to see Sir Thomas ffelton. Gloria Deo. What shall, or can, I give to God for all his blessings & benefits conferrd upon me?

JUNE 3.—Thursday, niece Elweses & their servants went from us to Stoke.

JUNE 14.—Munday, I made a vow to play no more, for ye following reasons, which I would have all my children consider seriously of. First, it occasions great mispense of time; 2dly, no mony prospers well that's gained by play; 3dly, Tis ten to one but that he who games upon ye square (and he who doth not is a downright Pick-Pocket) at long run suffers ye loss of his own mony; 4thly, it insensibly contracts habits of swearing, and leads a man generally into loose company & conversation; 5thly, Play necessarily makes one keep very ill hours, & setting up all night disorders ye health, and weakens ye memory, & renders one altogether unfitt for any sort of business either publick or private; 6thly, if a man of a great estate is known to love or follow gameing, ye sharpers never faile to form all sorts of plotts against him till they get his mony; 7thly, it naturally begetts quarrels, & altho' fighting in a good cause should never be declind by any man, yet tis one of ye last misfortunes to find oneself ingag'd therein upon these occasions, where murder may prove ye consequence of covetous desires; in fine this distich—on commence par estre dupe—on finit par être fripon—is ye best abstract of a gamester's character. Or thus : Le gross jeu est le renversement de toutes les bienseances; which is enough to cure any wise or honest man of so fatal a passion.

JUNE 19.—Saturday, dear wife, Sir Thomas ffelton & self went to Windsor to pay our duty to ye Queen before our going into country.

JUNE 22.—I was introduced into ye House of Peers by Lord Berkeley & Lord Ossulstone; & ye Parliament was then prorogued to ye 3d August following.

JUNE 30.—Dear wife, ye twins, Harry & myself went from London to Ickworth in 2 daies. We lay at Hockeril.

AUGUST 7.—Saturday, dear wife went without me from Ickworth to London, & ye XIth she sett out thence for Bathe, lay that night at Reading, ye 12th at Marlburrough, & next day arrivd there with Sir T. Felton, Bell & Tom.

AUG. 9.—Munday, I sett out from Ickworth, saw my running horses at Marham in Norfolke, lay that night at Wisbich, and arrivd next day at Aswarby, where I staid till Saturday the 21st, lay that night at Stamford, ye 22d at Northampton, ye 23d at Burford, & arrivd ye 24th at Bathe to meet dear wife, who I long'd to see most impatiently, haveing never been so long absent from her before.

OCT. 2.—Saturday, dear wife, Bell, Tom & I sett out from Bathe, lay that night at Cirencester, ye 3d at Oxford, ye 4th at Wooburn, ye 5th at Cambridge, & next morning to Newmarket.

OCT. 22.—Bury Election, Sir R. Davers 20, Mr. Weld 16 votes.

NOV. 27.—Saturday, ye most violent hurricane of wind that ever was known in England, whereby many ships perished at sea, several churches, houses, trees etc. blown down, & many people lost their lifes by ye falling of whole stacks of chimneys, etc.

NOV. 29.—My Wen beat ye Duke of Argyles roan, and won me above eleven hundred pounds.

NOV. 30—Dear wife & I went from Newmarket towards London & arrivd ye next day.

DEC. 15.—My niece Elwess with their servants came to live with me again at London from Stoke.

1 7 0 4 .

MARCH 13.—Munday, Mr. Hopes dyed.

MARCH 15.—Wednesday, Mrs. Fox dyed about 3 afternoon.

MARCH 17.—Friday, Carr, Jack, & Betty went from London to Ickworth.

APRIL 4.—Tuesday, dear wife, Tom, & I went from London towards Newmarket, and arrivd ye next day.

APRIL 7.—My niece Ame Elwes went from me to Stoke. My Spider beat Lord Granbys Yellow Jack, and won me near twelve hundred pounds.

APRIL 24.—Thomas Covell & my self executed ye deed for exchange of land in Buckstal.

MAY 14.—Dear wife & I went from Ickworth, lay that night at my house at Newmarket, ye next at Hockeril, & arrivd ye 16th at London.

JULY 2.—(N.S.) Ye Duke of Marlborough gained a considerable victory over ye French & Bavarians at ye post of Schellenberg near Donavert on ye Danube.

JULY 6.—Thursday, my dear wife was deliverd of a boy (still-born) about 6 in ye morning. A beautiful child, even in Death. Optimum non nasci, bonum vero quam citissime interire.

> Tis good not to be born ; but if we must,
> The next good is, soon to return to dust.

JULY 25.—My uncle Sir Algernoon May dyed at Hampton.

AUG. 4.—Dear wife & I went to Windsor to pay our duty to ye Queen, before we left London, & staied 6 daies there.

AUG. 13.—(N.S.) Ye Duke of Marlborough entirely defeated & routed ye French & Bavarians in a pitchd battle at Blenheim.

AUG. 25.—Dear wife, Sir Thomas ffelton & my self went from London to Ickworth where we arrivd next day, lying at Hockeril.

OCT. 6.—Spider beat ye Duke of Boltons horse calld Danger, & won me near five hundred pounds.

G

NOV. 1.—My Starer beat Lord Kingstons Red Robin.

NOV. 3.—Friday, dear wife & I went from Ickworth, took up Sir T. ffelton at Newmarket, lay that night at Hockeril, arrivd next day at London.

NOV. 29.—My niece Elwes's and their servants came from Stoke to live with me at London.

1 7 0 5.

APRIL 2.—I agreed with Mr. Scrope to give him eight thousand pounds, his wife one hundred guineys, and his son a fine young horse of my own breed, for all his right and interest, pretences or claim in, to, or out of my estates in Lincolnshire from ye death of Mrs. Fox, 15 March, 1703.

APRIL 6.—I received 325 guineys of Lord Kingston and others for Snouts forfeit to Wen.

APRIL 8.—Dear wife, niece Elwes and self went from London to Hockeril, and ye next day to Newmarket.

APRIL 10.—Ye Queen & Prince arrivd at Newmarket.

APRIL 13.—My Spider beat ye Marquiss of Granbys horse called Unicorn, & won me above thirteen hundred pounds.

JUNE 5.—Dear wife & I went from Ickworth to Newport, & next day to London.

JUNE 19.—I paid £3543 to my nephew Porter at ye Bank of England, in full of all Principal & Interest Money due to him by my father's will, pursuant to an order of ye Master of ye Rolls bearing date 30th March, 1705.

JUNE 25.—Munday, dear wife & I went to Windsor to pay our duty to ye Queen, & staid there till ye 5th July following.

JULY 10.—Dear wife and I went from London to Hockeril, and ye next day to Ickworth.

JULY 27.—I paid Peter Brooke £290 for Nichols Farm of £20 per annum at Staningfield.

JULY 28.—I paid Mr. Richard Gipps upon ye exchange of Clapgate wood for Leyton Leys and Pestle Piece ye sum of £295..9..4.

AUG. 5.—Munday, dear wife & I with Bell, Carr, Jack, Betty and Thomas Hervey went from Ickworth towards Aswarby, lay that night at Wisbich, & arrivd next day.

SEPT. 13.—My cousin Sir John Poley of Boxted dyed. (*Note* 18).

SEPT. 17.—Munday, (being my dear son Carrs birthday) my dearest wife & ye 5 above named children sett out from Aswarby, lay that night at Stilton, ye next at Newmarket, & arrived at Ickworth Wednesday ye 18th.

In October 1705 I planted Woolfleece Close & Parke-Grove with acorns. (*Note* 19).

DEC. 1.—Saturday, ye Corporation of Bury elected my brother Porter to serve with my Father Felton for their Burgess to Parliament. (*Note* 2).

DEC. 4.—Tuesday, dear wife, Harry & self sett out from Ickworth, lay that night at Newmarket, ye next at Hockeril, arrived ye 6th at London. My nephew Tom Porter dyed of a feaver at Vienna in Germany about 2 afternoon.

DEC. 10.—Munday, I paid Mr. Robert Scrope £3000, in part of ye £8000 I agreed to give him by articles dated 2nd April preceding for all his interests, claims or pretensions whatsoever in my Lincolnshire estate.

1 7 0 6 .

FEB. 12.—I paid Mr. Scrope £5000 more (in all £8000) besides 100 guineys to his wife (& £300 for ye interest of the mony since 2d April when ye Articles bore date) in full as aforesaid, beside a young horse I gave his son worth near £100 more.

MARCH 12.—Tuesday, dear wife and I went from London to Hockeril, next day to Newmarket.

APRIL 9.—Tuesday, my Wenn beat Lord Kingstons white mare called pipeing Peg, 8 miles for 500 guineys.

APRIL 11.—Thursday, Sir Gervase Elwes dyed at Stoke about 3 in ye morning. *(Note 14.)*

APRIL 15.—Tuesday, Wenn beat ye said mare 8 miles for 500 guineys more.

APRIL 23.—Tuesday, ye said mare paid Wenn a forfeit of 250 guineys more.

APRIL 30.—Tuesday, Wenn beat fframptons Toney 8 miles for 300 guineys.

MAY 1.—Wensday, dear wife & I went from Newmarket to Hockeril, & next day arrivd at London.

MAY 7.—Tuesday, Wenn beat ye Bury-mare 4 miles for 200 guineys.

MAY 12.—Whitsunday, ye Duke of Marlborough beat ye French, Spanish, & Bavarian forces in a pitched battle at Ramellies in Flanders.

JUNE 24.—Munday, dear wife was delivered of a son.

JULY 8.—Munday, he was baptized & named James Porter Hervey, ye Duke of Grafton, my brother Porter & Lady Isabella Turner answering for him.

JULY 28.—Dear wife & I went from London to Hockeril, next day to Ickworth.

AUG. 6.—On Tuesday morning about 1 a clock my sweet pretty son James was found dead in ye bed, being overlaid by his fatal nurse. The Lord gave, & ye Lord hath taken away, yet blessed be ye goodness of my most merciful God, who hath left me so many alive.

AUG. 8.—Thursday, dear wife, Jack & I went to Wisbich, next day to Aswarby.

AUG. 26.—Munday, dear wife & I, Jack, my two nieces & nephew Sir Hervey Elwes, sett out from Aswarby, lay that night at Chesterfield, ye next day (being my birthday) we dined with ye Duke of Devonshire at Chatsworth in Derbyshire ; ye 28th to Doncaster, ye 29th to Yorke, (seeing Mr. Leeds's studd at Milford by ye way) of whom I bought a 3 year old bay Filleé, gott by Lord Whartons famous horse called Careless out of a full sister to famous Leeds. A 2 year old bay colt gott by ye Barbe King William gave his father, out of bay Pegg (a daughter of young Spankers). And a yearing bay colt gott by ye said Careless under a daughter of ye said Barbes, which was out of an own sister to Lord Whartons Gallant.

SEPT. 1.—Sunday, we dined at Mr. Squires after hearing a sermon at Yorke Minster ; Wednesday we waited on ye Arch Bishop at his Palace at Bishops Thorpe. Friday we dined with ye Earle of Carlisle at Henderscelf, on Saturday back to Doncaster, Sunday to Newark, & next day arriv'd at Aswarby.

SEPT. 19.—Thursday, dear wife & I with ye said children & nieces lay at Stilton from Aswarby, ye next night at Newmarket, & ye next at Ickworth.

OCT. 7.—Pipeing Peg paid an other forfeit to Wenn of 250 guineys.

OCT. 30.—Wensday, my Wenn beat Lord Treasurers horse Chance 10 stone 4 miles for 600 guineys each side.

NOV. 21.—Thursday, dear wife & I, Carr & Jack went from Ickworth to Newmarket, ye next day to Hockeril, & ye next to London.

1707.

MARCH 25.—I stated & agreed all accompts with my nephew John, & my nieces Isabella & Ame Elwes, & there became due to them out of ye legacies left to thier mother by my Uncle Hervey's & my Father's wills for principal & interest of ye whole (all allowances made) to my niece Isabella £5200 ; to Ame Elwes £3600 ; & to John Elwes £1400 ; for which said several sums I gave them my bond respectively, dated ye same day at 5 per cent ; whereupon they severally executed general releases to me at Mr. Mill's Chambers in ye Temple.

MARCH 30.—Dear wife & I lay at Hockeril from London, next day to Newmarket.

APRIL 9.—Wednesday, my steward Will Covell dyed.

MAY 6.—Tuesday, my Chesnut Whigg won Ipswich Plate.

MAY 18.—Dear wife & I went from Ickworth.

MAY 19.—Ye Twins followd us to Newmarket.

MAY 20.—We lay all at Hockeril, & arrivd next day at London.

JUNE 14.—Dear wife & I & ye Twins went from London to Windsor being Saturday.

JULY 12.—Saturday, dear wife was brought to bed of a daughter about eleven at night at Windsor.   (My dearest Nann.)

JULY 16.—I went from Windsor to London.

JULY 17.—I insur'd my house & offices in St. James Square for £75 with ye Phœnix Society (at £5000) for 7 years. Ye same day I paid ye Bishop of Norwich £190 for ye renewal fine of my Church leases in Norfolke & Suffolke for 21 years from 10th July, 1707. Ye new lease from ye Dean & Chapter of Rochester is for 21 years from Midsummer 1706. I paid £159 .. 12 for my fine of this renewal.

JULY 27.—Sunday, my said daughter was baptiz'd by Mr. Thomas Dawson, Vicar of Windsor, & named Ann, our good, great & gracious Queen, ye Dutchess of Somerset (our cousin), & ye Marquis of Kent her said Majestys Lord Chamberlain answering for her.

JULY 31.—Thursday, Sir T. Felton & I went from Windsor to Woodstock to see Blenheim ; next day to Cornbury, from thence to Heathrop (ye

Duke of Shrewsburys), came back by Ditchley, (Lord Litchfields), & saw Emston Wells in our way again to Woodstock, & returnd to Windsor next day.

AUG. 10.—Dear wife and I, ye Twins & Ann, went from Windsor to London.

AUG. 13.—We lay at Hockeril, & next day arrivd at Ickworth my sweet center.

AUG. 22.—Dear wife & I & Bell went from Ickworth to Wisbich, & next day to Aswarby.

SEPT. 15.—Dear wife & I, Bell, Mrs. Burslem, & my young cousin Reynolds sett out from Aswarby, lay that night at Wisbich, & arrivd next day at Ickworth.

SEPT. 21.—Lady Harriet Ryalton came to Ickworth, & staid 10 daies.

NOV. 18.—Tuesday, my master Leeds dyed, having been 44 years School-Master at Bury.

NOV. 26.—Wednesday, my horse Gandergut beat Vane.

NOV. 27.—Dear wife & ye 7 eldest children lay at Hockeril, ye next night at London.

DEC. 9.—I paid my niece Isabella Elwes £3000 of ye £5200 due to her on my bond.

DEC. 31.—My good uncle Sir Edward Gage dyed at London.

1 7 0 8 .

APRIL 5.—Munday, dear wife & I went from London to Hockeril, & ye next day to Newmarket.

MAY 6.—Thursday, ye Corporation of Bury chose my father Felton and brother Porter (nemine contradicente) for thier Burgesses to Parliament.

MAY 8.—My horse Wenn beat Mr. Framptons Sparke. I won but 170 guineys by this match.

MAY 13.—The whole Corporation of Bury dined with me at Ickworth.

JUNE 3.—My dear wife was deliverd of a son, who lived but two hours after he was baptiz'd by Mr. Priest, & named Humphrey.

JUNE 4.—Friday, my dear son Carr went to Cambridg. I hope in God that he will prosper him in his studies there, & make him an useful instrument of his glory in this wicked generation.

AUG. 2.—Munday, my dear wife, Bell, Jack, Betty, Tom, & I, sett out from Ickworth ; lay that night at Wisbich, arrivd next day at Aswarby.

SEPT. 2.—Dear Carr came to see me at Aswarby from Cambridg.

SEPT. 17.—Friday, (being my dear son Carr's birthday,) dear wife & self & ye children above nam'd, sett out from Aswarby (in a very wett season), lay that night at Wisbich, & arrivd next day at sweet Ickworth.

OCT. 28.—Thursday, ye Prince of Denmark dyed.

NOV. 23.—Tuesday, dear wife & I left sweet Ickworth, lay that night at Newmarket, ye 24th at Hockeril, & arrivd at London on Thursday ye 25th with Sir Thomas Felton (from Newmarket).

DEC. 9.—Thursday, ye Corporation of Bury re-elected my worthy father in law Sir Thomas Felton (nemine contradicente) for thier representative to Parliament, upon her Majestys being graciously pleas'd to honour him with ye white-staff of Comptroller of her household, since he was first chosen by them to serve in ye same Parliament.

The same day my friend Major Norton of Ixworth dyed.

1 7 0 9 .

MARCH 3.—Thursday, my worthy friend & father in law Sir Thomas Felton dyed at his lodgings in White-Hall of the goute in his stomach, & was buryed at Playford ye 9th, Jack & I attending his hearse.

MARCH 10.—We went to Ickworth.

MARCH 26.—The Corporation of Bury chose Mr. Serjeant Weld thier Recorder to succeed Sir Thomas Felton as thier member to Parliament.

APRIL 4.—Munday, I lay at Hockeril from London, ye next night at Newmarket, & on Saturday ye 9th I went to Ickworth, & on Sunday ye 10th to Bury, on Wednesday ye 13th to Newmarket again, ye 14th to Hockeril, & ye 15th to London.

APRIL   .—My cousin ye Lord Dover dyed.

APRIL 26.—Tuesday, I went with Lord Ryalton & ye Earle of Crawford from London to Newmarket, & returnd to London May-day following.

MAY 19.—Thursday, dear wife was deliver'd of a daughter between 9 & 10 of ye clock at night.

JUNE 6.—I paid both my niece Elwess all interest mony due to ye 26th of March 1709, & they then allowd me for thier boarding with me to ye 7th of June 1709.

JUNE 8.—Wednesday, my aforementiond daughter was baptiz'd at my house in St. James' Square by Dr. Clarke, & named Barbarah ; ye Dutchess of Grafton (being represented by ye Countess of Grantham) ye Countess of Orkney & ye Lord Ryalton answering for her.

JULY 11.—Munday, dear wife and I (with ye Countess of Orkney) went from London to stay a week or 10 daies with ye Dutchess of Marlborough at her house at St. Albans ; but on Thursday about 3 afternoon, we receiving ye news there of Babs falling into convulsive fitts, we lay that night at Baldock, & arrivd at Ickworth (altho overthrown at Royston) ye next day; dineing with my son Carr at Cambridg by ye way.

JULY 21.—Dear wife & I sett out from Ickworth towards London where we arrivd ye next day.

JULY 25.—Sir John Playters paid in all ye principal & interest mony due upon his security.

H

JULY 30.—Dear wife and I sett out from London, & arrivd at dear Ickworth ye next day.

AUGUST 19.—Dear wife and I sett out from Ickworth, lay that night at Wisbich, & arrivd on Saturday ye 20th at Aswarby.

SEPT. 16.—Dear wife & I sett out from Aswarby, lay that night at Wisbich, & arriv'd on Carr's birth-day at sweet Ickworth.

SEPT. 24.—Saturday, ye Dutchess of Grafton & my cousin Sir Thomas Hanmer came to Ickworth, and staid with us till ye Wednesday following.

SEPT. 26.—Munday, ye Duke of Grafton lay at Ickworth.

OCT. 17.—I executed ye assignment of Dersingham great tythes in Norfolke to Mr. Walpole; & receivd £476 for ye consideration mony, being at ye rate of 14 years purchase, for ye remainder of my term in my lease from ye Bishop of Norwich. The same day I assign'd ye remainder of my term in Scotto & Hautebois lease (from ye said Bishop) to Mr. Durrant, & received £700 of him for ye consideration mony, being 14 years purchase also.

NOV. 2.—Wednesday, my colt called Thiefcatcher of Ickworth breed beat fframpton's fleet mare called Marguarita.

NOV. 9.—Ye said Marguarita paid her forfeit to my bay Betty of ye said Ickworth breed.

NOV. 17.—Dear wife & I went from Ickworth to Newmarket, lay ye 18th at Bishop Stafford, & arrivd ye 19th at London.

NOV. 24.—Thursday, both my niece Elwess & thier two servants came to board with us at London.

DEC. 26.—I seald new bonds to both my nieces, & nephew Jack Elwes, wherein was included all thier shares for principal & interest mony due to them out of Sir John Playters's morgage, given them by thier mothers will.

DEC. 31.—I assign'd Hoxne tythes (my share thereof) & ye remainder of my time in ye Bishop of Norwich's lease thereof to me, being about 18 years & a half, (ye same as in those for Dersingham, Scotto & Hautebois) to Mr. John Thruston for £466 13s. 4d. being at ye rate of 14 years purchase also for ye same.

1 7 1 0 .

MARCH 30.—I delivered to my niece Elwess thier receipts for ye 15 Lottery tickets I bought for them by thier order.

APRIL 5.—I reckoned with & adjusted accounts with my nephew Sir Hervey Elwes, & paid & allowd him therein all his share for ye principal & interest mony he was entitled to in Sir John Playters's mortgage by his mother's will.

APRIL 6.—Thursday, dear wife & I sett out from London, lay that night at Bishop Stafford, ye next at Newmarket, & on Saturday at Ickworth.

APRIL 11.—Tuesday, my Merryman beat Lord Treasurers single Peeper. I wonn 220 guineys.

APRIL 13.—Thursday, fframpton's Thief paid his forfeit to my Thief-catcher.

MAY 6.—My famous horse Wenn, bred in Barrow Parke by me, wonn his twentieth match, by beating the Whiteneck mare of Mr. Curwyns breed for 200 guineys.

MAY 8.—Dear wife, Carr, Jack, & I went from Ickworth to Ipswich, saw ye Plate run for on Bixley Chase, went afterwards to see Sir Compton Felton, who was ill of ye goute at Playford, and returnd to sweet Ickworth ye 10th.

MAY 24.—Wednesday, I paid £700 (part of ye mony I sold some of my Church-lease-hold estates in Norfolke for) to Robert Growse, Mr.

Rookwood, & ye Minister & Churchwardens of Great Saxham, for all ye lands in Barrow that were mortgagd by Mr. Heigham to his father Mr. Ambrose Rookwood & his Trustees.

JUNE 11.—Dear wife, sweet Nanny, & I sett out from Ickworth, lay that night at Newmarket, ye next at Stafford, & ye next at London. *(N. 20).*

JUNE 15.—Thursday, I took out mine & dear wife her lottery tickets, mine being 110 tickets, hers & her childrens 45, in all 155 lottery tickets, numberd from 32802 incl^{u}sive to 32956.

JUNE 19.—Dear Carr left Cambridg, & came to me at London.

JULY 3.—Munday, dear wife was deliver'd of a boy, between two & three of ye clock afternoon, & being ill was privatly baptiz'd ye 7th, & named Felton, & on Sunday ye 16th July my said son dyed between 11 & 12 at night.

AUG. 12.—Saturday, I had (by Gods good Providence) a benefitted tickett of five hundred pounds per annum come up in ye state-lottery against one of ye numbers of my ticketts, viz., 32847, commencing from Michaelmas 1710 for 32 years.

AUG. 16.—I purchasd £2000 Bank-stock of Nathaniel Halhid; & £1000 more of Thomas Holford, ye whole £3000 at £109 10s. per cent, which with ye brokerage cost me £3292 10s.

AUG. 17.—I bought £500 more of Thomas Engier at £109 per cent.

AUG. 19.—Saturday, one other benefitt tickett of £5 per annum for ye same terms of years came up in ye said lottery against an other of my tickets numberd 32868.

AUG. 31.—Ye Duke of Grafton, Sir Philip Parker, & ye whole Corporation of Bury St. Edmunds dined with me at Ickworth.

OCT. 9.—Munday, my famous horse called Wenn, bred by my self, wonn his one & twentieth match against ye Patty mare, on which I wonn 260 guineys. (The end of my old Almanack).

NOV. 15.—The Patty mare beat Pulleyns Slouch, on which match I wonn 165 guineys, beside £50 for Squirrels brother.

NOV. 22.—Dear, wife & I left sweet Ickworth, lay that night at Newmarket, ye next at Hockeril, & arrived ye 24th at London.

NOV. 25.—I attended ye managers ot ye State lottery who allow'd of my Benefitt ticket entitled to £500 per annum number 32847 drawn ye 12th of August 1710; & at ye same time they also allowd of my other benefit ticket ot £5 per annum number 32868 drawn ye 19th of August 1710. Both for 32 years.

1 7 1 1 .

JAN. 12.—My niece Elwess came to live with me at London.

JAN. 16.—I paid my nephew Jack Elwes all interest mony to this day, & £200 in part of ye principal.

FEB. 13.—Niece Isabella Elwes & Mary Arnold went from me.

MARCH 28.—Sir H. Furnese gave Mr. Masson his letter of creditt for £1000, for Carr's expence in travelling. *(Note 21).*

MARCH 31.—Jack, Tom, Will, Harry & my self sett out from London, lay that night at Hockeril, & arriv'd next day at Newmarket.

APRIL 3.—Niece Amee Elwes & her footman went from me.

APRIL 11.—I travelled all ye night between ye 11th & 12th of April from Newmarket to London to choose Governours & Directors of ye Bank *at the earnest request of the Dutchess of Marlborough. (Note 22).*

APRIL 15.—I returnd from London to Newmarket, & went ye next day to dear Ickworth.

APRIL 29.—I return'd from Newmarket to London with ye Duke of Kent.

MAY 6.—I paid niece Elwess in full of all interest money due to them to ye 26th of December 1710; & niece Amee Elwes the two years profitts of her benefitt tickets in ye first lottery due at Michaelmas 1710, when those payments ended.

MAY 12.—I transferrd £1000 of my Bank-stock to Mr. George Wanley in trust only, that his uncle Mr. James Chambers might make up therby such sums of mony as I should order him to pay into ye lotteries etc, which ye monies returned to him on my account would not extend to.

MAY 17.—Dear wife, Jack, Betty & I went from London to Hockeril, arrivd next day at sweet peaceful Ickworth.

JUNE 6.—Wednesday, my diligent just & faithful steward, Mr. John Burslem, dyed at Aswarby.

JUNE 25.—Munday, dear wife & I sett out from Ickworth, lay that night at Wisbich, & arriv'd ye 26th at Aswarby.

AUG. 9.—Thursday, dear wife & I sett out from Aswarby, lay that night at Spalding, where I saw all ye lands wherein I purchasd ye reversionary interests after ye expiration of ye several terms of years late Sir John Oldfield had therein : ye 10th we lay at Downham, & arriv'd at peaceful blessd Ickworth (ye sweet center of my humble soul), being ye most innocent quiet place it knows in all ye world.

AUG. 17.—Friday, dear wife & I sett out from Ickworth, lay that night at Hockeril, & arrivd next day at London.

AUG. 27.—Munday, (my birth-day) dear wife & I sett out from London, lay that night at Reading, ye next at Marlborough (where we saw our cousin ye Duke of Somersets house & ye mount,) & arrivd ye 29th at Bath.

SEPT. 26.—Wednesday, dear wife & I sett out from Bath ; lay that night at Marlborough, ye next at Reading, ye 28th at London ; where we rested ye 29th ; lay ye 30th at Hockeril, & arrivd ye first of October at Newmarket.

OCT. 14.—Sunday, my most pious, wise & dutifull daughter, Mrs. Isabella Carr Hervey fell sick of a feaver at Ickworth ; of which she dyed ye xith of November following ; & was interr'd at her most excellent mothers feet ye 15th after in Ickworth chancell.

> Si munera cœli bene computamus, diu vixit,
>
> Mortua obtinuit plurima quæ meruit.
>
> Those virtues which in her short life were shown
> Have equall'd been by few, surpass'd by none.

Quæ ita se gessit ut nunquam de illa etiam maledicorum quidquam auderet fama confingere.

> O happy child ! ta'ne from this wicked age
> Where nought but malice & hypochrisy does rage,
> A fitter time for Heaven no soul e'er chose,
> The only blessed place, now free from those.

NOV. 23 —Thursday, dear wife, my sans pareille daughter Ann, & I sett out from Ickworth, lay that night at Newmarket, ye next at Hockeril, & arriv'd ye 25th at London.

DEC. 4.—Munday, My niece Elwes's came to London.

1 7 1 2 .

On New years day $17\frac{11}{12}$, ye Duke of Marlborough, Baron Bothmar (ye Elector of Hannover's envoy), Lord Somers, Lord Cowper, Lord Godolphin, Lord Sunderland, Lord Hallifax, ye Duke of Devonshire, Lord Portland, Lord Wharton, & Lord Scarburrough, dined with me at my house in St. James' Square, ye day after ye queen had taken ye command of ye army from ye Duke of Marlborough.

JAN. 8.—Tuesday, Those two great men, ye Duke of Marlborough & ye Prince Eugene of Savoy, honourd me both together with thier company at my said house in St. James' Square.

JAN. 17.—Thursday, my sons Tom & Will went to Westminster School.

JAN 24.—Thursday, I paid my cousin Reynolds £200, in part of ye principal sum of £1200 due to him on my bond ; so there remains but £1000 due thereon ; & I at ye same time paid him all interest money due to this day.

JAN. 27.—Harry went to Westminster School.

JAN. 28.—Jack went to Westminster School.

FEB. 12.—Tuesday, my dear wife was deliver'd, by ye good Providence of Allmighty God, of her tenth son, by Sir David Hamilton ; for whose skilfull assistance we ought alwaies to thank God.

MARCH 3.—Munday, Jack & I went from London to Newmarket in a day ; & from thence to Ickworth ye 5th, & from thence to Hockeril ye 8th, & to London ye 9th.

MARCH 10.—Prince Eugene of Savoy supp'd with me at my house in St. James's Square.

APRIL 2.—Jack & I went from London to Newmarket with ye Duke of Bolton & his second son.

APRIL 3.—My bey colt calld Ickworth wonn ye Queens 100 guiney Plate there from all ye horses of ye same age ; *which said horse I gave to my particular friend Sir Thomas Hanmer.* (Note 22).

APRIL 13.—Jack & I returnd in a day from Ickworth to London.

APRIL 15.—Lord Godolphin dyed.

APRIL 26.—Dear wife, Jack, Ann & I lay at Hockeril from London, & ye next night at Newmarket.

APRIL 28.—My very pretty, witty twinn daughter Henrietta dyed at Ickworth of a consumption, between 1 and 2 in ye morning.

MAY 31.—Dear wife & I sett out from sweet healthful Ickworth, lay that night at Hockeril & arriv'd ye 1st of June at London.

JULY 7.—Dear wife & I sett out from London, lay at Hockeril, & arriv'd ye 8th at Ickworth.

JULY 28.—Munday, dear wife, Betty, my particular friend Anne, & I sett out from Ickworth, lay that night at Wisbich, & arrivd at Aswarby ye next day.

AUG. 24.—Dear wife, Jack & I sett out from Aswarby, lay that night at Stamford; ye 25th at Northampton; ye 26th we dined at Sir Edmond Dentons place Hilsden; lay that night at Lord Whartons seat Winchindon.

AUG. 27.—(My birthday) My grey horse Flanderkin beat all ye horses of his age for ye 200 guineys stakes at Quainton Meadow.

AUG. 29.—Friday, we went from Lord Whartons, lay that night at Burford, & arrivd ye 30th at Bath, where we mett Betty.

SEPT. 26.—Friday, dear wife, Jack, Betty & I left Bath; lay that night at Marlborough; ye 27th at Reading; & ye 28th at London, where we rested ye 29th; & on ye 30th lay at Hockeril, & arrivd on ye first of October at Newmarket.

OCT. 2.—Ye Dutchess of Cleveland came thither, & staid with us at Mr. Stutevilles till Saturday ye xith. (*Note* 23.)

NOV. 26.—I paid Mr. George Bird of Lawshall £250 for ye purchase mony of Dodds Farm in Whepstead.

DEC. 1.—Dear wife, Nann & I sett out from Ickworth, layd that night at Newmarket, ye next at Hockeril, & arriv'd ye 3d at London.

1713.

JAN. 12.—My niece Elwes's came to live with me at London.

MARCH 5.—Thursday, my dear wife was by ye mercy and blessing of Gods good Providence brought to bed of ye eleventh son she hath enrichd ye family of ye Herveys with.

I

MARCH 9.—Munday, I paid Sir Thomas Gery (a master in Chancery) £1101..7..3, by Sir Compton Feltons order, as executor to his brother Sir Thomas ; ye same being paid persuant to a decree of ye court obtaind by General Talmash's Creditors, so much being found by ye said Masters report in ye said cause to remain of ye said Mr. Talmash's estate in ye said Sir Thomas Feltons hands at his death, who was one of ye said General's executors.

MARCH 18.—I paid my niece Amee Elwes £300, in part of ye principal sum of £4300 I owed her on bond ; & then gave her a new bond for ye remaining £4000.

MARCH 25.—Wednesday, my said last mentioned son was baptizd by Dr. Clarke, & named James ; ye Duke of Rutland, ye Lord Ossulstone, & ye Countess of Essex answering for him.

APRIL 1.—Jack & I went from London to Bishop-Stafford, & arrivd ye next day at Newmarket.

APRIL 6.—Munday, my Union colt beat ye Duke of Rutlands Babylonian, & wonn me near £500.

APRIL 8.—Ye Marquiss of Dorchester, ye Earle of Godolphin, Mr. Charleton & I went from Newmarket ; lay that night at Hockeril & arrivd next day at London.

APRIL 9.—My horse Flanderkin won ye Queens 100 guineas Plate at Newmarket from all ye horses of his age ye second time.

APRIL 10.—Ye said company returnd with me to Newmarket.

APRIL 26.—Sunday, I was taken very ill of a fitt of ye stone or gravel at Ickworth Church, which lasted till nine at night ; ye next day hearing by an express messenger from London that my dear wife & youngest child were both ill there ; & she suspecting that I was not well at Ickworth ; we both mett on Tuesday ye 28th at Hockeril, going to see each other ; & on ye 29th came together to Newmarket ; & ye 30th to dear Ickworth.

MAY 3.—From Ickworth to Newmarket; ye 5th lay at Newport; ye 6th to London.

MAY 2.—Saturday, my last born son James dyed at London between 7 & 8 in ye morning of convulsive fitts; occasioned by an opening in his head which he was born with.

MAY 21.—Thursday, my niece Amee Elwes was marryed to Mr. Robert Meggott at my house in St. James's Square by Dr. Clarke, when I paid her £4080 in full of all interest & principal mony due to her on my forementiond bond, & of all other demands whatsoever. *(Note 14)*.

Then paid Jack & Tom thier blank lottery Tickets due Michaelmas 1712.

MAY 23.—I gave Thomas Manley one hundred pounds to sett up his trade with, for my dear Uncle Herveys sake & for my dearer Fathers, whose Godson he is. *(Note 24)*.

MAY 30.—Dear wife, Nann & I sett out from London, lay that night at Hockeril, & arrivd next day at sweet desireable Ickworth.

JUNE 20.—I conveyd away my lands in Burrough Marsh & Ashby Field in Lincolnshire to Mr. Thomas Kew for £322..10, being a very great price.

On Monday & Tuesday being ye 27th & 28th days of July, ye whole Corporation of Bury, with thier Burgess, Recorder & Town-Clerk, dined with me at Ickworth; & on Thursday ye 30th I visitted every member of ye said body, recommending my brother Porter & my son Carr as candidates at ye next election for Parliament men.

JULY 31.—Friday, dear wife & I left sweet Ickworth, lay that night at Hockeril, & arrivd next day at London, where we rested Sunday ye 2d of August, lay ye 3d at Reading, ye 4th at Marlborough, & arrivd (with Jack) ye 5th at Bath.

SEPT. 2.—Ye Corporation of Bury elected my son Carr Hervey & my brother Colonel Porter for thier representatives in ye new Parliament. My son had 31 votes out of ye 37 ; my brother Porter 24 ; & Mr. Jermyn Davers 12, & Mr. Afflick (ye other candidate) but 3.

SEPT. 18.—Dear wife, Jack & I left Bath; lay that night at Marlbro, ye 19th at Reading, & arrivd ye 20th at London ; where (she falling ill of ye Chollick) we stayd till Friday ye 25th, lying that night at Hoceril, & arrivd ye 26th at Ickworth.

NOV. 19.—Thursday, I & dear wife went with Jack to Cambridg, & left him at Clare-Hall (his brother Carrs Colledg) to persue his studies. May God prosper him therin, & all other his good purposes.

NOV. 27.—Friday, my dear wife her aunt ye Lady Poley dyed at London, & was buryed at Livermoor on Wednesday ye 16th of December following.

DEC. 16.—Wednesday, my dear son Carr arrived at Ickworth after almost three years Travels in France, Flanders, Holland, Germany & Italy etc.

DEC. 21.—Munday, ye Corporation of Bury waited on my said son Carr in thier formalities at my brother Porters house in Bury.

1 7 1 4 .

JAN. 5.—I & my whole Family left sweet Ickworth, lay that night at Newmarket, (where we mett ye Dutchess of Grafton & my Cousin Sir Thomas Hanmer) & went together next day to Hockeril, & arrivd ye 7th at London.

FEB. 6.—My son Charles went to Mr. Valet's school at Hampstead.

APRIL 8.—My niece Meggott was brought to bed of a son. (*Note* 14.)

APRIL 9.—Ye right of Bury-Election was heard by ye Committee of ye House of Commons ; who resolv'd that ye right of electing members to serve in Parliament for ye Burrough of Bury St. Edmunds is in ye Alderman, 12 Capital Burgesses, & 24 Burgesses of ye Common Council of ye said Burrough.

APRIL 27.—Tuesday, ye House unanimously confirm'd ye said resolution of ye Committee, & voted my son Carr & brother Colonel Porter both duely elected.

MAY 20.—I paid off all principal & interest mony due upon my bond to my cousin Robert Reynolds, being £616..15.

JUNE 19.—My niece Elwes went from us at London to Stoke.

JULY 15.—My good friend & honest neighbour, Mr. Samuel Battely, dyed at his house in Horringer.

	£	s.	d.
My expences from Midsummer 1695 to Lady day 1700 were	28236	11	02
From Lady day 1700 to Lady day last 1714 my expences were	88631	13	06
	116868	04	08

JULY 31.—My niece Isabella Elwes dyed at her brother Sir Hervey Elwes's at Stoke of a feaver.

AUG. 1.—Sunday, Queen Ann dyed about 7 in ye morning at Kensington.

AUG. 14.—Dear wife & I, with Tom, Will, Harry, & Charles, sett out from London, lay that night at Newport, arrivd ye 15th at charming Ickworth.

SEPT. 9.—Dear wife & I, with our son Jack, left sweet Ickworth, lay that night at Bishop Stortford, arrivd at London ye 10th.

SEPT. 18.—King George & ye Prince of Wales arrivd at Greenwich about 6 in ye evening ; where I had ye honour to kiss both their hands.

SEPT. 20.—Munday, I attended them from thence to thier Palace at St. James's in London ; being ye most magnificent entry that ever was seen.

OCT. 13.—Wednesday, ye Princess of Wales, with ye two young Princesses Ann & Æmilia, arrivd at St. James's.

OCT. 20.—Wednesday, King George was crowned, at which solemnity I walked in ye procession as Earle of Bristol.

NOV. 1.—Munday, (being just 26 years from ye day of my first marriage) his Majesty King George did me ye honour to supp with me at my house in St. James's Square.

1 7 1 5 .

FEB. 2.—Ye Corporation of Bury unanimously elected my brother Porter & my son Lord Hervey thier representatives for ye ensuing Parliament.

MARCH 2.—Wednesday, my dear wife was deliverd of her 5th daughter & 16th child.

MARCH 23.—Wednesday, she was baptiz'd by Dr. Trimnel Bishop of Norwich, & named Louisa Carolina Isabella; the King, ye Princess of Wales & ye Marchioness of Dorchester answering for her.

APRIL 27.—Wednesday, my young, yet old friend Nann, Bab, Felton & Louisa with myself went from London to Newport, & arrivd next day at sweet Ickworth.

MAY 8.—I left sweet Ickworth, lay at Hockeril, & arrivd next day at London.

JUNE 5.—Dear wife & I went from London to Newport, & arrivd ye next day at dear Ickworth.

JULY 18.—Dear wife & I left sweet Ickworth, lay that night at Hockeril, & arrivd ye 19th at London.

AUG. 16.—The King having named me to make his compliments to Seignior Tron, Ambassadour from ye Republick of Venice to his Majesty, I waited on him at Greenwich for that purpose, & conducted him from thence thro' London to his own house in St. James's Square.

SEPT. 19.—Munday, dear wife & I left London, lay that night at Hockeril, & arriv'd next day at sweet Ickworth.

SEPT. 26.—Munday, my cousin Sir Thomas Hanmer & ye Reverend Mr. Richard Hill came to Ickworth, & stay'd with me there till ye Thursday following.

DEC. 1.—Thursday, dear wife, Betty & I went to Euston, & stay'd there till ye Saturday sevenight after, returning to sweet Ickworth ye 10th.

1 7 1 6 .

JAN. 3.—Dear wife & I with our children sett out from Ickworth, lay that night at Newmarket (where we mett my cousin Sir Thomas Hanmer my cousin Ned Duncombe, & his sister Sophia) lay next night at Hockeril, & arriv'd ye 5th (my son Henry's birth-day) at London.

APRIL 3.—Tuesday, my self, with Lord Hervey, Jack, Nann, Bab, Felle & Louisa, went from London & lay at Hockeril; next day Lord Hervey, Jack & I went to Newmarket, ye others to Ickworth.

APRIL 12.—Thursday, Jack & I left sweet Ickworth in all its blooming beauties, & yet without regrett, returning to dear wife at London next day.

MAY 3.—Thursday, dear wife, Jack & I went from London to Epsom to see ye 3 Plates run for there; & returnd Saturday ye 5th.

JUNE 2.—Saturday, my son Will went on board Captain Agar in ye Rochester Man of Warr, to make the voyage of New-found-land, from thence to go up ye streights etc.

JUNE 4.—Munday, dear Jack sett out from London towards Paris, in order to his farther travels; wherin I beseech God Almighty to protect & perfect him ye man I wish to see him.

JUNE 7.—Thursday, several drunken officers of ye Guards with thier servants attackd my coach, (dear wife being in it very big with child) my self & servants in ye strand; for which affront his Majesty had ordered

Lord Cadogan to call a Court Martial to have them all broke ; but they coming all to my house and submitting themselves & severally asking pardon for ye same in ye presence of ye said Lord Cadogan, I humbly besought King George that thier prosecution might be stopp'd.

JULY 28.—Saturday, dear wife, Lady Betty & I went from London, lay that night at Hockeril, & arrivd at sweet Ickworth next day.

AUG. 23.—Thursday, dear wife, Felle & my self left sweet Ickworth, lay that night at Newmarket, ye next at Hockeril, & arriv'd ye 25th at London.

SEPT. 25.—Tuesday, my dear wife, by the goodness of my most merciful God, was safely & speedily deliver'd (according to our repeated joynt Prayers for that purpose) of a daughter (my twentieth child & her seventeenth) between four & five in ye morning ; who was baptiz'd on Sunday ye 7th day of October following by Dr. Clarke, and named Henrietta ; our Cousin ye Duke of Argyle, ye Dutchess of Cleveland & ye Lady Dalkieth answering for her.

OCT. 17.—Wednesday, my self with Betty & Felle left London, lay at Hockeril, & arriv'd ye 18th at my much belov'd Ickworth.

NOV. 1.—Thursday, my dear wife arrivd at Ickworth, making it much more agreeable than ever to me, being very much wanted & long'd for by me.

DEC. 17.—Munday, ye Dutchess of Grafton came to my house at Bury, & staid there till ye Friday following, untill the two Assemblees were over. Dear wife & I waited on her there to entertain her all ye time.

1 7 1 7 .

JAN. 19.—Saturday, ye King arrived at London from Hannover. My son Jack came over with his Majesty from thence.

JAN. 21.—Munday, dear wife, Betty, & all ye 5 youngest children, left dear Ickworth, lay that night at Newmarket, ye next at Hockeril, (where my son Jack mett us, being arrivd at London from his travels but ye Saturday preceding), and went all ye next day for London.

MARCH 29.—My conveyance of Digby, Catley & Walcott estates to Mr. William Thornton bears date.

APRIL 14.—Sunday, my brother Porter dyed at his house in Little Marlborough Street, & was buryed near his mother ye Lady Diana Porter in St. Gyles's Chancel ye 20th following. *(Note 2).*

APRIL 23.—Tuesday, my most dear son Tom went to Christchurch Colledg in Oxford ; may my most good & gracious God prosper him in his studies there, & give him grace to become as pious & as virtuous a man as his most excellent grandfather Sir Thomas Hervey was.

JULY 25.—Thursday, my son Will went on board Captain Jacob in ye Diamond Man of Warr, to go to Jamaica, Vera Cruze etc. God allmighty prosper him in this & all other expeditions.

JULY 26.—Friday, dear wife, Betty & I left London, & arriv'd next day at sweet Ickworth.

AUG. 14.—Wednesday, dear wife, Jack & I sett out from sweet Ickworth, lay that night at Wishich, & arrivd next day at Aswarby.

SEPT. 16.—Munday, dear wife, Jack, Betty & I sett out from Aswarby, lay that night at Wisbich, & arrivd ye 17th (my son Carr's birthday) at dear Ickworth.

SEPT. 24.—Sir Samuel Garth came from London to Bury to make me & dear wife a visitt.

SEPT. 26.—I carryed him to see sweet Ickworth, which he admir'd so much as to promise its celebration in poetry, if ever he wrote any more in verse.

OCT. 2.—Wednesday, ye King came to Newmarket, where I waited

K

on his Majesty, who honourd me with an audience alone in his Bedchamber on ye 5th.

OCT. 4.—Friday, I paid ye principal & interest mony for ye purchase of ye mannours of Chevington & Hargrave as followeth ;   viz.

	£	s.	d.
The purchase mony being	10942	08	05
& ye interest thereof from 24 June, 1715, to 25 July, 1717, ...	1140	13	09
In all	12083	02	02

which said sum was thus discharged

	£	s.	d.
By a mortgage I made of ye premises to ye D. of Marlborough for	7000	00	00
By a bill I drew on Messrs. Wanley & Cradock to Mr. Guidott for	3760	11	10
By a note of Sir Robert Child & Co. for	892	10	..
By four hundred guineas paid Guidott in specie (all at Bury)	430	..	..
	12083	01	10

OCT. 10.—Thursday, I paid Jack Bannister 50 guineas for my son Jack, on his most solemn promise passed to me that he would never ponte again at Bassett as long as he should live.

OCT. 25.—Friday, I narrowly escaped from being drowned in my new Canall at Spring Garden in ye parke ; for which & all other Gods great & wonderful mercies & protections towards me his most unworthy servant, his holy Providence be for ever adored by me & mine & our posterity after us. *(Note 25.)*

NOV. 2.—Saturday, the Princess of a Prince. *(Note 22.)*

NOV. 25.—Munday, dear wife, Jack, Betty, Nann, Bab, Louisa, Felton & Harriet left sweet Ickworth, lay that night at Newmarket, ye next at ye George at Bishop-sartford, & arrivd ye 27th at London.

DEC. 2.—Munday, ye Prince & Princess went from St. James's to Lord Granthams house in Albemarle Street.

1 7 1 8 .

FEB. 6.—Thursday, ye young Prince George William who was born ye 2d ult. dyed at Kensington.

MARCH 19.—I paid my son Jack ye ballance of my account (as residuary legatee of Sir Thomas ffelton), being £901..16..09½.

MARCH 28.—My conveyance of Branswel, Dunsby etc to my son Mr. John Hervey (Jack) bears date on ye 28th of March.

MARCH 31.—Munday, dear wife kissed ye Princess of Wales her hand, as one of the Ladies of her Royal Highness's Bedchamber.

MAY 24.—Saturday, my nephew Megott dyed at his place Marcham, near Abingdon in Berks, of a consumption. He was a very sober, sensible, honest man, & good husband. (*Note* 14.)

JULY 6.—Dear wife, Jack & I sett out from London, lay that night at Newport, & arrivd ye next day at sweet Ickworth.

JULY 16.—Wednesday, Sir John Vanbrugh came to Ickworth, and sett out ye scituation of my new house, leaving a plan with me for ye same, & went away ye 19th for Ely towards London.

JULY 19.—Dear wife & Jack sett out from Ickworth towards London to be at Richmond ye Munday following, when she went into her week of waiting.

JULY 31.—Thursday, my daughter Betty & I sett out from sweet Ickworth, lay at Hockeril; left her at London & arrivd at Richmond ye next night, where I found dear wife well there (thanks to my good & gracious God) tho' she had been ill there, which occasioned my journey thither.

AUG. 6.—Wednesday, dear wife, Betty, Jack & I sett out from London, lay that night at Reading, ye 7th at Marlborough & arrivd ye 8th at Bath, where we stayd till ye 19th of October, lay that night at Marlborough, ye 20th at Reading, & arriv'd ye 21st at London.

DEC. 31.—The Lord Commissioners of ye Admiralty signed my son Wills Commission constituting him 2d Lieutenant of his Majestys Man of Warr ye Defiance, a 4th Rate.

1 7 1 9.

JAN. 2.—Friday, he rode post to Portsmouth to go on board ye said ship.

APRIL 28.—Tuesday, my daughter Betty (who was & had been very ill), Babb, Louisa & Felle went from London (ye small pox having appeard ye day before on Harriet), lay that night at Harlow, ye next at Chesterford, & arrivd ye 30th at sweet Ickworth. The same day, being April 28, ye Prince & Princess went to stay at Richmond. The same day I borrowed £7000 of Mr. Le Bas at 4½ per cent, to discharge all other debts.

MAY 8.—Friday, dear wife, Nann & I sett out from London, lay that night at Hockeril, & arrivd ye 9th at sweet Ickworth.

MAY 16.—Saturday, Mrs. Eliz : Manley dyed at Erbistock (her husbands place in Wales) & was buryed there.   *(Note 24)*.

MAY 30.—Saturday, Mr. Joseph Alexander, Rector of Ickworth & Chedburgh, dyed at Bury, but was buried at Ickworth Church on Tuesday ye 2d of June.

JUNE 7.—Dear wife & I left sweet Ickworth, lay at Hockeril, & arriv'd ye 8th at London.

JUNE 15.—Dear wife, Jack & I left London, lay that night at Newport, & arrived the next day at sweet Ickworth.

JUNE 19.—I sign'd & seald ye presentation of Ickworth & Chedburgh to ye reverend Mr. Robert Butts.   *(Note 26)*.

AUG. 17.—Munday, dear wife, Jack & I went to Ipswich ; went to ye Assembly there ye 18th, where we mett near 200 gentlemen & ladies, all of Suffolke, & returnd ye 19th to Ickworth.

NOV. 18.—Wednesday, Sir Compton Felton dyed at his house in Ipswich.

NOV. 21.—Dear wife & I left sweet Ickworth, lay at Newport, & arriv'd at London ye next day.

NOV. 29.—I betted Colonel Campbell one hundred guineas that ye Missisippi stock at Paris would not be above 1000 on that day twelvemonth, which I won, & he paid me.

DEC. 17.—Thursday, dear wife, Jack, Tom, Will & I left London, lay at Newport, & arrivd ye 18th (being my most dear & entirely beloved wife her birth-day) at sweet Ickworth.

1 7 2 0 .

JAN. 8 —Dear wife, Jack & I left sweet Ickworth, lay at Newmarket, ye next night at Hockeril, & arrivd ye 10th at London.

APRIL 14.—Thursday, dear wife & I sett out from London, lay at ye Rein'd deer at Bishop-startford, & arriv'd ye 15th at Ickworth.

APRIL 21.—Thursday, my dear & hopeful son Mr. John Hervey was marryed to Mrs. Mary Le Pell. *(Note 27)*.

AUG. 20.—I left sweet Ickworth, lay at Hockeril, arriv'd ye 21 at London, & went ye 22d to Richmond.

AUG. 26.—I executed my articles of agreement with Mr. William Astell, altho' I could have had 16 years purchase more for ye estate of others than he was to give me for it.

SEPT. 2.—Dear wife & I sett from London, lay that night at Reading, ye 3d at Marlborough, & arriv'd ye 4th at Bath.

OCT. 9.—Dear wife & I sett out from Bath, lay at Marlborough, ye 10th at Reading, & arrivd ye 11th at London with Mr. Holt.

OCT. 19.—Wednesday, my wife her grandmother, the Countess of Suffolke, dyed.

OCT. 22.—My cousin ye Lady De Lorain dyed.

NOV. 9.—Wednesday, I mett Mr. Astell at Mr. Wards chambers in ye Temple, where, at his request, it was agreed that he would give me £2000 to discharge him from his articles with me for ye purchase of my lands at Hale magna & parva ; which in consideration thereof I did, wherupon ye said articles were cancelled, & mutual general releases executed ; ye value of lands being then fallen again to near 20 years purchase, & he being to give me 24 years purchase, I lost again by this bargain rather than have a suite.

NOV. 10.—I paid my son John £1500 in part of ye £6000 I gave him my bond for. Ye remaining £4500 I paid him on ye 16th of December following.

NOV. 11.—Dear wife & I sett out from London, lay at Newport, & arriv'd ye 12th at sweet Ickworth.

NOV. 19.—Saturday, dear wife & I went to Mildenhall, & staid with my most valuable kinsman, Sir Thomas Hanmer, & ye Dutchess of Grafton, till ye Tuesday following.

NOV. 25.—Dear wife & I, with our 4 youngest daughters, left sweet Ickworth, lay at Newmarket, ye next at Hockeril, & arriv'd ye 27th at London.

DEC. 16.—My mortgage to Dr. Arbuthnot bears date for £4500, with which I dischargd my bond to my son John.

1 7 2 1 .

APRIL 11.—Tuesday, my poor son Henry broke both the bones of his left legg by jumping over a hedg & ditch at Oxford.

APRIL 15.—Saturday, her Royal Highness ye Princess of Wales was deliverd of a Prince about 7 in ye evening.

APRIL 24.—Munday, Robert Wildman dyed, after having scrved my dear father & me 42 years as Coachman, without any ill accident in all that time.

APRIL 28.—I borrow'd £1000 more ot ye Duke of Marlborough.

MAY 8.—I borrow'd £1000 more (in all now £9000) of ditto.

AUG. 3.—Thursday, my daughter in law Mrs. Mary Hervey was brought to bed of a son about 4 afternoon, & was named George William; the King, ye Princess & my self answering for him.

AUG. 8.—Tuesday, my dear wife sett out from London towards Bath, where I found my self so very disconsolate without her, that ye next day, being Wednesday ye 9th of August, I sett out from London with my son Tom towards Ickworth, (which I found not sweet in her absence), lay at Newport & arrivd there ye tenth.

AUG. 21.—Munday, Tom & I went to Ipswich, saw my dear Heiress her estate at Sproughton by ye way, & ye next day those at Playford, and returnd to Ickworth ye 23d.

AUG. 28.—Sir David Hamilton dyed, an honest North-Briton.

AUG. 29.—My friend & fellow traveller Sir Henry Bond dyed.

AUG. 31.—Thursday, I entertain'd ye Corporation of Bury with a dinner of 27 dishes of meat. All were present but L. Wright & S. Ray.

SEPT. 23.—I left Ickworth to make my dear wife a visitt at Bath, lay that night at Biccleswade, ye 24th at Oxford, ye 25th at Cirencester, & arriv'd ye 26th at Bath.

OCT. 11.—Wednesday, dear wife, Mrs. Bradshaw & I sett out from Bath, lay that night at Marlborough, ye 12th at Reading at ye Crown Inn, & arriv'd ye 13th at London.

OCT. 21—My son Will returnd from ye Baltick.

1 7 2 2 .

JUNE 16.—That very great man & most serviceable of all English subjects, ye Duke of Marlborough, dyed at Windsor Lodg.

JUNE 19.—I borrowd £2500 of John Edwyn Esq.

JUNE 26.—Dear wife, Harry, Felle & I sett out from London, lay at Newport, & arriv'd ye 27th at sweet Ickworth.

JULY 22.—Dear wife, Mr. & Mrs. Hervey, & I went from Ickworth to Ipswich ; went next day to see Playford, ye 24th to see ye estate at Shotley, dined at ye Ferry-Farm, & returnd ye 25th to sweet Ickworth to keep our wedding-day there.

AUG. 4.—Dear wife, Harry & I sett out from sweet Ickworth, lay at Hockeril, & arrivd ye 5th at London, & carryed her ye 5th to Richmond, where I left her to waite for a fortnight,

AUG. 9.—Thursday, I (at ye desire of ye Dutchess of Marlborough) attended her late Lords funeral, as one of ye Pall-bearers,

OCT. 16.—Tuesday, Major Pack brought me a message from Mr. Jermyn Davers that Lord Hervey in his petition to the House of Commons had therein charged Mr. Davers with bribery & corruption to gett himself elected at Bury, and that if I would not make my son withdraw it, he expected satisfaction. To which my answer was in the very words following ; vizt, That as I had not seen the petition, I could not, nor would not, advise the withdrawing it ; did hope he had alleged nothing in it he could not make proof of ; if it should appear otherwise, I would then advise my son to make Mr. Davers all just & reasonable satisfaction ; which if he should refuse to do, I promisd the person who brought the message that I would be sure to do it myself.

OCT. 26.—I had ye honour of a private audience of ye King in his Closett at St. James's, where I told him as followeth : Sire, je me sens fort honoré de la permission que j'ay receve de rendre mes devoirs aupres de votre Majesté, et particulierement dans la conjoncture presente, puisque elle m'a fournie l'occasion que j'ay longtemps souhaittée d'assurer votre majesté de ma sincere fidelité, et de mon zele constant pour touts les veritables interests de vôtre Majesté et de vôtre Famille royale, et que je ne manqueray jamais de demontrer par toutes les actions de ma vie.

1 7 2 3 .

FER. 7.—Thursday, ye beautiful Dutchess of Grafton dyed at London ; in justice to whose memory I can strictly averr, that in above fourty years time that I had ye honour & happiness of her acquaintance I never heard her say anything of any absent person which, had they been present, they could have been in ye least offended at.

The small pox appeared upon my son Felton.

APRIL 13.—I sett out from London, lay that night at Newport, & arriv'd at sweet Ickworth ye 14th.

APRIL 15.—Munday, my daughter Hervey was deliver'd of a daughter, & named Le Pell. Mr. William Pulteny, my wife & Mrs. Brooke answerd for her. (*Note 28.*)

APRIL 18.—Thursday, my wife sett out from London to Bath.

MAY 20.—Felle & I left sweet Ickworth for London.

JULY 18.—I borrow'd £1000 more of Mr. Edwyn, in all £3500.

SEPT 5.—Felle & I went from London, lay at Newport, & arriv'd ye 6th at sweet Ickworth.

SEPT. 16.—Betty, Nann & I left sweet Ickworth, lay at Wisbich, & arriv'd ye 17th (it being Lord Herveys birth-day) at Sleaford.

L

SEPT. 26.—We sett out from Sleaford, lay at Leicester, ye next night at Stratford upon Avon, ye 28th at Cirencester, & arriv'd at Bath ye 29th.

NOV. 3.—My wife, Betty, Nann & I sett out from Bath, lay at Marlborough, next night at Reading, & arriv'd ye 5th at London.

NOV. 14.—Thursday, my dear son Carr Lord Hervey dyed at Bath between 9 & 10 at night.

NOV. 27.—*Mrs. Mary Williams (of a good family in Wales) came to serve my Lady Bristol, who continued with her till her death, which happen'd on May day, 1741, and was prevaild on to continue in the family after her death as the good genius of it.   (Note 22.)*

1724.

MARCH 17.—My aunt Mrs. Elizabeth Felton dyed.

MAY 7.—Thursday, my dear daughter Betty was marryed by Dr. Clarke at my house in London to ye honble Mr. Bussy Mansel son to ye Right honourable ye Lord Mansel.

MAY 13.—They, with Tom, sett out from London towards Bath.

MAY 19.—Tuesday, my daughter Hervey was deliverd of a son about one afternoon; & on Thursday, ye 18th of June following was christen'd, & named Augustus John, his Royal Highness ye Prince of Wales, ye Earl of Godolphin, & my daughter Mansel answering for him.   *(Note 29.)*

AUG. 12.—Wednesday, my wife, Nann, Bab, George, Jack & I sett out from London, lay at Hockeril, & arrivd ye 13th at sweet Ickworth.

OCT. 27.—Tuesday, my son Charles went to follow his studies at Queens Colledg in Cambridg, under ye Reverend Mr. William Geekie. God prosper him. *(Note 30.)*

The same day his mother sett out from Ickworth for London.

DEC. 1.—Tuesday, Lord & Lady Hervey, dear Nann, George, Le Pell & I left sweet Ickworth, lay at Hockeril, arrivd ye 2d at London.

DEC. 7.—Munday, her Royal Highness ye Princess of Wales was brought to bed of a Princess about 5 afternoon.

1 7 2 5 .

MARCH 12.—Friday, my daughter Mansel, her husband, Lord Hervey, Nann, Bab & I sett out from London, lay at Hockeril, & arrivd ye 13th at sweet Ickworth.

APRIL 2.—My son John Lord Hervey was chosen a burgess to serve in Parliament for ye Burrough of Bury St. Edmunds by every member of that Corporation.

APRIL 10.—Lord Hervey, my son Mansel & I left sweet Ickworth, lay at Hockeril, & arrivd ye next day at London.

JULY 27.—My wife, Lord Hervey, my son Will & I sett out from London, lay at Hockeril, & arriv'd ye 28th at sweet Ickworth.

OCT. 20.—Wednesday, my daughter in law Lady Hervey was brought to bed of a daughter, & on ye 19th of November. following was christen'd & named Mary; Sir Robert Walpole, ye Dutchess Dowager of Marlborough & her grandmother Mrs. Le Pell answering for her. *(Note* 31.*)*

NOV. 13.—My wife, Lord Hervey, my son Mansel, Nann, Will, Harry, Miss Hervey my grandaughter & I sett out from sweet Ickworth, lay at Hockeril, & arriv'd ye 14th at London.

1 7 2 6 .

APRIL 10.—Bab, Bell, Herriet & I sett out from London, lay at Newport, & ye next night at sweet Ickworth.

JUNE 2.—My faithful Fanny dyed, who, with a much more remarkable constancy than is common to most of her sex, loved me with a very particular affection from ye first day of our acquaintance to ye last, when leaving her little ones before her death just to come & take her last leave of

me, then returning to them again, immediatly expird.   *(Note* 32.)
Montaigne says, Nous pleurons souvent la perte des Bêtes que nous
 aimons, aussifont elles lanôtre.

> Post bellator equus positis insignibus Æthon
> It lacrymans, guttisque humectat grandibus ora.—*Æneid* L., XI.

> To close ye pomp Æthon ye steed of state
> Is led, the funeral of his lord to waite ;
> Stript of his trappings with a sullen pace
> He walks, & ye big tears run rowling down his face.

The famous orator Crassus, who had been Consul & Censor, having putt
on mourning for ye death of a lamprey (who knew him & would come at ye
call of his voice & eat out of his hand), & being reproachd for doing so in
full Senate, was so farr from denying or excusing what he had done as any
weakness, that he rather gloryed in it as a marke of singular humanity &
good nature. Lett this instance apologize for me. As also that of Argus
Ulysses's dog, who after twenty years absence rememberd his master, &
after having expressd his joy for his return, weak as he was, dyed at his
feet.

AUG. 1.—Munday, Lord Hervey, Nann & I left sweet Ickworth, lay at
Hockeril & arrivd ye 2d at London, where we mett my wife, who had then
compleated her months waiting at Richmond ; & on ye 6th we all sett out
from London, dineing that day with ye Dutchess of Marlborough at St.
Albans & lay at Dunstable that night ; ye 7th we lay at Northampton,
calling at Houghton (Lord Hallifax's) by ye way ; ye 8th we saw Althrope
(Lord Sunderland's seat) in ye morning, & went to Coventry that night ;
ye 9th we gott to Litchfield, where Lord Griffin mett us ; & on ye 10th
we took a view of ye estate which descended between him & my wife,
lying there & at Longden ; on ye xith we went to Hore-Cross, saw several
of ye farms that night, & spent ye 12th in looking over ye rest of that estate ;
ye 13th we passed our accompts in ye morning with Fieldhouse, & called

in ye afternoon at Inxtry (Lord Chetwynds seat), and lay that night at Stafford; & went ye 14th to Sir Thomas Hanmers in Wales, were we stayd till ye Wednesday sevenight after, being ye 24th, when we sett out thence, & lay that night at New-Inn, ye 25th at Worcester, ye 26th at Gloucester, & arrivd ye 27th (my birth-day) at Bath.

OCT. 24.—My wife, Nann, Bab (who mett us at Bath from Tunbridg) & I sett out from Bath, lay at Marlborough, ye 25th at Reading, & arrivd ye 26th at London.

DEC. XI.—Sunday, ye Lady Howard of Effingham dyed, leaving me one of her executors.

1 7 2 7 .

APRIL 3.—Munday, I went to ye Dutchess of Marlborough at Windsor Lodg, & staid with her till Sunday ye 9th, when I was forced to return to London, my wife not being well.

APRIL 26.—I paid off Mr. Auditor Harley all principal and interest mony due on Lady Effinghams mortgage to him of Rushmere, ye whole being £1176..17..8.

JUNE 11.—Sunday, King George dyed at Osnabrugh in his way to Hannover.

JUNE 17.—Saturday, I had an audience of King George ye 2d in his closett at Leicester-Fields-House; when I said as follows: Sir, I did not desire ye honour of this audience to renew the assurances of that zeale & steddy adherence I have alwaies had & shall ever have for your majesty & your royal family, hopeing my past conduct has made that unnecssary; but humbly to beseech your majesty that as I never intend to trouble your majesty for anything on my own account, whatever distinction your majesty may think fitt to shew to ye little meritt I can boaste in so uninterrupted an attachment to your majestys personal interests in ye most trying times, may be shewn to Lord Hervey ; whose establishment in your majestys favour is ye thing in this world I have most at heart, & therefore beg your majesty would on this happy * occasion promise some way or other to provide for him; his affection & fidelity I will stand bound for; his abilities I hope will answer for themselves.

JULY 19.—Lord & Lady Hervey & I sett out from London, lay at Hockeril, & arriv'd at sweet Ickworth ye 20th.

JULY 21.—The Daverians came to me to offer to choose my son Tom together with Lord Hervey for their representatives in ye ensuing Parliament, which I did not accept of on Colonel Norton's account.

JULY 25.—Tuesday, (ye day on which I was marryed to her mother) my dear daughter Barbarah dyed at Ickworth of a bilious feaver after a fortnights sickness.

AUG. 18.—The Corporation of Bury (nemine contradicente) chose my son Lord Hervey for one of their Burgesses to Parliament. Colonel Norton had 18 of their votes, & Sir Jermyn Davers but nine in all.

SEPT. 3.—Sunday, my dear daughter Mansel dyed at London about noone, and was buried at Ickworth ye 13th. *(Note* 33.)

OCT. 3.—Tuesday, my wife & I left sweet Ickworth, lay at Newport, & arriv'd ye 4th at London.

OCT. 18.—Charles & I sett out from London, lay at Newport, arriv'd at Ickworth ye 19th.

1 7 2 8 .

JAN. 3.—My wife, Nann, Isabella, Herriet, Felle, & I left sweet Ickworth, lay at Chesterford, ye 4th at Harlow, & arriv'd at London ye 5th.

---

* The death of his father ! S.II.A.II.

JULY 12.—Friday, my invaluable son Lord Hervey went on board ye William & Mary yacht with ye Duke & Dutchess of Richmond & Mr. Fox, bound for Ostend, to proceed thence to ye Spaw. Gods infinite goodness (in which I intirely have trusted) will, I firmly and humbly hope, prosper him both in this & all other things to his lifes end.

JULY 14.—My wife, Lady Hervey, Nann, Harry & I sett out from London, lay at Newport, & arriv'd ye 15th at sweet Ickworth.

AUG. 22.—My wife & I left sweet Ickworth, lay at Wisbich, & arriv'd ye 23d at Sleaford in Lincolnshire to take care of my estate there.

SEPT. 10.—My wife & I sett out from Sleaford, lay at Huntington, & arriv'd ye next day at sweet Ickworth, dear Nann lying ill of a feaver.

1 7 2 9 .

JAN. 18.—Dear Nann, Bell, Herriet, Felle, & I left sweet Ickworth, lay that night at Chesterford, ye 19th at Harlow, and arriv'd on ye 20th (my most dear first wifes & son Toms their birthday) at London.

APRIL 5.—Dear Nann, Bell, Herriett & I left London, lay at Hockeril, & arriv'd ye 6th at sweet Ickworth; ye 7th I went to Newmarket, and return'd on ye 13th to sweet Ickworth; & on ye 15th dear Nann & I left sweet Ickworth, lay that night at Hockeril, & arriv'd ye 16th at London.

APRIL 27.—Dear Nann & I left London, lay that night at Newport, & arriv'd ye 28th at sweet Ickworth.

OCT. 25.—Saturday, (that day twelve years I escap'd from drowning in my canal at Ickworth) my dear & valuable son Lord Hervey arriv'd at London from his travels in perfect health & safety according to my prayers; & for which great blessing I am bound to thank and praise the goodness of God as long as I live; & by his grace hope never to forgett his infinite mercy towards me & my family therin.

NOV. 3.—Munday, he came to see me at Ickworth.

NOV. 24.—I executed (at Ickworth) the articles on my son William's marriage with Miss Elizabeth Ridge.

DEC. 26.—My wife, Felle, dear Nann, Bell, Herriett & I left sweet Ickworth, lay at Chesterford that night, the 27th at Harlow, and arriv'd the 28th at London.

1730.

FEB. 10.—Mr. Thomas Ridge, father of my daughter in law Mrs. Hervey, dyed at Portsmouth.

MARCH 28.—Dear Nann, Bell, Herriet, Felle & I sett out from London, lay at Newport, and arriv'd the 29th at sweet Ickworth.

APRIL 4.—Dear Nann & I left sweet Ickworth, lay at Wisbech, and arriv'd the 5th at Sleaford in Lincolnshire.

APRIL 5.—My cousin germain the Lady Isabella Turnor dyed at Bury, & was interrd at Playford.

MAY 12.—Dear Nann & I sett out from Sleaford, lay that night at Stilton, the 13th at Baldock, & arriv'd the 14th at London.

MAY 16.—Saturday Lord Hervey & Colonel Norton were unanimously re-elected members of Parliament for Bury, my son having accepted of the office of Vice-Chamberlain to his Majesty, and Colonel Norton that of Deputy Governour of Chelsea Hospital.

MAY 29.—Friday, my wife, Nann, Felle, & I sett out from London, lay at Newport, & arriv'd the 30th at sweet Ickworth.

JULY 13.—Munday, my daughter in law Mrs. Hervey was deliver'd of a daughter, & dyed within an hour after at Portsmouth.   *(Note 34.)*

AUG. 1.—Saturday, my daughter in law Lady Hervey was deliver'd of a son.   The Prince of Wales, the Duke of Richmond, & the younger Dutchess of Marlborough answerd for him on ye third of September following, & named him Frederick.   *(Note 35.)*

1 7 3 1 .

JAN. 25.—Munday, my son Lord Hervey upon the justest provocations sent a challenge to his till then suppos'd friend, Mr. William Pulteney, & fought a duel with him in St. James's Parke.

The same day my wife, Felle, 3 daughters & I left sweet Ickworth, lay that night at Chesterford, the 26th at Harloe, & arriv'd ye 27th at London.

MARCH 24.—The honest, conscientious Dr. Baker, Bishop of Norwich, sealed a new lease to me of the estates in Norfolke I hold of him for 21 years, for which he made me pay £170 fine for the seven years elapsed on ye 11th of July, 1728, & £155 more for ye interest of ye said £170 (in all £325) from ye said 11th of July 1728 (we having some disputes about delivering up & cancelling my old lease) to this day, that is to say £155 for the forbearance of ye said £170 from 11th July, 1728, to this day. Jewish extortion.

MARCH 29.—I borrow'd £5000 of Mr. Frederick Frankland to discharge my bond to my son in law Mr. Mansel, given him for his late wife her marriage portion.

APRIL 25.—Louisa, Herriet, Felle & I sett out from London, lay that night at Newport, & arriv'd the 26th at sweet Ickworth.

MAY 27.—Ann Lady Powlett lent £3000 on Lady Effingham her estate at Rushmere to pay off Mrs. Paston & Mrs. Shaw, to each £1000 apiece; & Auditor Harleys mortgage for £1100, which I discharg'd; so £100 less upon it now than was charg'd by Lady Effingham.

SEPT. 23.—Thursday, my daughter Louisa Carolina Isabella was marryed to Sir Robert Smyth Barrt. by Dr. Butts, Dean of Norwich, in Ickworth Church.

1 7 3 2 .

JAN. 10.—Munday, my wife, Felton & I sett out from sweet Ickworth, lay yt night at Bornbridg, ye 11th at Harloe, & arriv'd at London the 12th.

M

APRIL 7.—My wife, Felton & I sett out from London, lay that night at Harloe, 8th at Bornebridg, & on the 9th arriv'd at sweet Ickworth.

MAY 5·—Mary the widow of Henry Howard of Clunn in the County of Salop departed this life at her house in London.

MAY 13.—Lady Hervey was brought to bed of a son & named William; the Duke, ye Earl of Chesterfield & ye Princess Royal answering for him. (36).

JULY 13.—Thursday, my dear daughter Henrietta dyed at Ickworth, & was buryed there in the same grave in the Chancel with her sister Barbarah.

AUG. 17.—I borrowd £1000 of Lord Hervey upon my bond to discharge my son Thomas's debts, which he had lost at play.

DEC. 29.—My wife, Felton, Lady Ann, my two grandaughters & I left sweet Ickworth, lay that night at Borne-bridg, ye 30th at Harloe, & arriv'd on the last day of the year at London.

1 7 3 3 ·

APRIL 2.—The reverend Mr. Thomas Seller executed a lease of the Prebendal tythes of Sleaford to me for my own life, & Lord Hervey's & his son George's life.

APRIL 26.—Thursday, my wife, Nann, George, Jack & I sett out from London, lay that night at Bishop-Stertford, & arriv'd the 27th at sweet Ickworth.

JUNE 29.—Thursday, came on the election of a new burgess for Bury in the room of my son Lord Hervey, call'd up by writt to the House of Peers, when my son Mr. Thomas Hervey was unanimously chosen by every mans vote in that Corporation for their representative in Parliament; tho' my said son could not appear there, by reason the small-pox was so much there at that time.

1 7 3 4 ·

JAN. 10.—Thursday, my wife, Will, Nann, Felle & I sett out from sweet Ickworth, lay at Bornbridg, the next night at Harloe, & arriv'd the 12th at London.

JAN. 24.—Thursday, Lady Hervey was deliver'd of a daughter.

APRIL 11.—Thursday, Nann, Felle, & I sett out from London, lay that night at Harloe, the 12th at Bornbridg, & arriv'd the 13th at sweet Ickworth.

APRIL 25.—Thursday, the Corporation of Bury chose my son Mr. Thomas Hervey & Colonel Norton for their representatives in Parliament, nem : con :.

MAY 30.—My daughter Smyth was deliver'd of son; & on ye 1st of July after he was christen'd by my son Charles at Ampton; Lord Hervey, my self & Mrs. Foubert answer'd for him & named him Hervey.

JUNE 14.—Friday, Lady Felton dyed at her house in Ipswich.

. JULY 29.—My wife, Felle & I went from Ickworth to Ipswich to see what condition Lady Felton had left her joynture estate in, stay'd there ye 30th & 31st, & return'd to sweet Ickworth on ye 1st of August.

1 7 3 5 .

JAN. 10.—Friday, my wife, Nann, Felle & I sett out from sweet Ickworth, lay that night at Bourn-bridg, ye next at Harlow, & arriv'd the 12th at London.

JAN. 24.—Lady Hervey was brought to bed of a daughter, and named Emily Carolina Nassaw; the Princess Emily, Princess Caroline, & the Prince of Orange answering for her.   *(Note 37.)*

APRIL 9.—My sons Charles & Felton & I sett out from London, lay that night at Harlow, ye 10th at Bourne-bridg, & arriv'd ye 11th at sweet Ickworth.

1 7 3 6 .

JAN. 6.—Thursday, my wife, Nann, Felle & I sett out from sweet Ickworth, lay that night at Bourne-bridg, ye 7th at Harlow, and arriv'd ye 8th at London.

FEB. 22.—Sunday, Lady Hervey was brought to bed of a daughter, & named Carolina; the Princess Mary, the Dutchess of Richmond & the Earl of Scarborough answering for her.   *(Note 38.)*

APRIL 17.—I paid Lady Powlett in full of all the interest & principal mony due on the mortgage which Lady Effingham left charg'd upon her estate at Rushmere, which amounted to the sum of £3076..8..9, beside £100 more which I had paid off before ; Lady Effingham leaving it charg'd with £3100 in all.

APRIL 18.—My dear daughter & I sett out from London, lay that night at Harlow, ye next at Bourne-bridg, & arriv'd ye 20th at sweet innocent Ickworth.

DEC. 30,—Thursday, my wife, Nann & I sett out from sweet Ickworth, lay that night at Bourne-bridg, ye 31st at Harloe, & on new years day arriv'd at London, with Miss Betty Hervey to be inoculated.

1 7 3 7 .

MARCH 31.—I paid Sir Robert Smyth £4083 in full of all principal and interest mony due to him for his wife her portion, when he executed the deeds settling a joynture of £500 per annum rent charge upon her, pursuant to the articles on his marriage.

APRIL 3.—Dear Nann, Felle, George & I sett out from London, lay at Harloe, ye 4th at Bourne-bridg, & arriv'd ye 5th at sweet Ickworth after my having pass'd a most sick & painful journey thither.

JUNE 5.—My invaluable son Lord Hervey, hearing I was ill, came to make me a visit at Ickworth, notwithstanding the Parliament was still sitting, & staid with me till Thursday ye 30th ; for which I hope & pray that God will please to reward him for this fresh instance of his piety towards an aged father, as well as for his constant, dutiful behaviour towards me ever since he was was born.

NOV. 20.—Sunday, the Queen dyed at St. James's Palace between 11 & 12 at night.

1 7 3 8 .

JAN. 20.—Friday, (my first most excellent wife her birthday), my wife, Nann, Miss Betty & I sett out from sweet Ickworth, lay at Bourne-bridg, ye 21st at ye Green Man at Harloe, & arriv'd ye 22d at London.

APRIL 9.—My wife, Nann, Miss Betty & I sett out from London, lay at the Green man at Harloe, ye 10th at Bourne-bridg, & arriv'd the 11th at sweet Ickworth.

JUNE 2.—Friday, my son Thomas having accepted of ye office of superviser of all the Kings gardens etc. in England, vacated his seat in Parliament, & upon a new writt issuing, he was this day re-chosen by every member of ye Corporation of Bury, nem : con :.

JUNE 9.—Chance, my wife her lap dog, dyed, who not two hours before his death open'd his eyes & wagg'd his taile on seeing me come home & speaking to him at my return from Hargrave. He was a very pretty spaniel & a good hunter.

SEPT. 7.—My hopeful grandson George sett forward from London on his journey towards Geneva (by Paris) to study there. God prosper him in all things.

SEPT. 25.—Munday, was the first night we laid at my wife her new house in Bury; where we staid till Saturday ye 7th of October, when we return'd to my center of rest sweet Ickworth.

1 7 3 9 .

JAN. 5.—My wife, Nann, my son Will & I sett out from Ickworth, lay that night at Bourne-bridg, ye next at Harloe, & arriv'd ye 7th at London.

APRIL 24.—Tuesday, my wife, Nann & I sett out from London, lay that night at the Crown at Harloe, ye next at Bourne-bridg, & arriv'd ye 26 at sweet Ickworth.

DEC. 6.—Thursday, dear Nann, Miss Betty & I left sweet Ickworth, lay at Bourne-bridg, ye 7th at Harlow, & arriv'd ye 8th at London, where my wife mett me the same night from Bath.

1 7 4 0.

APRIL 10.—Thursday, dear Nann, Charles & I sett out from London, lay that night at Harlow, ye next at Bourne-bridg, & arriv'd ye 12th at sweet Ickworth.

APRIL 23.—Wednesday, the king deliver'd the Privy-seal to my son the Lord Hervey, with many gracious expressions acknowledging his past services etc.

NOV. 19.—Wednesday, my wife & self with Nann & Miss Betty left sweet Ickworth, lay that night at Bourne-bridg, the next at the Green Man at Harlow, & arriv'd the 21th at London.

DEC. 25.—Thursday, my youngest son Mr. Felton Hervey was married to Dorothy the widow of Mr. Pitfield, by Dr. Secker Bishop of Oxford, at St. James's Church, about 10 o'th clock in the morning.

DEC. 31.—Wednesday, my son Charles was married to Miss Martha Maria Howard at Ickworth Church by his curate Mr. Jos. Leyton.

1 7 4 1.

FEB. 3.—Dyed dear Kickaninny, a perfect pattern to all her sex for constancy, fidelity & friendship, which she shew'd towards me in a most exemplary manner from her birth to her death.

MARCH 22.—Sunday, Lady Hanmer dyed at her lodgings in Kinsington.

APRIL 13.—Munday, dear Nann, my daughter in law Mrs. (Felton) Hervey & I sett out from London, lay at the Green Man at Harlow, next night at Bourn-bridg, & arriv'd the 15th at sweet Ickworth.

MAY 1.—Friday, my dear wife dyed of a fitt which seized her as she was taking the air in her Sedan in St. James's Parke, about 2 afternoon, after all sorts of means had been used to bring her out of it. We had been marryed and lived together above five and forty years, from the 25th of July, 1695; & was buried on Saturday ye 9th following in the same vault with my most invaluable & ever to be lamented first wife in Ickworth Church. Mortua obtinuit plurima quæ meruit.

MAY 4.—Munday, my most esteem'd friend, Sir Thomas Hanmer, on hearing my wife was dead, came to stay with me at Ickworth till the Thursday following.

MAY 5.—Tuesday, the Corporation of Bury elected my son Tom & Colonel Norton (nem. con.) to be their representatives again in the new Parliament.

MAY 11.—Munday, my kind & dutiful son the Lord Privy-Seal found time, tho' one of the Regency, to make me a visit at Ickworth after his mothers death, & staid with me till the Saturday following.

1 7 4 2 .

JAN. 15.—Friday, Mrs. Le Pell dyed at London. *(Note 27.)* Nann, George, his two youngest brothers & I left Ickworth, lay at Bourn-bridg, & the next night at Harlow, & arriv'd at London the 17th.

APRIL 13.—Nann, my 4 grandaughters & I sett out from London, lay that night at Harlow, the next at Bournbridg, & arriv'd the 15th at Ickworth.

END   OF   DIARY.

EXPENSES OF JOHN HERVEY.

1688—1742.

The volume begins with a forecast, and ends with a retrospect. The young man of 23, just married to his first wife, and just beginning house-keeping, sets down on the 1st page of his new book what he calculates his income and his expenses will be. Fifty three years later, with two wives and eleven children lying in Ickworth Church, he reaches the last page of the book, and he sets down thereon what his expenses have been during all that time.

1. This is the forecast. He has £1000 a year from his father. When Aunt Hervey dies, he will have another £1000. His wife has £512 a year out of ye lunatic's estate ; and an annuity of £400 payable from the estate recovered by Mr. Fox ; and another annuity of £400 payable from the estate of her late father, Sir Robert Carr. This last annuity is not being actually received, but is allowed to run on for the present as a debt. So his present income is £1912.

He then calculates his annual expenditure.

		£
" My dear wife her pin mony	....	400
" House-keeping one week with another my part comes to £10 per week	....	500
" House-rent & stable-rent, besides all taxes & duties	...	115
" The whole charge of my hunting stable, £10 per month	....	120

"   The charge of 7 coach horses, 1 pad for myself & 2 servants   £
        horses, being 10 horses at £25 per annum each horse   250
"   For my own cloaths & pockett mony   300
"   Servants wages. My share of ye stewards £10; of ye cooks⎫
"   £7..10; of ye butlers £5; of ye porters £4; of ye wash⎪
"   maids £2; house maid £2; skullion £1..10; to my valet de⎪
"   chambre £10; the nurse £20; her maid £5; my coachman⎬123
"   £8; 3 footmen to each £6; postillion £6; the house-keeper at⎪
"   Aswarby £5; my gardener there £14; one maid ther besides⎪
"   & old Towles £5; in all per annum,⎭
"   For 8 liveries at £6 a piece   48
"   To keep 3 coaches in repair per annum   20
"   Besides wine, firing."

The total of these sums I make £1876, though he makes it £1976.
During the time of his first wife I imagine that her mother, Lady Carr, more
or less lived with them, which would account for his speaking of "my
share" in the house keeping expenses and in some of the servants wages.
The lunatic was Rochester Carr of Aswarby, brother to old Sir Robert Carr,
who was his wife's grandfather.

2. This is the retrospect. All through the book the totals of each page
are carried forward from page to page till the sum gets inconveniently large,
and then a fresh start is made. After the last entry on the last page (which
is the payment of a bill of £7..18..0 to Mr. Galfridus Mann the woolen-
draper), the total is £60,581..5..9; "which sum of £60,581..5..9 being added
"to all the other summs mention'd in this book, from the first day of Novem-
"ber 1688 (when I was happily marryed to my most excellent first wife) to
"Lady day 1742, make together in all £284,779..17..11, which at an average
"amounts to £5320 per annum."

"The total sum of £284,779..17..11 mentioned on the other side as my
"expenses from Nov. 1, 1688 to Lady day 1742 accrued as follows:

N

		£	s.	d.
" From 1 Nov. 1688 to Midsummer 1695, ...	....	11,688..	6..	5¾
" From Midsummer 1695 to Lady day 1700,	....	28,236..11..	2	
" From Lady day 1700 to Lady day 1714,....	....	88,631..13..	6	
" From Lady day 1714 to Lady day 1720,....	....	38,673..17..	3	
" From Lady day 1720 to Lady day 1733, ...	...	56,968..	3..	9½
" From Lady day 1733 to Lady day 1742,....	...	60,581..	5..	9

Total ....   284,779..17..11½ "

On a fly leaf at the end of the volume is the following list of his household. Internal evidence shows it to have been made between 1703 and 1712, and probably in 1704.

Lord	 1	Squire	 18	Pad groom	34	At Aswarby,	
Lady	 2	Nurse Tuer	19	2 Rough-		Burslem	50
Carr	 3	Wett nurse	20	riders	36	ye maid	 51
Bell	 4	Martha	 21	Jackson	 37	ye gardiner	52
Jack	 5	2 Nursery		Jacob	 38	ye boy	 53
Betty	 6	maids	 23	4 ffootmen	 42	At London,	
Tom	 7	2 Landry		Page	 43	house-keeper	54
Will	 8	maids	 25	4 carters	 47	house maid	55
Henry	 9	House maid	26	Cow-boy	... 48	Porter	... 56
Harriet	 10	Kitchin maid	27	Jack Pool	 49	At Newmarket,	
Charles	... 11	Dairy maid	28			widow	 57
Beaulieu	 12	Skullion		The ffamily at		Thomas	
Isaac	 13	Mary	 29	Ickworth 49 be-		Stratton	58
Cocke	 14	Barricave	 30	sides D. Everard		Jack Fausett	59
Katherine	... 15	Coachman	31	& ye gardiner &		Peter	... 60
Morris	... 16	Postillion	 32	ye steward,		5 other boys	65
Edwards	... 17	Helper	... 33				

Barricave (No. 30) was tutor to the eldest son, Carr Hervey, from 1702 to 1704, and again to the youngest son Felton, after an interval of more than 20 years, from 1724 to 1726; though possibly the two are not the same man.

With regard to the extracts from the expenses which I print here, I have made an arrangement which is not to be found in the original book, and put them under 14 different headings. These are :—1, Books. 2, Bury Elections, Corporation etc. 3, His Children. 4, Coaches & Saddles. 5, His Grandchildren. 6, Horses & dogs. 7, Ickworth & Bury houses. 8, London houses. 9, Miscellaneous. 10, Music & plays. 11, Pictures. 12, Rents & legal expenses. 13, Wines. 14, Wigs.

John Hervey always reckons the year to begin on March 25. To prevent confusion I have always reckoned the year to begin on Jan. 1, so that e.g. what he would call Jan. or Feb. or March 1720 would be called in these extracts Jan. or Feb. or March 1721.

The words "and all demands" which are generally added to each item paid for, I have left out. They are merely formal. The expenses, like the diary, begin from the day of his first marriage. They are headed "My "whole expenses beginning from 1 November 1688 ; on which day & in "which year I married my dearest wife Mrs. Isabella Carr."

I.—BOOKS.

1688.—Nov. 27. For French books * £1..10..0.

Nov. 30. For English books * £1..12..0.

Dec. 17. For books of all sorts * £4..6..6.

1690.—March 25. Paid then for ye 2 last parts of Burnetts Theory of ye Earth, £0..8..6.

May 20. Paid Mr. Gilliflower for books, Bridgmans Conveyances, Miltons Poems, etc. £0..12..6.

July 9. Paid then to Phillip Lea for Mapps of England, Ireland etc. £1..6..0.

1691.—May 2. Paid ffox in full for pamphletts, news books, observators etc. sent to me into Suffolke, £0..14 .0.

---

* Entries of this sort are frequent, & will not be repeated, S.II.A.II.

June 22. Paid Gillyflower ye bookbinder for Cabala & Evelyns Kal. Hort. £0..17..6.

Nov. 12. Paid Gilliflower for Sir John Shardins Travels, £0..9..0.

1692.—May 30. Paid for 3 French books (Patins letters), £0..8..0.

June 10. For ye young Students Library, & Patrick upon ye Psalms, £0..15..6

Nov. 11. Paid for ye great mapp of ye World, a pair of globes, some books, etc., to James Moxon, £5.

Dec. 29. Paid Richard Blome for ye Gentlemans Recreation, and ye History of ye Bible in 2 tomes, £12.

1697.—Nov. 6. Paid for Drydens Virgil, & ffelthams Resolves (to Gilliflower), £2.

1701.—Jan. 9. Paid Mr. Hatley for ye Atlass etc. I gave dear wife, £33. [*I dont know whether this is literature or millinery. S.H.A.H.*]

1702.—Nov. 20. Paid Harris for ye new edition of his Historical Dictionary, £4..10..0.

1704.—Nov. 11.—Paid Christopher Bateman for Gravius & Gronovius of Greek & Roman Antiquities, £31.

1709.—June 16. Paid Mr. Christopher Bateman for 31 vol. of ye Acta Eruditorum, £10.

1712.—July 7. Paid Tonson for Jacobs Commentaries in ye large paper, £7..10..6.

1714.—Feb. 18. Paid Sam Tooke for Cicero's works by Gravius, £5.

July 16. Paid Graves for Mr. Lockes works in 3 vol., £2..13..9.

1719.—Jan. 1. Paid Graves ye bookseller for ye ffree-thinkers, & Fresiers Voyage, £1..5..6.

March 19. Paid Jacob Tonsons man, Thomas Glenster, in full for ye

2d payment to Rows Lucan, & ye 2d payment to Priors works, & for ye second part of Prideaux's Connection, in full of all demands, £4..2..0.

April 6. Paid Jacob Tonson in full for 2d & 3d volumes of Eachards History of England & all other demands to this day, £5.

April 25. Paid Bernard Lintot in full for Washingtons Abridgment, & Nelsons Continuation, £0..14..0.

1721.—Sept. 27. Paid Dardes for my French table-book, £3..3..0.

Oct. 29. I gave my cousin Mr. William Bond, as a present, upon his dedicating Buchanans History to me, tho' against my consent, £21.

Nov. 14. Paid Jacob Tonson in full for Addisons Works, £3..19..0.

1722.—Feb. 12. Paid Paul Vaillant for ye Dictionaire de Trevoux, £7.

June 13. Paid Paul Vaillant for Father Montfaucon's 10 tomes of L'Antiquité expliquée, & for ye Abbe's Reals Works, £12..12..0.

1723.—March 8. Paid Mr. Garrigues in full of his sallary to ye 19th inst. £10, & for ye two catalogues binding £1..1..0, & for Rosseaus works 6s., & for Boyers French Grammar 2s. 6d., in all £11..11..6.

Nov. 13. Paid John Parker, bookseller in Pell Mell, for Burnets History of his times, £1..6,.6, & 9s. for Clarke's Rohault, in all £1..15..6.

1724.—Feb. 25. Paid Lord Harcourt my subscription to Pope's Odysses, £3..3..0.

Dec. 8. Paid Paul Vaillant in full for what remained of my subscription for Montfaulcons supplement etc., £3..19..0.

1725.—April 15. Paid William Clarke by ye order & for ye use of Mr. A. Pope 2 guineas, on ye delivery of ye 3 first volumes of his translation of ye Odysses (besides ye 3 guineas to Lord Harcourt).

May 25. Paid Jacob Tonson for 2 setts of Montaignes Essays, being ye last payments to Mr. Coste's edition, & binding, £3..4..0.

June 12. Paid John Penn by ye order & for ye use of Rd. Stand-fast bookseller in Westminster Hall in full for Campbells Vitruvius Brittanicus at £9, Nelsons Abridgment etc., in all £10..13,.0.

June 17.   Paid John Parker bookseller for Winwoods Memoirs at £3, & for others, & binding Homers Odysses etc., in all £4..11..6.

June 17.   Paid Bowles in Pauls Churchyard for ye 2d volume of Westminster Antiquities & binding, £1..7..0.

June 25.   Paid Vaillant ye French bookseller in full for Rapin's History of England in 8 tomes, £4..14..0.

Dec. 16.   Paid John Parker bookseller in full for Boyles works in 3 vols. at 46s., Nelsons Lex Maner, & Cicero's Banishment, in all £3..2..0.

1726.—March 4.   Paid Thomas Wotton ye bookseller in full for Seldens works 6 vols. in folio of ye large paper, £12.

March 17.   Paid Paul Vaillant for Father Charentons translation of Mariana's History of Spain 5 vols. in 4to £4.

Aug. 4.   Paid Mr. Erasmus Philips my subscription for 2 setts of his works, £2..2..0.

Dec. 8.   Paid Eleazer Albin for his History of English insects. £3..13..6.

Dec. 28.   Paid Nicholas Prevost (who succeeded Vaillant) for ye Abbot Vertots History of Malta, £3..10..0.

1727.—June 4.   Gave Lord Hervey for my subscription to Voltair's Henriade, £2..2..0.

1728.—April 2.   Paid Nicholas Prevost for 9 & 10 vols. of Rapins History, £1..4..0.

June 3.   Paid John Jackson bookseller in Pell Mell for Chambers's Dictionary, & some pamphlets, together £4..10..0.

1730.—Jan. 10.   Paid John Jackson bookseller in full for Lord Bacons works £4..10,.0, & for others sent me to Ickworth, in all £5..8..6.

March 24. Paid John Hooke for ye 2d & 3d vols. of Nelsons Abridgment of ye common law, £2..10..0.

May 26. Paid T. Woodward in full for 4 volls. of ye Roman History, & 2 volls. of Dr. Clarks Sermons, in all £6..10..0.

1731.—Feb. 20. Paid George Hawkins, Thomas Woodwards servant, for Gordons 2d vol. of Tacitus, £1..5..0.

April 22. Paid Mr. Barricave for Ausonius in usum Delphini, £0..19..0.

1732.—Feb. 7. Paid David Scott for his History of Scotland, £1..6..0.

Feb. 16. Paid R. Franklin's servant Bartholomew Armstrong for a sett of the Craftsmans works in 7 vol. best paper & binding, £1..11..6.

1734.—Jan. 31. Paid Mr. White for copies of the House of Lords Journals sent to Ickworth, £2..2..0.

March 4. Paid William Waring for ye 2d volume of Burnets History £1..9..0.

March 23. Paid Arthur Collins for his book of Precedents etc., £1..5..0.

1735.—March 25. Paid P. du Noyer in full for 8 volls. of Rollins Histoire ancienne etc , £1..8..0.

1736.—Jan. 19. Paid P. Dunoyer in full for 16 tomes of Mr. de Thou's History in French, £9,.10..0.

Feb. 11. Repaid Lord Hervey which he had laid out for books for my library at Osborns sale, £13.

March 27. Paid Thomas Osborne for Lord Bacons works to give to my son Tom, £4..4..0.

April 3. Repaid Lord Hervey which he had laid out for a Diodorus Siculus Gr. ; & Latin, £4..4..0.

April 5.   Paid Du Noyer bookseller in full for 9 vols. of Rollins History for Miss Hervey, £1..11..6, & for Ramsays History of Mareshal Turenne 16s. for ye 4 vol., in all £2..7..6.

June 30.   Repaid my wife William Warings bill for Millers Dictionary, Celenia Scheme of Providence, etc. £1..17. 6.

Nov. 27.   I made my son Lord Hervey a present of 144 tomes of ye Classicks (variorum) which cost me three score guineas.

1738.—Feb. 18.   Paid Frances Franklin for ye 7 last volumes of ye Craftsman (to give Lord Hervey), £1..5..6.

Feb. 20.   Paid Mr. Henry Vanderesch for Stephens's Thesaurus in sheets, four guineas.

March 25.   Paid William Waring in full of his bill for binding Stephens's Thesaurus at 16s. & for ye votes & newspapers to this day, £2..15..6.

1742.—Jan. 20.   Paid Mr. Lewis Theobald for his new edition of Shakspears works, £2..2..0.

II.—BURY ELECTIONS, CORPORATION, ETC.

1697.—Aug. 11.   Paid Nath: Yarwood (Vintner) in full of his bill for wine at ye Election & Aldermans feast, Aug. 7 & Oct. 1, 1696, £11.

Oct. 25.   Paid Nath: Yarwood for wine deliver'd to ye Corporation Receiver (Mr. William Curtis Aug. 19, 97) by my order, £4..8..0.

1700.—Oct. 9.   Paid Mr. Battely which he had disbursed for me to Bayley ye Vintner for wine deliverd to ye 2 Corporation dinners, £7..17..0.

Oct. 9.   Paid Mr. Ray for ye buck Bell deliverd to ditto, £3.

1701.—Feb. 12.   Paid Sir R. Davers my half share of ye Election charges, £6..9..0.

1703.—Nov. 17.   Paid Mr. Westhropp for cloathing 40 poor children at Bury anno 1702, £20.

1706.—Oct. 23. Paid Mr. Matt: Burroughs my 6 months subscription to the new Charity Schooles in Bury, £2..13..9. [*This subscription goes on to the end of the book. S.H.A.H.*]

1709.—April 12. Paid Mr. Alderman Chamberlain for thirty eight mourning rings, which I gave to ye Corporation of Bury, their Recorder & Town-Clerk, upon ye death of thier Burgess Sir Thomas Felton, £37..10..0.

1712.—Nov. 27. Paid Mr. John Turnor for ye use of Bury ffree school, which he told me my father had receiv'd tor ye admissions of four country-schollars before his death, £2.

1713.—June 4. Paid Mr. Walter Rey, which I subscribed towards ye alter of St. James's Church at Bury, £10..15..0.

Dec. 3. Paid Mr. Ray ye Bury Apothecary half his bill of £16..17 which he laid out for wine, meat, ringers, beadles, musick etc. at Bury Election on Sept. 2 last for Carr & Colonel Porter, £8..8..6.

Dec. 30. Paid Gill Moody for 50 bushells of coales delivered to my Alms-Row at Bury, £1..7..6.

1714.—Jan. 2. Paid Mr. Walter Ray in full of his bill for ye meat etc. of the supper my son Carr gave ye Corporation at ye Guild-hall at Bury, Dec. 21, 1713, £26..5..5.

Jan. 2 Paid Alderman Lawrence Wright for 8 hogsheads of strong beer to give ye Poeple of Bury at ye same time, £22..4..6.

Jan. 2. Paid Hannibal Hill in full of his bill for wine at ye same time, £13..10..7.

Jan. 2. Paid Mary Sewell in full of her bill for wine at ye same time, £12..5..8.

Jan. 2. Paid Thomas Chesson in full for his bill for wine at ye same time, £10..1..8.

1725.—March 25. Repaid Lord Hervey which he gave ye ringers at Bury, £1..1..0.

O

April 2.   Gave Lord Hervey to give ye Town-Clerk of Bury when he was elected their Burgess to Parliament 5 guineas.

1727.—Oct. 2.   Paid Alderman Allen ye half of ye bills for ye Election & ye ball given at Eastlands, ye whole amounting to ye sum of £67..13..10, ye moytie wherof for my son came to £33..16..11.

1728.—June 4.   Paid Mr. Alderman Lawrence Wright in full of his bill for 2 hogsheads of strong beer given to ye populace of Bury on ye Kings Accession to ye throne, & 3 hogsheads more deliverd by ditto to ditto on ye Coronation day at £3..15 per hogshead, £18..15..0.

Dec. 21.   Gave Dr. Butts for ye Poor of Bury 5 guineas.

1731.—Nov. 4.   Repaid my son Tom what he had expended at Bury as Alderman, £3..18..0.

Nov. 6.   Paid ye Bury Musick for playing at the ball my son Tom gave ye Corporation, £2..2..0.

1734.—Oct. 8.   Paid Hannibal Hill my son Toms share for treating ye Corporation, £6..2..1.

1735.—April 27.   Paid Alderman Raye in full of what he disbursd to ye Serjeants, Hall-keeper, beadles, musick, ringers, drummers & morrice dancers at ye last Election, £7..15..0.

1738.—June 3.   Paid—Allen at ye Half Moon in Bury his bill for treating ye Corporation, £24..12..6.

Oct. 7.   Paid Mr. Grigby ye Town-Clerk for ye return of ye precept for Tom's re-election, £5..5..0.

1739.—Aug. 22.   Paid Allen at ye Half Moon Toms share of ye treat to ye Corporation, £8..7..6.

1740.—March 29.   Repaid my son Tom what he had paid Colonel Norton for his half part of the bills of charges accrued by the Mandamus etc. for Bury Corporation, £25.

III.—HIS CHILDREN.

[Of Lord Bristol's sons, Carr and Jack went to Clare College, and Charles to Queen's College, Cambridge, while Tom and Harry went to Christ Church College, Oxford. Jack, Tom, Will and Harry went to Westminster School, Felton to Eton, Charles to two private schools, whilst Carr seems to have gone nowhere. S.H.A.H.]

1689.—Nov. 6. Gave Mr. Thomas for christening Isabella Carr £2..3..0.

1690.—June 15. Dear wife had of me to give nurse Fleming when ye child cutt her first tooth a guiney.

June 19. Gave Doctor Lower a fee for coming to little Binny, £1..1..6.

1691.—June 23. Paid for stript musleen for ye child & for a necklace of henbane, £0..16..6.

Sept. 21. Gave Dr. Tenison for christening my son Carr Hervey 5 guineys.

1692.—May 13. Paid for asses milk for little Binny, £3..3..6.

1693.—Feb. 20. Paid Nick Burton in full for asses milk, £1..3..0.

1696.—Nov. 15. Gave Doctor Wake for christening my son & churching my wife, £5..10..0.

1698.—Jan. 1. Gave Dr. Wake at my dear wife her churching, £5..10..0.

1699.—Feb. 23. To Dr. Wake for christening my son Tom, 5 guineys.

July 22. Paid Mr. Philip Stotherd writing master for Carr & Bell, £8..10..0.

1700.—Jan. 27. Paid Dr. Wake for christening of Will, 5 guineys.

1701.—Aug. 27, 28, 29. Gave Doctor Gould, Mrs. Masters ye midwife, & Mr. Childe ye apothecary when dear wife miscarried of 3 children at Bath, £6..9..0.

1702.—May 28. Paid Mr. Ralph Courtivill in full for teaching my daughter Bell, £7..10..6.

May 29. Paid Mr. John Pujolas ye ffrench chaplain for reading prayers, £5..10..0.

Nov. 28. Paid Mr. Barricave his half years salary due Mich. 1702, £25.

1704.—Jan. 28. Paid Mrs. Mary Palmer for taking care of dear Bells shape, £30.

Nov. 27. Paid Mr. Barricave my sons tutor in full of all wages, £57..16..6.

1707.—Aug. 25. Paid L'Abbeé ye French dancing master for teaching Bell, Carr & Jack to dance 2 winters, 46 guineys & a half.

1708.—July 28. Paid Mr. R. Laughton his bill for my dear son Carr from Lady day to Midsummer quarter, £77..7..3.

July 28. Paid Mr. Priest his bill for Carr for ye same time, £40.

[There are eight more quarterly payments for Carrs expenses at Cambridge after this one, ending June 19, 1710, "when he came to me at London." They are to or by order of Mr. Priest. They range from £52 to £88, and average about £66 each. For Carr's parting gift to his College see further on. For a mention of Mr. Priest see Diary, June, 1708. S.H.A.H.]

1709.—July 2. Paid Dieupart for teaching Bell & Betty on ye harpscord last winter, £25..1..6.

1710.—May 13. Paid Mr. Curtis in full for Jacks & Charles's stuff suites, £4..18..0.

Aug. 10. Allowed Mr. Chambers upon account for ye candlesticks & snuffers Carr gave to Clare Hall in Cambridg when he came away, £17..14..0.

Aug. 17. Paid Ann Brathwayt for ye laced-head I gave dear Bell, £4..4..0.

Dec. 6. Paid Mr. Hinchley ye mercer in full of his bill for Carrs rich westcoat, £26.

1711.—Nov. 26. Paid Sir Henry Furnese in full discharge of 3 bills of exchange charged on me by Mr. Masson for ye expenses of Carrs travells, £404..9..8.

[Carr was abroad for nearly three years, returning home in December, 1713. (See Diary). Other payments are made for his expenses abroad amounting in all to about £2000. S.H.A.H.]

Dec. 6. Paid Mr. Dieupart for teaching Bell & Betty to sing & play, £10..15..0.

1712.—Jan. 28. Paid Doctor Friend (by dear Jack) for his, Toms, Wills & Harrys entrance-mony at Westminster School (a guiney each). £4..6..0.

Feb. 12. Gave Sir David Hamilton for delivering my dear wife of her 10th son, fivety guineys.

March 12. Gave Dr. Clarke for his christening, 3 guineys.

April 19. Paid Ruth Harvey in full of her bill for asses milk for ye children, £9..2..0.

April 25. Paid Mrs. Alice Berisford for my four sons board, & for Will Fiskes for a quarter ended this day, £35.

Dec. 12. Paid Mrs. Alice Beresford £40, which, with ye £30 paid her Sept. 29 last, is in full for my 4 sons & their servant's boarding to 25 Oct. last, being for six months.

[Mrs. Beresford has £35 each quarter for boarding four boys & their servant at Westminster up to July 25, 1713 ; then Jack leaves, and £27..10..0 a quarter is paid for three boys & their servant up to Jan. 25, 1716 ; then Will leaves to go to sea, and Tom & Harry only remain. S.H.A.H.]

1713.—March 5. Gave Sir David Hamilton for bringing dear wife to bed of this her eleventh son which she has enrich'd ye Hervey family with, £53..15..0.

May 25. Paid Francis Dieupart in full for teaching Betty on ye harpscord, £21.

Aug. 7. Repaid Jack what he laid out for his Doyley suit of cloaths, £3..4..6.

1714.—Feb. 6. Repaid dear wife which she paid to Mr. Valet ye schoolmaster of Hampsted for Charles's entrance mony, ten guineys.

Feb. 22. Paid William Springet of ye Bank who brought me Mr. Laughton's order to pay Mr. Herring of Cambridge so much to discharge Mr. Seatons first bill for Jack, £58..1..5.

May 22. Paid Barker ye bookseller in full for school books etc. for my sons at Westminster to this day, £12..18..0.

May 10. For Jacks quarters expenses at Cambridge from Christmas 1713 to Lady day 1714, £67..16..2.

[*Seven more quarterly payments for Jacks expenses at Cambridge are made after this, ending at Xmas* 1715. *They average about £66 a quarter. S.H.A.H.*]

Oct. 19. Paid Charles Mather for a gold snuff box for my son Carr, £19..14..6.

1715.—March 3. Paid Mr. Louis Vaslet in full for Charles's boarding & schooling at Hampsted for a year ending Feb. 6 last, £33.

March 25. Paid Arnold, Sir Richard Hoare's servant, a bill of £112..17..0 which Mr. Laughton drew on me payable to Mr. William Herring of Cambridg for Jacks half years expenses there, ending at Chrismas last.

April 14. Paid Mr. James Moore ye cabinet maker for my son Carrs desk and bookcase, £15.

July 30. Paid Bartholomew Pigeon in full for wiggs & cutting my sons hairs at Westminster to this day, £8..12..0.

Aug. 15. Paid Dr. Friend for my 3 sons schooling at Westminster for 5 quarters ending at Midsummer last, 1715, 21 guineas.

1716.—Jan. 25. Paid Mr. Dieupart in full for teaching my daughter Betty on ye harpsycord, £15..11..9.

Feb. 11. Paid Thomas Ford (Bill-man at ye Post office) Mr. Laughtons bills on me payable to Mr. Herring which he drew for Jacks last half years expenses at Cambridge ending at Xmas last, £135..18..8.

March 28. Paid Mr. Louis Vaslet for Charles's boarding & schooling etc. for a year ending Feb. 6 last, £33..5..0.

May 19. Paid Mrs. Beresford for Tom & Harrys quarters boarding ending April 25 last & for wax candles, in all £16..4..6.

June 1. Gave my son Will for his pocket when he went to sea, £5..7..6.

June 4. Jack had 10 guineas more of me for his pocket.

June 4. Paid for a portmanteau trunk for him £1..2..6.

June 4. Monsieur Jouneau received of me by bill on Mr. Chambers upon account towards my son Jacks travelling expenses, £50.

[There are other payments for Jack's travelling expenses between this and April, 1717. They amount in all to £705. I enter the last in its place. S.H.A.H.]

June 26. Paid James Wicks for 2 whips for Betty & Nann, & buckets etc., £2..10..0.

Sept. 17. Paid Doctor Friend in full for Toms, Wills & Harrys schooling at Westminster to Midsummer last, 1716, 12 guineas.

Sept. 25. I gave Sir David Hamilton fivety guineas for laying my dear wife of a girl this morning, being ye twentieth child God has been pleased to bless me with.

1717.—Jan. 29. My sonn Jack received thirty guineas of me towards his maintenance of £200 per annum, which is to be his allowance from 1st Feb. next, £32..5..0.

Feb. 1. Gave Sir David Hamilton for attending Harry in ye small-pox, £10..15..0.

Feb. 16. Paid Mr. Vaslet in full for Charles's boarding & schooling, £34..10..0.

Feb 23. Paid Barker ye bookseller in full for books for ye school-boys, £5..12..6.

April 18. I repaid Sir Theodore Jansen 2920 fflorins 10 stivers, which Messrs. Cliffords of Amsterdam furnished my son Jack with, while he was in Holland & at Hannover, and being reduced to our mony amounted to £269..3..4.

April 21. Gave dear Tom for his pocket when he went to Oxford, £5..7..6.

April 22. Paid Mrs. Beresford in full for a years boarding of my son Tom to ye 25th instant (when he went to Oxford), & for a quarter for Harry, ending ye 25th of July last at £30 per annum, in all £37..10..0.

May 21. Paid Captain Hagar £5..13..0, which he had given Will on account, & gave him 40 shillings more for Aunt Feltons fann, so in all £7..13..0.

May 24. Paid F. Harris, servant to Thomas Alexander, for the silver trimming I gave my daughter Betty, £15.

May 24. Gave Wills schoolmaster at sea, £3..4..6.

May 24. Paid Mr. Richard Foulkes (by my Goldsmyth Wanley) his brother Thomas Foulkes's bill for my son Toms Caution mony, furniture etc. at Oxford, £61..6..8. *[There are 7 more quarterly payments for Tom's College expenses at Oxford after this one, the last being made in March, 1720, They range from £22 to £40, averaging about £32. S.H.A.H.]*

July 4. Paid Joseph Valleng fencing-master, in full, for teaching Jack, £6..9..0.

July 21. Gave my son Will more for pocket mony, 5 guineas.

Dec. 9. Gave Betty, it being her birth-day, five guineas, £5..7 6.

1718.—July 23. Paid Mr. Arthur Kinsman for a years board and schooling for my son Charles ended 22 Feb. last, £22.

Oct. 25. Gave daughter Betty towards her birth-day cloaths, 10 guineas.

Nov. 6. Paid Mr. Samuel Pitt (a Spanish Merchant in Minceing lane) by ye order & for ye use of Captain Jacob, which ye said Captain advanced to my son Will whilst on board him £100.

1719.—Jan. 1. Paid Angel Burket for a new silver sword for Will, £3..10..0.

Jan. 1. Gave my son Will for his pocket when he went for Portsmouth £21.

Jan. 1. Paid E. Brierly for a leather-cloak-bag for Will £0..18..0.

May 6. Paid Dr. Friend in full for Toms & Harrys schooling, & ye allowance for Pocket mony, & to Mr. Nichols 2d master £30..9..0.

May 19. Gave my son Harry for his journey to and from Ickworth, when he went to Oxford, £5..11..0.

Dec. 10. Paid Benjamin Barker in full for Harrys school-books etc., £2..5..0.

Dec. 12. Paid Mr. White's first bill of disbursments for Harry at Oxford to Mr. Innys ye bookseller by my goldsmyth Wanley, £12..18..2.

[Only 3 payments for Harrys College expenses appear, viz. this one, and £11 in Dec. 1720, & £48 in Dec. 1721, which are both inserted among these extracts. I cannot account for there not being more. However, to make up for it, there is an abundance of bills run up by him with Oxford tradesmen. S.H.A.H.]

Dec. 12. Paid Thomas Davies taylor for my son Toms grey suite of

P

cloaths lined with scarlet shaggreen, (which I gave him over & above his yearly allowance) £10.

1720.—Jan. 21. Paid Jonah Boyer in full of his bill for books sent my son Henry to Oxford, (over & above ye Colledg allowance), £3..8..0.

Feb. 23. Gave my son Will all ye mony I then had in my pocket (which was twelve guineas, one half & a quarter one) ye night before he went to Rochester, in all £13. 7..9.

March 2. Paid Sergeant Edward Miller for my son Toms Chambers in Lincolns Inn £450; & to Messrs. Atwill & Hammond £16 for ye change of two lifes therein; & five guineas for ye new leases; in all £471..5..0.

April 9. Gave Will ten guineas more when he went down to his ship at ye Buoy in ye Nore.

June 22. Paid Mr. Arthur Kynnesman for two years board & schooling for my son Charles £44 due 22 Feb. last; & £2..2..0 for two maundyes; & £1..15..6 for books; & £5..5..0 in lieu of 2 pair of sheets, towells, napkins, silver spoons etc., £53..2..6.

Oct. 14. Gave my son Mr. John Hervey to buy him silver plates & dishes when he went to Housekeeping, £315.

Dec. 31. Paid Mr. John White of Christs Church, Oxford, in full of his bill of disbursments for my son Henry & tutoredg, £11..3. 0.

1721.—June 15. Gave Mr. Brown ye Surgeon for looking after dear Herriets forehead when she burnt it, £10..10..0.

Oct. 17. Paid Alexander ye lace-man for Wills silver galloon, £5..15..6.

Dec. 27. Paid Mr. Henry Child, linnen-draper near Temple-Barr, by ye order & for ye use of ye Rev. Mr. Thomas Folkes £48..3..2½, which he laid out for my son Harry at Oxford, & for Tutoredg etc.

1722.—March 14. Gave Will to take out his new commission 3 guineas.

March 26. Gave my son Will twenty guineas in mony, & a bank-bill of twenty pounds more, before he went down with his Captain Windham to Plymouth where their ship ye Falmouth was fitting out, in all £41.

Dec 21. Paid Mr. Garrigues (to make up what he had received before) his half years sallary at ye rate of £40 per annum due ye 19th inst., £16..19..0.

Dec. 21. Then also allowd him his board wages at Richmond, & his other disbursments on my son Feltons account, £4..6..0.

1723.—April 17. Paid Captain Gardiner for my son Henry's comission of Cornett of Dragoons in Brigadier Honywoods Regiment, vacant by Mr. Proctors sale thereof, £600.

June 16. Paid my son Henry which he laid out, 2 guineas to Captain Gardiner for entering his comission at ye Warr Office, £3..11..0 for a regimental sword & buff belt, & £3..11..0 more for a fuzee & silver shoulder knott for his red regimental cloaths, in all £9..4..0.

July 12. Paid Walter Turner for my son Henry's silver lace for his regimental hatt & cloaths, & for a scarlet sash etc., £6..5..0.

Aug. 30. Paid Nicholas Olivier ye taylor in full for my son Wills brown cloath suite trim'd with gold orris, £10..6..6.

Sept. 30.. Repaid my dear wife which she paid for Felle's boarding, washing, horse-hire etc. at Richmond, £19..1..0.

Dec. 18. Gave my son Henry to carry him to his quarters at Gloucester, £3..3..0.

1724.—June 2. Gave my son Henry five guineas more for his journey to Hereford.

June 30. Gave my son Henry more when he went a second time to Goucester, £5..5..0.

July 26. Paid my wife for Bettys new holland hoope Petticoate, £1..2..0.

Aug. 4.   Paid John Bates ye undertaker in full of his bill for ye Funeral of my dear son ye Lord Hervey, £150.

Aug. 11.   Paid Mrs. Elizabeth Callow widow in full of her bill for my daughter Bettys lace for her wedding etc., £73..10..0.

Nov. 28.   Paid Mr. Barricave by my note made payable to his sister (Rose Barricave) £42, which with . . . in all £75, ye same being in full for one year & an halfs sallary due to him as Governour to my son Felton, & ending on Oct. 8 last.

1725.—Feb. 11. Paid to Mr. Cornelius Crownfield by ye order of ye Rev. Mr. William Geekie, ye same being in full of ye quarterly bills due at Christmas last for Charles at Cambridge, £31..7..6.		[*For Charles's going up to Cambridge see Diary, Oct. 1724; and for his long stay there of 8 years see the note to that passage. S.II.A.II.*]

Feb. 24.   Paid John Vickers for 18 yards of pink-colour & silver stuff, which I gave dear Nann for her birth-day cloaths to dance at Court in ye 1st March next, £27.

March 19.   Paid Temple ye Bury taylor in full of his bill for my son Henrys brown suite trimmed with silver, £17.

May 8.   Sent my son Will by his boy, black Harry, 5 guineas more.

May 21,   Repaid my said son Mansel ye ninety six pounds which he had undertaken to (& did) pay to discharge Wickhams of Oxford bills due from my son Henry, for goods deliverd £96.

June 18.   Paid George Binckes mercer by his servant James Everard in full of their bill for what John Lord Hervey bought of him for Felle's grogram suite etc., £5..8..0.

July 8.   Paid Mr. Thomas Hinchliffe ye mercer in full for my daughter Bettys gold & silver manteau & pettycoat, £56..10..0.

Nov. 16.   Gave Dr. Andrews ye Civilian for his advice in my son Harry's contract with Mrs. Herriet Dunch, 2 guineas.

Dec. 22. Gave my son Will when he went down to his ship, 5 guineas.

1726.—Jan. 7. Gave my son Harry ye night before he went down to his quarters at Derby, 5 guineas.

Feb. 15. Paid Mrs. Elizabeth Smith in full of her bill for my son Wills shirts, table linnen etc. to carry with him to sea, £25..2..0.

Feb. 26. Paid Mr. David Willaume ye silver-smith in full for ye dozen of silver plates I gave my son Lord Hervey, £78.

March 26. Paid Richard Hill, servant to Walter Turner lace-man, in full for 17 yards of gold galloon for Wills new suite, £4.

April 2. Paid Mr. Fartial ye composition for my son Toms absent Commons at Lincolns Inn during ye time he had chambers there, £13..13..0.

April 6. Paid David Willhaume ye silver-smith in full of his bill for a new Tea-kettle & lamp, a cruet frame, a case for a dozen spoons, knives & forks for my son Will, boyling & mending etc., in all £67.

April 9. Paid Mr. William Barricave in full of his salary (as Tutor to my son Felton (from Oct. 8, 1724 to April 8, 1726, £75.

Sept. 20. Paid Mrs. Kitty Hayes her bill for ye expenses of ye private ball Lord Hervey gave Lady Walsingham, £13..19..6.

Oct. 13. Paid Eliz: Coward for a lace-head and ruffles for dear Nann at £25 which I gave her, & for 13½ yards of other lace, £31..13..0.

1727.—Jan. 21. Paid for ye silver cistern I gave my son & daughter Hervey weighing 317 ounces at 5s. 2½d. per ounce, £82..11..0.

Feb. 3. Paid my son Will one other quarterly allowance to be due at Lady-day next (being to sett forward as this day to Gibraltar), £25.

Feb. 13. Paid for a suite of Brussels lace night cloaths, ruffles & hand kerchiff bought of Mrs. Mary Wilkes, to make a present of to my daughter in law ye Lady Hervey, £42.

April 18. Paid Edmund Pemberton ye father, executor to James Pemberton his son, in full of what was due to his said son for teaching my daughters to dance, £14; and at the same time paid Lewis Pemberton in full of what was due to him for teaching them since his brother death, £38 more; so in all £42 (sic.)

June 13. Paid Thomas Vokins for Felle's fustian & shalloone, £2..10..0.

July 12. Paid my son Tom his charges to Eaton when he went to Felle, £1..2..0.

Oct. 12. Paid Mr. Sedgwick by bill on Fowler in full of Charles' bill at Cambridge for ye quarter ending at Mich : last 1727, & for ye charges of taking his degree of Master of Arts, £50..9..11.

1728.—Jan. 12. Paid Mr. William Bannister stationer at ye Kings Arms in ye Strand by ye order & for ye use of Mrs. Mary Young at Eton in full for half a years boarding for my son Felton there ending Dec. 20th last £12..10..0, & for his schooling £6..6..0 to Mr. George & Mr. Goode Bookseller, Apothecary, Shoemaker, Firing, Candles and other bills, in all £29..17..5.

April 19. Paid Mr. George Felle's entrance-fees to ye 2 masters at Eton, £2..2..0.

Nov. 30. Gave Dr. Burton ye Physician for coming from London & staying a week with dear Nann at Ickworth, £52..10..0.

1729.—Jan. 23. Paid Paul Girard ye Toy-man in full for rings etc. for Harry, £30.   [*Here and elsewhere are a number of bills entered, to each of which "Harry" is mournfully added in the margin. The wigs alone come to over £80. S.H.A.H.*]

April 22. Paid William Banister by ye orders & for ye use of Mrs. Mary Young of Eton in full of all her bills for my son Feltons board for three quarters of a year ending ye 20th March last, 1728'9, ye Doctors, Apothecarys, Tuition, etc., in all £61..11..9.

Oct. 13. Gave to Lord Hervey to please himself in purchasing some curiosities when upon his travels in Italy, by bill on Fowler, £150.

1730,—Feb. 6. Paid John Hodson ye upholder in full of his bill for my son Wills Callimanca cabbin-bed £10..10..0.

1731.—Feb. 22. Paid Major Foubert for all ye entrance-fees for my son Felton, £8..8..0.

April 15. Paid Mr. William Banister by ye order & for the use of Mrs. Mary Young of Eton in full of all her bills for my son Feltons boarding, schooling & tuition there; & also in full of Batemans, Sumners, ye book-sellers, Apothecarys, and all other bills & demands due & ending on 20th of December, 1730, before which time he left ye said school some weeks, in all £88..17..0.

April 20, Paid Lewis Pemberton dancing-master in full of his bill & all other demands to this day for teaching Louisa & Herriet, £9..19..6.

Nov. 6. Paid Mrs. Margaret Marsh in full of her bill & what she laid out for my daughter Louisa her white & gold lutstring at 23s. for ye wedding, her silver handkerchief, shoemakers bill, fann, etc., in all £34..9..0.

Nov. 6. Paid Mrs. P. Reed, partner with Mrs. Sarah Hopkins, in full of their bill for laces for my daughter Louisa her wedding, £75..10..0.

1732.—Feb. 2. Paid P. Siris ye danceing master for teaching my son Felton 2 months, £4..4..0.

Feb. 5. Paid Major Henry Foubert in full for my son Feltons rideing to Jan. 17 last, £9..9 .0.

Feb. 7. Paid Marius Mareyn fenceing-master for teaching ditto to ye same time, £3..10..6.

March 3.   Paid Samuel Trenoweth in full for my daughter Louisa her silver wedding trimming etc., £34.

April 3.   Paid Major Henry Foubert in full for Felle's rideing 2 months, £6..6..0.

April 3.   Paid Marcus de Mary in full for teaching him to fence for ye same time, £2..7..0.

April 5.   Paid P. Siris ye dancing master in full for teaching Felle, £6..0..6.

April 21.   Paid Sir Robert Smyth at Ampton in full for 6 months interest of the £4000 portion I covenanted to pay him by ye marriage Articles with my daughter Louisa, £80.

May 29.   Gave to Dr. Green Professor of Medicine at Cambridg 5 guineas, & 5 guineas more to Dr. Kerrich there for attending my son Charles when he spitt blood, £10..10..0.

Nov. 12.   Paid Mr. William Sedgwick, Master of Queens College in Cambridg, by a note I drew on my banker Fowler, by his order payable to ye Rev. Mr. Hotchkis of ye Charter-house, in full of all my son Charles's bills for one year ending at Michaelmas last 1732, when he left the University, in all £149..5..9.

1733.—July 23.   Gave my son Lord Hervey to discharge all the Fees for passing of his Patent when called up by writt to the House of Peers, £143.

1734.—Feb. 20.   Paid Lord Hervey the years interest of the £1000 I borrow'd of him to pay off his brother Tom's play-debts, £40.

April 10.   Paid Jos: Kelway in full for teaching my daughter Ann 8 months on the Harpsicord, & for entrance mony 1 guinea, in all 9 guineas.

1735.—Jan. 30.   Paid my wife for a mahogany scrutore I gave my dear daughter Ann, £3..3..0.

May 6. I paid into Sir Robert Smyths hands for ye use of my son Felton, to bear ye extraordiny expenses of his travelling with him, £100.

May 10. Paid Joseph Kelway Nanns musick master in full, £9..5..6.

1736.—Feb. 20. Paid John Conway for ye green & gold skreen in Lady Anns dressing-room, £2..3..6.

Feb. 24. Gave Lord Hervey for christening cakes etc., £21.

April 5. Paid Mr. Michael Leheup in full of his bill of fees for passing my son Charles's presentation to ye livings of Ickworth cum Chedburgh dated April 2, 1736. £15..14..6.

May 25. Repaid my tenant Thomas Woodward of Sproughton what he had paid by my order to Mrs. Bridget Beeston for goods I gave to my son Charles there, £33..18..0.

June 25. Paid my son Charles in full for the whole years Tythe of Ickworth, which will be due at Lady day next 1737, £40.

1737.—Jan. 10. Paid Mr. Harper on account what he paid Mr. William Hanmer for my son Charles for ye entire first-fruits of Kirkby Dennis, fees etc., £10..18..9. [*Like payments are made for Asgarby and Sproughton, from which I presume that Charles was appointed to all these livings. S.H.A.H.*]

Feb. 15. Paid Sarah Hopkins in full of her bill for a new suite of Brussels lace pinners, ruffles, etc. which I made a present of to Lady Anne, in all £26..17..0.

April 18. Paid my wife for the silver standish I gave to Lord Hervey, £34..14..10.

1738.—Nov. 22. Paid Mr. Rogers of Bury for a pair of silver candlesticks I gave Lady Anne, £13..4..6.

1739.—April 18. Repaid my son Felton which he paid Lady Folliot for cheese and for Spaw-waters, £7..10..0.

Q

April 21. Paid William Bradshaw the upholdsterer in full for my son Felton's new bed, £22.

April 21. Repaid my son Felton which he had paid to Robert Dunbar, Thomas Briggs and John Goodchild for the rest of ye new furniture of his bed-chamber, £12..1..6.

June 16. Paid John Shipman for the scrutore I gave my daughter Ann in full, £5..10..0.

1740.—Feb. 18.—Repaid my son Felton a bill which he paid John Elly when at Eaton £5..9..0.

Nov. 6. I gave to my son Mr. Felton Hervey towards furnishing his house upon marrying the widow Pitfield, £600.

1741.—Jan. 30. Paid Matt Cutler for a gold hankerchif I gave to Lady Hervey, £5.

Feb. 4. Paid Christopher Longwood for an embroidered apron I gave Mrs. Felton Hervey, £3..3..0.

May 12. Gave my dear daughter Ann to buy her mourning, 20 guineas.

July 15. Paid Mrs. Mary Williams for several things I bought of her for presents to Lady Hervey, my daughter Ann, & my 2 eldest grandaughters, £76..19..6.

Aug. 12. Repaid Lord Hervey for Nanns French white wine, & 2 pounds of tea, £6..12..6.

1742.—Jan. 25. Paid Lady Hervey for the two Pots-pourris which I gave her, £28..18..6.

Feb. 4. Gave my daughter Smyth a present of lace which cost me £14..10..0.

IV.—COACHES & SADDLES.

1689.—April 19. For a green hunting saddle, £2..10..0.

Same day. For a jocky whip, £0..10..6.

May 25. Paid Hutchinson ye sadler at Charing Cross for a crimson silver & gold hoose, & holster capps, £10.

Aug. 24. Paid John Godbee ye Coachmaker for a pair of green velvet hooses to lay on ye coach box, £7..10..0.

Sept. 27. Paid then to John Godbee my coach-maker, being in full payment for ye great glass coach & travelling coach & of all other accounts & demands to this day, £85.

1690.—May 29. Allow'd ye Duke of Grafton upon account 25 guineys for a calesh, he selling me that and paying me £25..15..0 in mony by Walsh evened my account with him of £52..12..6 (£31..2..6 of which I paid for him to Mr. Potts for wine, 10 guineys I paid my Father for him, and 10 guineys more of twenty I staked for him at my mares match when he was gone to Portugall ; ye other set off in a horse chop.

1691.—April 17. Paid for my black sadle with silver galloone & ye furniture, £1..7..0.

April 25. Paid for ye leaden sadle I rode for ye Plate with, £0..11..6.

May 29. Paid for a jocky velvett capp to Mrs. Rebecca Harrison, £0..9..0.

June 17. Paid Richard Wheigham a sadler for a plate furniture, and a sadle, hoose, capps and baggs with silver galloons & fringes, £40.

Oct. 1. Paid ye wheelwright of a runn of wheels for my chariot, £5.

1702.—March 24. Paid ye Newmarket Toy-man for Starers green silk bridle, purses, incorporaters etc., £2.

April 29. Paid Mr. Tatlocke ye lace man for silver ffringe for my padd saddle, etc., £20.

1703.—March 27. Paid John Hall ye coachmaker in full of all his bills for ye new coach etc. to this day, £151..10..0.

Aug. 7. Paid ye Thetford sadler for a yellow velvet sadle, £2..5..0.

1705.—Feb. 14. Paid A. Bignel sadler in full for D. W.'s (dear wife) saddle, £5..15..0.

1707.—Feb. 1. Paid Hall ye coach-maker in full of his bills for ye new chaise etc. £50.

1709.—Aug. 12. Paid John Goodwyn ye Bury sadler in full for 4 servants saddles, £8.

1713.—Oct. 3. Paid Freeman of Thetford in full for my green hunting saddle, £2..3..0.

Oct. 22. Paid Freeman of Thetford in full for dear wife her side-saddle, £8.

1714.—April 17. Paid Philip Humphreys for 33 yards & a half of crimson caffaw for my new travelling coach, 20 guineas.

Dec. 23. Paid Edward Sams ye coach-maker £36..5..0 more, which with £53..15..0 paid him 10th May last, makes £90 in full for my new travelling coach.

Dec. 24. Paid Edward Sams ye coachmaker in full for my son Carrs guilded charriot & Town harness, £110.

1717.—Aug. 10. Paid Edw: Freeman, ye Thetford sadler, in full for a blue velvet & a hoggs-leather saddle, £3..4..6.

1718.—Feb. 15. Paid William Tarver, for Chamberlaine & Co. Mercers, in full for 33 yards of crimson velvet for ye new coach at 26s. 11d., £44..2..0.

1723.—May 25. Paid John Bromley for 3 servants padd saddles by agreement at £12, and for mending ye old ones, 10s.

Dec. 13. Paid Eus: Treganey ye sadler in full for my son Harry's crimson velvet hoose & pistol-baggs, embroidered with gold & gold fringe, £6..12..6.

1724.—March 27.   Paid James Tickner ye sadler in full of his bill for a buff-seated saddle, holsters, bitt and other furniture, for my son Henry, £6..17..6.

1725.—Nov. 24,   Paid John Wylder ye coach-maker in full for my new travelling coach, for all things belonging to it as by agreement, £60.

1728.—July 31.   Paid William Brotherton for a Postillions leather coate, cap & saddle, & for a pair of Pole-Pieces, £3..13..0.

1730.—March 6.   Paid Thomas Basnett in full for a new coach by agreement, £70.

1731.—March 26,   Paid George Vaughan Sedan-maker as executor to his father Edward Vaughan for a new chair etc. he made for my wife, in full of that bill, £30.

1733.—April 16.   Paid John Bromley ye sadler for 3 Livery-saddles with housings, bitts & baggs, £12.

1735.—March 7.   Paid George Vaughan in full for my wife her new sedan, £14..10..0.

1736.—March 27.   Paid Edward Hooke for ye bitt & bosses for Lady Ann her new saddle, £0..17..6.

March 30.   Paid Susanna Bignell in full for Lady Anns new side-saddle, £10..10,.0.

1737.—March 11.   Paid Thomas Basnett Coachmaker in full for my new coach, a sett of harness & all things belonging to them, as saddle, postillions coat & capp etc., in exchange for my old coach valued at £10, & in ready mony £83..16..0.

1738.—March 6,   Paid William Campbell auctioneer for ye charriot Waters bought of him for me at £14.

April 5.   Paid William Low for painting the charriot with my arms, supporters etc. by agreement, £6.

April 7. Paid George Vaughan for putting my wife her sedan into mourning, £5.

1739.—Feb. 23. Paid John Bromley ye sadler in full for my quilted saddle and furniture, £4..1..0.

1740.—July 14. Paid John Brookshead for my new coach £75 & my old one, & 40s. for other worke, £77.

V.—HIS GRANDCHILDREN.

1721.—Oct. 31. I repaid my son Mr. John Hervey ye ten guineas which he gave ye nurses for me at ye christening my grandson George.

1725.—June 17. Paid Val : Grimstead for play-things for ye children, £1..1..0.

1727.—April 16. Gave my good grandson George to pay for his entrance mony at Mr. Le Place's french schoole, £10..10..0.

April 23. Paid Lady Hervey a guinea more for her sons entrance to ye usher.

1728.—Jan. 29. Paid Monsieur Delaplace his bill for 3 quarters boarding & schooling etc. for my grandson George ending Dec. 20 last, £26..17..6.

1729.—Feb. 8. Paid Monsieur De la Place for my good grandson George's years boarding & schooling, £34..13..0.

1730.—Feb. 13. Paid Mr. Denis Delaplace in full for my grandson George's boarding, books etc. from Jan. 18, 1728.9 to Jan. 18 last, £35..15..6.

1731.—Feb. 2. Paid Mr. Denis Delaplace his yearly bill for my grandson George's boarding, schooling, etc. to Jan. 18 last, £36..5..6.

June 21. Repaid Lord Hervey the bill for George's entrance fees at Westminster schoole, £11..11..0.

June 25. Repaid Lady Hervey a bill which she paid to Mr. La Place for George's boarding & schooling till he went to Westminster schoole, £8..8..6.

1732.—April 4. Paid Mr. Vincent Bourne in full of all his bills for my grandson George's boarding, schooling etc. at Westminster for 3 quarters ending Feb. 4 last, £42..2..6. [*These payments go on till Aug.* 1738. *Apparently George left Westminster at Midsummer,* 1738. *About £47 a year is the usual amount. Vincent Bourne was an usher at Westminster till his death in* 1747. *His poems, Latin and English, passed through several editions between* 1734 *and* 1840. *S.H.A.H.*]

1734.—July 1. Gave to ye midwife, nurses etc. when I answered for my grandson Smyth, £10..10..0.

July 6. Paid my son Henry 6 guineas to give for me to the midwife & nurse when I answered for his third child.

1735.—April 7. Paid Monsieur Pillissier for teaching my grandson George to speak French & write for 2 years to April 3, 1735, £21. [*These payments go on till Sept.* 1738. *S.H.A.H.*]

1736.—April 5. Paid Du Noyer bookseller in full for 9 vols. of Rollins History for Miss Hervey, £1..11..6.

Aug. 14. My grandson George's journey down & up this breaking up time cost me £2..10..6.

Oct. 20. Gave my godson & grandson Smith for a Bury fairing a Portugal-coyne of £6..15..0.

Oct. 20. Omitted to sett down a Portugal piece I gave him ye Bury fair before (1735) of £3..12..0.

1738.—Feb. 5. Repaid Lady Hervey which she paid for George's shoe and knee buckles, £4.

March 3. Gave Miss Hervey to buy herself & sister Mary & Mrs. Royrands fairings, £7..7..0.

April 8. Paid F. A. Pillissere for teaching my grandson George French & arithmetic to ye 3d instant, being for a whole year, £10..7..6.

1739.—April 2. Repaid Lord Hervey what he had laid out for my grandson George's expenses for the half year since he went from England to Geneva, £271..10..0.

1740.—May 15. Allowed my banker which he paid Lord Hervey by my order to answer the draughts my grandson George made to pay off his farther expenses at Geneva, £150.

May 17. I drew a bill for £150 more payable to Lord Hervey to answer other new draughts made by my said grandson for said expenses at Geneva, which with the two former sums amount in all to £571..10..0.

1741.—Sept. 5. Gave my grandaughters Emely & Caroline for singing a duo on my birthday to each a piece of 5 moydores Portugal coin, in all £13..10..0.

VI—HORSES & DOGS.

1689.—Jan. 17. Paid Lord Litchfield for seven brown coach horses, £150.

Jan. 17. Paid Lord Dover for three grey Dutch geldings, £64..10..0.

Jan. 19. Discharged my note to Jeffery Scotman upon death or marriage of forty guineys, which I was to have given him for a little brown Philley, £43.

Jan. 19. Discharged an other note of mine to Mr. Jarrett Russell of 25 guineys payable upon either of ye foresaid accidents in consideration of a bay crop horse, which note he assigned over to Lord Dover, & I discounted it.

March 5. Paid to Lord Renella's gentleman of his horse for two brown stoned coach horses, £41..10..0.

May 16. For a ball pad nag bought of Mr. J. Burslem, £18.

May 24. Paid Charles Hatton for a little bey pad nag, & a sorrel soldiers gelding bought in Smithfield, £29.

May 31. Paid Richard Hatton in chop for two bey padds bought also in Smithfield, £22..1..0.

June 14. For three black coach horses bought of Lady Carr, £30.

Aug. 25. For setting up horses at Twitnam, £0..10..0.

Aug. 28. For setting my horses at Eggum, £1..5..0.

Sept. 14. For setting up my horses at Eggum, & to ye maid at ye lodg, £1.

Oct. 18. Paid to John Knight in chop between 3 black mares & 2 black geldings of his, with one black stone horse, one sorrel gelding and one brown ball pad of mine, £40.

Nov. 21. Paid John Knight in chop between 2 old coach horses & two black mares, £16.

Dec. 14. Paid Mr. James Griffin for Picquerer a roan stone horse fifty guineys; thirty by a note on Chambers, ye other twenty I discounted with him, which were due to me from him, won upon ye match between the Duke of Sommersets grey marling & the brown mare called Sir Henry Bonds, run Oct., 1689.

Dec. 21. Paid then to John Knight in chop between a black resty mare of mine and two black young mares of his, £17.

1690.—Jan. 18. Paid then for a black coach mare to one Mr. Scott of Newington near Hackney, £17.

Jan. 29. Paid then to Arnold in chop between two black mares of mine & two black ones of his, £12.

May 6. Paid then to Mr. Frampton for 3 years contribution mony to Newmarkett Plate at 5 guineys per year, £16..2..6. [" *In the Church (at New-market) is buried Tregonwell Frampton, keeper of the running horses to*

R

William III, Anne, George I, and George II. He died in 1728, aged 86, the father of the Turf." Gent. Mag. S.H.A.H.]

May 6.   Paid him for mony in chop between a little grey nag of his & a grey mare of mine, £12..18..0.

Dec. 5.   Paid Knight ye horse courser in chop between two black mares and a black gelding of his, and two ball mares & a bey colt of mine, £12..5..0.

1691.—Jan. 30.   Paid Mr. Snapes man (Josiah Watts) a bill of £2 for keeping my roan horse att Hampton Court in hey & oates from Dec. 7, 1690 to Jan. 6 following.

April 7.   Paid Clerk of Barrow in full for looking after my stud there, £1..15..0.

May.   Paid Mr. fframpton at Newmarkett for Hawker to make a stallion of, £110.

May 22.   Paid Lord Ossulston for a black coach gelding, £15.

May 23.   Paid Banfield for a grey padd called Hogg, 16 guineys.

Oct. 23.   Paid ye scale-keepers at Newmarkett their fees for ye Plate I won there in ye spring with my brown horse Davers, £1.

1692.—May 28.   Paid John Taylor £3..1..0, which with ten guineys received of me at Burford ye 20th past is in full of all accounts for keeping my hunting horses from ye beginning of ye world to this day, in all £13..16..0.

June 17.   For a black coach mare at Smithfield, £8.

Oct. 22,   Paid Sir Adam ffelton his half share reserved upon my note of 40 guineys for a grey mare at ye birth of my first son, £21..10..0.

1693.—Feb. 23.   Paid Sir Adam ffelton 25 guineys which he had paid young Mr. Hodges for ye mare he bought of him for me.

1696.—Jan. 23. Paid Mr. Thomas Bond of Bury for ye old grey Downing mare & for her colt by ye Grafton Barb (called Spott) £25, for which he gave me a receipt, and in that receipt promisd to indemnify me against his brother Sir Henry Bond, or any claiming by him.

June 18. Gave Mr. ffelton to pay Collonel Mordaunt for Dunn 40 guineys.

July 2. Paid Banfield of Smithfield for my Isabella mare, £30.

1697.—March 30. Paid Mr. Charles May junior for six breeding mares that were my Uncle Baptists, by a bill on Chambers, £55.

April 16. Paid Mr. fframpton in chopp between bey Jack & Dunn, £50.

April 16. Paid Darloe ye farrier at Newmarket for fireing Cripple, £3..6..0.

April 24. Paid Charles Hatton ye horse courser in a truck between my grey Dutchman & a sorrel called Turke, £11.

May 29. Paid Edward Dixon for his master Charles Hatton in chop between my black coach mare & a black gelding of ye said Hattons, £12..10..0.

June 14. Paid Mr. fframpton between young Hawker & Hoboy in chopp, £50.

June 15. Paid Will Bamford ye horse-courser for my large grey gelding, £42..4..0.

June 18. Paid Arnold ye horse courser in chopp between two coach horses, £35.

June 24. Paid Mr. Mannours for a black ball coach horse, £22.

1698.—Feb. 16. Paid Sir John Woodhouse for ye Isabella mare, £80.

March 3. Paid Boucher for his horse called Hogg, 120 guineas.

March 23.   Paid Henry Holloway for a ratt-taile coach-horse, £22.

April 12.   Paid Sir Thomas Grosvenor for his brown horse called Glisterpipe, £50.

April 13.   Paid Sir Roger Mostyn for his bay horse called Bully, £110.

April 27.   Paid Mr. Cecill Bishop for his grey horse called Cobler, and for his yellow horse called Rawbones, £200.

June 30.   To Peter Ricard for a coach-horse, £15.

Oct.   Paid Parker of Thetford for Snowball that won ye Town plate, £15.

1699.—Feb. 23.   The book of expences for keeping my horses at Newmarkett from 6 Dec., 1695 to 25 Oct., 1698, comes to in all £674..10..5.

1700.—March.   The book of expences for do. from 25 Oct. 1698 to 1 Nov. 1699, £819..3..4.

1701.—Dec.   The book of expences for do. from 1 Nov., 1699 to 6 Dec., 1701, £946..14..10.

Aug. 25.   Paid for ye grey padd & black mare at Cawsham ffair in Wilts, £17..10..0.

1702.—March 20.   Paid Lieutenant Orpe for a roan mare, £10..15..0.

April 29.   Paid Mr. William Harvey of Chigwell for ye Scotch horses sister, £40.

1703.—June 10.   Paid my cousin James Griffin for young Sweetlips & his dun mare with her colt, £90.

Nov. 2.   Paid John Knightley Esq. for his chesnut mare called Female Antiquity; & Grashopper, £215.

Dec.   The book of disbursments from 6 Dec., 1701 to 6 Dec., 1703 for ye running horses at Newmarket, came to £771..1..1.

Dec. 20.   Paid Mr. William Lowther (by Mr. James Heriott) for his mare & colts, £100.

1704.—May 15. Paid Will Merrydew his bills for my running horses charges from 6 Nov., 1703 to 4 May, 1704, £279..14..11.

Nov. 2. Paid do. do. from 4 May, 1704 to this day, £345..3..4.

1705.—May 14. Paid Clement Darloe for keeping & cureing my Barbe of his foot, £13.

May 19. Paid John Richardson in full for horse-bread for ye racers, £29.

May 24. Paid Will Merrydew in full of his bills for their meat, boys board, etc., from 2 Nov., 1704 to 18 May, 1705, £299..7..9.

July 20. Paid for 2 horses bought at Cowledg Fair, £12,

Oct. 27. Paid Thomas Spedding for ye two young horses of Mr. Roger Crofts breed, (ye grey 6, ye brown 4 years old now past), £161..5..0.

1706.—April 11. Paid Mr. Leonard Childers for a large bey mare which was gott by ye same Arabian that gott ye Prince's Leeds, £40.

April 6. Paid John Dorling for a coach-horse, £13.

Sept. 3. Paid Mr. Anthony Leeds of Milford in Yorkshire for ye 3 year old bey Philley (gott by Careless under Leeds's full sister) & ye 2 year old bey colt (gott by ye brown Barbe King William gave his father under bey Peg, which was a daughter of young Spanker) & for ye bey yearling gott by Careless under a daughter of ye said Barbe's which was out of my Lord Wharton's Gallant's sister, in all £150.

Sept. 28. Paid Isaac Salvage for cureing ye Dun horse of ye Poll-evil, 15 shillings.

Nov. 2. Paid Mr. Thomas Broderick for my nutmeg String-holt 4 years old, £53..15.

Nov. 9. Paid ye Marquiss of Granby for my horse called ye Cooke, £53..15.

Nov. The expence of my running horses from 18 May, 1705 to 5 Nov., 1706, £1001..15..10.

1707.—May 19. Paid Hyam Cole (for ye use of his master Mr. Farrant) for a coach horse, £10.

Nov. 8. Paid Mr. Cotton in chopp between Longlegs & bay Croft, £53..15.

Nov. 8. Paid my cousin Griffin for Jonny Tasborough, £53..15.

Nov. 30. Paid my Cousin Griffin (by a bank bill) for ye roan mare & her stone colt & ye grey guelding, £100.

1708.—April 30. Paid John Young for ye chesnut nagg bred by Lord Stanhope, £43.

July 9. Paid William Marshal of Disneys Lodg for a black coach horse, £16.

July 27. Paid Will Headley for ye little black Galloway he brought me, £2..3.

Oct. 27. Paid Mr. Clayton of Newmarket for a black coach horse, £18.

1709.—March 5. Paid Mr. William Lowther, by ye order of his brother, 20 guineys, which with ten more paid his said brother at Newmarket in October last make together 30 guineys, in full payment (according to ye said Mr. William Lowthers judgment to whom ye value of ye horse was referred) for ye chesnut stone-horse left with me in April last.

Nov. The charge of my running horses from 21 Nov., 1706 to 15 Nov., 1709 amount to £1546. [*From Nov.*, 1709 *to Nov.*, 1710, £636 ; *from Nov.*, 1710 *to May*, 1711, £239. *See also entry in May*, 1713. *S.H.A.H.*]

1711.—March 3. Paid Mr. Minshul & Mr. Docminique for three horses & a mare, £350.

Nov. 2. Paid Abraham Goodwyn for Mr. Lawrence's chesnut mare (called Miss Ann) which Mr. Craven sold me, 30 guineys.

1712.—April 25. Gave ye Poor at Newmarket when my horse called Ickworth wonn ye Queens Plate of 100 guineys value there, £5.

1713.—May. The charges of my running horses from 17 Nov., 1709 to 5 May, 1713 (exclusive of Jack Faussetts bills of disbursments for them in that time) amounted to £1097..18..2, as by my Newmarket book appears.

July 1. Paid Mr. Henry Sorrel of Cavenham in full for a black coach-guelding 4 years old passed, £20.

1714.—Feb. 4. Paid Thomas Angell in full for a black coach-guelding, £20.

Oct. 27. Paid Lord Wharton & Mr. Childers my two subscriptions to Quainton & Newmarket great stake Plates which they won, £43.

1719.—May 6. Paid Sir William Gordon for two black gueldings, £30.

May 29. Paid William Tully by ye order & for ye use of his master, Mr. Jermyn Davers, in full for a black coach guelding, 4 years old past, 16 guineas.

1721.—July 10. Paid Welch Tom for his grey mare, 2 guineas.

1723.—May 1. Paid Captain Mosely of Owsden in Suffolk for the chesnut padd I gave ye Dutchess of Marlborough, £50.

1724.—July 16. Paid Major James Garth for Harrys black horse, £21.

Nov. 26. Paid & allowd Tom Harvey my coachman his bill for hey, oats, straw etc. when my wife went to London to ye Prince's birthday, & staid to bring her down again to Ickworth, £4..4..0.

1727.—June 9. Paid my son Henry for ye new guelding ye officers appointed for yt service bought for him, £25.

1728.—Aug. 12. Paid John Frost of Stoke for a large black mare, £20.

1734.—May 11. Paid Samuel Partridg of Wickham-Brook for a black mare 4 years old, £10.

1739.—April 2⁶. Paid James Courtney by ye order of Tetlow for ye use of Eliz: Blunt for ye hire of 8 coach horses from London to Ickworth for 5 daies, in all £11..5..0.

April 28. Paid John Guest for the hire of 4 saddle-horses for ye same journey, £5.

1740.—April 10. Paid Neale ye dog quack-doctor for not cureing but blinding my faithful friend dear Kick, for which he deserved hanging more than 5 guineas.

VII.—ICKWORTH & BURY HOUSES.

1699.—Aug. 1. Allowd Mr. Fisher £4 on account which he paid Row: Aython for Tim Styles use in full for painting my parlour at Bury.

1702.—May 6. Paid William Langham for 2 cowes for Ickworth Dairy, £8..15..0.

May 6. Paid Thomas Boyton for 2 cowes, £7.

May 6. Paid Thomas Abbot for 7 cowes, £28.

May 7. Paid Ambrose Nunn for 1 cowe, £3..15..0.

May 8. Paid Mr. Joseph Alexander, Rector of Ickworth for 4 cowes, £17.

May 8. Paid Mr. William Gilly brazier of Bury for ye brewing coppers, etc., £59..7..10.

May 9. Paid John Eljigood cooper of Bury in full for his bill of brewing & washing vessels, etc., £55.

June 13. Paid Richard Newton ye glazier in full for ye ffarm-house at Ickworth for our own dwelling, £16..2..0. [*See Diary April* 14, 1702, *and note thereupon. S.H.A.H.*]

July 11. Paid John Palfry for digging up ye orchard at Ickworth, £2.

July 25. Paid William Maning his bill for hodling ye cows, hey rakes, etc., £0..13..0.

July 28. Paid John Cornwall & James Dixen in full of their bill for ploughing etc. several lands for leying down in Ickworth Parke & for fetching oats from Worlington, £12..16..0.

Oct. 23. Paid John Summer ye collector of Ickworth for my self, wife, 7 children & 20 servants to ye Poll, £1..9..0.

Oct. 23. Paid John Jolley of little Saxham ye 1st and 2d quarter of ye land tax for my wood & land that lye within that parish, £0..6..0.

Oct. 26. Paid Arthur Goodchild for ye window tax ended Michaelmas 1702, 5 shillings.

Oct. 28. Repaid Mr. Battely which he paid Mr. Eldred for ye milch ass & foale, £5..7..6.

1703.—Nov. 11. Paid John Poulter of Barrow for six score weather sheep bought Sept. 20 at £51.

1706.—Feb. 21. Paid Mr. Richard Mostyn by ye order & for ye use of Mr. John Soame in full for ye 45 deer bought at Thurlow, £34..10.

April 20. Paid Thomas Drew ye Bury Stone cutter for my dear and excellent cousin Dons tomb-stone in Ickworth Church, £12.   [*Cousin Don means his first wife. S.H.A.H.*]

May 20. Paid Mr. John Turnor in full for ye deer bought of Mr. Braham, £21..1..6.

July 5. Paid Chambers in full of his bill for Ickworth Church fflaggon etc., £19.

Nov. 14. Allowed D. Everard for ye 16 fine colourd Deer bought at Glemham Parke, 17 guineys; & ye charges of bringing home, in all £21..5..4.

1708.—Oct. 27. Paid Ambrose Kempe ye chief rents due to Chevington for Watt Paynes ffarm & lands taken into ye Parke for 3 years at Mich: 1708, £4..19..4½.

S

1709.—Aug. 17.   Paid Poulter of Barrow for hey for Barrow sheep in ye hard winter 1708, £8..13..9.

1712.—May 19.   Paid Ned Fletcher in full for doing ye seat at Ickworth Church, £0..16..6.

1713.—June 5.   Paid Mr. Alexander six pounds, five shillings, in full for all ye Tythes of Ickworth Parish, due & ending at Lady day 1712, from which time he sealed a lease of them for 500 years to me at £40 per annum, that rent being much more than ye Tythes are worth, £6..5..0.

1714.—June 12.   Paid Smith, Mr. Wisa's partner, in full of his bill for ye several evergreen & other plants, for my new Spring Garden at sweet Ickworth, £16..2..6.

1717.—March 23.   Paid Mr. William Oram ye garden-nursery-man in full for all ye plants & flower-roots sent to Ickworth, £50.

1718.—April 26.   Paid William Oram (nursery-man) in full for my self & also for all ye greens & plants I gave my son for Aswarby, £31..10.0.

1720.—March 31.   Paid James Swaine (messenger) a foedary or Castle-guard rent issuing out of Ickworth & Horringer, at 4s. 6d. per term (accompting 20 weeks to a term) unpaid for 15 terms, ended 19th Dec. 1718, (with acquitt) due to ye Crown, £3..8..6.

March 31.   Paid ditto for do. issuing out of Picards in Read at 14 pence per term, for ye same time (with acquitt) £0..18..6.

March 31.   Paid ditto for do. issuing out of Wordwell at 9 pence per term, ended 23d Feb., 1718, (with acquitt) £0..12..3.

1729.—Oct. 29.   Paid William Haynes ye Bury Stone-cutter in full for dear Babbs tomb-stone, altering ye coronet on my own etc., and removing some others in ye church, £10..10..0.

1734.—March 25.   Paid William Bridgeman in full for new making & planting my garden, £7..10..0.

1735.—March 28.   Paid William Bridgman for a years keeping up my garden ending Lady-day 1735, £2.

April 5.   Paid ye Bishop of Norwich for ye pales of my son Toms house at Bury, five guineas.   Paid him also for wine he said my son Tom had of his, £6..10..0 more.

1737.—Feb. 15.   Paid Mr. Duncombe all ye rents for Ickworth & Horringer to 19 March 1736 & for Picards & Wordwell, £3..14..2.

Feb. 15.   Paid James Swaine ye small rents for Ickworth & Horringer due Michaelmas 1736, £3..14..2.

June 9.   Paid Robert Singleton in part of 30 guineas for ye arms at Bury-house, £22.

June 22.   Paid do. nine pounds ten shillings more, which with ye £22 make 30 guineas, in full for ye coate of arms and supporters which he putt up in ye pediment of my wife her new house at Bury.

1738.—Oct. 7.   Paid Thomas Complin of Bury in full for 109 deals at 2s. 3d. for a threshing floor for my barn, £12..5..0.

Oct. 20.   Paid Betty Williams ye house bills when we were at Bury Fair, £5..7. 1½.

1739.—Sept. 1.   Paid Robert Singleton in full of his bill for the new marble slabbs & chimney-pieces, tomb-stones etc. at Ickworth, £13..11..0.

1741.—Oct. 9.   Paid Mr. Duncombe ye receiver in full for the Foedary rent due out of lands in Ickworth & Horringer for ten terms ending 19 Jan. 1741, at 4s. 6d. per term with acquittances, £2..8..4.

Oct. 9.   Paid J. Saunders a fee-farm rent for Ickworth Hall due Mich : 1741, 2s. 4d.

Oct. 9.   Paid ditto another ffee-ffarm rent for lands in Ickworth ending ditto, 2s. 4d.

VIII.—LONDON HOUSES.

[From the date of his first marriage in 1688 to Midsummer 1689 John Hervey rented a house "at ye Pall-Mall." His half share of the yearly rent was £40. Apparently his wife's mother, Lady Carr, paid the other half. From Midsummer 1689 to June 1693 he rented a house in King Street of the Earl of Berkeley. The yearly rent was £140, of which his share was £80. After his second marriage, from Christmas 1695 to Christmas 1698, he rented a house in Jermyn Street at £70 a year. From Christmas 1698 to Christmas 1699 he rented the house in St. James Square (now No. 6) of " Aunt Hervey," paying £50 a quarter. This included a yearly ground rent of £15. Aunt Hervey died in 1700, when the house in the Square became his. He continued to pay ground-rent for it, to Lord Jermyn (1705), Lord Dover (1708), his executors (1709), Lady Dover (1714), Richard Gipps Esq. (1726), Lady Dover's trustees and executors (1727), her heirs Sir Jermyn Davers and Mrs. Silence Folkes (1733), Mrs. Mary Cook, who purchased it (1736-1741). The Lady Harvey who received Aunt Hervey's rent was Elizabeth wife of Sir Daniel Harvey, Knight, and daughter of Edward, Lord Montague of Boughton. Lady Harvey and her brother Ralph Montague were Aunt Hervey's executors.

St. James's Square was built between 1664 and 1676 on land belonging to the Earl of St. Albans, the site being till then part of St. James's Fields. The rate-books for the Parish of St. Martin in the fields, (St. James's Parish not having been formed till 1685,) show John Hervey, husband to " Aunt Hervey," paying poor-rate for a house on the North side of the Square in 1676. (See Cunningham's Handbook for London). This house has therefore had but one family to own it from the day of its first setting up until now. S.H.A.H]

1689.—June 3. Paid my half in ye house rent at ye Pall-Mall from Nov. 10, 1688 to May 10, 1689, being half a year, £20.

June 29. Paid Earle of Berkeleys steward for necessary utensils as coppers, grates, etc. left in King street house, £15.

Aug. 24. Paid Mr. Joseph Hayes carpenter in full of all those repairs which were adjudged necessary to be made by Lord Berkeley to make ye King street house tenantable for me, which mony I am to discount with his Lordship on ye first half years payment of rent, £15.

Oct. Due to Lord Dover for 26 weeks use of ye french Embassadours stables at 20 shillings per week, viz. from March 14, 1688|9 to Sept. 24, 1689, £26.

Nov. 26. Paid then to Walsh for ye last quarters rent due from me for ye Lady Carr her house in ye Pall-Mall, ending Midsummer 1689, when I came to live in ye King street house, £10.

1690.—Feb. 12. Paid then to Mr. John Heynes in full for half a years rent of ye King street house due at Christmas last the summe of £40, being my share of ye seventy.

1691.—June 11. Paid Thomas Stanes att ye Sadlers Arms in Swallow street ye sum of £30 in full for a years rent of ye 11 stall stable & 4 coach houses due Lady day past, 1691. *[These stables are rented for 2 years more after this. S.H.A.H.]*

1698.—Dec. 23. Paid Mr. John Molins £157..2..8, which with 15s. 4d. allow'd for ye street grate, & £2..2..0 for ye 6 first payments of ye Church debt, & £50 formerly paid him, makes up ye 3 years rent of my house in Jermyn street from Xmas 1695 to Xmas 1698, at £70 per annum.

1699.—May 8. Paid Lady Harvey a quarters rent of my house in ye Square ended Lady day last, £50.

1700.—Feb. 2. Paid Mr. John Chamberlaine by order & for ye use of Lady Harvey £34..11..8 in mony, which with £15..8..4 deducted for ye Ground rent, is in full for a quarters rent of my house, due Christmas 1699.

July 3. Paid Sam Tookie Esq. for ye insurance mony of my house & stables in St. James Square at £5000 value for 7 years, £75.

Aug. 1. Paid Chamberlain by Lady Harveys order for Aunt Hervey her use for ye quarters rent of my house due June 24, 1700, £50.

1702.—Jan. 15. Paid Mr. John Molins ye years ground rent for my house ended at Christmas 1701, in mony £13..13..6, which with £1..14..10 sett off for ye first three payments of this years tax, makes in all £15..8..4.

Jan 26. Paid my cousin Charles May £30 in mony (by a note of his own to me for so much dated anno 1687) & £5 sett off for taxes, in all £35, being in full for a years rent of his stables in Jermyn street due & ended on or about Christmas 1698.

Dec. 1. Paid Thomas Causey Churchwarden of St. James's for my wifes & my life in ye three Church-Galleries, £65.

1707.—July 17. Paid for insuring my house & offices in St. James's Square for 7 years at £5000 with ye Phœnix Society £75 & for ye stamp, £75..6..0.

1708.—Dec. 24. Paid Robert Clark bricklayer for repairing my house & stables etc. in St. James's Square, £67.

Dec. 24. Paid Robert Baddum ye plumber for new laying & repairing all ye gutters of ye said house & stables, £29.

1709.—Dec. 24. Paid John Smallwell ye joyner in part of his bill for making new sash windows etc. for my London house, £107..10..0.

Dec. 24. Paid Will Dissell ye painter in part of his bill for ye said house, £30.

Dec. 31. Paid Isaac Elles ye glazier in part for ye glass of ye new sashes, £21..10..0.   [*Further sums of £23, £37, £14 & £11 are paid in 1710 to Baddum, Smallwell, Dissell & Ellis or Eeles. S.H.A.H.*]

1719.—Dec. 5. Paid John Watkins bricklayer in full of his bill for re-building ye laundry chimney & all other works, £55.

1723.—July 26. Paid Samuel Thring ye blacksmith in full for my iron-rail pales in front of my house, weighing 30 cwt. o qr. 26 lbs., which at 28 shillings per cwt. for ye iron & stone-work included as by agreement came to £42..6..6.

Aug. 13. Paid John Colvart free-mason in full for new laying ye draines; setting up ye chimney-piece in ye porters hall, etc., £2..2..0.

1728.—Jan. 22. Paid Mr. William Benney receiver ye two quarters rates for cleaning & adorning St. James's Square at 8s. 6d. per foot for my house due Oct. 31, 1727, £10..14..7½.

May 11. Paid Mr. Philip Stotherd in full for ye half years assessment made for adorning St. James's Square due ye first instant, £10..14..7½. [*This rate continues to be paid till the end of the book. In " Round about Piccadilly and Pall-Mall" Mr. H. B. Wheatly quotes Macaulay's History of England as to the disgraceful state of St. James Square at the beginning of the 18th Century. And then he says, "In February 1725 6, the inhabitants of the east, north and west sides petitioned to be allowed to rate themselves in order to cleanse and adorn the Square." This same work contains a good view of the Square from an old engraving made in about 1727. S.H.A.H.*]

1731.—April 19. Paid William Frith the carpenter £255 more, which with the £100 receivd on account ye 8th of December last make together £355 in full of his bills to this day.

April 19. Paid William Blakesley bricklayer £140 more, which with ye £100 paid him on account ye 8th of December last make together £340 (sic) in full of all his bills to this day.

April 19. Paid James Collishaw ye painter in full of his bill to this day, £49..12..0.

April 21. Paid Mr. Roger Morris ye surveyor in full for surveying & measuring ye work of my new building in St. James's Square, £42.

April 22. Paid Francis Sanders ye plasterer in full cf his bill, £50.

1732.—April 5.   Paid Christopher Cass & Co. in full of their bill for free-masons worke at my house in London, £145.

1733.—Feb. 16.   Paid John Whittingham in full for my water-rent due to the proprietors of the London-bridg Water Works, & ending Xmas last, ⸴7.   [*The house was rated at £200 a year.   S.H.A.H.*]

IX.—MISCELLANEOUS.

1688.—Nov. 10.   For a Beaver hatt, £2..10..0.

Nov. 27.   To William Brownlow ye footman for Flambeaux £0..7..6.

1689.—Jan. 20.   Gave Orange Nan for a baskett of grapes she gave my wife, £1..1..6.

March 27.   Gave Deloné his little daughter, £0..10..9.

Aprill 10.   For a white Tea-pot & bason for dear wife, £4..16..9.

May 2.   For a scrutore, £8.

May 23.   Paid Orange Nann for ye use of her calesh into Lincoln-shire, & for cherries for dear wife, £1..6..6.

June 12.   Paid for two china basons for dear wife, £1..1..6.

July 6.   Paid to Katharine Scott for ye use of her mistress Mrs. Levena Cawne & by her order, being in full payment for twelve leaves of cutt Jappan skreens, two pieces of India Damask, & six Dutch chairs, & all other accounts, £65.

July 14.   Took ten guineys when we went to Bury with dear wife, Father & Lady Carr, £10..15..0.

Aug. 6.   The whole expences of Bury journey cost me besides, £36..5..10.

Aug. 8.   For an India trunk bought of Mrs. Ann Tabb, £7.

Aug. 30.   Paid Mary Billop for ye use & by ye order of Mrs. Jane Harrison for an India quilt for a bed, £38.

Aug. 30. Paid for wicker basketts for young Cozen Dons equipage, £1..15..0. [*Cozen Don was a nickname that John Hervey and his first wife gave each other, either to other. See entries in Jan. & Feb., 1690. S.H.A.H.*]

Sept. 27. To Mrs. Duncombs nurses when I christend Frederick, £9..13..6.

Oct. 4. Paid for a silver hanging candlestick for the nursery, weighing 17 ownces, 10 pennyweight, £5..11..0.

Oct. 5. Paid for 2 pounds of wax candles, two wax books, & five yards of yellow ribbon, £0..10..6.

Oct. 7. For a chest of drawers for ye nursery, £1.

Oct. 10. Paid then by Thomas Walsh my servant to John Bustan corn chandler in full for oats, beanes etc.; and that he may not defraud my posterity by after forged bills, I declare this to be the last time of my having any sort of commerce with him, £20.

Oct. 11. Paid then to Noul Tirpane a french varnisher in full for 10 chairs, a couch & two taboretts & of all other accounts to this day, £12.

Oct. 16. Paid then to Mr. Paul Clowdsley in full for 15 yds. & ½ of orange & silver stuff, a scarlet lining, & three yds. of scarlett satin, £44..1..6.

Oct. 16. Paid then to a semstress for necks of cruts & joyning lace, £0..7..0.

Oct. 31. Paid Mr. John Watson upholdsterer for ye Brokadel hanging in my wifes anti-chamber, £11..10..0.

Nov. 22. Paid Mrs. Rutland of ye old Exchange for two sutes of lace, for ye child, £55.

Nov. Remain yet due to Frenoye ye silkman for ye fringe of ye bed, edging for the window curtains, etc., £155.

T

Nov. Due to ye joyner who made the chairs, stools & squabs for my wife, £19.

Nov. Due to Mr. Morton for gold & crimson fringe for ye India bed quilt, £17.

Nov. Due to Chambers for ye change of my shaving pott for a new shaving bason & pott, £13.

Nov. 6. Paid Abraham Chambers for a silver hand candlestick, & then made even all accounts between us, £3..12..0.

Nov. 8. Gave Le Coque who was my valet de Chambre, £1..1..6.

Nov. 18. Gave my wife for nurse Plunkett, £1.

Nov. 29. For a pass, post-warrant, etc., £0..13..0.

Nov. 29. For a black velvet capp, £0..12..0.

Dec. 18. Paid then for a beaver muff, £1..15..0.

Dec. 19. Paid my cousen Barron which my dear wife had borrowed of her, £30.

Dec. 24. Paid to Ben. Ray mercer at ye Black Lion in Pater Noster Row for a brown & silver westcoat, & a lining for it, & a coat, £7..15..0.

Dec. 24. Paid for 6 dozen of Princes metal buttons, £1..10..0.

1690.—Jan. 7. *Given to me Is. Hervey by daer cosen donn a five pound piece of gold, £5..7..6.

Jan. 24. Paid for a pair of silver andirons for my dear wife her closett chimney, £13..5..0.

Jan. 24. *Then given me by daer cosen donn five halfe guineys being £2..13..9.

---

* This entry is made by his wife Isabella.   Her handwriting and spelling are of a piece.

Jan. 24. Paid then for a gold snuff box, which be it here rememberd ye goldsmith Mr. Howerd, of whom I bought it, is obligd whenever I return it to allow me for it again six pounds & a crown, £6..10..0.

Jan. 25. Paid then for a glass skreen for my niece Elwes, £1..1..6.

Feb 3. *Daer cosen donn gave me a sillver ege thing worth tenn ginnes, £10..15..0.

* The same day he gave me a halfe gienny £0..10..9.

Feb. 6. Lost at Lady Ossulstons lottery, £1.

Feb. 17. Paid then to Medina ye Jew for a Tea-table, & 2 pair of china cupps for dear wife, £10.

Feb. 27. Paid then for china cupps etc. for dear wife, £4..10..0.

Feb. 28. Paid then to the same woman, viz. Eliz: Genua, for 2 pair of basons for dear wife, £1..12..0.

March 1. Paid then for a large china punch-bowl, with a large jarr & two white cupps for dear wife, £3..5..0.

March 3. Paid then for a sett of cupps & saucers for dear wife, £2.

March 4. Paid for six other saucers for her, £0..10..0.

March 5. Paid then to Mrs. Genua for two china beakers for dear wife, £2..11..0.

March 5. Paid then for 2 great jarrs of china, & 2 other less, with one very little one, bought of Mrs. Devett for dear wife, £7..3..0.

March 8. Paid then to Medina ye Jew for a parcell of old china for my dear wife, £21.

March 11. Paid to Mr. Green ye potter for a parcel of old china for dear wife, £6..10..0.

* This entry is made by his wife Isabella.

March 11.   Paid then to one Mrs. Sarah Terry for an other sett of old china for dear wife, £22.

March 13.   Paid then to Medina ye Jew for a pair of old china rowl-waggons for dear wife, £7..10..6.

March 13.   Paid more to him for a pair of china cupps and a little jarr for dear wife, £1..6..0.

March 14.   Paid then to Mrs. Harrison for a china tea-pott bason for dear wife, £1.,1..6.

March 14.   Paid then to Abraham Chambers for a corrail sett in gold, £1..10..0.

March 29.   Paid then for 2 pair of beaver gloves, £0..8..0.

April 30.   Paid then for an old china bottle & two china dishes for dear wife, £1..15..0.

May 20.   Paid for dear wife at curiosity shop, £0..10..0.

June 13.   Paid then to John Van Colina for a parcel of old china for dear wife, £3..2..6.

July 11.   Paid then to George Caldicot ye mercer for 12 yards & a half of lutestring for dear wife, £3..10..0.

July 16.   Dear wife had of me to pay for pinking of her mantoe and petticoat, £0..12..0

Oct. 19.   Paid Mr. Morris of Euston for a piece of gold I had of him upon marriage or death to pay 5 guineys, £5..7..6.

Oct. 30.   Gave my Fathers servants when I came away, £3.

Nov. 4.   Paid Mrs. Cawne for a rich piece of India Atlas for dear wife, £13..10..0.

Nov. 6.   Paid Mrs. Cawne for a parcell of Indian things for dear wife, £5..7..6.

Nov. 19.   Paid Bend ye Italian for wax candles, £2..2..0.

Dec. 3.   Gave dear wife two Jacobus's, 2 half guineys, 1 pistol, they make together, £4..10..0.

Dec. 19.   Paid Mrs. Harache for a silver standish, £15..10..0.

Dec. 29.   Paid John Green ye potter for a pair of china jarrs, £1..4..0.

1691.—Jan. 2.   For a dozen of fflambeauxs, £0..14..0.

Jan. 15.   Paid Peter Remy for a Jappan travelling strong water cellar, £5..7..6.

Jan. 17.   Paid Sutton a whole-sale man of ye new exchange for an Indian gowne, £2..10..0.

March 20.   Paid Mrs. Barron in full of what dear wife ought her, £10..16..6.

April 5.   Gave att Mr. Battely's childs christening att Bury, £3..4..6.

May 27.   Paid Bleiberg ye gunsmith for a pair of servants pistolls, £2..7..6.

June 20.   Paid Medina ye Jew for a Persian carpett (all of silk) to lay under a bed, and for an old china Rowlwaggin, 22 guineys.

June 22.   Paid Mrs. Harrison for a piece of blue Indian stuff for dear wife, £2..15..0.

Oct. 10.   Paid Mrs. Hicks for a cradle-skreen, £1..6..0.

Oct. 28.   Allowed for what I ordered to be given for me at Mrs. Brackenburys christening, £2.

Nov. 12.   Paid a furrier for altering dear wives Palatine, £1.

Nov. 12.   Paid Mrs. Du Kelly a Tyre woman for capps & cutting hair, £1..10..0.

1692.—Jan. 1.   Paid Mrs. Harrison for 2 china rice potts for dear wife, £5.

April 23. Paid Garfoot of ye Temple for a watch with seconds, £4..15..0.

May 24. Gave Mr. Steward Lord Cornwallis's Secretary when he brought me a commission for a Deputy Lieutenant of Suffolke, 3 guineys.

May 31. Gave Welch Tom for a little diamond ring, £1..10..0.

June 17. ffor ye chest of drawers bought at Stow-Green ffair, £1..17..6.

Nov. 26. Paid Mrs. Harrison for a china-jarr for dear wife, £2..10..0.

Nov. 26. Allowd dear wife for a parcel of china she bought, £2..14..0.

Dec. 10. Paid John Deards for a silver headed cane, £1..15..0.

Dec. 16. Paid Mr. Robert ffowle in full for a pair of large andirons, and a silver pair of scales. £88..5..6.

Dec. 17. Paid Mr. Morton for ye change of my silver fringed gloves, £2.

1693.—Feb. 2. Paid Leeds ye mercer in full of his bill for ye damask of my wives ffield-bed, etc., £17.

Feb. 9. Paid Mr. Robert ffowle in full of his bill for several pieces of plate, £420.

March 7. Gave Dr. Stockham for coming to my dear wife that morn she died, £5..7..6.

March 7. Paid Walsh his first bill of ye mourning, carrying down ye corps, etc., £155..14..9.

April 29. Paid ffr: Kercher for hair rings etc., £10.

June 20. Paid John Marshall for my two microscopes, £6.

June 27. Paid Mr. Hornbault ye jeweller for rings, locketts etc., £20.

1695.—June. Paid Charles Mather (ye cane-man in ffleet street) for a silver snuff-box, a table-book, a pockett-case & a silver wove hatband, by bill on Chambers, £11..15..0.

July 11.   To Mr. Martyn ffolkes for drawing ye articles of marriage, 10 guineys.

Dec. 7.   Paid Mr. ffrancis Ferris (for ye use of his master Mr. Thomas Tompion) ye sume of sixty pounds in full for a gold repeating watch for my dear wife.

1696.—Jan. 11.   Paid Calamar ye Dutchman in Green street for a parcell of china for my dear wife, £31..8..4.

April 18.   Paid Mr. William Sherrard ye mercer for ye camlett & lineing of my blue sur-tout, £4..2..0.

April 22.   Paid Mr. Tompion for ye gold chain of my dear wifes repeating watch, £7..15..0.

April 22.   Gave to my dear wife her self a double guiney, £2..10..0.

May 4.   Paid Collema ye Dutchman for an other parcel of china, £10..4..0.

May 6.   Paid Mr. Chambers & Partner in full of their bill for plate exchanged & made for me to this day, £115.

May 18.   Paid Mr. James Seamer ye goldsmith for 2 table stands, £15.

May 18.   Allowed Mr. James Chambers & Partner upon accompt this day stated for an other dozen of silver plates, £62..2..6.

May 23.   Paid Mr. James Seamer ye goldsmith for eight diamond buckles which I gave my dear wife (for bodies), £51.

May 25.   Paid Mr. Gerreit Johnson ye Cabinett-maker in full of his bill for ye black sett of Glass, table & stands, & for ye glasses, etc., over ye chimneys & elsewhere in dear wife's apartment, £70.

June 12.   Paid Mr. Ed : Waldegrave ye goldsmith for a bason & ewer, weighing 244 ounces & a half, at 5s. 2d. per ounce, £63..3. 2.

June 23.   Paid Mr. Chambers & Partner in full of their bill for ye silver stand & salvers, etc., £30.

Oct. 5. Paid a work-woman in Half-moon street for finishing ye crimson and yellow quilt (for a toilette-cloath) which my dear Isabella begun, £5..10..0.

Oct. 7. Paid Mr. James Seamers ye goldsmiths man Thomas Outlaw for ye great silver chased baskett, weighing 128 ounces, 4 dwt., at 5s. 5d. per ounce, £34..10..0.

Oct. 13. Paid Joseph Bindé ye Italian for wax candles & parmazan cheese, £7.

Oct. 17. Paid Mr. James Seamer for a monteth weight 75 ounces at 5s. 4d. per ounce, and a chafindish weight 24 ounces 15 dwt. at 6s. 6d. per ounce, together £28..5..0.

Nov. 5. Paid Mr. Richard Hoar ye goldsmith for a pair of branch candlesticks weighing 78 ounces 2 dwt., & for a pair of gilt sconces weighing 46 ounces 14 dwt., both at 7s. 6d. per ounce, £46..15..6.

Nov. 5. Paid William Nodes at ye Crown by Fleet ditch for 2 looking glasses, £6.

Nov. 7. Paid Mr. Edw: Waldegrave, a goldsmith in Russel street, for 11 dishes, 1 dozen of plates, a coffee pott, & a porridg laddle, weighing 802 ounces, at 5s. 3¼d. per ounce, & for ye graving, £211..7..0. [Paid] £7..3..0 in mony, ye rest in old plate of my dear fathers.

Nov. 19. Paid John Kinsei ye auctioner for a large piece of Bramer's, £5..12..0.

Nov. 19. For 2 dishes made by Mr. Chambers weighing 154½ ounces at 4d. per ounce fashion, & 10 shillings for graveing them, & ye plate at 5s. 2d. per ounce, £42..19..9. Gave him ye weight in old plate.

Dec. 2. Paid Mrs. Devett for half a pound of Keiser Tea, £2.

1697.—Jan. 14. My dear wife had 100 guineys of me (which summe she is to receive on ye first day of every Kalendar month) to find herself, ye children & all other necessarys in Housekeeping, to commence from new years day last part, £110.

April 2. Paid John Whiston ye dyer for 4 pieces of Scotch plodd, £11.

May 7. Paid Mr. Duncombe & Mr. Pigeon (as executors of Mr. Baptist May) for a large silver cystern, 2 dozen of nurld plates, 1 large cup & cover, 1 bason, 1 chamber pott, 1 laddle, & 1 skimmer, all weighing 1128 ounces 15 pennyweight, which at 5s. 4d. per ounce come to £301.

1698.—Feb. 22. Paid my subscription towards ye Combination in Suffolk, £10.

July 19. Paid Mr. Paman ye under-sheriff my 2d contribution on ye new Combination account, £10.

Dec. 7. Paid Mr. Chambers his bill in full for a Tea-kettle & lampe, weight 90 ounces 11 dwt. at 6s. 2d., & for a chafin dish with a cawdle-heater, weight 51 ounces 18 dwt. at 5s. 6d. per ounce, in all £42..19..10.

Dec. 31. Paid John Van Collema in full for an Indian trunk etc., £35.

Dec. 31. Paid Watt Compton goldsmith in Lincoln's Inn ffields for 2 pair of Andirons & 2 little knobbs for tongs & shovel weighing 307 ounces 14 dwtt. at 5s. 4d. per ounce, £82..1..0.

1699.—Jan. 17. Paid David Williams for ye silver borders of 8 glass sconces for ye drawing room weighing 231 ounces 13 dwtt., £75..5..0.

Jan. 20. Paid ditto for a pair of ye same borders for ye chimney weighing 53 ounces 13 dwtt. at 6s. 6d., & for a pair of chimney sconces all of silver weighing 90 ounces 3 dwtt. at 7 shillings per ounce, in all £47..6..0.

Feb. 21. Paid David Williams for ye 8 great silver sconces weighing 491 ounces at 7 shilling per ounce & for graving etc., in all £175.

July 21. Paid Mr. Henry Tatlocke ye lace-man (Pierce's partner) in full, £97.

V

1700.—Jan. 23.   Paid Collonel William Parsons in full for ye Italian painted glass cabinett, £21..10..0.

Jan. 27.   Paid George Lewis, silversmith, for 2 pair of plate Andirons being French plate at 5s. 5d. per ounce intrinsick value & 1d. fashion, in all 5s. 6d. per ounce, ye large pair weighed 135 ounces 2 dwtt.; ye doggs 28 ounces 9 dwtt., so cost £45.

March 18.   Paid Mrs. Porter for ye lace of two cravatts, £12.

July 6.   Paid Williams ye French silversmith for 2 pottage & 4 ragow spoons, £15..15..0.

Oct. 26.   Paid Lanseter for 2 silver jarrs etc. deliverd Bury ffair 1699, £3..9..0.

Nov. 18.   Paid Peter Rochfort for ye Iron-chest in my closett, £9..13..6.

1701.—Jan. 13.   Paid Mrs. Medina for china etc., £40.

Jan. 24.   Paid Mrs. Medina for a pair of Indian cutt Jappan skreens, £60.

March 22.   Paid Jonathan Mayne jun. in full for ye carv'd work in my closett, £80.

July 10.   Gave Mr. Warley, Minister of Witham in Essex, to refresh ye tomb of my ancestor Mr. ffrancis Hervey buried in that Church, £5..7..6.

July 11.   Gave ye servants & ringers at Stoke, £3..4..6.

1702.—Jan. 16.   Paid Colonel Parsons for ye black bureau, £6.

April 27.   Paid Isaac Blieberg for a pair of pistols & 2 musquetoons, £14.

April 30.   Paid Gumley for my bureau & some china ware, £11..10..0.

Dec. 1.   Paid Mr. Chambers for ye present of Plate I gave Mr. Vanbrook £65.

Dec. 16.—Paid Peter Gumley for China & Japan ware, £29.

1703. June 23. Paid Mr. Chambers & Comp. in full of their bill for new plate (besides 1236 ounces they had of me in old plate) £209..16..0. Ye 22 new dishes & 3 dozen of plates weighed in all 1668 ounces 5 dwtt. at 10 pence per fashion.

June 24. Paid Henry Bolton in full for Ermyn & making my robes, £14.

Dec. 21. Paid Colonel Parsons for an antique seale, a head of Socrates, £5.

1704.—Jan. 24. Paid Dan Dargent for dear wifes jewels, loopes & buttons, £125..10..0.

June 22. Paid Bourguet for ye egg-marine stone for my seale, £7.

Dec. 18. Paid Mrs. Eliz : Harrison for ye Jappan scrutore, £50.

1705.—Feb. 21. Paid Mr. Chambers for 12 spoons, 12 fforkes & 12 knives, etc., £29..13..0.

March 8. Paid Tho : Phill upholdsterer in full for ye Turkey leather chairs, etc. £30..2..6.

July 9. Paid Charles Mather in full for my seale, chess board, etc., £20.

July 18. Gave at ye christening of Mr. John Turner, £6..9..0.

Sept. 22. Paid Morgan Herbert for ye gold watch I gave Aunt Poley, £21..10..0.

1706.—Dec. 3. Paid Mr. Vernon ye mercer in full for ye damask window curtains of ye great bed-chamber, etc., £71..10..0.

1707.—Dec. 17. Paid Mr. Chambers for ye two new pair of Candlesticks, & for a dressing weight for dear wife etc., £20..10..0.

1708.—March 9. Paid Mr. Thomas Brydon for a pair of candlesticks, snuffers & stand which I made a present of to Monsieur Masson, £16..13..6.

April 5.   Paid Anthony Harrison for my silver watch, £11..16..6.

Dec. 2.   Paid Mr. Chambers for a great silver nurld dish etc. in full, £18..15..7.

Dec. 2.   Paid Charles Mather in full for my pocket case of knife cizers etc., £3..4..6.

1709.—Jan. 11.   Paid Pierre Platel ye French silver-smyth, more than ye office allowd for Nanns silver frame & ye 5 covers to it, £63..10.0.

March 22.   Paid for dozen of Dutch chairs Will Lovegaune bought for Sir Thomas ffelton in Holland, £2..18..10.

June 16.   Paid Mr. Chambers for ye 3 gold medalls of ye Princess Sophia, ye Elector of Hannover her son (which I exchanged for a larger of him, & paid £12..14 more for it, so they cost in all £62..14) & ye Prince Electoral his son, £50.

July 14.   Gave ye Dutchess of Marlborough's servants 10 guineys when dear wife & I were some daies with her at her house at St. Albans.

Dec. 3.   Paid James Hayes ye stone cutter in full for 98 foot of marble at 5s. 6d. for ye Beufette & for other work, £31.

1710.—Feb. 12.   Paid James Moore in full of his bill for glass peers, sconces, etc., £33..10..0.

May 16.   Paid Henry Manning for ye use of his mother ye widow Ann Manning for 21 yards of green cloath, £6..16..6.

June 1.   Paid ye said widow for 21 yards more of green cloath for ye boys liveries at Newmarket in September last, £6..16..6.

June 15.   Paid Mr. Devett for six muslyn cravatts (which I made 12 of), £3.

July 15.   Paid Luke Nightengal ye taylor in full for 8 liveries & ye page's cloaths, £36.

1711.—Jan. 27. Paid John Smith for holland for my own shirts, & for lawn kenten, muslin & holland for ye boys etc., in all £38.

April 13. Paid for a pink colourd manteau & pettycoat for dear wife, £8..16..o.

May 16. Paid Luke Nightengale ye taylor in part of his bill for nine livery suites at £4 per suite, 20 guineas.

July 26. Paid Mr. Chambers for mending ye silver toaster, £1..2..o.

1712.—Jan. 14. Paid Nurse Edwards for ye black french lace scarfe & ye fflanders lace, which Lady Albemarle bought for her, & which I gave my dear wife for a new years guift, £58..15..9.

June 7. Paid Luke Nightengale ye taylor for 2 suites & ye 3 blue surtouts, £15.

July 26. Sent Mrs. Manley by her son Tom into Wales, £5..7..6.

1713.—May 25. Dear Fathers birth-day, gave Tom Manley to sett up his trade, for my good uncle's sake, & for my dear fathers, whose godson he is, £100.

May 27. Paid Charles Mather in full for dear wifes gold snuff-box, & all demands, £20.

1714.—Jan. 14. Paid Mr. Obrian six guineas given for me at Mrs. Elwes's christening.

Jan. 21. Paid Sir Henry Bond in full for a Jappan cabinet, £35.

March 2. Paid Charles Mather for my new gold snuff-box, £22..6..o.

March 2. Paid Hussey ye hatter in full for beaver, £1..10..o.

April 18. Gave at ye christening of my niece Meggots son, £10..15..o.

Sept. 14. Paid Thomas Hinchliffe ye mercer in full for a piece of Dutch crimson velvet (32 yards) for my Coronation robes, £30.

Sept. 16. Paid Mrs. Pitronella de Vlieger & Son for my new lace cravat, £10..15..o.

Oct. 15.   Paid Mr. Tully ye mercer in full for 8 yards of rich brocade stuff, & lineing for my Coronation westcoat & breeches, £44..15..6.

Oct. 19.   Paid Charles Mather for a pair of gold buckles for my self, £6..1..10.

Oct. 19.   Paid Louis Cuny for my Earls Coronet, £14.

Nov. 4.   Paid Philip Pinkney in full for ye Ermin & Furring of my Coronation robes, 15 guineas.

1715.—March 16.   Paid & allowed Mr. Mills on account his bill of disbursments for passing & solliciting my Patent for ye Earldom of Bristol, £395..18..7.

April 9.   Paid Walter Davis ye bill of fees due upon my being introduced into ye House of Peers as Earl of Bristol, £17..10..0.

April 14.   Paid Quinton Watson in full of his bill for flambeauxs, £12..15..0.

Aug 2.   To Mr. Roger Manley to sett up his trade as an Apothecary, £10.

Sept. 19.   Spent at Bury-Fair, 13 guineas.

Dec. 10.   Gave to Sir Thomas Hanmers servants when we lay at Euston, £10..15..0.

1716.—Jan. 25.   Paid Andrew Carpenter in full for 2 lead flower potts, £2..13..9.

April 18.   Paid Andrew Carpenter for ye 4 Figures representing ye 4 seasons in full (except for ye cases), £20.

June 2.   Paid David Wynn gunsmith in full for 3 Carabines etc., £3..18..6.

Aug. 29.   Paid Mr. Chambers for a silver stew-pan weighing 67 ounces 14 dwt., & for a silver chamber pott weighing 30 ounces, both at 6s. 6d. per ounce, & for graveing them etc , in all £32..7..3.

1717.—Feb. 16. Paid West & Vickers in full for ye blue burdett hangings & nurses gown, £35..9..6.

Sept. 25. Spent & gave away at this Bury Fair, 13 guineas.

1718.—Feb. 12. Gave to Susan Manley five guineas.

March 10. Gave dear wife to buy her a new watch, £31..10..0.

Oct. 13. Paid Mrs. Eliz: Wharton in full for 10 weeks lodging at ye Abbey in Bath, £46.

Nov. 29. Paid Dan. Delander in full for my gold chain & swiffles, £5.

1719.—April 25. Paid Mr. Playters & Co. in full for my black cloath, & for my Drap de Berry great Coat, & all other demands, £7..18..0.

Nov. 17. Paid Sir Thomas Hanmer £15, which his steward in Wales paid by my desire to Bell, Kez, & Mall Manley to buy them mourning for thier good mother Mrs. Eliz: Manley.

Dec. 19. Gave Parson Millicent towards his loss by fire, £5..5..0.

1720.—Jan. 20. Gave Nurse Plunkett for dear cousin Dons sake, £2..2..0..

April 7. Paid West, Vickers & Eyre in full of their bill for my blue damask nightgowne & two shagreen linings for myself & Will, in all £10..15..0.

April 13. Gave dear wife to make up ye mony she gave to Mrs. Manley for her poem 20 guineas, £10..10..0 (sic). [*At the end of the 2nd of 2 MSS. volumes containing letters between Lord and Lady Bristol is a poem to Lady Bristol by Mrs. Manley. It seems to have been printed in* 1719. *Probably that is what is here alluded to. S.H.A.H.*]

Nov. 22. Gave to Sir Thomas Hanmers servants at Milden-hall, £5..5..0.

1721.—Jan. 20. Gave Nurse Plunkett for dear cousin Donns sake, 2 guineas.

Sept. 25.   Paid for an etuy for a fairing at Bath for Mrs. Bradshaw, £2..2.,0.

Sept. 27.   Paid for ye ring I gave Lady Lucy for a fairing, £1..11..6.

Sept. 27.   Paid Dardes for my French table-book, £3..3..0.

Oct. 25.   Paid Mr. William Wilson ye draper for 5½ yards of ratteen, £5..10..0.

1723.—July 7.   Paid Benjamin Brooke ye Gun-smith in full for a pair of pistols made up with silver knobbs etc., 10 guineas.

1724.—May 20.   Paid Ben Godfrey, for ye use of his master John Craig, in full for ye silver Tea-pott I gave Mrs. Sellars of Sleaford, £4..10..0.

1725.—June 16.   Gave at ye christening of Tom Manley's son at Mr. Gansells at Low-Leyton, £5..8..6.

June 26.   Gave ye poor woman at whose house Moratt was found, £1..1..0.

July 22.   Paid William Pearcy ye taylor for black Harrys new suite, etc., £9..15..0.

1726.—April 9.   Paid John Sibthorp in full for a copy of Rubens Bacchanal at £5, 10 black leather chairs at £12..3..0, a sett of knives & forkes at 18s., a case of 12 agatt handled knives, 12 forkes ditto, & 12 silver spoons at £10..10..0, in all £28..11..0, bought at Brigadier Mundens Auction of goods.

Aug. 6.   Gave 5 guineas to Kezia Manley, & a Jacobus to Bell & Susan each, £7..17..0.

Aug. 6.   Gave to ye ringers at Hanmer, & to ye old gardiner there, 13 shillings.

Aug. 23.   Gave to Sir Thomas Hanmers servants at Bettisfield in Wales where I had been ten daies to see him, £10..10..0.

Aug. Gave at ye Dutchess of Marlboroughs at St. Albans, & at Lord Sunderlands at Althorpe, & Lord Chetwynds at Inxtree, £1..15..0.

Aug. To ye bells & musick at Worcester & Gloucester, £1.

Oct. 14. Paid Dardes for a gilt etuy for Mrs. Williams, 2 guineas & ½.

Oct. 21. Paid for ye snuff-box I gave to my Saint Hayes, £1..10..0.

Dec. 7. Gave John Frost ye Lady Howard of Effingham her servant when he brought me ye gold cupp as a present from her which she desird I would accept to remember her by, £1..1..0.

1727.--April 12. Paid Mr. John Vickers ye mercer in full of his bill for ye green mantua window curtain, Wills scarlet chagrine & my own, my new blue damask night gown, £31..10..0.

April 13. Paid Andrew Regnier ye taylor in full of his bill for my own & my son Wills double-breasted cloaths which were trim'd with gold, my camlett surtout, etc., £17..10..0.

April 17. Paid David Willaum ye silversmith for ye case of 12 gilt knives, 12 spoons & 12 forks, weighing 131 ownces at 5s. 8½d., bought at ye D. of Shrewsburys sale, & for boyling & mending old plate, in all £37..10 .0.

April 23. Paid & allowed for ye several pieces of plate I bought which were Lady Effinghams, (besides ye cistern of £82..11..0 I gave my son Lord Hervey & charged before) in all £58..4..0, which made ye whole I was chargeable for £140..15..0.

May 13. Paid Robert Leigh ye Cabinet-maker in full for putting in new glasses to ye silver sconces, & India cutt jappan frame, & for a dumb waiter, £10..10..0.

June 6. Paid Peter Ducasse for a piece of cambrick to make me necks, ruffles, etc., £6.

Dec. 8. I repaid my wife ye seventeen guineas she paid for me to Mrs.

W

Moren for ye rich brocade stuff for my westcoate to be wore at ye Coronation, which I gave my son Tom.

1728.—July 30. Paid John Wilson for 7 snuff-colourd pocket handkerchiefs, £1..4..6.

Oct. 19. I gave Mrs. Mary Spalding of Bury fifty pounds out ye mony she paid me as executrix to her father Mr. Roger Spalding, for her own separate use, being left poor by her said father, who was (all but once) my friend there.

Nov. 22. I repaid my wife six pounds she allowd Mathews to putt himself into mourning for ye late king.

1729.—Jan. 23. Paid John Vickers ye mercer in full for my new red night-gowne, £5..10..0, & for shagreen for lining etc., in all £16..11..0.

1730.—Feb. 20. Paid Thomas Rawlinson for 27 dozen of common candles at 6s. 6d., & for 3 dozen of moulded ones at 7s. 6d., in all £9..18..0.

March 6. Paid Messrs. Vicars & Eyre in full of their bill for my new crimson nightgown £5, & lineings for Felle & self, in all £10..4..0.

April 11. Paid John Holford for my bureau I bought at Sleaford, 3 guineas.

May 11. Paid Mrs. Eliz: Kinsey for my lodging at Sleaford, 7 guineas.

1731.—Feb. 11. Paid John Sharpe ye upholder in full of his bill for 98 yards of crimson harretine for my new bed chamber at 2 shillings per yard, £9..16..0.

Feb. 18. Paid John Sharpe ye upholder in full of his bill & all demands for more goods bought of him, as a correspondent of Isaac Olivers of Bury, £19..5..6.

April 2. Paid William Basnett in full of his bill for ye Livery shoulder-knotts, 6 at 10s. delivered in 1727, & seven at 6s. each delivered 27 Feb. last, £5..2..0.

April 22. Paid Ben Tassell by his servant George Hewett for my new hatt, £1..1..0.

1732.—Feb. 4. Paid Isaac Fernandes ye Jew in full for a pound of Havannah snuff, £1..1..0.

April 5. Repaid Lady Hervey for a pound of tea 28s., & a fee to Dr. Hollins, £2..9..0.

1733.—April 3. Paid Ben. Tassell in full for my last Beveret-hatt, £1..1..0.

April 6. Paid George Wickes & Mr. Craig for a silver Coffee-pott at 5s. 9d. & all demands, £11..18..0.

April 25. Paid E. Scarlet for ye perspective-glass & handle of my cane trimmd with gold, £3..13..0.

1735.—Jan. 24. Paid Mr. John Vicars in full for my blue gown, chagreen, etc., £9..5..0.

March 5. Repaid Lord Hervey what he laid out for ye gold lace of my cloaths, £6..18,.0.

March 14. Paid Thomas Robinson shoemaker in full for a pair of red morocco slippers, 10 shillings.

April 27. Paid Mr. Peter Rogers of Bury for a silver Coffee-pott, £6..18..0.

Oct. 17. Paid Peter Rogers for a silver mugg I gave Williams for a Bury-Fairing, £3..10..0.

1736.—Jan. 9. Paid Perigal for ye repeating watch which my (wife) trucked with him for her new one, £21.

Nov. 11. Paid John Shipman of Bury for a large scrutore, £12.

1737.—Jan. 21. Paid Mr. John Turner table keeper at court in full for wax candles etc., £6..7..6.

April 1. Paid Christopher Cock ye auctioneer in full for a silver epargne weight 497 ounces 12 pennyweight at 6s. 8½d. per ounce, bought at Lord Scarsdales sale, £166..17..0.

April 2. Paid Perigal for mending my Tompion repeating watch, & ye clock on ye stairs head, £1..11..6.

1738.—Feb. 24. Paid Thomas Colebrand in full for twenty pieces of paper-hangings for Ickworth at 3s., £3.

March 31. Paid William Bradshaw upholder for ye table-bed, & lineing ye needle-work carpet, £3..5..0.

1739.—Feb. 2. Paid Mr. John Turner for 8 dozen of wax-candles at 2s. 4d. per pound, £10..8..0.

Feb. 16. Paid Mrs. Margaret Marsh for my dark-colourd damask night-gowne, £4..18..0.

April 23. Repaid Mr. Jer : Lewis for 2 pounds of Tea bought of Mrs. Churchil at 32s., boxes etc., £3..7..0.

April 23. Paid Pye ye grocer, by Mrs. Benney, for 2 pounds of Tea, £2.

Oct. 9. Gave King ye Collector towards ye losses by fire at Tuddenham 24 Aug. last, £5..5..0.

Oct. 26. Gave my Godson John Oliver when he went to Cambridg £15, to pay for his caution-mony & for the furniture of his chambers.

Dec. 24. Paid John Hopkins for a silver sugar canister I gave Williams for a fairing, £5..13..6.

1740.—Feb. 8. Paid Mr. John Turner for 20 papers of wax candles at 13s. each, £13.

1741.—March 21. Paid Richard Gurney & Comp. for four gaudroned silver dishes weighing 155 ounces 7 pennyweight at 7s. 6d. per ounce, ingraving at 5s. each, £59..5..3.

March 26. Paid Scarlet jun. for ye change of my reflecting telescope, 3 guineas.

Nov. 3. I gave to the poor sufferers by the fire at Lakenheath in this County, £5..5..0.

1742.—Feb. 8. Paid Williams in full of her bill for tea, Mrs. Charles Herveys China gown, etc., £13..17..0.

X.—MUSIC & PLAYS.

[John Hervey added music to his other accomplishments. In a letter to his wife written from Ickworth in July, 1719, he says he has just come back from Hawstead, " where I carried my flute and fiddle to compare notes with honest innocent Sir Dudley Cullum." And in a letter from his wife written from Richmond in July, 1719 she says that they had had some fine music on the terrace; " but I would willingly have exchanged it all to have heard you pipeing in the Summer-house." One of the following extracts shows him still keeping his violin in order when close upon three score years and ten. S.H.A.H.]

1689.—Aprill 18. Gave Mr. Finger for his sonnatas, £1..1..6.

Sept. 9. To ye Basson Hautboy for a sett of tunes, £0..10..0.

1699.—Nov. 25. Paid Mr. John Player for my dear wife her Harpscord, £40..10..9.

1700.—March 1. Paid Vaillant ye Bookseller for French & musick books, £10..5..6.

1704.—May 30. Paid Mr. Vanbrooke ye first payment of my subscription mony for building ye new Theatre in ye Hey-market (ye whole being one hundred guineys) for which I am to have ye priviledg of ye House gratis dureing my life, £26..17..6.

1705.—Jan. 15. Paid Mr. Vanbrooke my 3d payment, which with ye 2d paid Mr. Vice-Chamberlain Bertie 25 Aug., 1704 by Chambers is £53..15..0.

1712.—Nov. 29. Paid Mr. Battely Mr. Westhrops bill which he paid him for me June 11, 1708, for 5 blue cloaks, which I gave to Bury-musick, £15..7..8.

1715.—June 28. Paid Mr. James Eastland my subscription to his danceing room, £2..3..0.

1717.—Sept, 24. Paid Mr. James Eastland four guineas more, in all six guineas, in full of my subscription to his danceing-room building, £4..6..0.

1721.—June 5. Gave ye two Castruchis & Weiber ye lutenist, to each 2 guineas, for playing to Bononcini & Senezini & Mrs. Robinson, when Crispo was performd at my house, £6..6..0.

1731.—March 31. Gave Mr. Smith for his concert-ticketts, 2 guineas.

Sept, 26. Paid Colonel West for 6 tickets on the musick-subscription, £3..3..0.

1732.—Jan. 30. Gave Mr. William Bond towards his play without taking any tickets, £2..2..0.

March 19. Gave Mr. Smith for tickets to go into his Concert on Wednesday next, £5..5..0.

Nov. 12. Paid Mr. Eastland my subscription for 5 tickets to his Assemblies, £2..12..6.

1733.—March 31. Paid John Barret in full for mending & stringing my Cremona violin, £0..12..0.

1734.—April 11. Paid B. Schudi for tuneing the harpsichord, £0..17..6.

1735.—March 29. Gave Mr. Lyell for the tickets I took of him for his benefit-play, 7 guineas.

May 10. Repaid Lady Ann which she paid B. Schudi for tuneing her harpsicord, £1..4..6.

Nov. 18. Paid Mr. Eastland for 6 tickets to his new subscription for 8 Assembleys, £3..3..0.

1736.—Nov. 13. Paid Mr. Eastland my subscription for 4 tickets to 8 Assembleys for next year, £2..2..0.

XI.—PICTURES & TAPESTRY.

[For a list of family portraits see the Appendix. S.H.A.II.]

1689.—Feb. 14. Paid Mr. Dixon ye painter for my picture which dear wife desird of me, £17..7..0.

June 6. For a Picture of Madames with gilt frame, £3..10..0.

July 5. Paid to Mr. Van Heythuysens nephew & agent, Gerard Van Heythuysen, for his uncles use in full payment for four pieces of Tapestry hangings, & all other accounts, £200.

1690.—Feb. 27. Paid then to John Le Sage carver for two gilt picture frames, half lengths, £8..15..0.

Feb. 27. Paid him for four little pictures with carved work gilt in oyl gold frames, pictures & all £11..5..0.

March 6. Paid then to Mr. Henry Pert for copying my Fathers picture drawn by Brook, £10.

Aug. 1. Paid for ye carriage of my wife her picture from Bury 5s., and for bringing of it from Bishopsgate street 1s. 6d.

Sept. 27. Paid Mrs. Elwes att Bury which she paid Brook ye painter for drawing dear wives picture for me, £10.

1692.—Nov. 1. To Mr. Gerard Van Heythuysen for two pieces of tapistry-hanging for dear wives drawing-room, £52.

Nov. 11. Paid to John Bullard for pictures, £5..18..0.

Nov. 26. Paid for 2 fruit pieces & a fframe, £5..5..0.

Dec. 10. Paid for ye Prospect picture of St. Andrews Chappel, £7..10..0.

Dec. 3. Paid Bullord for an other parcell of pictures, £16..3..6.

1693.—May 11. Paid Mr. Henry Peart for copying Mrs. ffox her picture of dear wife, £10.

June 27. Paid Mr. Cross ye limner for dear wife her picture, £16..5..0.

1697.—June 21. Paid Mr. Richard Soames for a parcell of pictures (No. 74) & for a hogshead of old Canary, £80.

1699.—Jan. 2. Paid Mr. Gerard Van Heythuysen for 4 pieces of tapistry, £110.

Jan. 5. Paid Mrs. Elizabeth Davis for ye 4 great pictures of Beasts etc., £80.

Jan. 5. Paid ditto for a small Madona, £5..11..0.

June 10. Paid Sir Godfrey Kneller for Sir T. ffeltons picture & frame, £35.

1700.—Nov. 5. Paid Spanger ye Dutch carver in full for picture frames, £37.

Dec. 6. Paid Cotton for his Mr. Daula for my wife her ¾ picture, £10..15.

1701.—Oct. 4. Paid Brook ye Bury painter for ye 7 children's pictures, £5..7..6.

1702.—April 30. Paid Francis Barlow ye painter for St. Lawrence (by Carlotto Titians disciple) and St. Michael (by Guido), £35.

1702.—Nov. 9. Paid Mr. Joseph Brooke ye painter in full to this day, £17..17..0.

1703.—Jan. 7. Paid Peter Verelst for pictures I bought at that auction, £27..18..0.

Jan. 25. Paid Thomas Robinson for ye Banquet of ye Gods, a picture, £13..10..0.

1709.—Sept. 19. Paid Brook ye painter for dear Nan her picture, £2..10..0.

Nov. 21. Paid Edward Cooper for 50 of my dear wife's prints & my uncle Mr. John Herveys picture, £5..2..0.

Nov. 25. Paid Mr. Charles D' Agar for my dear wife her picture with ye twins, twenty two guineys.

1710.—Dec. 23. Paid Mrs. Ann Brown in full for copying of pictures etc., £13.

1711.—Feb. 17. Paid Mr. Lens for ye copy of Raphael's Madona at Kensington, £7..10..6.

March 24. Paid Bernard Lens for ye copy of dear wife her picture, £5..7..6.

May 17. Paid Michael Dahl ye Swedish painter for dear wifes picture, £21..10.

1712.—Jan. 25. Paid Lens ye limner in full for my wifes & my ring-pictures, £5..7..6.

1714.—April 15. Paid Hans Hyssen ye painter for several copies of pictures, & altering others, & an original portrait of Babel ye musician, £16..2..6.

May 12. Paid Lentz ye limner for dear wife & Feltons picture, £8..12..0.

1715.—April 16. Paid Mr. Peter Lentz ye limner for Raphaels & Rubens pictures (when he made me a present of his own), £6..9..0.

Aug. 27. Paid Hyssing in full for my dear wifes picture which I gave ye Countess of Pickbourg, & all cther demands, £6..9..0.

X

1716.—June 29. Paid Michael Hue for ye frame of my wifes picture which I gave ye Countess of Bucenburgh, £2..10..0.

Dec. 8. Paid Mr. Brook for Louisas, Felles & Wenns pictures, in full, £8..12..0.

1717.—Dec. 20. Paid Mrs. Brown in full for copying ye 2 half lengths of dear wifes & my pictures, for my son to send to Aswarby, & for a 3 quarters copy of mine for Ickworth, in all £12..10..0.

1719.—Feb. 21. Paid Christopher Cock ye painter in part of his bill of £25, which by agreement he was to receive for cleaning & mending my whole collection of pictures, 10 guineas.

May 2. Paid Thomas Tenant for lineing Carlotto's picture of St. Lawrence with canvass, & of all demands, £2..10..0.

1720.—April 6. Paid Mr. Richardson ye painter in part for my son Toms picture, which I am to make a present of to Mr. Harcourt, £12..12..0.

June 22. Paid Richardson ye painter ye remaining twelve guineas (by my son Tom) for his picture which I gave Mr. Harcourt, & three pounds more for ye frame, so more £15..12..0.

Oct. 22. Paid Mrs. Ann Howard for copying my picture for Jack, £5.

1721.—July 26. Paid Mr. Bernard Lens ye limner in full for six pictures of Vandyke, Sam Cooper, Sir Peter Lely, Greenhill, Dobson, & Sir Isaac Newton, 18 guineas.

1725.—Sept. 26. Paid Mr. Joseph Brook ye Bury-painter for copying my wife her picture at half-length drawn by Daule, £5..5..0.

1726.—July 29. Gave Lord Hervey what he paid Mr. Harman for his subscription for 12 cutts of ye survey of Bury, £3..12..0.

1727.—March 6. Paid Arthur Calcott for two pictures of Churches, which were part of ye goods he bought of Lady Effinghams executors, £6..10. 0.

April 28. Paid William King frame-maker for that of my wife her half-length picture at Bury, & for ye case 7s., in all £2..9..0.

May 19. Paid Count Viane my subscription to his fine picture, £10..10..0.

Dec. 8. I took in & discharged ye note my son Tom gave his mother for ten guineas dated Sept. 2 last in lieu of paying Faram ye painter for his picture and frame which he gave his Oxford Tutor Mr. Folkes, £10..10..0.

1728.—June 3. Paid Mr. John Fayram ye painter in full for three half length pictures, of Lord Hervey, Tom, & Nann, & all demands, £21.

July 13. Paid John Fayram for ye copy of Lord Herveys picture which he promised to Mr. Winnington, £4..4..0.

1729.—Feb. 22. Paid Fayrum ye painter in full for ye copies of dear Bettys & Lady Herveys their pictures from Richardsons & Knellers, £7..7..0.

1731.—Feb. 5. Paid Mr. Henry Peart for a picture of my most excellent first wife drawn soon after our marriage by his father 3 guineas.

1733.—April 10. Paid Fayram ye painter for ye copy of my picture for Saint Squire, £2..10..0,

1734.—April 10. Paid John Fayram the painter seven pounds for my son Felton's picture; & 20 shillings more for altering mine at ye Guild-hall in Bury, in all £8.

1735.—April 7. Paid John Fayram ye painter for my dear mothers & son Wills pictures, £10..10..0.

1736.—March 25. Paid Fayram for ye 3 quarter length copy of Lord Herveys picture, 2 guineas.

1737.—Jan. 8. Paid Knapton for the copy which he drew in crayon of Lord Herveys picture by Fayram, which I made a present of to Lady Hervey, 8 guineas.

Jan. 19. Paid J. Fayrum ye painter in full for a half length copy of Lord Herveys picture, £3..10..0.

April 2. Paid Fayram for ye 2 copys I gave my wife of her father & mothers pictures, £7.

1738.—March 1. Paid Mr. J. Fayram for copies of mine, my fathers & mothers pictures for my wife, £7..17..6.

April 1. Paid Mr. Fayram for 3 copies of my picture, 1 a half length, ye other two 3 quarters, £7..17..6.

April 8. Paid Mr. Enoch Seemans in full for copies of mine & my wife her pictures, being both whole lengths, (at 10 guineas each), £21.

1740.—Jan. 25. Paid William Waters by the order & for the use of Mrs. Penelope Jarvis, executrix to her husband Charles Jarvis, in full for my daughter Louisas picture, £13..13..0.

1741.—April 11. Paid J. Fayrum for the copy of my picture which I gave my son Felton, £3..13..6.

1742.—Jan. 20. Paid J. Fayram for the copy of my most dear 1st wife her picture, £3..13..6.

XII.—RENTS & LEGAL EXPENSES.

[John Hervey was frequently at law. He was at law with "Aunt Hervey." The Lincolnshire property was a fruitful source of legal disputes ; so was the Felton property in Suffolk ; so was an estate in Staffordshire which came to his second wife. In addition to which there were frequent disputes about annuities, wagers, etc. which had to be decided in the courts of justice. The very first page of this volume contains a list of " Fees given by me in Lord Holles's suit commenced by "me John Hervey (for the benefitt of my wife her estate) on ye 16th February, "A.D. 1688'9." Sergeant Rawlinson, Sergeant Hutchins, Sir Charles Porter, Mr. Hennedg Finch, Sir William Whitlock, Mr. Paul Jodrell, Mr. John Gardiner our sollicitor, are the recipients. Then follow half a page more of fees

paid in the Hetley case. Both the Holles and the Hetley cases were connected with the Carr property in Lincolnshire. S.H.A.H.]

1695.—May 4. To Mr. Poley for drawing a bond etc. between me and Ralph Blackall concering a discovery one Nicholas Roe should have made as to Aunt Herveys death and disposition of her estate, whereby if £10,000 or upwards was recovered I obliged my self to pay him £1000, £2..10..0.

1699.—June 10. Paid Mr. Andrew Card in full for ye writings of Chedburgh & Griffins house, £11..19..6.

1707.—June 28. Paid for ye renewal fine of my Rochester Church Lease from Midsummer 1706 for 21 years £159..12..0, which with ye ffees came £163..10..10. [*This estate is described as the Farm and Manor of Darenth in Kent, and was leased of the Dean and Chapter of Rochester. The 21 years lease was renewed every 7 years, viz. in* 1714, 1722, 1728, 1734, 1741, *on payment of a fine of about* £160. *S.H.A.H.*]

July 17. Paid ye Bishop of Norwich for ye renewal of Norfolke & Suffolke leases for 21 years from July 10, 1707, £190, & £21 for ffees, £211.

Expences in law from ye 14th of July, 1696 to ye 14th August, 1709, amount to £603..8..10, as by ye particulars following, as they were entered in my long narrow booke. *Amongst the particulars are these :—*

1696.—Dec. 4. Gave Mr. Poley upon Aunts lease to E. Montague, £2..4.0.

1697.—Feb. 17. Paid a bill to Henry Lord ye Attorney for ye ejectment from ye Copyhold land in Ickworth, & for sueing Stutville & Suttertons bond, £7..5..0.

1698.—March 14. To Mr. Poley when he settled my case to be printed on Mrs. Herveys petition to ye House of Commons, £3..6..0.

1700.—Feb. 28. To Sir B. Shower when he made his award between Lord Mountague, Aunt Hervey & me, £26..17..6.

March 1.   To Mr. Poley in ye release I was to sign to Aunt Hervey, £1..1..6.

April 27.   To Mr. Poley for advise on Aunt Herveys death, £2..3..0.

April 29.   To Mr. ffolkes on ye same & other matters, £3..4..6.

May 17.   To Mr. Poley about her estate, £2..3..0.

1722.—Nov. 26.   Paid Mr. Richard Minshul £250, (pursuant to ye agreement between us dated ye 15th instant) in part of ye £500 he recovered upon ye wager relating to ye King of Spains successes etc., ye other £250 being to be paid him on ye last day of this session of Parliament, he remitting to me all costs in ye suite beween us thereupon.

1723.—May 30.   Paid Mr. Richard Minshul £250 more, which together with ye £250 paid him in Nov. last is in full payment & satisfaction of ye judgment he recoverd against me in ye Court of Common Pleas upon ye wager of £500 to £400 I laid him on ye present Emperours succeeding in his expedition to Spain, ye costs of suite being remitted by agreement, & he this day executed a warrant of Attorney to acknowledg satisfaction on ye said judgment upon record.

1722.—Dec. 12.   Paid Mr. Hugh Mills (as one of ye executors to ye late Earl of Tankerville) in full for ye years ffee-ffarm rent due out of ye Castle of Sleaford at Lady day last, (taxes deducted), £51.

1723.—Sept. 25.   Paid ye Reverend Mr. Thomas Sellar for ye adding of one life & exchanging an other, in ye lease which I hold of him of Sleaford tythes, as he is Prebend thereof, £70.

Dec. 20.   Paid Mrs. Sarah Hetley as executrix of her husband Major John Hetley, who was executor of Elizabeth English, ye last surviving annuitant of ye five lives to whom Sir Robert Carr granted an annuity of £100 per annum dated in 1638, pursuant to an order of Chancery of ye 19th instant, as in part of my proportion of ye arrears chargeable on my lands, £560.

Dec. 20. Paid Mr. F. Pemberton by ye said order of Court in part of what is due to him for what he has overpaid of his own proportion due from his lands on account of ye said annuity in arrear, £440.

1724.—July 31. Gave Mr. Jacob for 2 attendances at Mr. Lamb's Chambers when Sir Francis Whichcote & Mr. Martin paid ye mony, £2..2..0.

Aug. 1. Paid Mrs. Sarah Hetley ye farther sum of £1436..9..5½, which with ye £560 paid her 20 Dec. last make together £1996..9..5½, ye same being in full of her share decreed to be due to her by virtue of an order of Chancery of 12 March last, out of ye arrear of ye rent-charge of £100 per annum granted by old Sir Robert Carr in 1638 to his half brothers & sister & chargeable on his whole estate.

Aug. 11. Paid Mr. Francis Pemberton pursuant to a decree in ye Court of Chancery what remained due to him of my average towards making good what he paid on accompt of ye arrear of Hetley's annuity of £100 per annum granted by old Sir Robert Carr anno 1638, & charged upon ye lands purchased by my self, ye late Lord Holles, and Sir Francis Pemberton, £1203..6..10½, which with ye £440 paid him 20 Dec. last is in full of all ye principal and interest mony due to him by virtue of ye said decree.

1725.—Oct. 11. Paid Mr. Samuel Burroughs ye attorney at Newmarket 3 guineas for ingrossing counterparts of ye conveyance I made of my house there to Captain Hawkins.

Nov. 26. Gave my cousin Reynolds for his opinion on Shotley advowson, £2..2..0.

Dec. 9. Gave my said cousin Reynolds more in ye same affair, £2..2..0.

1728.—Aug. 21. Paid Mr. James Goodalle for ye use of Mrs. Ann Stuteville, executrix of her husband Thomas Stuteville, 10 guineas for ye hire of his house at Newmarket.

1729.—March 20. Repaid Lord Griffin my moytie of ye bill which he paid to Thomas Peach ye attorney of £185..19..6, for getting possession for us of ye Staffordshire estate (late Mrs. Giffards) & making ye tenants to attorn to us as heirs at law to Mr. Robert Howard, £92..19..9.

1731.—March 24. Paid the Bishop of Norwich, Dr. William Baker, £170, being ye fine agreed on for renewing 7 years in my leases ending 11 July 1728, £170 being one full years value of my estates; but some disputes & difficulties arising between us till this day, he had the true episcopal conscience to ask & insist on (without which he would not seal a new lease) £155 more as interest for ye said £170 fine from 11 July, 1728 to this time; so in all I was forced to pay him £325. Besides his Secretary's fees which amounted to £10..9..0 more.

1733.—May 30. I then repaid William Clarke £60 which he paid to ye Reverend Mr. Seller as a fine upon his adding my grandson George's life to his fathers & my own in a new lease dated April 2, 1733.

XIII.—WINES.

1689.—May 23. Paid three fifths of ye Hogshead of Clarrett which I bought at Locketts, £9..12..0.

Oct. Due to Mr. Potts for my share in two Hogsheads of Duncomb wine, £12.

1690.—March 8,—Paid then for a pinte of spiritt of black cherries etc. for dear wife, £0..10..6.

Aprill 28. Paid then to Mr. Potts for Duncomb wine in all seventy four pounds, fourteen shillings; £31..2..6 was ye Duke of Graftons share, which I paid for him, for 5 half hogsheads, my lady her share being two fifths in 6 half hogsheads came to £14..8..9; my father for one half £6..4..6, and my share being 3 fifths in ye 6½ hogsheads my Lady Carr is to pay the other two fifths of comes to at £12. 9..0 per hogshead, £22. 8..3.

Dec. 27. Paid Sir John Shardin (by Walsh) my 3 fifths for a hogshead of Hermitage wine bought of Longueville, £10..16..0.

1691.—March 4. Paid Mr. Longueville for my share in half a hogshead of Hermitage Clarett, £5..8..0.

1692.—May 10. Paid for ye Lucina wine I sent my father to Bury in March, £7..4..0.

May 23. Paid Goudette ye wine merchant in full of my share for a hogshead of Hermitage wine, £10..5..2½.

July 9. Paid Jacob ffranklin for 6 gallons of sack, 3 of Rhenish and for 5 dozen and four bottles, £4..1..6.

Oct. 26. Paid Rycroft of Ipswich for wine I gave my ffather, £2..2..10.

Dec. 16. Paid my share to Mr. Long for ye hogshead of Gallicia wine at £17..10. & ye charges of corking, bottelling etc., £11..1..10.

1696.—Feb. 8. Paid Rowd Harris ye vintner att ye Queens Head in Bishop-Gate-street for a parcell of sack, £8..15..0.

Feb. 17. Paid Mr. Abraham Beake, by a bill on Mr. Thomas Gibson, for a hogshead of red french wine, £17.

April 22. Paid Mr. Peter Reneu for 3 pipes of Navarre wine, £96.

Oct. 24. Paid Mr. Robert Rowse of ye Rose Tavern for 6 dozen pints of sack, £3..12..0.

Dec. 22. Paid Mr. Renew ye wine merchant, in full of his bills for 3 pipes of Navarre at £32 per piece; bottles, cooperidge etc. to this day, £106..19..0.

1697.—Feb. 16. Paid Jacob ffranklin ye Quaker for 2 dozen pints of Palme, £1..17..0.

June 18. Paid Mr. Richard Soames ye merchant in part of £80 agreed for 2 pipes of Fayall & 1 pipe of Canary, ye sum of £40.

June 21. Paid Mr. Richard Soames for a parcell of pictures (No. 74) & for a hogshead of Canary, £80.

Y

July 1.   Paid John Astell in full for Syder, bottles etc., £13..10..0.

1698.—March 28.—Paid Richard Lissiman in full for 10 dozen of Syder, £11.

Nov. 17.   Paid Richard Wilcox, Mr. Dades Book-keeper, for ye tierce of Burgundy wine by bill on Chambers, £35.

1699.—May 4.   Paid Mr. de Sartre for a pipe of wine, £50.

July 10.   Paid Mr. Peter Reneu ye merchant in full for 3 pipes of Navarre wine, bottles, corks etc., £105.

July 22.   Paid Mr. Sabatier for ye pipe of Languedoc wine (for which Sir Thomas ffelton paid me his half) £50, for 30 bottles of St. Laurent at 10 shillings per bottle £15, & for 3 dozen of Languedoc £3..12..0, in all £68..12..0.

1700.—June 24.   Paid La Roche in full of his bill for Champaigne & Burgundy, £12..9..0.

Sept. 26.   Paid Judith Millegan (by Sir R. Davers order & for his use) £32 for ye 2 hogsheads of wine Glover sent from Ipswich to Bury.

Nov. 13.   Paid Michael La-Roche in full for Champaigne & Burgundy, £16.

1701.—Feb. 5.   Paid Mr. Laroche for Champaigne & Burgundy, £48.

1702.—March 26.   Paid Mr. Robert Harrison for 4 hogsheads of obrian wine, £101..10..0.

April 24.   Paid Mr. Hatley for Mrs Auchmoutys tierce of Burgundy, & bottles, £22..2..0.

1703.—Dec. 13.   Paid Mr. Keene merchant for a hogshead of Margoose Clarett, £27..10..0.

1704.—June 9.   Paid Bourguet for 3 chests of wine fromAvignon, £16..10..0.

Nov. 7.   Paid Mr. Hatley (by Mr. Chambers) for ye sack he sent to Ickworth, £11..15..7½.

Dec. 14.   Paid Thomas Thatcher for Mr. Manwayrings hogshead of wine, £28..10..0.

1705.—Jan. 15.   Paid Hen: Johnsons servant Bicknel for a hogshead of wine, £27..10..0.

Jan. 22.   Paid Osenda for 6 doz. pint bottles of non-pareil wine, £6.

July 9.   Paid Mr. John Hatley for ye ½ hogshead of claret his brother George divided with me, £16..18..9.

July 9.   Paid ditto for 9 gallons 1 quart Canary he bought for me, £4..15..0.

July 10.   Paid Nath: Torriano for 3 hogsheads of wine, 2 of Obrian & 1 of white Langoon, bought of Mr. Dutry, Peter Reneu & himself at £80.

Aug. 18.   Paid Mr. Gabriel Smith for ye 2 chests of Florence wine, £11..2..0.

1706.—April 23.   Paid Mr. Gabriel Smyth (by Chambers) for 2 chests more of Florence wine, £11..2..0.

July 12.   Paid Mr. Gabriel Smith for ye chest of Florence I sent Captain Felton, £5..6..0.

Dec. 9.   Paid Bonnet & Binet for one hogshead of Margous claret-wine, £43.

1707.—May 24.   Paid Mr. Gabriel Smyth in full for 3 chests of Florence wine, one sent to Mr. Macro 27 ffeb ; & 2 to Ickworth 26 Mar. 1707, £15..18..0.

May 31.   Paid Sir Henry Furnese, by a note on Chambers, payable to his servant Beranger, in full for 2 hogsheads of Obrian wine, £56.

1709.—June 9.   Paid Mr. Gabriel Cheney in full of his bill for Houbrion French wine, after ye rate of £48 per hogshead, £27..8..6.

Dec. 16.   Paid Lord Orkney for a hogshead of Clarett he bought for me in Holland £22..0..6, which with £17..2..2 paid Mr. Walker for ye Customs & other charges cost me in all £39..2..8.

1710.—Jan. 12.   Paid John ffell in full of his bill for Portugal wine etc., £19..10..0.

Feb. 2.   Paid Frederick Standert for an ame of Moselle wine, £17..2..3.

Feb. 17.   Paid Robert Jeffe merchant for a 4th part of a pipe of Canary, £15.

Aug. 9.   Paid Mr. Francis Chay in full for 2 chests of Florence wine, £11..13..0.

Dec. 7.   Paid Mr. Robert Jeffes in full for a hogshead of red moncon wine, & a hogshead of French white-wine, £40.

Dec. 29.   Paid John Andrews in full for 15 dozen of ffrench clarett, £24..5..0.

1711.—Feb. 7.   Paid Mr. Robert Jeffes for 60 gallons of Palme & Canary wine etc. £33..10..0.

May 3.   Paid Mr. Robert Brookes for 5 doz. & 6 quartes of ffrench Clarett, £14..17..0.

Sept. 29.   Paid Bonet & Bennet in full for 100 Flasks of french Clarett, £25.

Dec. 14.   Paid Robert Witham for a hogshead of Red-Port wine, £16.

1712.—Jan. 24.   Paid Matt: Chavin for 3 dozen flasks of French Clarett, £9.

Feb. 2.   Paid Matt: Chauvin for 34 flasks more of ye said wine, £8..10..0.

April 19.   Paid Edward Fargée for 7 half chests of Florence, £17..10..0.

1713.—Jan. 12.   Paid Robinson in full of his bill for 3 dozen of Champaign wine etc., £12..4..2.

May 28. Paid Sir Thomas Hanmer for half a hogshead of Chaos wine, £12..2..6.

Sept. 23. Paid James Razer in full of his bills for French Clarett, £16..7..6.

1714.—Jan. 2. Paid Simon Webster of Bury in full for 6 gallons 1 quart of Red-Port wine, £1..11..0.

Feb. 6. Paid Messrs. Bonet & Benet in full of thier bill for French red & white wines to this day, £46.

April 23. Paid La Roche for 18 bottles of Hermitage - wine, £5..8..0.

July 17. Paid Mackenzie (Brokes servant) for 4 dozen Flaskes of wine, £10..15..0.

July 23. Paid Mr. Robert Jeffes in full for a hogshead of Red-Port, etc., £16..5..0.

July 23. Paid Mrs. Mary Taylor in full for 3 dozen of white Lisbon wine, £2..14..6.

July 30. Paid A. Amiand, Michael La Roche's servant, in full for 12 Flaskes of Burgundy wine for dear wife at 6 shillings, £3..12..0.

July 30. Paid Manaux at ye Queens Arms in Pell Mell for 2 Flaskes, £0..13..0.

Aug. 9. Paid Mr. William Beger in full for 6 dozen of French wine, 3 of Hermitage, & 3 dozen of Pontac, & 2 flasks of Burgundy, £18..13..0.

Aug. 11. Paid Gabriel La Cheney & Partner in full for a hogshead of new French Clarett £30, & Tastes of other sorts, in all £34..8..0.

Nov. 6. Paid Mr. Henry Milles for 6 dozen of Obrian wine, £12..12..0.

Nov. 23. Paid Baltazar Reclan for 18 gallons of white Coindrieux wine, £14..6..6.

1715.—Jan. 18.   Paid Mrs. E. Beger for 25 Flasks of St. George-wine, £6..5..6.

June 25.   Paid Thomas Chesson of Bury for 12 gallons of Port-wine, £3..13..6.

Aug. 20.   Paid Sam Hatton in full of his bill for cyder, £6..10..0.

Sept. 3.   Paid Mr. J. Fauvell in full for 10 dozen of Clarett, £21..10..0.

1716.—March 23.   Paid Nicholas Bernaudeau (by Thomas Mason) in full for white Lisbon, £9..13..6.

March 24.   Paid Alex: Delmay in full for Rhinish wine (10 gallons) bottles etc., £5..10..0.

May 2.   Paid Mrs. Ellenor Beger in full for 6 dozen of Hermitage wine at 4s. 6d., & some other tastes, £16..18..0.

May 19.   Paid Peter Hattanville for a hogshead of Margoo Clarett £34, & for tastes of other wine, in all £37..10..0.

June 5.   Paid William Leech (Mr. Sheppards Cellar-keeper) in full for a hogshead of Port-wine, £14.

June 17.   Paid Mrs. Renault for 3 dozen of Burgundy at 5s. 9d., £10..7..0.

July 6.   Paid John Stone in full for 4 Kilderkins of strong ale, £4.

Sept. 29.   Paid James Bennet in full for 10 dozen Flasks of Chateau Margou wine at 4s. per flask, £24.

Oct. 9.   Paid Mr. Thomas Parry for a hogshead of Port wine £14, & for bottles, corks etc., so in all £17..10..6.

1717.—March 23.   Paid Mr. William Parry in full for a hogshead of Port wine, £14, & for 2 gross of bottles etc., in all £17..6..0.

March 30.   Paid William Beger for 10 dozen of French Clarett, £21.

April 19.   Paid Mr. Alexander Dilman in full for Rhenish wine, £8..4..0.

May 23. Paid James Soleirol in full for 6 dozen fflasks of Pontack Clarett at 3s. 6d., £12..15..0.

June 15. Paid James Razer for 4 dozen of Champaigne wine etc., £13.

June 29. Paid Messrs. Chaplyn & Batson in full for 9 gallons of sack etc., £4..4..0.

July 25. Paid James Soleirol for 6 dozen flasks of Pontack Clarett, £13..2..0.

Dec. 12. Paid James Perrott in full for six dozen bottles of Champaigne wine at 5s. 3d., & for one of Burgundy at 5s., £19..3..0.

Dec. 14. Paid Mr. Soleirol in full for 6 dozen flasks of Chateau Margou wine at 3s. 3d., & for tastes to this day, £12..3..9.

Dec. 14. Paid Sam Hatton in full of his bill for Cyder, £5..16..8.

1718.—Feb. 1. Paid Will: Leech for a pipe of Red-Port, & 4 gross of Corkes, £28..8..0.

Feb. 1. Paid Adam Maes for 18 dozen of French Clarett, £35..2..0.

March 8. Paid Mrs. Alice Minshul in full for 30 gallons of Canary, £12..1..6.

March 21. Paid Robert Jeffes wine-cooper in full of his bill for Port-wines, Canary, & all other demands to this day, £114..17..6.

April 26. Paid Mrs. Honor Renault for 18 dozen of Margou-Clarett-wine at 3s. 10d. per flask, £41.8..0.

Dec. 6. Paid Joseph Renshaw, by ye order & for ye use of Mr. Henry Gardie, for half a hogshead of French white wine, £15.

1719.—Jan. 17. Paid James Rasier in full for 5 dozen 7 bottles of white Muljo Burgundy at 3s. 6d., & of all other tastes of wine, £14..18..6.

April 11. Paid David Chovet for 10 dozen of Claret & all demands, £18..8..0.

May 5.   Paid Mr. Powel (by dear wife) ye Prince's Clerk of his kitchin in full for an aume of Rhinish wine, £16..10..0.

1720.—Jan. 23.   Paid Peter Hattanville for 6 dozen Flasks of La Tour Claret, £14..8..0.

Dec. 23.   Paid James Soleirol in full for Palm-wine, £7..7..0.

1721.—April 22.   Paid Peter Hattanville for 3 dozen & a half of La ffitte Clarett at 50s. per dozen, & for 2 tastes, in all £9..1..0.

July 26.   Paid John Sharvey by ye order & for ye use of his master Mr. John Fell jun. in full for 60 gallons of Mountain wine at 5s. 6d., & for bottles etc., in full of all demands to this day, £19..9..0.

1722.—Jan. 3.   Paid Robert Sharpe in full for 30 gallons of Palm-sack at 7s. per gallon, & for 22 dozen of pinte-bottles, £12..12..0.

June 9.   Paid James Soleirol in full for 4 dozen & ten Flasks of ffrench clarett at 3s. 3d. per flask (he at ye same time taking back & allowing for 26 flasks of bad wine he sent me in to ye Country), so there remain (which I paid him) £6.

Nov. 28.   Paid John Fell jun. in full for 20 gallons of mountain wine at 5s. 6d., bottles etc., £6..13..0.

1723.—April 1.   Paid Gedion L'Eglize for 16 dozen flasks of Chatteau Margou Claret at 4s., & bringing in 5s., £38..13..0.

Aug 9.   Paid William Lissiman in full of his bill for 13 dozen of Cyder at 12 pence per bottle, £7..18..0.

Aug. 10.   Paid Alexander Dylmane for 10 gallons of Rhinish wine at 10s. per gallon with bottles etc., £11..3..0.

Aug. 26.   Paid Cowper my butler in full of his bill for Bristol waters for dear wife, tasts of wine, corks etc., £3..8..0.

1724.—Jan. 10.   Paid Mr. Thomas Parry ye wine-merchant in full of his bill for 3 parcells of Canary, a pipe of Porte at £28, bottles, corks etc., £62.

March 14. Paid Mr. William Rollison for a hogshead of Chasteau-Margoux at £43, & for bottles, corks & carriage £4..7..0 more, so in all £47..7..0.

March 28. Paid Alderman Allen of Bury in full of his bill for wine, bottles etc., when I was at Bath, for Jack & his wife, £8..17..6.

July 15. Paid Mr. Peter Diharce ye French merchant in full of his bill for 2 dozen of Champaigne at 54s., & 1 dozent of Burgundy wine at 45s. per doz., in all £7..9..0.

1725.—Jan. 11. Paid Mr. Le Blanc for 14 dozen of French Clarett at 3s. per bottle in full to this day, £23..4..0.

Feb. 20. Paid John Harrington, by ye order & for ye use of John Fell, in full for 20 gallons of mountain wine, £5..10..0.

March 8. Paid Charles Le Blanc for a pipe of Port-wine at £29, & for ye charges of bottling £1..9..0.

May 29. Paid Mrs. Jane Whalley in full for half a hogshead of Lucina white-wine at £8..10 & bottles, corks, etc., in all £10..3..6.

Nov. 24. Paid Elias Perricaud for 37 Flasks of La Fitte Clarett at 4s. per flask, £7..8..0.

Dec. 25. Paid Elias Perricaud for 37 Flasks of Pontac Clarett at 50s. per dozen, £7..14..0.

1726.—March 12. Paid Mrs. Jane Whalley in full for Lucina-wine, bottles etc., £5..12..6.

Oct. 4. Paid Daniel Vigneau for 6 dozen of Burgundy wine, £12..12..0.

Nov. 29. Paid Mr. William Beger for 10 dozen Pint-bottles of old Palm sack at 10s. per gallon, & for other tastes of wine, in full £8.

1728.—June 8. Paid to John Fell jun. for ten gallons of sweet Mountain wine at 5s. 6d. per gallon, £2..15..0.

1729.—Dec. 25. Paid Alderman William Allen of Bury in full of his

z

bill for wine, strong beer, bottles etc. delivered at Ickworth & to ye Guild Hall, & 3 dozen of Port for Tom, & 2 dozen & a half to Harry, from ye 6th of May last to this Christmas day 1729, in all £74..12..0.

1730.—May 22. Paid Antoine Solleirol in full for Methuen-wine, £4..2..0.

May 27. Paid Mrs. Ellinor Beger in full of her bill for Palm sack, Moselle wine for Nann, oyle etc., £8..15..0.

1731.—March 17. Paid Edmund Meyrick for 9 gallons of red Port at 5s. 6d., £2..9..6.

March 17. Paid John Turner for 2 dozen bottles of French Clarett, £3..12..0.

April 14. Paid Mr. Ed. Fontaine for 20 dozen of French Clarett at 42s. per dozen, £42.

1732.—Feb. 16. Paid my son Will for 3 dozen of red Madera wine for his mother, £3..12..0.

March 28. Paid Patrick Allan for 2 tastes of Clarett Sir Thomas Hanmer sent me, 7 shillings.

March 28. Paid Edward Fountaine for 2 tastes of French wine, 7s. 6d.

1733.—Jan. 4. Paid for 20 dozen of Bristol-water, freight & all other charges, to Richard Keinton & John Baylie, Daniel Morgue & Thomas Rice, in all £4..10..0.

1734.—March 29. Paid Mr. George Fitzgerald in full for a pipe of Canary, £30.

1735.—Jan. 25. Paid William Gibson for a hogshead of Madera at £15..15, corks and bottles, in all £19..14..6.

Feb. 14. Repaid Day my butler what he paid Soleirol for 12 gallons of Mountain wine, £3..4..0.

1736.—July 2. Paid Captain Davers for ye duty & charges of ye hogshead of White Lisbon Will sent us, £6..1..0.

1737.—Jan. 21. Paid Mr. John Turner, table-keeper at Court, in full for a dozen bottles of French wine at 3s., £1..16..0.

March 23. Paid William Gibson for sixty gallons of Madera wine at 7s., £21.

April 23. Paid Sir Robert Smyth for my share of the hogshead of Côte Rôty wine, £20..5..8.

1738.—Feb. 10. Paid John Page in full for a dozen of Hermitage & 1 dozen of Cotterottie, £4.

Feb. 10. Paid Mr. James Towers in full for 3 dozen bottles of Rhinish wine at 2s. 6d., £4..10..0.

April 7. Paid Roger Williams for a hogshead of French wine & a bottle of Port wine, £40..2..0.

1739.—Jan. 18. Paid John Butler in full for 5 dozen of Burgundy wine £10.

April 20. Paid James Soleirol for 60 gallons of Palm-sack 7s., £21..17..0.

1740.—Feb. 15. Paid Mr. John Towers, by the order & for the use of his father, in full for 10 dozen of Steiner wine at 42s. per dozen, & 1 of Rhinish at 30s., in all £22..10..0.

Dec. 12. Paid Mr. John Hastings in full for 60 gallons of Port-wine £21.

Dec. 25. Paid Mrs. Alice Judgson for 3 dozen bottles of Champaigne-wine, £7..10..0.

Dec. 25. Paid Mr. Dupont in full for a dozen bottles of Burgundy wine, £3.

1741.—March 26. Paid Mr. John Chalie for a hogshead of Canary at £31..10..0, bottles, corks & for tastes of several sorts of wine, in all £37..17..6.

Oct. 9. Repaid my son Felton what he had paid Mr. John Tomlinson by his agent William Richardson for a pipe of old Madeira wine, bottles, corks, etc., £40..18..6.

XIV.—WIGS.

1689.—Aprill 15. Paid ye Perriwig maker, £3.

May 22. For a Perriwig of Du Perré, £4..12..6.

1690.—Aprill 15. Paid then to G. Collier for a Perriwigg, £2..5..0.

1691.—March 2. Paid Du Perry in full for a Perriwigg & all accounts, £5..7..6.

1692.—June 10. Paid du Perry for a Perriwig, £5..7..6.

Oct. 3. To du Perry for a long Perriwigg, £5..7..6.

1697.—May 7. Paid Daniel Marigeot for a new perruque & mending an old one, £7..10..0.

1698.—Feb. 5. Paid Fouchers ye Perruque maker for a Perruque, £10.

1699.—Jan. 24. Paid Stephen Fouchers for a long Perriwigg, £12.

June 16. Paid Ralph Lagg for my son Carr's * Perriwig, £2..3..0.

1701.—July 4. Paid Stephen Fouchers for a long Perruque, box etc., £20..14..0.

1702.—Dec. 16. Paid Stephen Fouchers in full for my Campaigne Perruque, £12..18..0.

1704.—Jan. 24. Paid H. Foucher for a long Perruque, £20.

1707.—March 8. Paid Fouchers in full for my long Perruque, & all accounts, £23..1..6.

---

* Carr was then under 8 years old.—S.H.A.H.

1709.—Jan. 15. Paid Isaac Bucket for my new long Perruque, £19..7..0.

1712.—April 25. Paid Peter Saraillat for my new long Perruque, £8.

1714.—Jan. 11. Paid Stephen Foucher in full for a long Perruque, £10.

1716.—June 20. Paid John Allen & La Serre in full for a long Perruque, £16.

July 6. Paid Thomas Wildman in full for making a wig of Will's * hair, £0..15..0.

Sept. 29. Paid W. Vignon in full for a tying Perruque, £10.

1717.—Dec. 20. Paid Thomas Ward for a bob-Perruque for my son Henry, £1..1..6.

1718.—Nov. 15. Paid William Vignon in full for two Perruques, ye one for my self, ye other for my son Will, £10 & £4..10, in all £14..10..0.

1721.—April 29. Paid Stephen Mathew for a Perruque for my son Will, £3..3..0.

1722.—Feb. 7. Paid Monsieur Vignon for a new Perruque in full, £10.

1725.—May 6. Paid Robert Bowie in full for a Bob-wigg, £3..3..0.

Dec. 14. Paid Robert Bowie Perruque maker in full for a long tyed wigg, £9..10..0.

1727.—March 4. Paid Robert Bowie for a new Bob-Perruque, 3 guineas.

1728.—Feb. 12. Paid Robert Bowie for a new long Perruque in full, £10.

June 15. Paid Robert Bowie in full for a bob-Perruque, £3..3..0.

* His son Will had just left Westminster School and gone to sea. —S. H. A. H.

1729.—Jan. 23.   Paid James Whitfield ye Perruque-maker in full of his bill for Harry's Perruques to this day, £50.

Jan. 25.   Paid George Gordon Perruque-maker in full for Harry, £7..7..0.

Jan. 25.   Paid Stephen Mathew Perruque-maker in full for Harry, £25.

1735.—Jan. 31.   Paid Robert Bowie in full for a bob-wig, £3..3..0.

March 1.   Paid Robert Bowie Perruque-maker in full for a tye-wigg, £7..7..0.

1736.—June 7.   Paid Daniel Crosman of Bury for a bob-perruque, £3..3..0.

1738.—March 25.   Paid Noel Protin in full for a new Tye-wigg & a Bob-perruque, £10..10..0.

1740.—March 18.   Paid John Elliot for a Tye-wig at £7, & a bob-wig at £3, in all £10.

ADDENDA.

So much for the fourteen headings under which I have placed the extracts.   It repents me now that I did not print the expences bodily and just as they are in the original volume.   It would have taken much less time, and been much less troublesome, and much more satisfactory.   However, repentance has come too late to be of much use.   A few more facts may be gleaned from the volume as to John Hervey's domestic affairs; though, as it contains only the sums total of several other books of expences, and things are here often lumped together, not so much can be made out as might have been.

HIS DOMESTIC TUTORS AND CHAPLAINS.—In 1692 Mr. Rome or Roome was receiving a salary, though it does not appear what he did for it. In 1702 Mr. John Pujolas, "ye ffrench chaplain," had a salary for reading prayers. In 1702-3-4 Mr. Barricave was receiving £50 a year as tutor to Carr Hervey. In 1722 Mr. Garrigues had £40 a year as tutor to Felton Hervey, who I think at that time was a Royal page. In 1724-6 Mr. William Barricave was Felton's tutor with a salary of £50 a year.

HIS BANKERS.—Payments are made through " my goldsmith " till 1726, when I first notice "my banker," and " my goldsmith " is seen no more. Wanley and afterwards Fowler were " my goldsmith"; Fowler and afterwards Simpson were "my banker." Other goldsmiths mentioned as being employed as bankers are Sir Richard Hoare, Drummond and Chambers.

HIS STEWARDS.—In 1688 and the following years Mr. Thomas Burslem and his nephew John Burslem were associated in collecting the Lincolshire rents and dues. John Burslem continued to act as steward of the Lincolnshire property till his death in 1711. He was succeeded by one Chapman, who was gone by 1731, when William Clarke held the office. He was still holding it in 1742 when this volume closes. The Ickward steward in 1695 was William Covell who died in 1707. [A Thomas Covell had been steward many years before, in 1665. John Covell, 1638-1722 one of the same Horringer family, was chaplain to the Embassy at Constantinople, and published an account of the Greek Church.] It is not clear what happened immediately after William Covell's death ; but in December, 1712, William Oliver is mentioned as "going to take care of my affairs at Ickworth." He was still steward in 1742, with a salary of £40 a year. He had a son John who went up to Cambridge. [See page 156.]

HIS DOMESTIC SERVANTS.—Wages and other expences are so often lumped together, that it is not easy to make out what the household consisted of, nor what it cost.

The COOK, excepting during the last 10 years covered by this volume, was always a man, with wages of £30, sometimes £35, a year. Mary Burford had £18 a year. This is the succession of them, so far as they chance to be mentioned here, with the year in which they are mentioned. Stephen, 1692. Edward Varney, 1704. William Atkinson, 1705. Peter Mellot, 1711. Alexander Tullouch, 1712. Charles Byrne, 1718. Edmund Varney, 1720. Michael Morell, 1722. William Webb, 1723. John Walsh, 1724. Philip Macguire, 1729. Mary Burford, 1732-34. Ann Griffin, 1735-36. E. Llloyd "the woman cook," 1735.

The BUTLER had £10 a year. This is the succession of them so far as they chance to be mentioned. Richard Mathews, 1689. Robinson, 1712. Hugh Heny, 1719. Robert Cowper, 1722-3-4. Benjamin Cole, 1726. Edward Day. Edward Day came in 1727, and was still at his post in 1741. His tombstone is in Ickworth Churchyard, with those of several other old servants of the same master. (See Ickworth Registers, p. 65. No. 18.) The long inscription on his tomb which is given in the Cullum Notes in that volume, I do not recollect to have seen, and do not think it is there now.

The VALET DE CHAMBRE had £10 a year. This servant is certainly sometimes and probably always he who keeps an account of what he disburses for his master, which amounts to some hundreds of pounds in the year. This is the succession of the disbursers : Le Coque. Thomas Walsh, 1689. Charles Kirby, 1697 Grey, 1700. Aberlaine, 1701. Beaulieu, 1703. William Carus, 1705-1710. Tewer or Tuer, 1714. Webster, 1715. Cuthbert Cornforth, 1718-1724. William Jenkins, 1728. William Mathews, 1728. Jeremy Allen, 1729, 1732. William Jones, 1732-1734. Sam Brentnall 1735 to March 6, 1742, "when we parted."

The footmen had £6 and £5 a year, and the postilion had £5. The Diary, April 24, 1721, mentions the death of Robert Wildman, who had been his and his father's coachman for 42 years. He had £8 a year. After him came Tom Harvey, with £7 a year. In his early days, 1688, there was one calle Scotch Jacob or James the Scotch coachman, who had £6 a year.

Robert Price and afterwards Josiah Long were the London porters. Their wages are not stated clearly. Other servants are mentioned, but too confusedly to get much information from the mention of them. There was one called Welch Tom, who seems to have had some of the privileges of the mediæval fool or jester. (See Index to Letters.) He may be the Thomas Aubrey, whose long service of over 50 years is recorded on his tombstone in Ickworth Churchyard. (See Ickworth Registers, p. 65.) Nurse Fleming, "my little girl's nurse," in 1690, had £20 a year. Elizabeth Morris, whose long service of 50 years is recorded on her tombstone in Ickworth Church-yard, (see Ickworth Registers, p. 65) was having £6 a year in 1732 and thereabouts. Mrs. Mary Williams, the lady of a good family in Wales, whose coming into Lady Bristol's service is recorded in the Diary under Nov. 27, 1723, was receiving £10 a year in 1734. There was Bridgman the gardener in April, 1735, and earlier, and there was Thomas Ranny the gardener in November, 1735; and Firmin, the gamekeeper; what their wages were does not appear.

Other account books casually mentioned are " my great account book," May, 1696; " my long narrow book," July, 1696; " the Ickworth Bybook," constantly.

AA

APPENDIX No. 1.

I.

Here ev'ry line does sacred prove
To friendship, gratitude and mutual love;
They with such energy of thought are writ,
They show what love can do when joynd with wit.

—————

II. *Mrs. Ramsey on Mr. Hervey.*

(1.)

Why, Strephon, did you charm my heart
From soft repose and downy rest;
Free'd and secur'd from any art,
Had you kept stranger to my breast,
My thoughts no anxious cares had known,
Nor me love's victim had not made,
But pass'd those quiet hours alone,
Which Strephon's merit has betrayd.

(2.)

In vain we strive against our fate,
Tho reason is it self in view,
When mighty love turns advocate,
Reason becomes a party too;
Dissolves all force, with love contends,
Secures our doubts, still sooths us on
By flattering hopes, the cause defends;
Too late we find we are undone.

---

* The lines in this Appendix are all in the two quarto volumes containing Lord and Lady Bristol's correspondence. The first four lines refer to that correspondence, and rightly describe it. Mrs. Felton is of course the future Lady Bristol.—S.H.A.H.

III. *Mrs. Ramsey to Mrs. Felton upon Mr. Hervey's owning he was in love
with her.*

(1.)

Amintor ownd to me his flame
  For your too conquering charms,
Says all resistance was in vain
  Against your power to arm ;
He tells the story with such grace,
  So reasons for his love,
That who e're hears the matchless swain,
  Such passion must approve.

(2.)

Ah ! happiest nymph to gain a heart
  That merits such return ;
Tho' all your charms augmented were,
  Tis pride for him to burn.
To make him blest as he deserves,
  And you the envyd she,
Is but to love and think on him
  By imitating me.

———

IV. *A copy of verses by Mr. Hervey upon Mrs. Felton.* *Bury Fair,* 1694.

When bright Armida gracd this happy place
With her attractive charms, it wore a face
*(In spite of sickness and disease) of joy,
Which nothing but her absence coud destroy.
Twas feard our fair would be a solitude,

* Marginal note says, The small pox.—S.H.A.H.

But she being there it provd a multitude.
Instead of catching she the infection spread
Of a contagion worse than that she feard ;
That seizing only here and there a heart,
Her eyes an universall ruine dart ;
All car'd, then sigh'd, and whereso'ere she movd
Made thefts of hearts that never else had lovd ;
The play-house throng'd with emulating beauxs,
(Streets cant be more so where a triumph goes ;)
Each day produc'd agreeable delights,
Sweet dreams and serenades employd our nights ;
Gay were the hours, but swiftly seemd to haste;
Pleasures so exquisite do never last ;
For but a now our hungry eyes she fed,
And then the short livd blessing disappeard,
Leaving our town the dismall revers'd scene
Of that prosperity it late had seen ;
For she'd no sooner left the wondring Fair
But all like statues look'd of deep despair,
Proving the place suspected by their fears,
Unpeopled and abandon'd it appears ;
No soul peeps forth of its neglected home,
Unless (like dead men at the Resurrection,
Fearfully jealous of their coming doom,
With conscious dread,) t'enquire if she be gone ;
Which was no sooner learnt but even the wise
Cold Stoicks felt invincible surprise ;
Their boasted apathy they found was lost,
And the unlikelyest regretted most,

The melancholly prospect by it shown
(Like Egypts when their fears of grain were gone)
Of plenty past but long dearth now to come,
For tis a tedious penance we must bear,
Before the leaden-heel'd revolving year
Can bring her back, if she will then appear,
To be of virtue, breeding, witt and truth
Th' exactest standard for our female youth.

V. *Verses by Mrs. Felton on Mr. Hervey upon her leaving of Suffolk. Anno 1694.*

When first I saw the charming Suffolk swain,
I felt a pleasure which created pain ;
In every look he did my wonder move ;
I knew but coud not help my growing love ;
His pleasing image haunted every thought,
Each coming hour a farther conquest wrought ;
Sweetness with truth were seated in his face,
Wisdom and virtue shin'd in every grace ;
His talk was musick to my listening soul.
And did all passions but its own controul ;
Whate'er he said or did th' infection spread,
Even when he told his sorrows for the dead,
Which with such faith, such love, he did express,
As make me envy her (yet) happyness,
And wish my self the Nymph that coud his grief redress ;
But that's a bliss too great for me to expect,
And since I fear he cannot love, will shunn neglect.

VI.*

What magick power in mighty love their lies ;
What wonderous miracles can it not do ;
The wise it makes a fool, the fool seem wise,
And even of me has made a poet too.

VII. *An imperfect sketch of the Earl of Bristol's character collected from several authors by the Countess of Bristol.*

Oft turning others leaves I hop'd t'indite
Something like him that might be exquisite.
Fool, said my Muse, consult thy heart, then write.
Yet look not every lineament to see ;
Some will be cast in shades, and some will be
So lamely drawn, you'll scarcely know tis he.
In every virtue his rich furnishd mind
Excells in each, as if to one confind ;
For he has all in that supream degree
That as no one prevails so all is he ;
The several parts lye ready in the piece,
The occasion but exerting that or this ;
His actions all so willingly do tend,
By ev'ry thing he does he gains a friend ;
Mirth never makes him say a thing unfit,
Virtue his will and Prudence rules his wit.
All human worth is center'd in his breast,
Not one rough passion does his soul molest,
But is all truth, and so from vices free,

---

* This was wrote by Lady Bristol under her own verses.　(Lord Bristol's note.)

As if not out of choice but from necessity.
When often urg'd, unwilling to be great,
His country calls him from his lov'd retreat
And thence to Senates charg'd with common care,
Which none less seeks and none can better bear,
Where coud they find another form'd so fit
To poise with solid sense a sprightly wit ?
Were these both wanting (tho' they both abound)
Where coud so firm integrity be found ?
Well-born & wealthy, wanting no support,
He steers betwixt his country and the Court,
Nor gratifyes whate'er the Great desire,
Nor grudging gives what publick needs require ;
Good senators (and such is he) so give
That kings may be supply'd, the people thrive ;
He does with hands unbribd & heart sincere
Twixt Prince and People in a medium steer ;
Preserves that ballance which supports the state,
Making the people safe & monarch great.
O true descendant ! from a patriot line,
Who whilst thou shar'st their lustre lend'st them thine ;
So many virtues joynd in him as we
Can scarce pick here and there in history ;
More than old writers practice e're could reach,
As much as they by rules could ever teach ;
Just, good & wise, contending neighbours come
From his award to wait their final doom,
Who foes before return in friendship home.
He courteous is by kind, and justly proud

With friendly offices to help the good ;
No porter guards the passage to his door,
T'admit the wealthy & exclude the poor ;
For God who gave the riches gave the heart
To sanctifye the whole by giving part ;
To help all wants he only seems to live,
To do much good his soul's prerogative ;
To all relations their just rights he pays,
And deals rewards where'ere he worth surveys ;
The tenderest husband, master, father, son,
Yet these by sacred friendships still outdone ;
His love to friends no bounds does ever know ;
What he to Heaven all that to him they owe;
All who deserve his love he makes his own,
And to be lov'd himself needs only to be known ;
Each in his turn; the rich may freely come
As to a friend, but to the poor tis home ;
Such multitudes he feeds, he cloathes, he's nurs't,
That he himself may fear his wanting first ;
Of his five talents other five he's made,
Heaven that has largely given is largely paid ;
And in few lives, in wond'rous few, we find
A fortune better fitted to the mind ;
The distant hear by fame his pious deeds,
And lay him up for their extreamest needs,
A future cordial for a fainting mind,
For what was n'ere refusd all hope to find,
The hunger-starv'd, the naked & the lame ;
Want and diseases fly before his name ;

He feels a greater joy in doing good
Than they to whom the benefits accru'd ;
As never more by Heaven to man was given,
So never more by man was paid to Heaven ;
Business may shorten, not disturb, his prayer ;
Heaven has the best if not the largest share ;
An active life long oraisons forbids,
Yet still he prays, for still he prays by deeds.
This, this is he in whom doth mixt remain
All that fond mothers wishes can contain ;
No power nor pomp can sway his steady mind,
He's truly great, yet affable and kind.
Since then kind Heaven has been so much my friend,
To have such bliss on my first choice attend,
All my ambition I will here confine,
Still to preserve this treasure only mine.

July   Thro' each returning year may that day be
25,   Distinguish'd in the rounds of all eternity,
1695.   That joyn'd my heart to one of such fidelity.
Gay be the sun that day in all his light,
Let him collect his rays to be more bright,
Shine all that day, though all the rest be night.
Happy that Nymph who, when her stars incline
Her soul to love, can make a choice like mine ;
Heaven's rarest blessings has adorn'd his mind,
A lover far beyond his faithless kind ;
To him for ease I all my griefs impart,
His pleasant converse always chears my heart ;
In his chaste love my wishes meet their end,

BE

Pleas'd & secure in such a faithful friend;
Watchful I'll guard him, & with midnight prayer
Weary the Gods to keep him in their care,
And joyous ask at morn's returning ray
If he has health, and I may bless the day.
Witness, you everlasting powers above,
That never mortal bore a truer love;
But as no faith did ever mine excell,
So never any man deserv'd so well;
The same our hopes, our fears, & our desires,
Love is our life, & one love both inspires.
Thrice happy we, of whom no one does know
Which first began to love, or loves most now;
Fair course of passion, where two lovers start
And run together, heart still yokd with heart;
For me each lover sigh'd and sued in vain,
He had my heart, but they my cold disdain.
O poor return for all thy wond'rous love!
That to no other youth I kind coud prove;
Without injunction I'd have made that vow,
Immortal passion is his merit's due,
No heart can love again who once loves you.
No, thou dear idol of my conquer'd soul,
Thy empire in my breast no pow'r shall ere controul;
That knot must sure for ever last,
Which fancy ty'd & reason has made fast;
His merits are avow'd by publick voice,
And ev'ry tongue does justify my choice;
His constancy, his truth & worth alone

Shall for the falsehood of his sex atone ;
Gracious to all, but where his love was due
So fast, so faithful, tender, and so true,
That bless'd we live & happy in content,
Save Heaven's-self nought can our joys augment ;
To greatness he so little did incline,
His heart ask'd never any thing but mine ;
His story I for ever will preserve,
From whence let constant lovers learn to serve,
Let sighing virgins endless praise rehearse,
Crown him, ye poets, with immortal verse ;
For even when death dissolves our human frame,
Tho' earth the body, verse preserves the fame.
Vouchsafe this picture of thy soul to see,
Tis so far good as it resembles thee ;
The beauties to the original I owe,
Which where I miss my own defects I show.

VIII.   *These four lines were compos'd by Lady Bristol to be written
          under the foregoing verses.*
Cou'd I like Cowley think, and Dryden write,
In Otway's tender words my soul indite,
I then in verse might hope to soar above
All other mortals, as I do in love.

IX.   *To the Right Honourable the Countess of Bristol.**
Long had my mind, unknowing how to soar,
In humble prose been train'd, nor aim'd at more ;

---

* Some one has written in pencil, *By Mrs. Manley*. If so, this is probably the poem for which Mrs.
Manley was paid 20 guineas. See page 151 of this printed volume, April 13, 1720.—S.H.A.H.

Near the fam'd sisters never durst aspire
To sound a verse or touch the tuneful lyre ;
Till Bristol's charms dissolv'd the native cold,
Bad me survey her eyes, and thence be bold.
Thee, lovely Bristol, thee with pride I choose,
The first and only subject of my muse,
That durst transport me, like the bird of Jove,
To face th' immortal source of light above !
Such are thy kindred-beams ;
So blessings with a bounteous hand they give,
So they create, and make creation live.

When charming Felton of a beauteous race,
Adorn'd in blooming youth with ev'ry grace,
First saw the lovely Suffolk swain her prize,
The noblest conquest of the brightest eyes,
How many wretched nymphs that union made !
What cold despair the warmest hearts invade !
What crowds of lovers, hop'less and undone,
Deplore those charms which brought their ruin on !
Rich in themselves—all excellence they find,
Wit ! beauty ! wisdom ! and a constant mind !
No vain desire of change disturb their joy ;
Such sweets, like bliss divine, can never cloy ;
Fill'd with that spirit which great souls inflame,
Their wondrous offspring start to early fame ;
In their young minds immortal sparkles rise !
And all their mother flashes from their eyes !

From thence such scenes of beauty charm the sight,
We know not where to fix the strong delight !
Hervey's soft features —next, Eliza bright !
Anna just dawning, like Aurora's light !
With all the smiling train of Cupids round,
Fond little loves, with flowing graces crownd !

As some fair flow'rs who all their bloom disclose,
The Spanish Jasmin or the British rose,
Arriv'd at full perfection charm the sense,
Whilst the young blossoms gradual sweets dispense,
The eldest born with almost equal pride,
The next appears in fainter colours dy'd,
New op'ning buds, as less in debt to time,
Wait to perform the promise of their prime,
All blest descendants of the beauteous tree,
What now their parent is themselves shall be.
O ! coud I paint the younger Hervey's mind,
Where wit and judgment, fire and taste refin'd,
To match his face with equal art are join'd ;
Oh best belov'd of Jove ! to thee alone,
What wou'd enrich the whole, he gives to one !

*In Titian's colours, whilst Adonis glows,
See fairest Bristol more than Venus shows;
View well the valu'd piece, how nice each part ;

* This is not design'd as a parallel of the story, but the painting from a piece of Titian's at my Lord Bristol's.—M.S. note.

Yet Nature's hand surpasses Titian's art!
Such had his Venus and Adonis been,
The standard beauty had from thence been seen!
Whose arbitrary laws had fix'd the doom
To Hervey's form and Bristol's ever-bloom!

*As once Kazeia, now Eliza warms,
The kindred-fair bequeath'd her all her charms,
Such were her darts, so piercing and so strong,
Endow'd by Phœbus both with tuneful song;
But far from thee, Eliza, be her doom,
Snatch'd hence by death in all her beauty's bloom;
Long mayst thou live, adorning Bristol's name,
With future heros to augment his fame.

When haughty Niobe with joy and pride
Saw all her shining offspring grace her side,
She viewd their charms exulting at each line
And then oppos'd 'em to the race divine!
Enrag'd Latona urged the silver bow,
Immortal vengeance laid their beauties low.
No more a mother now—too much she mourn'd,
By grief incessant into marble turn'd.

But lovely Bristol with a pious mind
Owns all her blessings are from heaven assign'd,
Her matchless lord—her beauteous num'rous race!

---

* A sister of Lord Bristol's, who was a lady of most extraordinary beauty.—M.S. note.

Her virtue, modesty and ev'ry grace !
For these devoutly to the Gods she bows,
And offers daily praise and daily vows ;
Phœbus well-pleas'd the sacrifice regards,
And thus the grateful mother's zeal rewards ;
" Beauty and wit to all of Bristol's line !
" But each in some peculiar grace shall shine !
" Or to excel in Courts and please the fair !
" Or conquest gain thro' all the wat'ry war !
" With harmony divine the ear to charm !
" Or souls with more melodious numbers warm !
" By wondrous memory shall some excell
" In awful Senates, and in speaking well !
" To hold Astræa's scales with equal hand,
" And call back justice to that happy land !
" To teach mankind how best the Gods to praise !
" To fix their minds in Truth's unerring ways !
" Thus all her honours Bristol's sons shall wear,
" Whilst each his country's good shall make his cheifest care !

Printed in the year 1719.

APPENDIX No. 2.

A copy of the Earl of Bristol's Memorandum of the births of all his children by his wife Elizabeth, Countess of Bristol.

15 Oct. 1696. Thursday.	My said dear wife was brought to bed of a son between 3 and 4 in the afternoon having been in a painful perillous labour near 17 hours, & on Sunday ye 28th of the said month he was baptizd by Doctor Wake at my house in Jermyn-street and nam'd JOHN; my father-in-law Sir Thomas Felton, my uncle Mr. Baptist May, & the Dutchess of Laudedale answer'd for him.
Thursday 9 Dec. 1697.	My dear wife was brought to bed of a daughter about 11 at night, & christen'd 23d of the same month by Doctor Wake at my said house in Jermyn-street; my cousin Mr. William Duncombe, the Countess of Suffolk, & Lady Howard of Effingham answer'd for her and nam'd her ELIZABETH.
Friday 20 Jan. 1698/9.	My dear wife was deliverd of a son near midnight and on Thursday ye 23d of February following he was baptiz'd by Doctor Wake at my house in St. James's Square, and nam'd THOMAS; the E. of Jersey, my cousin Sir Thomas Hanmer & Lady Pooley of Boxstead answer'd for him.

---

* This memorandum is in the second of the two quarto volumes containing Lord and Lady Bristol's correspondence.—S.H.A.H.

Xmas day. 25 Dec. 1699.	Between 2 and 3 in the morning my dear wife was brought to bed of a son being about 13 hours in labour, and on Saturday the 13th of Jan. following he was christen'd at my said house in St. James's Square by Doctor Wake and nam'd WILLIAM ; the Duke of Somerset, Duke of St. Alban's & Aunt Felton answer'd for him.
Sunday. 5 Jan. 1700/1	My dear wife was brought to bed of a son about 8 in the morning ; he was born with a cawl about his face and round about his head, and on Thursday the 6th of February following he was christen'd by Doctor Wake and nam'd HENRY ; the Duke of Bedford, Lord Godolphin & the Countess of Marlborough answer'd for him.
Monday, 5 April, 1703.	My dear wife was brought to bed of a daughter between 9 and 10 at night, & about half an hour after she was deliver'd of a son, and on Thursday the 18th of the same month they were both christen'd by Doctor Wake ; the girl was nam'd HENRIETTA, the Lady Henrietta Godolphin, the Lady Fitzharding & the Earl of Sunderland answering for her ; the boy was nam'd CHARLES, the Dutchess of St. Albans, the Duke of Bolton & the Marquess of Hartington answering for him.
Thursday, 6 July, 1704.	My dear wife was deliver'd of a male child still-born about 6 of the clock in the morning, a beautiful child even in the arms of death. Optimum non nasci; bonum vero quare citissime interire.

> 'Tis good not to be born, but if we must,
> The next good is soon to return to dust.

<table>
<tr><td>Monday,
Midsummer Day
24 June, 1706.</td><td>My dear wife was brought to bed of a son between 2 and 3 in the morning, and on Monday the 8th day of July following he was christen'd by the Reader of St. James's Parish (in the absence of Doctor Wake, then Bishop of Lincoln,) and nam'd JAMES PORTER HERVEY, the Duke of Grafton, my brother Colonel Porter & Lady Isabella Turner answering for him ; & on the 6th of August after about midnight was found dead in the bed, being overlaid by his fatal nurse.</td></tr>
<tr><td>Saturday,
12 July, 1707.</td><td>My dear wife was deliver'd of a daughter about 11 at night at Windsor after a very safe & easy labour scarce an hour long, and on Sunday the 27th of July she was baptiz'd and nam'd ANN, our good & gracious Queen, the Dutchess of Somerset, & ye Marquess of Kent, her Majesties Lord Chamberlain, answering for her. The Minister who christen'd her was Mr. Thomas Dawson, Vicar of the said parish of Windsor.</td></tr>
<tr><td>Thursday,
3 June, 1708.</td><td>My dear wife was deliver'd of a boy, who liv'd but two hours after he was christen'd by my chaplain Mr. Priest at Ickworth and nam'd HUMPHREY, my good and honest grandfather May being so call'd.</td></tr>
<tr><td>Thursday,
19 May, 1709.</td><td>My dear wife was deliver'd of a daughter between the hours of 9 and 10 at night and was baptiz'd on Wednesday the 8th of June following by Mr. Clarke, the Dutchess of Grafton, the Countess of Orkney & my Lord Roylton answering for her, named BARBARA.</td></tr>
</table>

Monday, 3 July, 1710.	My dear wife was deliverd of a male child between the hours of 2 and 3 in the afternoon, and on Friday the 7th he was privately baptiz'd being ill & nam'd FELTON, who dyed on Sunday the 16th of July 1710 between the hours of seven and twelve at night.
Tuesday 12 Feb. 1711.	My dear wife was deliverd of her tenth son between the hours of 5 and 6 in the afternoon, and on Tuesday ye 26th of the said month he was baptiz'd by Dr. Clarke & nam'd FELTON, the Earl of Portland, Sir Compton Felton & the Countess of Burlington answering for him.
Thursday, 5 March, 1712/13.	My dear wife was deliver'd of her eleventh son between the hours of 9 and 10 at night, and on Wednesday the 28th of March 1713 he was baptiz'd by Dr. Clarke & nam'd JAMES, the Duke of Rutland, the Lord Ossulston and the Countess of Essex answering for him.
Wednesday 2 March 1714/15	My dear wife was deliver'd of a daughter about two a clock in the morning, and on Wednesday the 23d of the same month she was baptiz'd by Doctor Trimnel Bishop of Norwich, and nam'd LOUISA CAROLINA ISABELLA, his Majesty King George, Her Royal Highness ye Princess of Wales & the Marchioness of Dorchester answering for her.
Tuesday 25 Sept. 1716.	My dear wife was deliverd of a daughter between 4 and 8 a clock in the morning, and on Sunday the 7th of October following she was baptiz'd by Doctor Clarke and nam'd HENRIETTA, my wife's cousin the Duke of Argyle, the Dutchess of Cleaveland & Lady Dalkeith answering for her.

APPENDIX No. 3.

The case of the Honourable Elizabeth Hervey, widow. *

That she having brought a great fortune to John Hervey Esq. her late husband, he made his will and appointed £20,000 to be laid out in a purchase of land to be settled on her for life; and until that was done did appoint interest to be paid her for the same at 4 per cent per annum half yearly; and made Sir Thomas Hervey, his brother, executor of his will, who had assets come to his hands very much beyond that value, yet never made the said purchase.

But pursuant to an order in Chancery he and John Hervey Esq. his son and heir, now a member of the Honourable House of Commons, gave security by recognizance to pay the said interest half yearly; and the said Sir Thomas did duly pay the same during his life.

That Sir Thomas dyed about four years since, leaving his said son his sole executor, who hath suffered the said interest to run so much in arrear that there is now due about £3000 which he refuseth to pay, and insists on his priviledge as a member of the said House of Commons.

Whereupon Mrs. Hervey having leave of the Court of Chancery to sue the said Recognizance, and having likewise the order of the House of Commons of the 30th November, 1696, That no member should have priviledge longer than the House was actually sitting (except for his person only), she soon after the last Session of Parliament sued out a Scire facias upon the said Recognizance directed to the Sheriffs of Middlesex, returnable n Chancery the first return of Trinity term last; but she cannot get the

---

*I am indebted to Lord John Hervey for copying this document for me from the printed copy in the British Museum. Elizabeth Hervey is the Aunt Hervey sometimes mentioned in the diary, daughter of William, Lord Hervey of Kidbrook.—S.H.A.H.

Sheriffs to return the said Writ, for that Mr. Smith the Under Sheriff saith, the said Mr. Hervey insists on his priviledge.

And she hath moved the Chancery to compel a Return, but cannot have any effect thereby, being told by the said Court she must apply to the House of Commons.

It is therefore humbly desired that the said Sheriff may be ordered by the House of Commons to return the Scire facias, that so the said Mr. Hervey may have the benefit of the said order of the 30th of November, 1696.

APPENDIX No. 4.

The case of John Hervey Esq; heir and executor of Sir Thomas Hervey his father, who was brother and heir and executor of John Hervey, Esq; deceased, husband to Elizabeth Hervey (widow) the Petitioner. *

John Hervey, who was Treasurer to the Queen Dowager, married (in the late troublesome times, viz. in the year 1658,) with Elizabeth, the daughter and heir of the Lord Hervey, who had an estate of inheritance of about £1300 or £1400 per annum. And the said Mr. Hervey being obnoxious to those times, a settlement was made of her said estate in Trustees to cover and protect it from the violence of the then powers, and to add the greater colour to the said contrivance, and make it seem the more real, and less subject to question or suspicion, and not be look'd upon as a design to keep it from being seized or sequestred for Mr. Hervey's delinquency, it was advis'd and accordingly directed, That Mr. Hervey should covenant with the said Trustees (the late Earl of Leicester and others) that the profits should be answered to her.

---

* I take this from a printed copy at Ickworth. It throws light upon several matters ; amongst others upon the disappearance of the old manor house that stood by the Church, Ickworth being the jointure-estate alluded to. See Section v.—S.H.A.H.

After the Restauration (when all was quiet) the said Mr. Hervey and Mrs. Hervey (the Petitioner) liv'd together until the year 1679, when he died ; and during all that time he received all the profits of the estate, without any contradiction of her self or the said Trustees, and he maintain'd her all along, and they liv'd upon their estate.

In the year 1679 the said Mr. Hervey died without issue, and having setled upon his wife the seat of his Family in Suffolk, and about £800 per annum out of his estate there, for her joynture did (over and above what he was obliged to by the settlement of his marriage) by his will give unto the Petitioner the interest of £20000 at £4 per cent amounting to £800 per annum more; and also all his lease-hold estates, to the value of £600 per annum; and likewise his house in St. James's Square, worth £300 per annum, besides all his plate, jewels, goods, and houshold-stuff, worth above £15000 more, and all this out of his estate, besides her paternal one of £1400 per annum, as aforesaid; and made her one of his executors, but in trust for Sir Thomas Hervey, his brother and heir, whom he made residuary legatee.

But notwithstanding he made such large provisions for her, and gave her such great gifts, she (after his death) having possest her self of all her husbands writings, and the securities he had taken for above £50000, and also of a great collection of gold, silver and brass medals, together with a Library of books to a great value, and considerable sums of money in old gold, etc, set up her claim to all the profits of her own estate, which her husband had receiv'd during the Coverture, to the value (as she pretended) of £30000, and sued Sir Thomas upon his brother's (her husband's) said covenant (so entred into as aforesaid) to recover the said £30000 out of his estate.

Upon which Sir Thomas Hervey exhibited his bill in Chancery, as well to be relieved against that pretence and suit, as to discover and have the said writings and securities of his estate; and upon several hearings and rehearings, the Court adjudging her pretence very unjust and unreasonable, decreed against it, and ordered, That she should discover upon her oath and account for and deliver up all the writings and securities, and all the rest of her husband's estate, to the said Sir Thomas Hervey, except such parts of it as was devis'd to her by will.

And she refusing to discover the said writings, securities etc on oath, or deliver them as the Court directed her, was prosecuted with contempt to a Sergeant at Arms and sequestration; and after the sequestration was actually laid upon her house in St. James's Square, wherein she and all the said securities, writings, medals and books were, the said house was (by night) broken into and ransack'd, and the securities, writings, medals and monies carried away by means of the now Earl of Montague (then Mr. Montague) and Dame Elizabeth Hervey his sister, part of the spoil being carried to his house, part to hers, some part to one Justice Dewy's, other part to one Henry Baker's, and she her self, by the said Baker, by the said Lord and Ladies advice, direction and procurement, as it was then taken, and as Mr. Hervey does not still doubt to make appear, sent beyond sea.

This outragious procedure was so resented by the Court of Chancery, that the Lord Montague and his sister, and Dewy, and Baker, and every person any wise concern'd therein, were prosecuted with contempts for it, and ordered to make a full discovery touching the securities, goods etc. so violently by them taken out of her husband's house; and also all her own estate and joynture, leases etc. were sequestred till she yielded obedience to the said decrees of the Court, which prosecutions cost the said Sir Thomas Hervey above £1500.

At last, when the Lord Jeoffries was Chancellour, all her estate being so under sequestration, her agents here desired the original cause might be re-heard; but before the Court would grant a re-hearing, they would have a discovery from the said Mrs. Hervey (the Petitioner) upon oath, and the securities etc brought into Court, whereupon she was examind beyond sea, and several of the securities, medals etc brought into Court.

Upon which the cause was re-heard, and the former decrees confirm'd ; after which her said agents desir'd to have the sequestration taken off her estate, and an account was taken of as much as Sir Thomas Hervey could then make appear she had possest her self of in his wrong ; and upon full satisfaction thereof (which she hath not at this day made as to several particulars wherein the said Sir Thomas was injured) and delivering up the said securities and other estate then discovered, Sir Thomas was to account for what had been receiv'd out of her estate under sequestration, and re-deliver what goods etc belonged to her, which had been seized by virtue of the said sequestration.

Upon an account taken, Sir Thomas Hervey had such securities, writings, moneys, books and medals as he could then recover out of her hands (altho not all of either kind are restored), and thereupon (willing to yield all obedience to the Court) delivered back the jewels and estate under sequestration, and paid her agents £8000 and upwards, which had been received out of her estate, by vertue of the sequestration.

After this Sir Thomas Hervey having married his son (against whom Mrs. Hervey now petitions the Commons) anno 1688, and made a settlement of most part of his estate upon that marriage ; Mrs. Hervey (the Petitioner) by her agents here petitioned the Court, That the said Sir Thomas and his said son might enter into a recognizance for securing the payment of the said £800 per annum, the interest at £4 per cent (of the said £20 000), by half yearly payments, which being held reasonable by the said Court of Chancery, the said Sir Thomas and Mr. Hervey his son did accordingly enter into a recognizance of £4000 for payment of the said £800 per annum, and constantly paid the same for some years, from January 1679 to July

1693, to the said Dame Elizabeth Hervey, who hath an authority by a letter of Attorney from the Petitioner Mrs. Hervey to receive both that and all other the profits of her estate, amounting in the whole to near £4000 per annum, which the said Lady Hervey hath done for 14 or 15 years last past.

Now the reasons why Mr. Hervey hath not paid the said £800 per annum as he used to do, are as follow.

I. Because she the said Petitioner (by her agents here) hath made use of a Flock of sheep (consisting of thirteen hundred ewes and sixty two hoggets) belonging to Mr. Hervey (but going upon a farm in her joynture-estate), for the use of which stock (the property whereof they never controverted) the said Sir Thomas Hervey and Mr. Hervey have all along demanded a deduction of £50 per annum out of the said £800 per annum, (and accordingly had such an allowance made for them for the first four or five years, from January 1679,) but there being now twelve or thirteen years rent in arrear for the use of the said sheep, and they (after several promises to satisfie them, but never suffering any defalcation to be made for the same out of the many payments Sir Thomas and his son made of the said £800 per annum) altho they have constantly enjoyed the benefit of the sheep, refusing to continue the said allowance of £50 per annum for the sheep, the same was one reason he was advised to stay the money in his hands, until they made him satisfaction for the same.

II. There being several Copy-hold lands which the said Agents have for above fifteen years last enjoyed with her jointure, but (by the custom of the Manor they hold of) descending to the younger brother, and so consequently the profits thereof, from Mr. Hervey's decease in 1679, belonging to Sir Thomas Hervey, who actually paid his fine of admission, and the Lord's rent annually due for the same; and they likewise refusing to account for the said profits, (notwithstanding he hath judgment in ejectment for the same,) he is also advised to insist upon a just allowance for the same, before he pays the money she petitions for.

DD

III. There being several quantities of Gold and other monies which she and her agents possess'd themselves of when the house was rifled, as aforesaid, for which there has yet been no compensation made; he is advised they ought to make restitution out of the said money they would have him pay them.

IV. There being yet several writings undelivered, belonging to the titles of his estate of inheritance, and others relating to other parts of his estate, (particularly touching some shares in the Duke's Play-house,) and several securities for moneys, especially one relating to a debt of £700 due from the heirs of Sir Robert Holt to the said Mr. Hervey, which money he cannot recover for want of the writings belonging thereto; he is likewise advised not to pay the money in question, until they procure for him, or deliver to him the said writings, securities, etc., through the want of which he is damnified to the value of £1400 or £1500.

V. Mrs. Hervey's agents having committed great wasts upon her jointure-estate, in cutting down several hundred loads of wood and timber in one spring (about the year 86 or 87) and selling them off the estate; by reason whereof the Tenants, not having sufficient fuel left upon their farms to carry on their Dairy-business, were forced to cut down several bodies of trees, and great arms of timber trees, for firing; and in the wood so taken down there was very good timber for building, which had never been cut within the memory of man; and not only this, but several little groves they stubb'd up, and made pasture, and broke up several pieces of feeding-ground, and have converted into arable, upon the same jointure-estate; and have also suffered the seat of the family to run into such ruine and decay, that daily the tiles, sometimes by loads, fall off the Mansion-house, whereby the timber-roofs have lain so expos'd to the sun and rain, that they being rotten fall down, and have destroyed the planchard floors, which now in some places lie one upon another; and when he hath threatened to bring his action, they have cut down sixteen or eighteen timber trees at a time, under a pretence that they designed them for repairs ; but having sold or disposed of their tops and bark, they let the trees lie unemployed, and the repairs undone, although the trees were taken down several years since, and so even those timbers spoil'd likewise. Besides all this, there are some barns and out-houses quite fallen down, which her agents will not rebuild, but say, they wish all the houses on her jointure-estate in the same condition.

In any of which matters, by reason of the said Mrs. Hervey's being kept beyond the seas, Mr. Hervey hath not been nor is able to have his right, the same belonging now to him in his own right, as heir and executor of his father Sir Thomas Hervey ; and therefore he is advised, it is but just to stay the payment of the said £800 per annum, till he can have justice and right done him in the premisses.

Note, The Petitioner, Mrs. Hervey, hath been kept beyond the seas ever since she was conveyed away, as aforesaid, and still continues so ; and that the said Lady Hervey, the said Lord Mountague's sister, has, by a letter of Attorney from her, had and possess'd all the jewels and houshold-stuff of such great value as aforesaid, and has received the profits of her own estate of the values aforesaid ; in all amounting to £4000 per annum, for this fourteen or fifteen years.

Note also, There was a petition of the same nature the last session ; and upon Mr. Hervey's acquainting the House with his case to the effect aforesaid, the said petition was rejected. After which, Mr. Hervey proposed a reference to the Lord Mountague of the said matters ; which he at first accepted of, but afterwards declined. And since the Lord Mountague has taken a lease himself of Mrs. Hervey's jointure-estate from her for one and twenty years (as given out), and by his agent threatens to make all destructions imaginable, to the prejudice of Mr. Hervey, to whom the reversion and inheritance of the estate belongs ; and by virtue of that lease his Lordship protects the tenants by his privilege, so that Mr. Hervey cannot punish them for the several wastes they daily commit on the jointure-estate.

Wherefore Mr. Hervey humbly hopes, That unless he may have right done him in the matters aforesaid, he may justly insist on his privilege still.

APPENDIX No. 5.*

The curious unparallell'd Hunting New Machine :

That was shewn at the King's Palace, St. James's, and to Members of both Houses of Parliament, at Parliament Coffee-House, in the Court of Request, Westminster-Hall, when Parliament sat, may now be seen elsewhere on Occasion, paying for the Projector's Trouble of shewing the same : Being the original Model of a complete Hunting-Chair or Travelling-Chaise, for one Horse, and with one Wheel, and to follow the Horse safely any where, even over Hedge, Ditch or Stiles on Occasion, most safe from overturning, as the little Model with the artificial Horse in sufficiently shews to the Satisfaction of the most Curious ; the like Model being, it is thought, not before made. The Model being so small and so easy to carry from Place to Place, that those Gentlemen who desire to see it at a Coffee-House or Tavern may be so far pleasured as to have it brought them to View, if about the Heart of the City at Change Time, or if at the other end of the Town towards Evening, by leaving notice.—Now may be seen at ye Vine Inn by ye Market Cross in Bury, or other Inns where Gentlemen pleasis.

N.B.—Any Gentlemen who hath seen this Model may have of the Garden Machines made with the like artificial Horse therein ; which for Curiosity,

---

* This printed advertisement is lying loose in the Diary, and is apparently of about the same date as that part of the book where it lies, viz. 1714. The machine would seem to be a rude forefather of the bicycle.—S.H.A.H.

Sightliness, and Conveniency of Riding in Gentlemen's Fields, Yards or Gardens, have been much approved of by the greatest Nobility, who have had of the same.

APPENDIX No. 6.*

Debts due to me from ye Crown.

	£ s. d.
To an arrear due to Barbarah Countess of Suffolke as Groom of ye Stole to Queen Katharine of	5600..00..00
To £1000 principal mony upon a Tally & order payable out of ye new ffarm of ye Customs at Christmas 1672, beside interest	1000..00..00
To £1000 more principal mony upon a Tally & order payable out of ye collection of ye Customs dated 8 Dec. 1671 in repayment of so much lent	1000..00..00
	7600..00..00

250 Guineys due from Queen Dowager to my Uncle Hervey for a sett of Gold Counters bought in ffrance.

Sir Thomas Felton laid out above £1500 in building several new rooms & repairing all ye Lodgings (now Mr. Dunch's), & altho' he never liv'd to enjoy ye new rooms at all as Comptroller of ye Household, yet ye Queen never allowd Jack one farthing as his residuary Legateé.

Her Majesty was pleasd likewise to take away Sir Hervey Elwes's office from him of Prothonotary of ye Dutchy of Lancaster, which had been in his

---

* This paper in Lord Bristol's writing is lying loose in the Diary.—S.H.A.H.

family 50 years, whose father & grandfather had constantly servd ye Crown without any other reward.

The granting a Licence to destroy ye Patent for acting Plays in Drury Lane, whereby I lost an interest which formerly yielded constantly upwards of £300 per annum to my family.

APPENDIX No. 7.*

The case of St. Edmund's Bury. The Honble Carr Hervey Esq. and Aubrie Porter Esq., sitting Members, against Jermyn Davers Esq. and Gilbert Affleck Esq. Petitioners.

King James the first by letters-patent in the fourth year of his reign ordained that the Town of St. Edmund's Bury should be from thenceforth a Free Borough, and thereby incorporated the inhabitants of the said Town by the name of Alderman and Burgesses, and constituted an Alderman, 12 Capital Burgesses, and 24 Burgesses of the Common-Council for the government of that Corporation.

And by Charter in the 12th year of his reign he granted that there should be two Burgesses to serve in Parliament for the said Borough, to be elected by the Alderman, 12 Capital Burgesses and 24 Burgesses of the Common Council, or the majority of them.

In pursuance whereof the Elections and returns thereupon were constantly made by the Alderman, Capital Burgesses and Burgesses of the Common Council, without any interruption by the Populace upon any pretence whatsoever till the year 1680.

---

* I copy this petition from a printed sheet in the British Museum. Several allusions to the matter will be found in Lord Bristol's Letterbooks.—S.H.A.H.

In 1680 some persons (who had had a considerable share in the
government of that Corporation in the times immediately preceding the
year 1660) upon some general notions that all elections by a select number
alone were derogatory to the freedom of Parliaments, (which opinion had
indeed receiv'd some sort of countenance from a pretended ordinance of the
usurping powers about the year 1656,) prevailed upon some of the inhabitants to assume to themselves a right of electing the Burgesses to serve in
Parliament ; who proceeded thereupon to elect Sir Thomas Cullum and
Mr. Rotheram in opposition to Sir Thomas Hervey and Mr. Jermyn,
grandfather to one of the present petitioners, who were elected and returned
by the select number alone ; whereupon Mr. Rotheram petitioned the then
House of Commons, and insisted upon a pretended right of election residing
in the Populace ; but upon hearing the merits of that petition, twas resolved
that Sir Thomas Hervey and Mr. Jermyn were duly elected, as by the
Journal of that House doth appear ; and the Elections have ever since been
accordingly made conformable to that determination without any dispute
until this present election, when the Petitioners insisted that they were
elected by some of the Populace of the said Town in opposition to the
sitting-members, who were elected and returned by the select number as
usual.

So that the single question will be, In whom the right of Election
resides, whether in the Freemen and inhabitants of the said Town, as is
asserted by the petitions, or in the Alderman, Capital Burgesses and
Burgesses of the Common Council, agreeable to the words of the Charter,
to constant usage, and the determination abovesaid.

Twas formerly objected by Mr. Rotheram's Councel that there could be
no such thing as a right of Election subsisting by Charter ; and admitting
there could, yet it could not be vested in the governing part of the
Corporation alone, exclusive of the Populace.

But to this was opposed, first Co. 4, Int. 49, 2 Rolls abr. 198, Hob. 14, 15.   Secondly constant and universal experience ; and thirdly the constitution of two thirds of the Parliamentary Boroughs in England, who elect at this day in several manners by force of their several Charters.

But tis observeable that even supposing the truth of what the then petitioner urged, yet no right could result from thence to the petitioner ; for since it can never be proved that we did elect by prescription, and tis asserted that we cannot elect by our Charter, the plain consequence of it must be that this Borough has no right to elect members at all, a consequence which would not only divest this Borough of the best of its franchises, but would render precarious the rights of above half the Parliamentary Boroughs in England.

Then twas objected that Bury sent Burgesses to Parliament by prescription ; but there being no evident traces of any such right, they produced an old memorandum or two endorsd only upon some old writs of summons as long ago as the reign of Edward I, wherein mention is made of the Senaschallus Libertatis Sancti Edmundi, though no elections were ever pretended to be made thereupon.

But it being plain that the Liberty of St. Edmund was a franchise, comprehending 7 Hundreds and an half, entirely distinct from the Borough ; that the Steward of that Liberty was not the person to whom the precepts for electing Burgesses to serve for this Borough had at any time been directed ; nor did ever any Steward of the Liberty (which is an office enjoyd at this day by grant from the Crown) pretend to be the Returning Officer for this Borough ; that piece of evidence was dropped as utterly inapplicable to the dispute then on 'foot ; and according the Alderman is admitted to be the Returning Officer by the present petition.

N.B —That St. Edmund's Bury was not anciently a Town of any considerable note ; the inhabitants were called Homines or Vassalli Sancti

Edmundi, and generally belonged to the Abbot, who was a Lord of Parliament; but it began to increase as the Abby grew great, by whose reputation and protection it chiefly subsisted; and this is the reason no mention is made of this Town as a Borough either in Dooms-day Book or any other ancient record.

TIS therefore humbly insisted upon that the right of electing Burgesses to serve in Parliament for the said Borough depends upon the same common foundation with the rights of the greatest part of the Parliamentary Boroughs in England; which in consequence must be equally affected by any 'thing which may invalidate the effect of this Charter, or render precarious the right of Election depending thereupon, especially since the determination of Parliament has added the highest authority to the privileges of this Corporation.

APPENDIX No. 8.

List of Members for the Borough of Bury St. Edmunds from the first return to 1859.*

King's Reign.	A.D.	
12 James I.	1614.	Sir Thomas Jermyn; Robert Crane.
18 James I.	1621.	Sir Thomas Jermyn; John Woodford.
21 James I.	1624.	Sir Thomas Jermyn; Anthony Crofts.
1 Charles I.	1625.	Sir Thomas Jermyn; Sir William Spring.
1 Charles I.	1626.	Sir Thomas Jermyn; Emanuel Gifford.

* I have made out this list from a Parliamentary Return printed in 1879. My father has given a list in his History of the Hervey family. There are slight differences between the two. The names for 1614 ear in my father's list, but are not in the Parliamentary Return.—S.H.A.H.

EE

King's Reign.	A D.	
3 Charles I.	1628.	Sir Thomas Jermyn ; Sir William Hervey.
16 Charles I.	1640.	Sir Thomas Jermyn ; John Godbold, Recorder of Bury.
16 Charles I.	1640.	Sir William Spring ; Sir Thomas Barnardiston.

These two were probably elected vice Sir Thomas Jermyn and Mr. Jermyn, disabled to sit. (Commons Journals. Aug. 21, 1645.)

Cromwell.	1654.	Samuel Moodye ; John Clarke.
	1659.	John Clarke ; Thomas Chaplin.
12 Charles II.	1660.	Sir Henry Crofts ; Sir John Duncombe.
13 Charles II.	1661.	Sir John Duncombe ; Sir Edmund Poley.—Feb. 1673, William Duncombe vice Poley deceased.
31 Charles II.	1679.	Sir Thomas Hervey ; Thomas Jermyn.
31 Charles II.	1679.	Sir Thomas Hervey ; Thomas Jermyn.
33 Charles II.	1681.	Sir Thomas Hervey ; Thomas Jermyn.
1 James II.	1685.	Sir Thomas Hervey ; William Croftes.
Convention.	1689.	Sir Robert Davers ; Sir Thomas Hervey.
2 William & Mary.	1690.	Sir Robert Davers ; Henry Goldwell.—March, 1694, John Hervey vice Goldwell deceased.
7 William III.	1695.	John Hervey ; Sir Robert Davers.
10 Will : III.	1698.	Sir Robert Davers ; John Hervey.
12 Will : III.	1701.	Sir Robert Davers ; John Hervey.
13 Will : III.	1701.	John Hervey ; Sir Thomas Felton.
1 Ann.	1702.	John Hervey ; Sir Thomas Felton.—Nov. 1703, Sir Robert Davers vice Hervey called to the Upper House.
4 Ann.	1705.	Sir Thomas Felton ; Sir Robert Davers.—Dec. 1705, Aubrie Porter vice Davers, who elected to serve for the County of Suffolk.

King's Reign.	A.D.	
7 Ann.	1708.	Sir Thomas Felton; Aubrey Porter.—March 1709, Joseph Weld vice Felton deceased.
9 Ann.	1710.	Joseph Weld; Aubrey Porter.—Feb. 1712, Samuel Battely vice Weld deceased.
12 Ann.	1713.	Carr Hervey; Aubrie Porter.
1 George I.	1715.	Carr, Lord Hervey; Aubrie Porter.—May, 1717, James Reynolds vice Porter deceased.
8 George I.	1722.	James Reynolds; Jermyn Davers.—April, 1725, John Hervey vice Reynolds made a Judge.
1 George II.	1727.	John Hervey; Thomas Norton.—June, 1733, Thomas Hervey vice Hervey called to the Upper House.
8 George II.	1734.	Thomas Hervey; Thomas Norton.
15 George II.	1741.	Thomas Hervey; Thomas Norton.
21 George II.	1747.	William Stanhope, Lord Petersham; Felton Hervey.
27 George II.	1754.	Lord Petersham; Felton Hervey; Augustus John Hervey. Felton Hervey vice Augustus John Hervey, whose election was declared void.—Dec. 1756, Earl of Euston vice Lord Petersham called to the Upper House.—May, 1757, Augustus John Hervey vice Lord Euston called to the Upper House.
1 George III.	1761.	Colonel Charles Fitzroy; Augustus John Hervey. Feb. 1763, Captain William Hervey vice his brother Augustus John, who accepted the Stewardship of the Manor of Old Shoreham, Sussex.
8 George III.	1768.	Col. Charles Fitzroy; Augustus John Hervey.
15 George III.	1774.	Augustus John Hervey; Sir Charles Davers.—March 1775, Henry Seymour Conway vice Hervey called to the Upper House.
21 George III.	1780.	Sir Charles Davers; Henry Seymour Conway.

King's Reign.	A. D.	
24 George III.	1784.	Captain George Ferdinand Fitzroy ; Sir Charles Davers.—Feb. 1787, Lord Charles Fitzroy vice George F. Fitzroy who accepted the Stewardship of the Chiltern Hundreds.
30 George III.	1790.	Lord Charles Fitzroy ; Sir Charles Davers.
41 George III.	1801.	Frederick William, Lord Hervey; Sir Charles Davers.
42 George III.	1802.	Lord Charles Fitzroy; Lord Hervey.—Aug. 1803, Lord Templetown vice Hervey called to the Upper House.
47 George III.	1806.	Lord Charles Fitzroy ; Lord Templetown.
48 George III.	1807.	Lord Charles Fitzroy ; Lord Templetown.
53 George III.	1812.	Lord Charles Fitzroy ; Frederic Thomas Hervey Foster.
58 George III.	1818.	Earl of Euston ; Arthur Percy Upton.
1 George IV.	1820.	Lord John Fitzroy ; Arthur Percy Upton.
7 George IV.	1826.	Earl of Euston ; Fred William, Lord Hervey.
1 William IV.	1830.	Earl of Euston ; Earl Jermyn.
1 William IV.	1831.	Earl Jermyn ; Charles Augustus Fitzroy.
3 William IV.	1833.	Lord Charles Fitzroy ; Earl Jermyn.
5 William IV.	1835.	Earl Jermyn ; Lord Charles Fitzroy.
1 Victoria.	1837.	Lord Charles Fitzroy ; Earl Jermyn.
5 Victoria.	1841.	Earl Jermyn ; Lord Charles Fitzroy.
11 Victoria.	1847.	Earl Jermyn ; Edward Herbert Bunbury.
16 Victoria.	1852.	Earl Jermyn ; John Stuart.—Dec. 1852, James Henry Porteus Oakes vice Stuart appointed Vice Chancellor.
20 Victoria.	1857.	Earl Jermyn ; Joseph Alfred Hardcastle.—March, 1859, Lord Alfred Hervey vice Jermyn called to the Upper House.

Reign.	A.D.	
22 Victoria.	1859.	Lord Alfred Hervey ; Joseph A. Hardcastle.
29 Victoria.	1865.	Joseph A. Hardcastle ; Edward Greene.
32 Victoria.	1868.	Edward Greene ; Joseph A. Hardcastle.
37 Victoria.	1874.	Edward Greene ; Lord Francis Hervey.

WILLS.

APPENDIX No. 9.

The will (nuncupative) of John Hervey of Ickworth, who died 1630 aged about 70 years. His wife was Frances Bocking of Ash-Bocking, Co. Suffolk. His father was William Hervey of Ickworth, and his mother was Elizabeth Poley of Boxted. His eldest son was Sir William Hervey. The will is at Somerset House, 39 Audley. P.C.C.

Memorandum, that upon Satterday being the six and twentieth day of June in the yeare of our Lord God 1630, John Harvy of Ickworth in the County of Suffolk, Esquire, being of perfect minde and memory did in the tyme of his late sickness whereof he dyed and with a full minde and intent to make his will utter these words following or the like in effect ; that is to say the said Testator takeing the lease of the house and ground wherein the said Testator dwelt which he had in his possession at the tyme of his death made from Sir William Harvy Knight his sonne to him the said Testator, and holding of it in his hand, did deliver the same lease into the hands of Robert Harvy sonne of the Testator, saying, I give the this and all that I have in the world besides; saying further speaking to the said Robert, Pardon mee, Robin, I have not to bestowe on the as I would; if I had the world I would bestowe it on thee. Then Nathaniel Castericke speaking to the Testator and putting him in minde of a hundred pounds which the said Sir William Harvey did owe unto him, the said Testator said, I give it him alsoe, meaning the said one hundred pounds to the said Robert his son. And moreover the said Testator said, I have fower servants, and have nothing to give them, but there is one in Horningerth that owes me a hundred pounds ; take that among them.

Being then and there present Robert Harvey, gent ; sonne of the said Testator, and Marian his wife ; Nathaniel Casterick ; Anne Pilborough and Anne Frost.

APPENDIX No. 10.

The will of John Hervey of Ickworth, eldest son of Sir William, whose will is not at Somerset House. He married his cousin Elizabeth Hervey, and died without issue in January 1680. This will is at Somerset House, 70 Bath.

In the name of God Almighty, Amen. The eighteenth day of August, 1676, I John Hervey of Ickworth in the County of Suffolke Esq. Treasurer to the Queens most excellent Majestie that now is, being in good health, perfect mind and memory, (God be praysed) doe make this my last will and testament in manner and forme following. First I humbly resigne and present to God Almighty the Creator and preserver of all things my poore sinful soule, beseeching him threw the all sufficient meritts of his sonne Jesus Christ my alone intercessor and redeemer to receive the same into everlasting Blisse ; and for my body I doe desire it may be interred in the Chancell of the parish Church of Ickworth aforesaid where my anchesters lye, and where I doe earnestly desire my deare wife Elizabeth Hervey would alsoe be buried when it shall please God to call her out of this life. And for all my worldly goods whereof God Almighty hath abundantly blessed me above my deserts I dispose as follows after funeral charges and all my just debts fully satisfied I doe out of a tender care and pious regard to the last will and testament of my ever deare father Sir William Hervey deceased, of which he left me sole executor, will ordaine and enjoyne the executors of this my last will to have a care and see that the said last will of my said deare father fully exactly and punctually performed and fulfilled in every clause, and if there should be any debts of my said deare father unpaid (of which I know not any at present) to see them fully satisfyed. And whereas my said deare father gave unto Penelope Gage his grandchild a legacie of seaven hundred and fifty pounds to be paid upon some conditions at her time of marriage, which not haveing been performed nevertheless upon her marriage with Mr. Sullyard of Hawley in Suffolk I did pay her the legacy left her by my father as aforesaid, gave her over and above five hundred pounds more of my own bounty and love to her in remembrance of my father's recommendation of her to me, I doe by this my last will give her five hundred pounds more to be paid her within six months after the death of my dear wife, if the said Mrs. Penelope Sulyard shall be then liveing, and not else.—Alsoe I give and bequeathe unto Mary Gage one other daughter of my sister Gage deceased the sum of five hundred pounds to be paid at such time and in such manner as the legacie left her by my said dear father ought to be paid by my executors, that is within six months after her day of marriage, and not otherwise.—Alsoe I give to William Hanmer eldest son of my sister Hanmer the sume of five hundred pounds to be paid within one year of my decease, if he be then liveing, and not otherwise.—Alsoe I give to Thomas Hanmer second sonne of my said sister and now Solicitor to the Queen's Majesty the sum of five hundred pounds to be paid him in the like time of one year after my decease, if he be then liveing, and five hundred pounds more to be paid him within six months after my decease to help to support him in the study of the law, which course God blesse him in.—I also give and bequeath to Susan Tyrell the eldest daughter of my dear sister Tyrell deceased the sume of one thousand pounds to be paid her within six months after her marriage or when she shall attain the age of twenty five years, the money to remayne in my brother Sir Thomas Hervey's hands till the day of her marriage or the death of Thomas Tirell her father, Sir Thomas Hervey paying her the use for the same for her support.—I likewise give to Kezia Tirell the second daughter of my said dear sister Tirell one thousand pounds likewise to be paid her in the same manner the former thousand pounds is to be paid her sister, and not otherwise.—Alsoe I doe give and bequeathe unto my dear sister Reynolds the sume of one thousand pounds to be paid to her within six months after my decease if she be then liveing, and if not then to her sonne Robert Reynolds within six months after the decease of my dear wife, if he shall then be living and not else.—Alsoe I give and bequeathe unto my ever faithfull true and constant freind Sir John Coell of Debden Co. Suffolk Knt the sum of one hundred pounds to buy him a ring or what else he please to keep as a rememberance of my true affection and love to him.—I doe also give unto my ever faithful servant Edmond Seymour the like sum of one hundred pounds for the paines care and fidelity he has always shown in my service.—I doe alsoe give and bequeath unto my intirely beloved and ever deare wife Elizabeth Hervey all my jewells, plate, household stuffe and implements of household, only desiring her that my brother Sir Thomas Hervey may at her decease have all my gold, silver and brass medals which I here bequeath unto him after her life, that they may remayne to him and his heirs and the owners of Ickworth.—I doe also give and bequeath unto my said dear brother Sir Thomas Harvey all and singular my leases which I hold of the King's Majesty or of any Bishops, Deans and

Chapters, Bodyes Politick or Corporate or of any other person whatsoever, the same to be enjoyed by him, his executors and assignes for ever from and after the decease of my dear wife, Elizabeth Harvey, and not before, my intent and meaning being that she my dear said wife should have, hold, receive and enjoy the whole and entire benefitts, proffitts and rents of all and singular the said leases for and during her natural life, and that my said brother nor any other person whatever clayming by this my will do not meddle with nor disturb my dear said wife in the sole possession and quiet enjoyment of all the said leases and the profitts thereof during her life time, but peaceably to suffer my said dear wife without trouble or molestation to receive all the profitts and issues of the said leases soly and intirely to her own use during her natural life.—I do also give and bequeath to my dear freind the Lord Halifax twenty pounds to buy him a ring; and the like sum to my dear freind Sir John Duncombe.—I alsoe give and bequeath to every servant of myne at the time of making this my will and that shall be in my service at the time of my decease one years wadges over and above what shall then dew to them.—I doe further nominate and appoint executors of this my present will and testament my ever dear wife Elizabeth Hervey and deare brother Sir Thomas Hervey, desiring and conjuring them by the true love they ever bare me to be kind and friendly one to another in the performance of this my last will, injoyning my brother to beare the same rare respect and kindness to my wife that he would do to my selfe, and desiring her to be both kind and freindly to him and our family, of which she is a part by blood as well as marriage.—I doe further desire my ever kind freinds Henry Earl of St. Albans, Phillip Viscount Lisle, Sir John Coell Knt. and James Reynolds Esq. to be overseers of this my last will and testament, giveing to each of them fivety pounds a peece for their care and paines in seeing the same performed so farr as in them ly.—In witnes whereof I have hereunto sett my hand and seale to this my last will

FF

and testament contayned in foure sheets of paper the day and year abovesaid.
J. Hervey.

Sealed, signed and published for my last will and testament in the
presence of Jo: Coell, Edm: Seymour, Wm Masemore.

Whereas since the makeing my last will and Testament I have purchased of Mr. Abraham Story a capitall messuage with the appurtenances
scituate on the North side of St. James Square in the County of Middlesex
in the names of Sir Thomas Hervey, Sir Thomas Hanmer, Mr. James Reynolds and Mr. Thomas Coell, but in trust for me and my heirs and to be at
my dispose, I doe by this codicil (which I have annexed to my said will
and doe hereby declare to be part of my will) give and devise unto my dear
wife Elizabeth Hervey the said capitall messuage with all and singular the
appurtenances to have and to hold the same unto my said dear wife for the
terme of her natural life.   And I doe alsoe hereby give, devise and bequeath
unto my said dear wife all such household stuffs and furniture as shall be
in the said capitall messuage at my decease.—And I doe hereby give and
bequeath unto Elizabeth Manley wife of Cornelius Manley the sume of five
hundred pounds to be paid into her own hands for her own seperate use
within six months after my wife's decease, if she shall be then liveing and
not otherwise.—In witnes whereof I have sett my seale and subscribed my
name and published the same to be part of my will in the presence of the
witnesses whose names are hereunder written, August 15, 1677.   J. Hervey.

Published in the presence of Jo: Coell, William Masemore.

A codicill made December 12, 1679 to be annexed to my will bearing date
August 18, 1676, and to be taken as part thereof.

I doe hereby declare by this codicil that after my debts, funeralls and
charges about the probate of my will and the legacies sume and sumes of
mony in and by my said will and the survayors of them and the executors
of the survevor of them doe lay out the full sum of twenty thousand pounds

in the buying and purchasing manors, lands, tenements and hereditaments in fee simple either by one entire purchase or severall purchases as they shall find oportunity as soon as conveniently they can, and to settle the same or cause the same to be setled or conveyed unto or to the use of my deare wife for her life and from and after her decease to or to the use of my deare brother Sir Thomas Hervey and his heirs and assignes for ever, but untill such purchase or purchases shall be made and conveyed to the severial uses aforesaid, my will is and doe by this codicil give unto my dear sister the Lady Hanmer the sume of five hundred pounds to be paid within twelve months next after my decease. And to my nephew John Hervey, eldest son of my brother Sir Thomas Hervey, the sume of two thousand pounds; and to my nephew Thomas Hervey, my neices Isabella and Kesiah Hervey, to every of them one thousand pounds a peice: the same sumes soe given as aforesaid to my said brother's children I will shall remayne in their fathers hands untill his sonnes attaine unto their respective ages of twenty one yeares, and his daughters their respective ages of twenty yeares or days of marriage, their father to take the benefitt that he can make thereof in the meane time for and towards their maintenance and education. I doe further give and bequeathe unto my servants Mr. Hall and Mrs. Hall to each of them one hundred pounds, and to my servant William Chamber the sum of four score pounds, and to Mrs. Edgar the yearly sume of twenty pounds dureing her life. The rest and residue of my personal estate that shall remayne after debts, legacies, funeralls, sume and sumes of money in or by my said will, this codicill, or any other codicill annexed or to be annexed to my said will, be satisfied and discharged, I give unto my dear brother Sir Thomas Hervey.

In witnes whereof I have sett my seale and subscribed my name and published the same to be part of my will in the presence of the witnesses whose names are hereunto written the day and year above written. J. Hervey.

Signed, sealed and published in the presence of Apsley, Jo : Coell William Jevers, Edm : Seymour.

This will was proved with one codicill in P.C.C. at London Feb. 14, 1679, by Sir Thomas Hervey Knt, the brother and an executor nominated in the will, to whom administration was granted; power reserved to make like grant to Elizabeth Hervey the relict.

Proved at London with two codicills June 3, 1680, by Elizabeth Hervey the relict and executrix.

APPENDIX No. 11.

The will of Sir Thomas Hervey, Knight, son of Sir William Hervey, and father of John, 1st Lord Bristol. He died 1694, æt. 69 years. This will is at Somerset House, 127 Box.

The last will and testament of Sir Thomas Harvey of Ickworth in the County of Suffolke Knt written with my own hand the fifth day of October in the yeare of our Lord God 1689.—Whereas my brother Mr. John Harvey by a codicill made Dec. 12, 1679, to be annexed to his last will bearing date Aug. 18, 1676, and to be taken as parte thereof, did give unto my now daughter Elwes by the name of Mrs. Isabella Harvey one thousand pounds, now my will is that my executor pay unto her the said one thousand pounds, and seaven thousand pounds more, in all eight thousand pounds, in full of her pencion money.—To my grandson Thomas Porter for the love I beare to his mother I add to the thousand pounds given to her by my brother Mr. Harvey (as witnesseth the foresaid codicill) by the name of Mrs. Keziah Harvey three thousand pounds, in all four thousand pounds, and noe more for this reason, that in her life time I was out for her on severial scores above one thousand pounds.—To my younger son Thomas Harvey his thousand pounds given to him in like manner I give foure thousand pounds more, in all five thousand pounds, to be paid to him by my executor within six months after my decease.—I give unto my dearest grandchild Mrs. Isabella Elwes one thousand pounds to be put out to interest in her name and to her sole use, the interest to goe towards her maintenance untill she be eighteen yeares of age, and then the said thousand pounds to be paid into her (hands) as an addition to her pencion for the love that I beare unto her, as alsoe for the great affection my dearest wife had for her. But in case the said Isabella Elwes my grandaughter shall happen to departe this life before she shall have attained to eighteen yeares of age, then my will and meaning is that the said thousand pounds shall revert to my executor and his heires male for ever.—I give unto my deare daughter Elwes the relict of Gervas Elwes Esq. the use of my house I now live in scituate in the streete knowne by the name of School Hall Street in St. Edmonds Bury, together with all the plate, household stuffe and implements of household during the terme of her naturall life, and after all to my executor and his heirs male for ever.—As for the four thousand above mentioned to be given to my grandson Thomas Porter, my will and meaning is that it be under the limitations following and not otherwise, that is to say that the four thousand pounds doe remaine in the hands of my executor untill the said Thomas Porter shall have attained eighteene yeares of age, or by him put out at interest in the meane time, that the increase thereof may go and be laid out for the education of him the said Thomas Porter; but if it shall happen that he the said Thomas Porter shall dye before that he shall attaine to eighteene years of age, then the principall money of foure thousand pounds doe revert to my executor his use and to his heires male for ever.—To John Poole I give twenty pounds.—To the use of the poor of each parish in St. Edm: Bury ten pounds.—I doe hereby constitute, nominate and appoint my eldest son John

Harvey Esq. to be executor of this my last will and testament, and I doe give unto him and his heires male the residue of my estate real and personal, and alsoe all my copyhold lands, he paying my debts and legacies above mentioned, and not failing to see me buryed or by his direction causeing my corpes to be laid in the same grave with my dearest wife and buried in lynnen.—In witnesse whereof I have hereunto sett my hand and seale the day and yeare above written.   Tho: Harvey.

Memorandum.   The words *male* in the first sheet, and the words *male and his heirs male* in this sheet were by me interlined before the sealing and publishing hereof.   Signed, sealed and published to be my last will and testament in the presence of Cha: Crofte Reade, Edm: Cosman, John Wadkin.

Proved at London in P.C.C. June 26, 1694, by John the son and executor nominated, to whom administration was granted.

APPENDIX No. 12.

The will of Elizabeth Hervey, widow of the above John Hervey. She died abroad in 1700, and was buried, not at Ickworth, as her husband had desired in his will, but at Lee in Kent, on April 25, 1700. This will is at Somerset House, 75, Noel.

In the name of God, Amen. I Dame Elizabeth Hervey, widow and relict of John Hervey late of Ickworth in the County of Suffolke Esq. deceased, do make this my last will and testament in manner following, that is to say, Whereas by my deed bearing date on or about the second day of March, in the two and thirtieth year of the reign of his now Majesty King Charles the second, reciting that I was then possessed of and interested in divers goods, chattles and personal estate as one of the executors of the said John Hervey, to the end and for the consideration and upon the trust therein mentioned I did bargain and sell unto Thomas Hall then one of my meniall servants the said goods, chattles and personal estate and all goods, chattles, leases for years and personall estate of what kind soever to me belonging either in my owne right or as one of the executors as aforesaid or as executrix or administratrix to any person or persons; and whereas the said Thomas Hall hath behaved himselfe and dealt unfaithfully and treacherously with me as touching the said goods; Now my desire and will is that in case I do not in my life time that my executors hereinafter named do call the said Thomas Hall to an accompt for the said goods, and receive or recover the same from the said Thomas Hall or any other persons or person in whose hands or custody the same shall be. And my will is that my said executors pay such money as I shall owe or give away. And I make the Hon. Ralph Mountague Esq. son and heir apparent of the right honble Edward Lord Mountague of Boughton in County of Northampton, and the honble Dame Elizabeth Hervey widow and relict of Sir Daniell Hervey knt and one of the daughters of the said Lord Mountague, my executors in case I do not hereafter revoke this my will and make some other disposition to the contrary.

In witness whereof I have hereunto set my hand and seal the fifth day of November, in the three and thirtieth of his said now Majesties reign, A.D. 1681.   E. Hervey.

Signed, sealed and published by the above named Dame Elizabeth Hervey to be her last will and testament in the presence of Mary Page, Henry Baker, Cha: Bland, Fran: Cane.

Proved in the P.C.C. at London May 11, 1700, by the most honble and noble Ralph Earl of Mountague and the honble Dame Elizabeth Hervey the executors nominated in the testament, to whom administration was granted.

APPENDIX No. 13.

The will of Elizabeth, 2nd wife of John, Earl of Bristol. She was only child to Sir Thomas Felton, and died in 1741 aged 64 years. This will is at Somerset House, 114, Spurway.

In the name of God, Amen.—I Elizabeth Countess of Bristol, wife of the Right Honourable John Earl of Bristol, in pursuance of certain powers given to me by my dear lord and husband and of all and every power and powers me thereunto enabling, do make and ordain this to be my last will and testament for the disposition of such estates real and personal whereof I have power to dispose in manner and form following; that is to say, I do hereby give, devise and bequeath all that my messuage or dwelling house in Saint Edmonds Bury in the County of Suffolk with the gardens, orchards, outhouses, yards and appurtenances thereto belonging in as large and ample manner as the same is now enjoyed or used by me and my said dear lord and husband, and the use of all the plate, goods, pictures, china and furniture which now is or are or shall be therein at the time of my decease of whatsoever kind the same be (except my gilt etoilet and all the furniture and things thereunto belonging) unto my dear lord and husband for and during the term of his natural life, he signing a memorandum at the bottom of an inventory of my said goods, plate, pictures, china and furniture that his executors or administrators shall be accountable for such goods and furniture at his death, the reasonable use and wear thereof excepted, and immediately from and after his decease I do hereby give and devise my said house with the gardens etc. and the use of all my goods, plate, pictures, china and furniture unto my youngest son the Honourable Felton Hervey Esq. for and during his natural life; and from and immediately after the determination of that estate unto the Honourable Busby Mansell of Briton Ferry in the County of Glamorgan Esquire and John Howell of Lincoln's Inn in the County of Middlesex gentleman and their heirs during the life of the said Felton Hervey in trust to preserve the contingent remainders herein after limitted from being defeated and destroyed, and for that purpose to make entrys and bring action as occasions shall require, yet nevertheless to permit and suffer my said son Felton Hervey to hold and enjoy my said house, gardens and premises for and during his natural life; and immediately from and after the decease of my said son Felton Hervey unto the first son of my said son Felton Hervey lawfully to be begotten and the heirs male of the body of such first son lawfully issueing;* in default of such issue to every other son of the said Felton Hervey lawfully to be begotten severally, successively and in remainder one after another in order and course as they shall be in priority of birth and seniority of age, and the several heirs male of such sons; and in default of such issue unto my son the Honourable Thomas Hervey Esq for and during his natural life; and after the decease of my said son Thomas Hervey to his first son and heirs male; in default to his second and other sons and their heirs male; in default of such issue unto my son the Honourable William Hervey Esq. (etc. etc. as above); in default of such issue unto my son the Honourable and Reverend Charles Hervey Esq. (etc. etc. as above;) in default of such issue unto my son the Honourable Henry Hervey Esq. (etc. etc. as above); in default of such issue unto my grandson the Honourable Augustus John Hervey, (second son of my eldest son the Right Honourable John Lord Hervey, Lord Privy Seal,) (etc. etc. as above); and in default of such issue unto my own right heirs for ever, provided always nevertheless and it is my true intent and meaning that each and every of my said sons and also my said grandson as they shall respectively come into the possession of my said

---

* Here for brevity's sake I leave off giving the ipsissima verba of the will.—S.H.A.H.

GG

house, gardens and premises by vertue of this my will shall have the use of all my said goods, plate, pictures, china and furniture for their lives respectively, and shall respectively sign such memorandum as is herein before mentioned at the bottom of an inventory of all my said goods etc., to be accountable for the same from time to time, that so the goods etc. may from time to time go along with my said house and premises as heir looms and as belonging thereunto, and shall be reputed to be part and parcel thereof; and in case any of my said sons or said grandson shall refuse or neglect to sign such inventory, then in such case the devise and limitations herein before mentioned for his and their benefit respectively and for the benefit of his and their respective heirs male shall cease and be utterly void and of none effect; and it is my request and desire that all the issue male of my said sons and grandson to whom the said premises are hereby limitted do and shall add or have added to their Christian names the name of Felton in remembrance of my family. It is also my will and desire that my said younger sons and grandson and their issue male to whom my said messuage in Bury shall go and belong by virtue of this my will shall keep and use the same for their own residence, and not let the same to any tennant.—I also give unto my said dear lord and husband my large emerald ring, which I intreat him to wear for my sake; and I give to my daughter the Right Honourable the Lady Ann Hervey my said gilt etoilet herein before excepted, and all the furniture and things thereunto belonging. I also give to my said daughter the Lady Ann that snuff box with her father's picture in it ; and to my daughter the Lady Louisa Carolina Isabella Smith my ring with my lord's picture, and another ring set with the late Queen's hair, as also the said Queen's picture now in my house at Bury. And I do hereby give all the rest of my jewels, watches and rings unto my trustees and executors to sell and dispose of and apply the produce thereof as part of the residue of my estate hereby devised. I also give to my said eldest son the Lord Hervey my cabinet chest, large skreen and small skreen being white japan of my own work, in confidence that he will preserve them for my sake.—And I do hereby give, devise and bequeath unto my said son Felton Hervey and to the Right Honble Sir Thomas Hanmer of Milden Hall in the said County of Suffolk, Baronet, their executors and administrators, all my ready money and all securitys for money in any wise belonging unto me, and all other my personal estate of what nature or kind soever not herein before given and devised upon trust that they shall thereout raise to and for my said grandaughter Elizabeth Hervey, eldest daughter of my said son Henry Hervey, the sum of one thousand pounds to be paid at her age of twenty one years or day of marriage, which shall first happen, provided such marriage shall be had with the consent of my said dear lord and of my executors, or the major part of them, or of the survivor of them if living; and it is my will that my said trustees shall place out the said one thousand pounds upon good Government or other good security or securities and pay the interest and produce of the said one thousand pounds towards my said grandaughter's maintenance and education; and it is my request to my dear lord that my said grandaughter may be under his care untill her age of twenty one years or her marriage as aforesaid; but if my said grandaughter shall die before her age of twenty one years or marry without such consent, in either case it is my will that the said one thousand pounds shall be applied as the residue of my personal estate is hereafter directed to be applied; and I do further desire my said trustees to lay out the money arising by the sale of my diamond ear ring and all the rest of my personal estate above devised to them in a purchase of freehold lands, tenements or hereditaments in Suffolk in as advantageous a manner as can be done, and that the same be settled to the use of my said son Felton Hervey for his life, with like remainders and limitations as my said house in St. Edmonds Bury, and to place out such residue of my said personal estate in the mean time at interest upon Government or other sufficient security, and to pay the interest thereof to my said son Felton Hervey, and such persons as will after him in succession be entitled to the lands & hereditaments when purchased.—And I do hereby constitute and appoint my said son Felton Hervey and the said Sir Thomas Hanmer executors of this my last will and testament, hereby revoking all former wills by me at any time heretofore made, and declare this to be my last will and testament; and I do hereby declare it shall be lawful for my said trustees and executors from time to time to pay and reimburse themselves out of my said estates all such costs, charges and expences which they shall at any time be put unto in respect of the trust hereby in them reposed. In witness whereof I the said Elizabeth Countess of Bristol have to this my last will and testament contained in four sheets of paper set my hand and seal this fifth day of December, 1740. E. Bristol.

Signed, sealed etc. in the sight and presence of us, who in her sight and presence and at her request have attested the same.

Samuel Brentnall. Ed. Day. John Edwardes.

Proved at London in the P.C.C. May 8, 1741 by the oath of the Honourable Felton Hervey Esq., the son and one of the executors nominated to whom admon was granted. Power reserved to make like grant to Sir Thomas Hanmer, Bart. when he shall apply for the same.

APPENDIX No. 14.

The will of John Hervey, 1st Earl of Bristol.   This is at Somerset House, 38 *Busby.*

In the name of God, Amen. I John Earl of Bristol, being in good health considering my great age (being now in my eighty sixth year) and in perfect mind and memory (God be praised), hereby revoking and making void all former and other wills by me at any time heretofore made, do make, publish and declare my last will and testament of the same tenor and date with duplicate hereof executed at the same time with these presents and before the same witnesses.—In the first place I will and devise that all my just debts and legacies hereby given be duly paid and discharged, and to that end I do hereby give, devise and bequeath all my castles, manors, messuages, farmes, lands, tenements and hereditaments whatsoever wherein I or any person or persons in trust for me have or hath any estate in fee simple as well within the several counties of Lincoln and Suffolk as elsewhere in England unto Sir William Bunbury of Mildenhall in the said County of Suffolk, Baronet, and my son in law Sir Robert Smith, Baronet, their executors, administrators and assigns, from and after my decease for the term of five hundred years from thence next ensuing, without impeachment of waste upon special trust and confidence and to the intent and purposes and subject to the determination herein expressed, limited and declared of and concerning the same term, and from and after the expiration or other sooner determination of that estate, and subject thereunto and to the several powers, provisoes and appointments hereinafter declared, limited and contained, I give, devise and bequeath all the said castles etc., and also all and singular my copyhold of inheritance in the said counties of Lincoln and Suffolk or elsewhere in England unto my most beloved grandson George William Lord Hervey and his assigns for and during the term of his natural life without impeachment of waste ; and from and after the determination of that estate unto the Right Honourable James Earl of Northampton and the Right Honourable Lyonel Earl of Dysert and their heirs during the life of the said George William Lord Hervey upon trust to preserve the contingent uses and estates hereinafter limited from being defeated or destroyed, and for that purpose to make entries or bring actions as occasion shall require, yet nevertheless to permit and suffer the said George William Lord Hervey and his assigns to receive and take the rents, issues and profits thereof for and during his natural life ;* with remainder to his sons lawfully begotten and to their sons ; in default of such unto my grandson Augustus John Hervey, brother of the said Lord Hervey, and his sons ; in default of such unto my grandson Frederick Hervey, brother of the said Augustus John, etc.; with remainder to my grandson William Hervey brother of the said Frederick, etc. ; with remainder successively to my son Thomas Hervey, to my grandson William son of said Thomas and his sons, to other sons of Thomas that may be begotten, to my son William Hervey, to his sons that may be begotten, & their sons, to my grandson Henry Hervey Aston son of my son Henry Hervey otherwise Aston, to his son to be begotten and his son, to my son the Reverend Doctor Charles Hervey, to his son, to my son Felton Hervey & his sons, and in default of such to my own right heirs for ever. And I do hereby will and declare that the estate and term hereby devised to the said Sir William Bunbury and Sir Robert Smyth as aforesaid is so devised to them upon trust and to the intent in the first place that they do and shall by sale or mortgage of such part or parts of my said castles, manors etc. as to them shall seem convenient and shall be sufficient for that purpose (except only my mansion house, park and estate at Ickworth aforesaid) pay and discharge all my just debts whatsoever and also the sum of two thousand pounds hereinafter mentioned to be bequeathed to my said son Charles Hervey upon certain contingencies (if those contingencies happen and the said sum shall be to be raised at all) pursuant to my intent and meaning hereinafter declared ; and likewise the legacy of four thousand pounds hereinafter bequeathed to my said son Felton Hervey ; and upon this further trust, that they, the said Sir William

---

* Here I abbreviate and condense. — S.H.A.H.

Bunbury and Sir Robert Smyth, their executors etc., do and shall by and out of the rents, issues and profits of the residue of the premises over and above what shall be sufficient for the payment of my debts and legacies as aforesaid raise and pay to my son Thomas Hervey and his assigns for the term of his natural life one annuity or yearly sum of two hundred pounds free and clear from all parliamentary and other taxes, payments and deductions whatsoever which are or may hereafter be charged or chargeable upon such annuities by any Act of Parliament heretofore made or hereafter to be made or otherwise howsoever by four equal quarterly payments in every year upon the feast days commonly called Christmas day, Lady day, Midsummer day and Michaelmas day, the first payment thereof to be made upon such of the said feast days as shall first and next happen after my death; and also shall raise and pay unto my said son Charles Hervey and his assigns for and during his natural life (if the sum of two thousand pounds herein before and after mentioned shall not in the mean time become payable, and if the said sum of two thousand pounds shall in the mean time become payable, then until such time as the said sum of two thousand pounds shall become payable,) one annuity or yearly sum of one hundred pounds clear of all deductions for Parliament taxes or otherwise howsoever by four equal quarterly payments upon the several feast days hereinbefore mentioned, the first payment thereof to be made upon such of the said feast days as shall first and next happen after my decease; and I do hereby will, give and bequeath unto my said son Charles Hervey the sum of two thousand pounds to be raised by my said trustees as before mentioned at such time and upon such conditions as are hereafter mentioned and not otherwise, that is to say in case the said Charles Hervey shall have any issue by Martha Maria his present wife that shall survive him the said Charles, then from and immediately after the death of the said Charles Hervey the said sum of two thousand pounds shall be raised and paid unto

such of the said issue and in such proportions as the said Charles Hervey
by his last will and testament in writing or by any other writing for that
purpose signed in the presence of two or more credible witnesses shall
direct and appoint; and for want of such directions or appointment unto
and among all and every the sons and daughters of the said Charles and
Martha Maria and their respective issues then surviving equally to be divided
among them per stripes and not per capita; or in case the said Martha
Maria shall depart this life without leaving any issue by the said Charles, or
such issue should afterwards depart this life during the life of the said
Charles, and the said Charles should after the decease of the said Martha
Maria and such issue (if any such issue there shall be) take unto him a
second wife, that then forthwith upon such second marriage the said sum
of two thousand pounds be raised and paid, applied, laid out, settled or
secured in such manner for the benefit of the said Charles and such second
wife and the issue of such second marriage as by the Councel of the said
Charles and such second wife by and with the direction and approbation of
the said George William, Lord Hervey, shall be thought most meet, secure
and expedient; and from and after the raising and paying of the said sum
of two thousand pounds as aforesaid the annuity of one hundred pounds
hereinbefore given to the said Charles Hervey for his life from henceforth to
cease and be no longer payable.. And I do hereby will, give and bequeath
unto my said son Felton Hervey the sum of four thousand pounds to be
raised and paid by my said trustees as herein before mentioned as soon as
conveniently may be after my decease, with interest for the said sum of four
thousand pounds after the rate of four pounds by the year for every one
hundred pound from the time of my decease until the said principal sum
shall be paid unto him, his executors etc. And it is my further will and I
do hereby declare that the said term of five hundred years so as aforesaid
limited to the said Sir William Bunbury and Sir Robert Smith is upon this

further trust, that they do and shall by and out of the rents, issues and profits of the residue of the premises over and above what shall be sufficient for the payment of my debts and legacies as aforesaid raise and pay to my daughter Ann Hervey and her assigns for and during the term of her natural life one annuity or yearly sum of six hundred pounds free and clear from all parliamentary and other taxes, payments and deductions whatsoever which are or may hereafter be charged or chargeable upon such annuities by any Act of Parliament heretofore made or hereafter to be made or otherwise howsoever by four equal quarterly payments in every year upon the feast days commonly called Christmas day, Lady day, Midsummer day and Michaelmas day, the first payment thereof to be made upon such of the said feast days as shall happen first or next after my decease ; which said annuity I have made the larger in consideration of the bad share of health my said daughter is now in, and finding by experience that the daily use of taking the air in a coach hath very much contributed to the improvement of her health, and the better to enable her to support and maintain herself in the way she now is.—And also shall raise and pay unto Mrs. Mary Williams who lived many years with my late dear wife as her waiting woman and behaved herself to my said wife as the most faithful and excellent servant that ever was, and as my said dear wife earnestly desired me to make some provision for her, the said Mrs. Williams, in case she should happen to survive me, I do therefore give unto her and her assigns for the term of her natural life one annuity or yearly sum of one hundred pounds free and clear etc. (as above) by four equal quarterly payments etc. (as above).—And also shall raise and pay unto John Goodall my servant who is immediately attendant upon my person for his faithful services one annuity or yearly sum of fifty pound free and clear etc. by four equal quarterly payments etc.—And shall also raise and pay to my nurses Mary Spencer, widow, and Sarah the wife of Henry Everard, and to my

HH

coachman Thomas Hervey, respectively the several annuities or yearly sums of five pounds a piece during their respective natural lives free etc.—And I do hereby declare that the said term of five hundred years so as aforesaid limited to the said Sir William Bunbury and Sir Robert Smyth is upon this further trust, that such person or persons respectively to whom the next immediate reversion or remainder of the same premisses expectant upon the determinations of the same term shall for the time being belong shall and may receive the residue and overplus of all the profits of the premises comprised in the same term over and above what shall be sufficient to answer, pay and satisfye the several other trusts, annuities and payments hereinbefore and hereinafter appointed, directed and declared of concerning the same term, and also that when and so soon as all and every the said other trusts, annuities and payments herein declared of and concerning the same term shall be fully answered, paid and satisfied then and from thenceforth all the said term of and in the premises or so much and such part thereof as shall then remain or be unsold or undisposed of according to the true intent and meaning of this my will shall cease, determine and be utterly void, anything hereinbefore contained to the contrary notwithstanding; and I do hereby likewise declare that my said trustees or either of them, their executors or administrators, shall not be charged or chargeable with or accountable for the acts or omissions of the other of them, or with any sum or sums of money besides what they or either of them respectively shall actually receive, or for any loss or losses that may happen in the execution of their trust without their or either of their privity or wilfull neglect or default, and that they shall respectively be paid and satisfied out of the rents, issues and profits of the premises comprised in the said term all such losts (sic) charges and expences as they or either of them shall necessarily and reasonably sustain or be put unto for and by reason of all or any of the trusts hereby reposed in them.   And I do hereby further will, declare, limit and appoint that it shall and may be lawfull for my said grandson, George William, Lord Hervey, and for all and every other person and persons to whom any estate for life or greater estate of and in the castles, manors, lands, hereditaments and premisses hereby given, devised or limited when and at such time as he and every of them respectively shall be in the actual possession of the same premisses or any part thereof by indenture or indentures under his and their respective hands and seals respectively to limit and appoint any part or parts of the premisses so in his or their actual possession (other than and excepting my mansion house, parks and estate at Ickworth aforesaid) unto and to the use of any woman or women that he or they shall respectively marry for the life or lives of such woman or women as and for a jointure or jointures ; so, nevertheless, that the manors, lands, and hereditaments so as aforesaid to be limited and appointed do not exceed the yearly value of eighty pounds for every one thousand that such person so limiting and appointing shall and do actually receive for the portion of such woman or women respectively. And I do hereby likewise will, limit and declare that it shall and may be lawfull to and for the said Lord Hervey and all and every the persons aforesaid when and at such time as he or they respectively shall be in the actual possession of the premisses or any part thereof pursuant to this my will to demise or leave by deed or deeds indented to be executed in the presence of two or more credible witnesses any part or parts of the premisses so in his or their actual possession (except my mansion house, park and estate at Ickworth) unto any person or persons for any term or number of years not exceeding twenty one years to commence in possession and not in remainder, reserving upon every such lease the best improved yearly rent that can be reasonably had for the several lands and hereditaments to be comprised in every such respective lease without taking any fine or other consideration to abate the rent, and so as no such lease shall be made dispunishable of waste, and that in every such lease there be contained a clause of re-entry for nonpayment of the rent or rents to be thereby respectively reserved, and that the lessees do execute counterparts thereof.—And whereas upon the marriage of my said son William Hervey with Elizabeth the daughter of Thomas Ridge Esq. since deceased, by certain articles indented bearing date on or about the 24th day of November which was in the year of our Lord 1729, and made between my self of the first part, the said Thomas Ridge of the second part, my son Thomas Hervey and Thomas Ayles of the City of London, Merchant, of the third part, and the said William Hervey and Elizabeth Ridge of the fourth part, I did covenant for the payment of three thousand pounds within twelve months after my decease by my heirs, executors or administrators to the said Thomas Hervey and Thomas Ayles as trustees for the purposes of the said articles expressed, by which articles amongst other things I likewise covenanted for the payment of interest for the said sum of three thousand pounds after the rate of four pounds by the year for every one hundred pounds unto my said son William Hervey from the time of the celebration of the said marriage until the said three thousand pounds shall be actually paid in case my said son William should so long live ; and whereas the said marriage was duly solemnized, and the said Elizabeth is since deceased, leaving no other child but one daughter by my said son William, so that pursuant to the terms of the said articles and the true intent and meaning of all the parties thereunto in case the said sum of three thousand pounds should be raised by my trustees, the said Sir William Bunbury and Sir Robert Smyth, and paid to the said Thomas Hervey and Thomas Ayles for the purposes in the said articles mentioned, the same sum or the produce thereof according to the purport of the said articles from and after the decease of the said William Hervey would be to be repaid or assigned and transferred to such person or persons as I should either by deed or my last will executed in the presence of three or more credible witnesses direct or appoint, and for want of such direction or appointment to my executors or administrators ; now I do hereby direct and appoint, if the said sum of three thousand pounds shall be raised and paid to the said Thomas Hervey and Thomas Ayles pursuant to the terms of the said marriage articles, that immediately from and after the decease of my said son William the said sum of three thousand pounds or the pioduce thereof shall by the said Thomas Hervey and Thomas Ayles or the survivor of them or the executors or administrators of such survivor by and with the approbation and consent of the owner or owners of Ickworth Park aforesaid for the time being be conveyed and settled to and for such uses and estates and in such manner and for the benefit of such persons successively as I have limited and devised my freehold estate unto in and by this my will ; but if my said son William shall think fit to waive the raising of the said principal sum of three thousand pounds, and shall be willing to accept of interest for the said sum after the rate before mentioned during his natural life, and signify such his intention and willingness by writing under his hand within twelve months after my decease, which I recommend him to do as most for the ease of all the trustees and for the common benefit of my family in general, then and in that case I do hereby will and declare that the said term of five hundred years hereby given and devised to the said Sir William Bunbury and Sir Robert Smyth is so given and devised to them upon this further trust, that they do and shall out of the rents, issues and profits of the before mentioned residue of the premisses remaining unsold raise and pay unto my said son William Hervey so much as shall from time to time become due to him for the interest aforesaid during the term of his natural life ; and in that case I do will and appoint that the said principal sum of three thousand pounds shall not be raised out of my real estate, but shall wholly sink into the same for the benefit of the several devisees of my said real estate before mentioned successively and according to their several estates and interests therein pursuant to the true intent and meaning of this my will : and direct that my funeral shall be as private as possible, and free from all manner of pomp and unnecessary expences; and I give and bequeath unto the poor of the two parishes of Bury St. Edmunds in the County of Suffolk two hundred pounds, that is to say one hundred pounds to each parish, to be disposed of to the worthiest objects of charity within each parish respectively at the discretion of my very good friends the Alderman and Burgesses of the said town for the time being.— And likewise I give and bequeath unto the poor of the parish of Ickworth aforesaid the sum of fifty pounds to be laid out and disposed of at the dis- cretion of my executor in placing out ten poor children of the same parish apprentices to trades. Also I give and bequeath unto the said James, Earl of Northampton, and Lyonel, Earl of Dysert, Sir William Bunbury and Sir Robert Smith, one hundred pounds apiece to buy them rings in remem- brance of me.—Also I give to the said Mrs. Mary Williams the further sum of two hundred pounds towards furnishing her house at Bury which I lately gave her.—Also I give to Jane Tuer and Ann Guilliam my servant one hundred pounds a piece ; and to Clomdia D'Assanville, now servant to my two grandaughters, daughters of the late Lord Hervey deceased, one hundred pounds for her better incouragement to serve my said grandaughters faithfully.—Also I give to my servant Sarah Barnett thirty pounds, and to Elizabeth How, wife of Stephen How of Norton, who was formerly my servant, ten pounds.—Also I give to all the servants who shall be in my service at the time of my death, including the stewards of my Lin- colnshire and Shropshire estates, one years more than shall be then due to them respectively, and mourning; and subject only to the payment of my funeral expences, the expence of proving this my will, and the payment of the several legacies herein mentioned subsequent to the mentioning of the aforesaid small life annuities of five pounds a piece, I give and bequeath unto my said most beloved grandson George William, Lord Hervey, his executors, administrators and assigns, all my leasehold estates, and all my goods, chattels, cattle, books, medals, pictures, plate, jewels and personal estate whatsoever, to his and their sole use and benefit, subject only as aforesaid, and I do constitute and appoint him sole executor of this my last will and testament.

In witness whereof I the said John Earl of Bristol have to this my last will and testament contained in three skins of parchment affixed together at the bottom set my hand and seal the first day of December, in the year of our Lord Christ 1750. Bristol.   Signed, sealed etc. in the presence of us who have subscribed our names as witnesses thereof in the presence and at the request of the said testator, John Symonds, Edwd. Is. Jackson, Thomas Knowles, Joshua Grigby.

Proved at London in the P.C.C. Feb. 23, 1750, by the oath of the Right Hon. George William, Earl of Bristol and Lord Hervey, the grandson of the deceased and sole executor nominated in the will, to whom admon was granted.

APPENDIX No. 15.

This is a list of Hervey portraits which enter into John, Lord Bristol's Book of Expences. (See p.p, 159—164.) I have given painter, size, destination, date and price where I can. On comparing this list with the next (Appendix No. 16), it will be seen how many of them I have not been able to trace. One wonders where they all are now. Perhaps hanging up somewhere with no name, or a wrong one, attached to them. If every portrait had the name of the subject put plainly upon it as soon as it was painted, this would not be possible.

PORTRAITS OF JOHN HERVEY, EARL OF BRISTOL. Nos. 1 to 12.

1. Painted by Dixon; for " dear wife"; in 1689; £17..7..0 being the price.

2. By Lens ye limner; a ring picture; in 1712 ; £5..7..6 being paid for it and No 22 together.

3. A copy by Mrs. Brown; half length ; for Carr Hervey to send to Aswarby; in 1717; £12..10 being paid for it & Nos. 4 & 25 together.

4. A copy by Mrs. Brown ; 3 quarters ; for Ickworth ; in 1717.

5. A copy by Mrs. Ann Howard; for Jack ; in 1720 ; £5.

6. A copy by Fayram ; for " Saint Squire"; in 1733; £2..10..0. Mrs. Squire was a servant of Lady Bristol's, whom, ironically or otherwise, he canonizes.

7. A copy by J. Fayram ; for Lady Bristol ; in 1738; £7..17..6 for it with Nos. 47 & 49.

8. 9. 10. Copies by Fayram; one a half length, the other two 3 quarters; in 1738; £7..17..6 for the three.

11. A copy by Enoch Seemans; whole length; in 1738; ten guineas.

12. Copy by Fayram; for my son Felton; in 1741; £3..13..6.
    See also Letter to Mrs. Manley, No. 503.

ISABELLA, 1ST WIFE OF JOHN HERVEY. NOS. 13 to 17.

13. By Joseph Brook, the Bury painter; in 1690; £10.

14. A copy by Henry Peart of Mrs. Fox's picture; in 1693; £10.

15. By Mr. Cross ye limner; in 1693; £16..5..0.

16. By late Mr. Peart; bought of his son in 1731 for 3 guineas.

17. A copy by Fayram; in 1742; £3..13..6.

ELIZABETH, 2ND WIFE OF JOHN HERVEY. NOS. 18 to 27.

18. By Daula; 3 quarters; in 1700; £10..15..0.

19. By Charles D'Agar; with ye twins; in 1709; 22 guineys.

20. A copy by Bernard Lens; in 1711; £5..7..6.

21. By Michael Dahl ye Swedish painter; in 1711; £21..10.

22. By Lens ye limner; a ring picture; in 1712; see No. 2.

23. By Lentz ye limner; with Felton; in 1714; £8..12.

24. By Hyssing (Hans Hyssen?); for the Countess of Pickbourg alias Bucenburgh; in 1715; £6..9..0.

II

25. A copy by Mrs. Brown; half length; for Carr Hervey to send to Aswarby; in 1717; see No. 3.

26. A copy by Joseph Brook of picture by Daule; half length; in 1725; 5 guineas.

27. A copy by Enoch Seemans; whole length; in 1738; 10 guineas.

JOHN, LORD HERVEY. NOS. 28 to 32.

28. By John Fayram; half length; in 1728; £7.

29. A copy by Fayram; for Mr. Winnington; in 1728; 4 guineas.

30. A copy by Fayram; 3 quarters; in 1736; 2 guineas.

31. A copy in crayon by Knapton of picture by Fayram ; for Lady Hervey; in 1737; 8 guineas.

32. A copy by Fayram; half length; in 1737; £3..10. 0.

MARY, LADY HERVEY.

33. A copy by Fayram of picture by Kneller; in 1729; 7 guineas with No. 41.

LORD BRISTOL'S CHILDREN. NOS. 34 to 45.

34. Ye 7 children ; by Brook of Bury; in 1701; £5..7.6. It is not clear whether this is a group, or seven different pictures.

35. Tom ; by Richardson ; for Mr. Harcourt ; in 1720; 24 guineas.

36. Tom ; by Fayram ; for Mr. Folkes, his Oxford tutor ; in 1727 ; with frame 10 guineas.

37. do ; by Fayram ; in 1728 ; £7.

38. William ; by Fayram ; in 1735 ; 5 guineas.

39. Felton ; by Brook ; in 1716 ; £8..12 with Nos. 44 & 53.

40. do ; by Fayram ; in 1734 ; £7.

41. Betty (Lady Elizabeth Mansel) ; a copy by Fayrum of picture by Richardson ; in 1729 ; 7 guineas with No. 33.

42. Ann ; by Brook ; in 1709 ; £2..10.

43. do ; by Fayram ; half length ; in 1728 ; £7.

44. Louisa ; by Brook ; in 1716 ; see No. 39.

45. do ; bought of Penelope, widow of Charles Jarvis ; in 1740 ; 13 guineas.

SIR THOMAS HERVEY.

46. A copy by Henry Pert of picture by Brook ; in 1690 ; £10.

47. A copy by Fayram ; for Lady Bristol ; in 1738 ; see No. 7.

ISABELLA, WIFE OF SIR THOMAS HERVEY.

48. A copy by Fayram ; in 1735 ; 5 guineas.

49. A copy by Fayram ; for Lady Bristol ; in 1738 ; see No. 7.

SIR THOMAS FELTON, FATHER TO LADY BRISTOL.

50.   By Sir Godfrey Kneller; in 1699; with frame £35.

51.   Copy by Fayram; for Lady Bristol; in 1737; with No. 52 £7.

LADY FELTON, MOTHER TO LADY BRISTOL.

52.   Copy by Fayram; for Lady Bristol; in 1737; with No. 51 £7.

WENN, A FAMOUS RACE HORSE OF LORD BRISTOL'S.

53.   By Brook; in 1716; see No. 39.

APPENDIX No. 16.

HERVEY PORTRAITS.

This is a chronological list of all Hervey portraits, painted, engraved or cut on brass, whose existence I know of. I have not included busts. The list has been made out with a great deal of help from others, for which I am much obliged. I have begun with the generation to which Thomas Hervey belonged, who married Jane Drury, and died about 1467, because that marriage was the origin of the connection between Ickworth and the Hervey family.* And I have left off with the generation to which the first

---

* Had I begun with an earlier generation, before the connection with Suffolk had begun, there would of course have been no painted portraits to add, but two monumental brasses ; the one of John Hervey, of Thurleigh, who died about 1420, the other of Margery, his wife, afterwards wife of Sir William Argentein. The one is in Thurleigh Church, the other in Elstow. Both have been engraved for Lord Arthur Hervey's History of the Hervey family. They were the grand parents of the Thomas from whom I start.

Marquis of Bristol belonged, whose long life extended from 1769 to 1859. From that Thomas Hervey to the first Marquis of Bristol, there were (including both of them) 11 generations. Only two of those generations have no representative in this list, viz. the second and fifth, whilst others have a great many. I have included all who bore the name, whether by right of birth or of marriage, but I have confined myself to the Suffolk branch. On comparing this list with the previous one, it will be seen how many in that list cannot now be traced. I am indebted to Mr. Gage (History of Thingoe Hundred) for descriptions of some of the earlier pictures at Ickworth, and have not in every case verified his descriptions.

GENERATION I.

I.—*Elizabeth Hervey, daughter of John Hervey, of Thurleigh, and sister of Thomas Hervey, who married Jane Drury. She was Abbess of Elstow from 1501 to 1524.*

1. Her portrait on brass is on her tomb in Elstow Church, and has been engraved for Fisher's Collections for Bedfordshire, 1817 ; for Wigram's Chronicles of Elstow, 1885 ; and for Lord A. Hervey's History of the Hervey family, 1858.

GENERATION II. Unrepresented.

GENERATION III.

II.—*Sir Nicholas Hervey, younger son of William Hervey, of Ickworth ; Ambassador at Ghent ; died 1532.*

1. A doubtful portrait of him at Ickworth; half length, in bonnet and cloak, with sword; arms of Hervey quartering Niernuyt: Nulla motus fortuna.

2. His portrait on brass is on his tomb in Ampthill Church, and was engraved some years ago for a short paper on him by Lord Arthur Hervey.

GENERATION IV.

III.—*Sir Thomas Hervey, Knight Marshal to Queen Mary, son of the above Sir Nicholas.*

1. Evans Catalogue of British Portraits (issued about 1850) contains a drawing in colours from an original portrait of him at Marks Hall, Essex. But I have not been able to make out where either portrait or drawing is now.

IV.—*Francis Hervey, younger son of John and Elizabeth Hervey of Ickworth, died in 1601, and was buried at Witham in Essex.*

1. His portrait is at Ickworth; dated 1564, æt. suæ. 30: half length, on panel; a partizan is in his right hand, his left is in his belt: arms of Hervey quartering Niernuyt. Humilem mentem crea in me, Deus.

GENERATION V. Unrepresented.

GENERATION VI.

V.—*Sir William Hervey of Ickworth, son of John and Frances Hervey; born 1585, died 1660.*

1. Portrait at Ickworth; three quarters, on panel; ruff round his neck, red scarf over his shoulder.

VI.—*Susan, daughter of Sir Robert Jermyn, and first wife of above Sir William.*

1. Portrait at Ickworth, in a ruff and bonnet.

VII.—*Lady Penelope Gage, 2nd wife of her 3rd husband, Sir William Hervey; she died in* 1661.

1. Her portrait is at Hengrave, and has been engraved for Gage's History of Hengrave.

GENERATION VII.

VIII. *John Hervey of Ickworth, eldest son of above Sir William:* 1616—1679.

1. Portrait at Ickworth, full length, by Lely.

2. Another portrait of him by Lely has been engraved in mezzotint by Thompson; 3 quarters length, standing, with his hand on a classic bust; but where this portrait is I know not. I presume that the picture given to the first Lord Bristol by Lord Bathurst (see Letter 450) was the first of these two.

IX.—*Elizabeth Hervey, daughter of Lord Hervey of Kidbrook, and wife of above John Hervey; she died abroad in* 1700. *By right of her husband I put her under Generation VII; by her own right she would be in Generation VI, being to him third cousin once removed.*

1. A portrait of her by Vandyke was engraved by Hollar at Antwerp in 1646, and also by Gaywood ; half length, standing, to right, holding some portion of her dress in her left hand ; but where this portrait is I know not.

X.—*William Hervey, 2nd son of Sir William ; died of small pox at Cambridge in 1642, and lamented by Cowley.*

(1) A portrait of him at Ickworth was engraved by Van der Gucht for an edition of Cowley's poems ; half length, full face.

(2) Another portrait of him at Ickworth.

XI.—*Sir Thomas Hervey, 3rd son of Sir William ; succeeded his brother John at Ickworth ; 1625—1694.*

1. A Portrait of him at Ickworth; has been photogravured for Lord Bristol's Letter-books.

2. Miniature at Ickworth, supposed to be of him.

XII.—*Isabella, daughter of Sir Humphry May, and wife of above Sir Thomas Hervey ; died 1686.*

1. Portrait at Ickworth; photogravured for Lord Bristol's Letterbooks.

2. Miniature at Ickworth, half length, by Mathew Snelling.

XIII.—*Mary, daughter of Sir William Hervey, and first of the five wives of Sir Edward Gage ; died 1654.*

1. Portrait at Hengrave.

GENERATION VIII.

XIV. *John Hervey, eldest son of above Sir Thomas ; 1st Earl of Bristol ; died 1751 æt 85.*

1. Portrait at Ickworth, as a young man ; originally quarter but afterwards enlarged to halflength; at the back has been written in Lord Bristol's large clear handwriting, *This picture I have given to my daughter Ann. Bristol.* This picture has been photogravured for Lord Bristol's Letter-books. It is in bad condition.

2. At Ickworth; young.

3. At Ickworth ; whole length, in peer's robes; photogravured for Lord Bristol's Letter-books.

4. At Downhill (Sir Hervey Bruce); copy of No. 3.

5. At the Guildhall, Bury St. Edmunds.

6. At Ickworth ; in old age, holding a book, oval, half length; photogravured for the Letter-books.

XV.—*Isabella, daughter of Sir Robert Carr, and first wife of above John Hervey; died* 1693.

1. At Ickworth; three quarters, by Michael Dahl; photogravured for the Letter-books.

2. At Ickworth ; large miniature, half length, by Lewis Cross, with Latin inscription.

XVI.—*Elizabeth, daughter of Sir Thomas Felton, and second wife of above John Hervey, 1st Lord Bristol; died* 1741.

1. Half length, with book, oval, by Dahl; this picture belonged to Lord Howard de Walden who died in 1868 ; it was sold at Christie's not long after his death, but I have not been able to trace it. It has been engraved in mezzotint by Simon, and the engraving has been photogravured for the Letter-books.

KK

2. At Ickworth; full length; photogravured for the Letter-books.

3. At Downhill (Sir Hervey Bruce); copy of No. 2.

4. At Ickworth; three quarters.

5. At St. James' Square; three quarters, with a book in her left hand, in a white dress with blue scarf; by Kneller.

6. At Ickworth; miniature, by Bernard Lens.

7. At Aston Hall, Cheshire, (Mr. Hervey Talbot). I have not been able to get exact information as to this portrait.

GENERATION IX.

XVII.—*Carr, Lord Hervey, eldest son of John and Isabella; born* 1691, *died unmarried in* 1723.

1. At Ickworth; seated, with hand on a globe; photogravured for the Letter-books.

2. At St. James' Square; half length. This is uncertain.

XVIII.—*Isabella Carr Hervey, daughter of John and Isabella;* 1689—1711.

1. At Ickworth; on panel, three quarters, with bird; photogravured for the Letter-books.

XIX.—*John, Lord Hervey, eldest son of John and Elizabeth;* 1696—1743: *educated at Westminster and Clare Coll: Cambridge.*

1. At Ickworth; full length, as Lord Privy Seal.

2. At St. James' Square.

3. Presented to the National Portrait Gallery in 1863 by Lord Bristol; size 6 feet 8 inches by 5 feet 1 inch; painted in 1741 by Van Loo.

4. At the Bishop's Palace, Wells; bought at Christie's in 1888; formerly belonging to Mr. Hanbury Williams, of Coldbrook, Monmouthshire.

5. At Downhill (Sir Hervey Bruce).

N.B.—These five pictures (Nos. 1, 2, 3, 4, 5,) are all very alike, but it is not clear whether they were all painted by Van Loo. One of them has been engraved in mezzotint by Faber; and the upper part has been engraved by Harding for (I think) an edition of Walpole's Royal and Noble Authors.

6. At Ickworth; small oil painting, as a child.

7. At Ickworth; three quarters; standing.

8. At Ickworth; three quarters; in a snuff brown coat; oval frame.

9. At Melbury (Lord Ilchester); as a young man, full length, to left, dressed in a white coat and green waistcoat, white stockings, a cap in his hand; by Enoch Zeeman: brought from Redlynch in 1872.

10. At Mulgrave Castle (Lord Normanby); with Lady Hervey.

11. There is a satirical engraving of the duel between Lord Hervey and Pulteney. The duel is being fought in a courtyard; Sir Robert is standing in a doorway and saying, Let them cut one another's throats. There are some verses underneath, and it is entitled, A consequence of the motion.

12. An engraving of a bust of Lord Hervey (at St. James' Square) is given in each of the three editions of his Memoirs of the reign of George II.

13. An engraving of another bust was done for the Letters between Lord Hervey and Dr. Middleton concerning the Roman Senate, published in 1778.

*XX.—Mary, daughter of Brigadier-General Nicholas Lepel, and wife of
John, Lord Hervey; 1700—1768.*

1.   At Ickworth; three quarters.

2.   At Ickworth; chalk drawing.

3.   At Ickworth; in oval frame; three quarters; hands in a muff.

4.   At St. James' Square; copy of No. 3.

5.   At Hengrave Hall; by Dronais, done in 1750.

6.   Lent by Lord Lifford to the Exhibition of National Portraits in 1867,
     and formerly at Strawberry Hill; half length; as an elderly lady,
     grey hair, with muff and furred red dress; 30 by 25 inches; by
     Allan Ramsay.

7.   At Melbury (Lord Ilchester); small full length, in a white dress, looks
     young, a dog on a cushion, by Hogarth; brought from Redlynch
     in 1868.

8.   At Melbury; head and shoulders, in a pale red silk cloak edged with
     fur, small lace cap tied over the ears with black lace; 2 ft. 6 inches
     by 3 feet; by Allan Ramsay.

9.   At Ickworth; miniature.

10.   At Ickworth; miniature.

11.   At St. James' Square, very small miniature.

12.   At the Bishop's Palace, Wells; pencil sketch of head, profile to left,
     elderly.

13. In the Strawberry Hill Sale Catalogue, 1842, 18th day, is a portrait of
Lady Hervey by Miss Reade; bought by Richard Preston Esq. for
10 shillings.

14. Also on the same day of the same sale, portrait of Lady Hervey in an
old carved frame; reserved by Lord Waldegrave.

15. Also on the 22nd day of the same sale, a portrait of Mary Lapelle
afterwards Lady Harvey, in an elaborately carved frame by Gib-
bons; bought by Money for £ 13..2..6.

16. Also on same day of same sale, miniature portrait of Lady Hervey, in
a finely carved and gilt frame; bought by Strong of Bristol for
£2..10..0.

17. There is an engraving by Watelet from a drawing by Cochin filius in
1752; head and shoulders, profile, to right.

18. At Mulgrave Castle; with Lord Hervey.

XXI.—*Thomas Hervey, 2nd son of John, Lord Bristol, and Elizabeth his
wife; 1698—1775, educated at Westminster and Christ Church Coll: Oxford.*

1. At Ickworth; half length.

XXII.—*William Hervey, 3rd son of John, Lord Bristol; educated at Westminster; naval officer; 1699—1776.*

1. At Ickworth; standing, three quarters, with telescope, by Hudson.
2. At the Palace, Wells; replica or copy of No. 1.

XXIII. *Henry Hervey, 4th son of John, Lord Bristol; 1700—1748;
educated at Westminster and for a short time at Christ Church Coll: Oxford;
went first into the army, then into the Church; was Rector of Shotley; preached*

a sermon at St. Paul's in 1745 *at the Festival of the Sons of the Clergy, which has been printed; married in* 1730 *Catherine, daughter of Sir Thomas Aston of Aston Hall, Cheshire, and heiress of her brother, Sir Thomas, who died in* 1744, *whereupon Henry Hervey took the name of Aston, the baronetey passing to another branch. His descendants in the male line remained at Aston till the death of his great grandson, Sir Arthur Aston, in* 1859, *when Aston passed to Captain A. C. Talbot, who had married Sir Arthur's niece Harriet Hervey Aston.*

1.   I believe there is one or more portrait of him at Aston, (Mr. Hervey Talbot,) but I have not been able to get exact information of them.

XXIV.—*Felton Hervey,* 9*th son of John, Lord Bristol, July* 3 *to July* 16, 1710.

1.   At Ickworth; as a baby lying dead on a bed, with a cherub above.

XXV.—*Felton Hervey,* 10*th son of John, Lord Bristol; educated at Eton;* 1711—1773.

1.   At Ickworth; half length.

2.   At St. James' Square; three quarters.   This picture is uncertain.

XXVI.—*Elizabeth Hervey, eldest daughter of John, Lord Bristol, and Elizabeth his wife, and wife of Hon. Bussy Mansel;* 1697—1727.

1.   At Ickworth; small oil painting, as a child, companion to XIX, 6.

2.   At Ickworth; three quarters.

3.   At Ickworth; miniature, half length, by Bernard Lens.

XXVII.—*Ann Hervey,* 3*rd daughter of John, Lord Bristol; died unmarried;* 1707—1771.

1. At Marston, Somerset, (Earl of Cork); small half length, as a child, with large brown eyes ; catalogued as being by Lely, but unfortunately he had been dead 27 years before Lady Ann was born.

2. In the possesion of Mr. Arthur Brookes of Eltham ; a miniature painting, head and shoulders, full face.

XXVIII.—*Barbara Hervey*, 4*th daughter of John, Lord Bristol*; 1709—1727.

1. At Rushbrooke, near Bury St. Edmunds.

2. At Rushbrooke.

XXIX.—*Louisa Carolina Isabella Hervey, 5th daughter of John, Lord Bristol, and wife of Sir Robert Smyth*; 1715—1770.

1. At Ickworth ; half length.

GENERATION X.

XXX.—*George William, 2nd Earl of Bristol, eldest son of John, Lord Hervey ; died unmarried ;* 1721—1775.

1. At St. James' Square ; whole length, standing, in robes, under life size, by Zoffany. This picture has been engraved in mezzotint by J. Watson.

2. At Ickworth ; head and shoulders, in pastel ; by Raphael Mengs ; bought at Rome in 1868.

XXXI.—*Augustus John, 3rd Earl of Bristol, 2nd son of John, Lord Hervey ; an Admiral ;* 1724—1779.

1. At Ickworth ; whole length, standing, in naval uniform leaning on an anchor, telescope in left hand, sea and ships in the background ; by Gainsborough. This picture has been engraved by J. Watson.

2. At St. James' Square; half length; the head is like the head in No. 1

3. At White's Club; head and shoulders; apparently copied from No. 1. This has been engraved for a History of White's, 1892.

4. At the Guildhall, Bury St. Edmunds; three quarters, standing, with hand on a plan of a sea-fight, which is half spread out on a cannon; sea and ships in the background; by Sir Joshua Reynolds. This picture has been engraved by E. Fisher.

5. At Ickworth; miniature by Cosway.

XXXII.—*Frederick William, 4th Earl of Bristol, 3rd son of John, Lord Hervey; Bishop of Cloyne and Derry; 1730—1803.*

1. At Ickworth; whole length, seated, in episcopal dress, by Angelica Kaufman. This has been engraved for Gage's History of Thingoe Hundred.

2. At Ickworth; as a young man, oval.

3. At St. James' Square; three quarters, seated, with Vesuvius in the distance; by Madam Le Brun.

4. At Downhill (Sir Hervey Bruce); three quarters, seated; by Madam Le Brun.

5. At Downhill; three quarters, in episcopal robes, by Pompeius de Batconi, Rome, 1778.

6. At Downhill; small full length, sitting, in chalks.

7. At Downhill; presenting his eldest son, John Augustus, to Lord Chatham; three quarters, life size, signed William Hoare, 1771.

8. At the Palace, Wells; a miniature painting in oval frame, half length, sitting, holding a plan of Ickworth, with Vesuvius and Bay of Naples in the background.

9. Satirical engraving, whole length, standing, in episcopal dress, a fire-brand in his right hand, the devil seated on his shoulder, a pedestal inscribed, The Irish Patriot. 8 lines underneath. Published Nov. 5, 1784.

XXXIII.—*Elizabeth, daughter of Sir Jermyn Davers, and wife of the above Earl-Bishop; died* 1800.

1. At Rushbrooke. Whole length, in green silk dress, with a child (Louisa, afterwards Lady Liverpool) standing in front of her.

2. At Rushbrooke. Leaning on her hand.

XXXIV.—*William Hervey, 4th son of John, Lord Hervey, a general, died unmarried;* 1732—1815.

1. At Ickworth; small half length, in red coat, as a young man, oval.

2. At Wortley (Lord Wharncliffe); half length, in military uniform, with one epaulette only, life size; by L. F. Abbott. This has been engraved in mezzotint by Valentine Green.

3. At Sandringham Rectory (Rev. F. A. J. Hervey); a replica or copy of No. 2.

4. Another replica or copy of No. 2 is in the possession of Miss McDonnell, of Liverpool.

5. In the possession of Mr. Algernon Hervey; bust portrait, as a young man, in scarlet uniform, life size, oval frame.

XXXV.—*Lepel Hervey, eldest daughter of John, Lord Hervey, and wife of Constantine Phipps, 1st Baron Mulgrave in Ireland;* 1722—1780.

1. At Ickworth; small half length.

LL

2.   At Ickworth; small miniature supposed to be of her.

3.   In the possession of Mr. Samuel Joseph; catalogued in the Burlington House Winter Exhibition of 1893; half figure, seated, with her arms round a boy (her son), who is leaning against her; blue-grey dress, dark back-ground; painted about 1758 by Sir Joshua Reynolds.   Canvas 35 by 27 inches.

4.   Lent by Mr. James Price at the Old Masters Exhibition in 1885; bust to right, head turned over the right shoulder, white dress, black mantle, which she holds up with her left hand, powdered hair, sky background; oval, 28½ by 24 inches; by Gainsborough.

5.   At Mulgrave Castle.

XXXVI.—*Mary Hervey, 2nd daughter of John, Lord Hervey, and wife of George Fitzgerald of Turlough, Co. Mayo : 1726—1815; burnt to death at the age of* 89.

1.   At Ickworth; small half length.

2.   At St. James' Square; small three quarters, sitting.   This is uncertain.

3.   At Sandringham Rectory (Rev. F. A. J. Hervey); small oval, half length, in oils.   This is uncertain.

4.   There is an engraving of her in old age, head and shoulders, in an oval, very small, on a folio sheet with an account of her death below.

XXXVII.—*Emily Caroline Nassau Hervey, 3rd daughter of John, Lord Hervey ; died unmarried ; buried at Preston, near Brighton ; 1735—1814.*

1.   At Ickworth; small half length.

XXXVIII.—*Caroline Hervey, 4th daughter of John, Lord Hervey; died unmarried; buried at Preston; 1736—1819.*

1. At Ickworth; small half length

GENERATION XI.

XXXIX.—*Augustus Hervey, naval officer, natural son of Augustus, 3rd Earl of Bristol.*

1. At Ickworth; small head, by Gainsborough. This picture also appears in a life-size picture of Lord Mulgrave by Gainsborough, formerly at Mulgrave Castle.

XL.—*John Augustus, Lord Hervey, 2nd son of the Earl-Bishop; naval officer; died before his father in 1796, leaving one daughter, afterwards Lady Seaford.*

1. At Ickworth; whole length, leaning against a cannon, with a dog; by Gainsborough.

2. At Ickworth; miniature, by Cosway.

3. At St. James' Square; small full length, standing, water-colour, done by Day at Rome, 1795.

4. At the Bishop's Palace, Wells; miniature.

5. See xxxii, 7.

XLI.—*Elizabeth, Lady Hervey, daughter of ——— Drummond, and wife of the above John Augustus; died 1818.*

1. At Ickworth; half length, seated, with her child, who was afterwards Lady Seaford; by A. Kaufman.

2. At Megginch, in Perthshire; (Mr. Malcolm Drummond;) full length, by A. Kaufman.

XLII.—*Frederick William, 5th Earl and 1st Marquis of Bristol, 3rd son of the Earl-Bishop; 1769—1859.*

1. At Ickworth; three quarters, seated, with book on his knees, by Sir T. Lawrence. This has been engraved for Gage's History of Thingoe Hundred.

2. At Ickworth Lodge (Mr. George H. W. Hervey); a copy of No. 1.

3. At Ickworth; half length, under a tree, with Ickworth dome in the background; by Hoppner. This has been engraved in mezzotint by Young.

4. At Ickworth; a miniature, as a boy, in red page's Court dress.

5. At Ickworth; head and shoulders, crayon, life size.

6. At the Palace, Wells; chalk drawing, as a boy, half length, profile to left, inscribed, "Frederic William Hervey, 3 years old, Chriskna, May 22, 1773."

7. At the Palace, Wells; three quarters, sitting in a library, with hand on writing table, a book on his knee, life size; by Sir Francis Grant. This has been engraved by Henry Cousins.

8. At Ickworth; a small copy of No. 7.

9. At 19, Sussex Square, Brighton; small whole length, standing, with horse and dog.

10. At Downhill (Sir Hervey Bruce); half length.

11. At Rushbrooke; by Lawrence.

XLIII.—*Elizabeth Albana, daughter of Clotworthy Upton, 1st Lord Temple-town, and wife of the first Marquis of Bristol : died 1844.*

1. At the Palace, Wells ; three quarters, standing, facing spectator, with column in background ; by Sir Francis Grant. This picture has been engraved by Henry Cousins.

2. At Ickworth; small copy of No. 1.

XLIV.—*Mary Caroline Hervey, eldest daughter of the Earl-Bishop, and second wife of John, Earl of Erne.*

1. At the Palace, Wells; chalk drawing, as a child.

2. In the possession of Miss Mary Hervey ; half length, in a small oval, with a child on her knee, (her only child, afterwards Lady Wharncliffe,) water-colour by Downman, dated 1781.

3. In the possession of Miss Mary Hervey ; miniature on ivory, half length, $5\frac{1}{2}$ by $4\frac{1}{2}$ inches, dated.

4. At Wortley (Earl of Wharncliffe); miniature.

5. At the Exhibition of Old Masters, 1885 ; a picture containing two half figures, seated to left, in a landscape, the one in a yellow dress, the other in a pink dress, with her hands clasped over her companion's shoulder; 39 by $45\frac{1}{2}$ inches ; by Gainsborough. These ladies were Lady Erne and Henrietta Maria, Lady Dillon, who being a daughter of the 1st Lord Mulgrave, they were consequently first cousins.

XLV.—*Elizabeth Christian Hervey, 2nd daughter of the Earl-Bishop ; married firstly in 1776 John Thomas Foster of Dunlee, Co. Louth, and secondly in 1809 William, 5th Duke of Devonshire. She died in 1824.*

1. At Ickworth ; three quarters, seated ; by A. Kaufman.

2. At Chatsworth ; half length ; by Sir Joshua Reynolds. This has been engraved by Bartolozzi.

3. At the Palace, Wells, there is a miniature painting.

4. There is an engraving of her as Lady Elizabeth Foster by Caroline Watson "after an original drawing made by Mr. Downman for the scenery at Richmond House Theatre." Where the drawing is I know not.

5. There is an engraving of her as Duchess of Devonshire by F. C. Lewis from a painting by Sir Thomas Lawrence ; half length, seated, with hat and feather.

6. There is an engraving of her as Duchess, head only, profile to left ; Carl. T. Lawrence dip ; G. B. Borani dis ; D. Marchetti inc.

7. Lent by the Duchess of St. Albans to the Exhibition of Fair Women (1894) is a picture by Romney; but it does not seem to be absolutely certain whether this is Elizabeth or Georgiana. This picture has been slashed, and the slashes are attributed to George, Prince of Wales in a fit of temper.

8. At Wortley (Lord Wharncliffe) there is a miniature by Cosway, young, in white dress.

9. A miniature was sold at Christie's in 1894 ; white dress and black sash, fair hair not powdered; on the frame is written, *The gift of Elizabeth, Duchess of Devonshire, wife of William, 5th Duke of Devonshire, to Sir Walter Farquhar.*

There are probably more portraits of her somewhere.

XLVI.—*Louisa Theodosia Hervey, 3rd daughter of the Earl-Bishop; married in 1795 Robert Banks, Earl of Liverpool, died s.p. 1821.*

1. At Ickworth ; full length, standing, by Romney.

2. At Downhill ; head and shoulders, with a dove, by Sir J. Reynolds.

3. At Downhill ; copy or replica of No. 2.

4. At Kingston Church where she is buried, a marble bust.

5. See xxxiii, 1.

XLVII.—*Sir Felton Elwell Bathurst Hervey, eldest son of Felton Lionel Hervey, who was son of Hon. Felton Hervey, 10th son of John, Earl of Bristol; A.D.C. to the Duke of Wellington at Waterloo ; he lost an arm at the passage of the Douro ; he married in 1817 Louisa Caton of Baltimore, and died s.p. in 1819 æt. 36. There is a monument to him in Egham Church.*

1. At Clarendon, (Sir Frederick Bathurst) ; in uniform, with one arm ; 49 by 39 inches.

XLVIII.

1. At Ickworth ; a political group in 1738, by Hogarth, representing John, Lord Hervey ; Charles, 2nd Duke of Marlborough ; Stephen Fox, afterwards Lord Ilchester ; Henry Fox, afterwards Lord Holland ; Mr. Villemain ; Rt. Hon. Thomas Winnington.

2. At Melbury ; replica of No. 1.

XLIX.

1. At Ickworth ; a family group by Zoffany, representing Captain Augustus Hervey taking leave on his appointment to the command of a ship. The other figures are his mother, Lady Hervey ; George and Lady Mary Fitzgerald ; Constantine and Lady Lepel Phipps.

EXPLANATORY NOTES TO JOHN HERVEY'S DIARY.

Note 1, p. 1.   Ye Bishop of Exeter was Bishop Lamplugh.   See Macaulay's History of England II. 488, 502.

Note 2, pp. 5, 43, 65.   John Hervey's youngest sister, Kezia, married Aubrey Porter.   She was baptized in St. Mary's Church, Bury St. Edmunds, April 24, 1664, and buried at Ickworth in June 1689.   His death and place of burial will be found at p. 65.

Note 3, p. 7.   John Hervey's aunt, Kezia, had married Thomas Tyrell of Gipping.   Their daughter, Ada, is the Mrs. Tyrell here mentioned as marrying Mr. Auchmouty.   Another daughter, Kezia, married her first cousin, Robert Reynolds.   (See Note 4.)

Note 4, p. 7.   Judith, eldest child of Sir William Hervey, and aunt to John Hervey, married James Reynolds of Bumpsted, Co. Essex.   They had a son Robert, who married her first cousin, Kezia Tyrell.   (See Note 3.)

Note 5, p. 11.   Little Binny, afterwards called Bell in the Diary, was John Hervey's eldest child, Isabella Carr, who died in 1711.   (See Diary Oct. 1711.

Note 6, p. 22.   From a paper on the Carr family, read by Mr. Maurice Moore at a meeting of the Lincoln Diocesan Architectural Society in 1863, I gather that John Hervey's father-in-law, Sir Robert Carr, had three sisters ; viz. (1) Elizabeth who married Sir William Trollope, and whose only child, Elizabeth, was the Mrs. Fox here mentioned, wife of Charles who was son of Sir Stephen Fox and half-brother to Lords Ilchester and Holland ; (2) Mary who married Sir Adrian Scrope ; (3) Lucy who married Lord Hollis. The shares of the two elder sisters were bought up by John Hervey. "The lunatic" sometimes mentioned in John Hervey's accounts was Rochester Carr, uncle to these three ladies, and younger brother of old Sir Robert, their father. Lady Carr, wife of the second Sir Robert, John Hervey's mother-in-law, who is often mentioned in the Diary, was Elizabeth, sister of the Earl of Arlington. This second Sir Robert died at Aswarby in 1682, and Lady Carr in 1696. Their only son, Sir Edward, died a minor in 1683, when his sister, Isabella, John Hervey's wife, succeeded to a portion of the estates.

Note 7, p.p. 22, 23. John Hervey's aunt Elizabeth, widow of his uncle John, and daughter of Lord Hervey of Kidbrook, spent the latter part of her life in Holland, and died there in 1700. She was buried at Lee in Kent on April 25, 1700. The entry on p. 33 explains the reason of Robert Reynolds' trip abroad. See Appendices 3 and 4. See also her will, Appendix 12.

Note 8, p. 29. Amongst some old family books belonging to my father, which were left at Ickworth Lodge in 1830 when the move was made into the Round house, is one called " *The Devout Christian instructed how to pray and give thanks to God, or A book of devotions for families*, etc. by SY. Patrick, D.D., 4th edition, London, 1681. This book has belonged to Thomas & Isabella Hervey, and then afterwards to their children Kezia and John, all of whose names are written in it. Amongst the prayers in this volume is "*A thanksgiving for any public or private mercies.*" In the margin John Hervey has written, *Run away with, 6 Oct.* 1698. 25 *Oct.* 1717 *ye*

MM

Canall. This second mercy will be found mentioned in the Diary.
(See Note 25.)

Note 9, p. 29. This house, now No. 6, had been built about 1676, and before
August 1677 had been bought by Lord Bristol's uncle, John Hervey,
(See Codicil to his will, Appendix 10.) John the uncle left it to
his widow Elizabeth for her life, of whom John the nephew rented
it till her death in 1700, paying £50 a quarter. At her death it
became his. The house was rebuilt from the ground by the first
Marquis of Bristol during his absence abroad from 1817 to 1822.
(See page 132.)

Note 10, p. 29. John Hervey's aunt, Mary, daughter of Sir William Hervey,
married Sir Edward Gage of Hengrave. One of their daughters,
Mary, married William Bond of Bury St. Edmunds, brother to Sir
Thomas Bond, Bart. ; and their eldest son, Sir William Gage,
married Mary Charlotte, daughter of Sir Thomas Bond. Mention
of the Bonds will be found in John Hervey's letter-books, from
which it appears that they were great sufferers from impecuniosity.
The above William Bond was an author. Expenses, p.p. 93. 158.
a list of his works see Allibone's Dictionary of Authors.

Note 11, p. 30. According to Lord Arthur Hervey's History of the Hervey
family, a John Hervey who died in 1292 became possessed of
Thurleigh in Bedfordshire through his wife ; and his descendants
remained there till the time of Sir George Hervey who died in 1521,
when the estate passed to his natural son Gerard, from whom this
Major Hervey was descended. Thomas Hervey who married the
heiress of Ickworth, and from whom Lord Bristol was descended,
was uncle to Sir George. It appears from Lord Bristol's letter-

books that he at one time contemplated buying Thurleigh Hall. (See Vol. I. Letters 187, 243, 270.)

Note 12, p. 31.   See Appendices 3 and 4, though I am not sure that they refer to the same case as the one here referred to.

Note 13. p. 32.   In one of his account books John Hervey sets down as follows ; *June* 14, 1700, *I granted a rent charge of £80 per annum to Mrs. Elizabeth Peart for ye collection of pictures which were her husbands ; £40 for her own life, £20 per annum for her son Henry's, & ye other £20 for her daughter Jane.* This Mrs. Peart was the widow of Mr. Henry Peart, a painter, who had not been dead very long.   He had copied a portrait of Sir Thomas Hervey in 1690, and one of John Hervey's first wife in 1693.   (See p.p. 159, 160.) The payment of the annuity is entered every year in the By Book of expenses.   By the death of Jane Peart in 1709, it was reduced to £60.   By the death of Mrs. Peart at some time between 1725 and 1728 it was reduced to £20, which Henry Peart was still receiving in 1741, when the By Book closes.   In 1725 and other years Mr. Henry Sedgwick receives it for the use of his aunt Mrs. Peart.   In 1737 Mrs. Mary Peart receives it for her husband.   Redgrave (Dict. of Artists) says that Henry Peart or Paert was an indifferent artist, chiefly employed as a copyist, and copied most of the historical pictures in the Royal collections ; and that he died in 1697 or 1698.

Note 14, p.p. 33, 44, 59, 60, 67.   "My niece Elwess" always means my two nieces Elwes, whilst "My niece Elwes" means one of them only.   John Hervey's eldest sister, Isabella, married Gervase eldest son of Sir Gervase Elwes, who died before his father, who died

(p. 44.) in 1706. Gervase and Isabella had four children : viz. (1) Sir Hervey Elwes, who succeeded his grandfather, and died unmarried in 1763 ; he is said to have been a great miser ; (See Topham's Life of John Elwes, 12th ed. 1805); (2) John Elwes who is sometimes mentioned in the Book of Expenses and in the letter-book as Captain Elwes, and who seems to have died young, leaving 8 children unprovided for. See letter 1150. (3) Isabella, who died unmarried in 1714; (p. 61.); (4) Amy, who married Robert Meggott, by whom she had two children ; viz. a daughter who married Mr. Timms, and a son, John, who inherited the Suffolk estates of his uncle, Sir Hervey Elwes, took the name of Elwes, and died unmarried in 1789. This John, whose birth is mentioned at p. 60, and whose christening is mentioned in the expenses (p. 149), was the well-known miser. But according to his Life by Topham, his mother, his uncle Sir Hervey, and his grandmother Isabella Hervey, had all been misers.

Note 15, p. 33. Brother of Sir Dudley Cullum of Hawstead and Hardwick, and younger son of Sir Thomas, the purchaser of that estate. He was 38 at his death. There had been some flirtation between him and John Hervey's sister, Isabella Elwes, who died in October, 1696. Two letters from John Hervey to him will be found, Nos. 85 and 106, written in two different states of mind.

Note 16, p. 34. This Francis Hervey was a younger brother of William Hervey of Ickworth, who was grandfather to Sir William, who was grandfather to our diarist. He is described in the Pedigree as a Gentleman Pensioner to Queen Elizabeth, and there is a picture of him at Ickworth. See Expences, July 10, 1701, p. 146.

ICKWORTH, SOUTH FRONT, *circa* 1780 TO 1830.

Note 17, p. 36. 1702 *April* 14. *Ye first night dear wife and I lay at Ickworth.*
I must make these words the text for a few notes on the successive
Halls. The old Ickworth Hall of the 17th and previous centuries
had stood within a stone throw of the Church, just outside the east
wall of the churchyard. The foundations are still in the ground,
and a few hot dry days in the summer shew them out very distinctly.
An engraving* of Ickworth Church will be found in this volume
shewing the marks made on the turf by the foundations that lie
beneath it. Apparently soon after 1620, and probably after having
been somebody's residence for not less than five centuries, this
house was deserted by the Herveys of that time. Up to 1621 the
Hervey infants were baptized in Ickworth Church. John, Mary
and Susan, three of the children of Sir William Hervey, were
baptized there between 1616 and 1621 ; others of his children were
baptized at Bury. After 1642, when he married Lady Penelope
Gage, Sir William lived at Hengrave. John Hervey, his eldest
son, had a lease from the Crown of Oatlands, and lived at Court
and elsewhere, and Sir Thomas his brother lived at Bury, if one
may judge by the fact that his children were baptized there. So
what with Hengrave and what with Bury and what with Court,
Ickworth seems to have been more or less completely deserted by
its owners after 1621 ; they only came there to be buried ; and so the
entry in the diary on which this note is hung tells of a return to it
after 80 years absence. But not a return to the old Hall by the
Church. Apparently during the greater part of those 80 years the
Hall had been left to take care of itself, and we know what sort of

* It is done from a drawing made for me by Mrs. George Hervey, who stood for that purpose exactly
where the house once stood. A plan of these foundations will be found accompanying a paper on the old
house read by the Rev. Lord Arthur Hervey, Rector of Ickworth, at a meeting of the Bury & West
Suffolk Archæological Institute in December 1848.—S.H.A.H.

Note 17.—*continued.*

care that is which a house takes of itself ; and so in this year 1702 it was no longer fit for habitation. A picturesque though melancholy account of its condition at about this time, will be found in Appendix No. 4, p. 210 : "*they have suffered the seat of the family to run into such ruine and decay that daily the tiles, sometimes by loads, fall off the Mansion House, whereby the timber roofs have lain so expos'd to the sun and rain that they being rotten fall down, and have destroyed the planchard floors, which now in some places lie one upon another.*" After reading that account it does not require a very lively imagination to hear the owls hooting there night after night. Where then does John Hervey bring his wife to in this year of grace, 1702 ? There is at Ickworth a Survey book (which has lately been privately printed) made in 1665, showing what is now the park divided into so many farms, with farm houses dotted about, of most of which there is at present no visible sign. I imagine that disparking of the park and letting it out to farm must have been the result of the 80 years desertion of the Hall, and, perhaps, also of the previous poverty of John Hervey, father to Sir William. (See his piteous will, Appendix No. 9.) One of those farm houses, apparently one of a group which stood round what was then called Ickworth Green, had just been enlarged and fitted up and smartened by John Hervey, to serve for a time as the Hall, and thither on April 14. 1702, he brings his wife for the first time. Amongst the extracts from his expenses for this year 1702 printed in this volume, will be found some relating to this new residence at Ickworth ; cows for the dairy, deer for the park, glass and brewing vessels for the house, etc. (p. 128.) For difficulties that occured while the transformation of the farm-house into a mansion-house

Note 17.—*continued.*

was going on see Letters Nos. 204 and 206. It is evident that this new residence was only intended to be a temporary one, a stop-gap or make-shift. In July 1718 he mentions in his diary a visit from Sir John Vanbrugh, the architect of Blenheim, who set out the situation and made the plan of an intended new house. From the fact that John Hervey had enlarged the kitchen-garden and made the Canal near the Church, and from the fact of his removing the old Rectory and what there was of a village near the Parson's pond, I should imagine that this new house was intended to be on or near the site of the old Hall. But the plan was never carried out. A large family sprung up, more numerous than profitable, as he describes them in one of his letters, and money for the new house was not forthcoming. So the converted farm house at Ickworth continued to be the Mansion house to the end of his long life, and for 80 years after his death. There, sick of Courts, hating London, hating Bath yet more, he spent all the time he could, and we may be sure that the endearing epithets which he bestows upon it in his letters were bestowed in all sincerity, and came from the fulness of his heart. There his son John Lord Hervey died in 1743, and there death found the old Earl seven years later.

Somewhere about 1790, Frederick, 4th Earl of Bristol and Bishop of Derry, began the building of a new house, standing half way between the old Hall by the Church and the converted farm house or Ickworth Lodge as it is now called. The work having been sufficiently carried on by his son Frederick William, 1st Marquis of Bristol, a move was made into it in or soon after the year 1830, and the Lodge became empty. In 1832, Lord Arthur Hervey became Rector of Ickworth and Chedburgh ; the converted farm-

Note 17.—*continued.*

house was partly pulled down and became his residence, and so
continued till his promotion to the Bishoprick of Bath and Wells in
1869.   After that there was dead silence in it for about 20 years,
which silence has only lately been broken again.

Of the first and earliest of these three successive Halls, I have
given in this volume the only possible illustration that I can give,
viz. one showing the effect of its foundations upon the turf above
in a dry summer.

Of the second I have given three illustrations.

(a) The folding one, showing the East side of the house, is done
from an old oil painting given me about 30 years ago by Mrs. Byford
of Horringer, who had been a servant girl in the house in the early
part of the century, as her mother had been before her in the last
century.   There is a companion picture of Rushbrooke, from which
one might infer that they were done in the time of the Bishop of
Derry, who married the heiress of Rushbrooke.   The artist has not
allowed himself to be fettered and hampered and restrained by any
rules ; he brings in the bows on the South and North sides ; from
no point of view could both of them be seen at once, and from his
point of view neither of them could really be seen at all ; but with
a happy contempt for mere technicalities he shews both.   In fact
he must have sketched walking up and down a length of about 100
yards sideways, and bringing in everything that he saw in the
course of his walk.   The bow on the north or right hand side (as
you face the picture) was what was called the Alcove room, and
was till 1830 (when it was demolished) the best guest's bedroom.
I imagine that this may have been the room which Lord Bristol
says he was building for Lord Hervey in May 1742, (see Letter

Note 17.—*continued.*

1166,) though it is not the room in which Lord Hervey is tradition-
ally said to have died. The bow on the south or left hand side is
one of the two which appear in the next illustration. The sundial
which is to be seen in the painting within the garden inclosure is
still not far off, and appears again in the third illustration, that
of 1861.

In Gage's History of Thingoe Hundred there is an engraving of
the house done from this same point of view, or near about. It is
from a drawing made in 1828, not long before the house was partly
demolished. Some differences will be noticed between this drawing
and my oil painting. The difference of 50 years or more in their
respective dates may account for these differences ; but more
probably the reason for them is that the one artist was accurate,
the other not ; the one drew to show the building as it was, the
other drew a fine house to please (as he thought) his patron. In
my oil painting there are battlements and a general appearance of
heighth and grandeur which are absent in Gage's illustration ; and
my father speaking from his early recollections of it says that Gage
represents the house better than the other, it being a plain un-
pretentious building. Gage's artist stood still and did not walk
about as he sketched, so only the bow on the north side (containing
the Alcove room) is to be seen ; but this bow comes out so faintly
in the engraving in Gage's History that if one did not know it was
there one would never see it, and even then it is hard to see it.

(b) The second illustration, showing the south side of the house,
is from a sketch by Mrs. George Hervey. The sketch is done
partly from what is still standing, and partly from my father's
memory and description. There is a little doubt as to whether

NN

Note 17.—*continued.*

there should be battlements or not, and a few minor points are uncertain; but in the main the drawing is correct. I have dated it circa 1780 and not circa 1710, because the tradition is that in John Lord Bristol's time there were two stories, and that the upper story was removed by Augustus, Lord Bristol, to heighten the rooms below. This sketch represents the house with the upper story gone. John, Lord Hervey, is said to have died in one of those rooms upstairs which were afterwards thrown by Augustus into the room below, viz. one in the left hand bow as you face the picture. Where John, Lord Bristol, died tradition does not say; probably the left end room on the ground floor. In the early years of this 19th century, and up to the move in 1830, the rooms were as follows. Beginning from the right hand side (as you face the picture), there was first the ante-room with its two windows; then the drawing-room lightened by the three windows in the bow; then the dining-room with its four windows; then Lady Bristol's room, occupying the other bow; then Lord Bristol's study lightened by the two remaining windows.

It must have been somewhere about where the two imaginary figures are standing in this illustration that Lady Ann Hervey had one of her many fits in May 1736, for she had been walking in the Home-Garden, and her father saw her, "being a reading in the dining-room." See Letter 1025. The Home-Garden would be so called as opposed to the Kitchen or Spring Garden near the Church.

Which was the Pladd-room, offered to Lady Effingham in 1724 (Letter 808), and which was the room built for John, Lord Hervey, in 1742 (Letter 1166), I cannot say.

Note 17.—*continued.*

Mary, Lady Hervey, spent a good deal of time at Ickworth after the deaths of Lady Bristol and her own husband, writing letters for old Lord Bristol, listening to his prophecies of the country's ruin, and pleasantly arguing with him thereon, as well as amusing herself with books, birds and roses. (See her Letters to Rev. Edmund Morris.) She seems to have had a room on the South side of the house, and upstairs, therefore one of the rooms which Augustus threw into the room below. I say upstairs, because writing to Mr Morris on Feb. 1, 1749, she says, *I am in a very chit-chat disposition, and should have spun out this letter much longer, but that Sir Robert Smythe is just come up-stairs to your rescue.* And I say on the south side, because writing to Mr. Morris on April 5, 1749, she says, *I am luckily situated here, in a little room where I enjoy it (the sun) in its full meridian. It gilds and beautifies a scene that is as pleasing as lawn, trees, extent and diversity can make it. Nor is my sight the only sense that is gratified in this situation : a profusion of flowers and sweet shrubs perfume the air ; and a variety of beautiful birds whilst they please my eye delight my ear.* We may therefore imagine her as writing in a room whose window looked out on the spot where Lady Ann had her fit, though that window is gone by the time to which this illustration (*b*) belongs, and the room is thrown into the one below. Possibly it was the room in which tradition places the death of her husband.

In a letter to Mr. Morris written Oct. 24, 1747, she gives an account of her labours in the garden at Ickworth, and of her rosery with fifty different sorts of roses.

How much of this South side of the house was pulled down in 1831 (or thereabouts), and how it was then heigthened and otherwise altered, will be seen by comparing this illustration *(b)* with the third *(c)*.

(c) The third illustration is from a photograph taken in 1861, and represents the house as it still is. The figures are not typical or imaginary as they were in the other one, but represent those who were actually standing there when the photograph was taken.

I only wish I could give two more illustrations of the house; one showing it as it was in 1702, when John Hervey, not yet a peer, had just converted it from a farm house to a mansion house, and had just begun his long residence there of 50 years; and another showing it as it was up to 1700, when he had not yet touched it, and it was still a farm house looking out upon Ickworth Green.

It is possible that the whole of the South front, as shown in the second illustration, may be John Hervey's work, and that the farm house may be represented by that part of the house which lay (and more or less still lies) behind it, where the kitchen and nursery and staircase is.

Note 18, p. 43.   This Sir John Poley was second cousin to John Hervey, their paternal grandmothers, Ann and Susan Jermyn, being sisters. He was also first cousin to John Hervey's mother, his aunt Judith Poley being the wife of Sir Humphry May, one of whose daughters was Isabella, wife of Sir Thomas Hervey. Sir John Poley was also uncle by marriage to John Hervey's second wife, his (Sir John's) third wife being Dorothy, daughter of Sir Henry Felton.   (See Lord Arthur Hervey's Paper on Boxted and the Poleys, read before the Suffolk Institute of Archæology in June 1859.)

ICKWORTH LODGE, SOUTH FRONT, 1861.

Note 19, p. 43. A loose bit of paper has the following note on this passage in the writing of the 2nd Marquis of Bristol : "*so that the trees in the grove between Arthur's house* (i.e. Ickworth Lodge) *& Little Horringer Hall are just* 150 *years old ;*" thus identifying Park-Grove with the grove near the present cricket ground.

Note 20, p. 52. Stafford means Bishop's Stortford.

Note 21, p. 53. Mr. Masson was Carr's travelling tutor. Amongst some old books belonging to and kept in Wedmore Church, Co. Somerset, there is a life of Horace in Latin by John Masson, A.M & E.A.P, printed at Lyons in 1708. There is a long dedication in Latin of the usual fulsom kind to John Lord Bristol, then Lord Hervey

Note 22, p.p. 53, 56, 66, 74. The words printed in italics are not written by John Hervey's hand, as the rest of the diary is. They are all by the same hand, probably additions made at his dictation when reading his diary in his old age, after that his failing sight made writing difficult. Possibly the hand is the hand of the lady of a good family in Wales, mentioned at page 74.

Note 23, p. 57. John Hervey rented a house at Newmarket belonging to Mr. Thomas Stuteville. See Extracts from Expenses, p. 167. The Stutevilles had lately parted with Dalham, where they had been seated for some time.

Note 24, p.p. 59, 68. Besides these two entries in the Diary there are the following allusions to the Manleys in the Expenses.
1712 July 26.   Sent Mrs. Manley by her son Tom into Wales, £5..7..6
1713 May 25.   Gave Tom Manley etc. (as at p. 59).
1715 Aug. 2.   To Mr. Roger Manley to sett up his trade as an Apothecary, £10.

Note 24.—*continued.*

1718 Feb 12. Gave to Susan Manley five guineas.
1719 Nov. 17. Gave Sir Thomas Hanmer £15, which his steward
               in Wales paid by my desire to Bell, Kez. & Mall
               Manley to buy them mourning for their good
               mother Mrs. Eliz: Manley.
1725 June 16. Gave at ye christening of Tom Manley's son at Mr.
               Gansell's at Low-Leyton, £5..8..6.
1726 Aug. 6.   Gave 5 guineas to Kezia Manley, & a jacobus to
               Bell and Susan each, £7..17..0.

It would seem that Elizabeth, the mother of the above-mentioned
children, had been a servant of some sort to John (the uncle) and
Sir Thomas Hervey. She is mentioned in a codicil to John Hervey's
will, Appendix 10, p. 226.   I am indebted to the Rev. Philip
Sparling, Rector of Erbistock, Co. Flint, for the following information ; that she was the wife of Cornelius Manley of Erbistock ;
that Kezia was baptized there in 1680, and Thomas in 1684 ; that
she was buried there in 1719, and her husband in 1722 ; that in the
time of Thomas, her son, the Erbistock Quillets, "the hardest in
North Wales to account for," were marked out ; that the Manleys
continued to reside at Erbistock till about 1760 ; that the estate is
still in the possession of the family, the present representative
living near Lichfield ; that the estate consists of a manor house, a
farm of 160 acres, a wood 7 acres, and 10 cottages with holdings of
from 1 to 10 acres attached. Not far from Erbistock is Bettisfield,
where Sir Thomas Hanmer had a house, who is conseqently
sometimes made the vehicle to convey John Hervey's gifts.
Allusions to the Manley's will also be found in the Letter-books.

Note 25, p. 66. A fuller account of this second escape will be found in Letter 815. See also Note 8. The Canall still exists at Ickworth called by the same name ; but I do not think that the Kitchen Garden is ever now called the Spring Garden. An allusion to " ye intended kitchin garden," whose laying out he is superintending, will be found in Letter 410.

Note 26, p. 68. Robert Butts, son of William Butts, Rector of Hartest, was educated at Bury School and Trinity College, Cambridge ; in 1731 appointed Dean of Norwich ; in 1732 Bishop of Norwich ; in 1738 Bishop of Ely ; died in 1748. Several letters to him from Lord Bristol will be found in the Letter-books. His son, Eyton Butts, was afterwards Dean of Cloyne.

Note 27, p.p. 69, 87. In his preface to Lord Hervey's Memoirs, Mr. Croker says that there was some mystery about his marriage, and that it was not publicly announced till the following October, and he gives a guess at the reason thereof. (p. xxiv.) That guess may or may not be right ; but another guess of Mr. Croker's was certainly quite wrong, and this must now be made clear once for all.

In 1821 there was published " *Letters of Mary Lepel, Lady Hervey, with a memoir and illustrative notes.* The Rev. Edmund Morris, tutor to Frederick and William, Lady Hervey's two youngest sons, was the correspondent to whom the letters were written ; Mr. Croker was the editor. Lady Hervey's tastes were in some respects French, and her sympathies seem to have been strongly French, insomuch that in these letters she occasionally, apparently in jest, speaks of *us* and *our friends*, meaning thereby the French. In a note to one of these passages Mr. Croker says : *I suspect that Lady Hervey's family were originally from one of the islands on the coast of France ;*

as I find that about this period a Mr. Lepel was the proprietor of Sark. This may have been the foundation both of her French taste, and the joke of considering her as a French woman. (p. 64.) That was of course a mere guess, good for very little till some evidence could be found to support it; but it got to be repeated and accepted as a certainty. It often happens that a man makes a statement with a question stop after it, but those who repeat the statement leave out the question stop. In Wharton's Wits and Beaux of Society we are told without the least suggestion of doubt that Lady Hervey *"derived from her father, Brigadier Lepel, who was of an ancient family in Sark, a considerable fortune."* Being in Guernsey not long ago, I saw in the Catalogue of a public library there a list of authors who had been natives of Sark ; amongst them was Lady Hervey. I believe that her descendants of the present and last generation have never doubted but what she came from Sark, insomuch that that charming island has thereby had an additional charm given to it in our eyes. It had never occured to me to doubt it, and I had fully intended giving in this volume an illustration of the old Seignurie of Sark, now used as the Rectory, and entitling it, The Birth-place of Molly Lepel. Being in Sark in the summer of 1892, I called at the present Seignurie to see what I could learn there of Lady Hervey's family. The Seigneur very courteously told and showed me everything he could. Looking about on the outside of the old part of the present Seignurie, we found a leaden water-pipe with initials that fitted Nicholas Lepel, and the date 1690 or thereabouts, just about the time when he was supposed to have married, and might have entered into possession of his Sark property. Instantly that water-pipe became a thing worthy to be sketched and engraved, and almost embraced and adored.

Note 27.—*continued*.

On coming home, before I got the drawings of General Lepel's water-pipe and Lady Hervey's birth-place done, I thought I would just look to see what evidence there was that the water-pipe was his, and that the birth-place was hers; and I was then astonished to find how slight was the evidence to support Mr. Croker's guess, and how great was the evidence to upset it.

I here marshal the former evidence, viz. that connecting Lady Hervey with Sark, under the letters *a*, *b*, *c*, *d*, and the latter evidence, viz. that disconnecting her from it, under the figures 1 to 8.

(a) There is the fact that Lady Hervey in her letters sometimes says *our friends* and *us*, meaning thereby the French.

(b) There is the fact that her maiden name, Lepel, and the name of the Seigneurs of Sark in the last century, Le Pelley, are something like each other.

(c) There is the fact that her father's name was Nicholas, and that Nicholas was also a name borne by several generations of the Le Pelley family, one of them being contemporary with her father.

(d) There is the fact that Lady Hervey had some French tastes and sympathies.
There is that much to support Mr. Croker's guess, but nothing more that I can think of. Against that evidence there is this to be opposed.

(1) The name of the Sark family is not Lepel or Le Pel, but Le Pelley, which is quite different.

(2) The Le Pelleys of the present day, and other antiquarians of the Channel Islands, are quite convinced that Lady Hervey had nothing to do with Sark. Colonel Ernest Le Pelley, now residing

OO

Note 27.—*Continued*.

in Guernsey, has been good enough to send me a very full pedigree of the family, apparently made with care and accuracy and on good authority, wherein there is no room to be found for Lady Hervey. He, however, says there are Le Pelleys in France with whom she might be connected.

(3) Lady Hervey herself, though rather ignorant of her parentage, yet was satisfied that she was not connected with the Le Pelleys of Sark. In 1742 the Gentleman's Magazine announced the death of Nicholas Lepelle, Lord Proprietor of Sark. It would seem that this announcement was brought to Lady Hervey's notice as being possibly of some family concern to her, her father's name being Nicholas; and it would seem that she could not say offhand that it was of no family concern to her; but on Aug. 17, 1744, she writes as follows to Mr. Morris from Ickworth : *You have given yourself a great deal of trouble, Sir, to procure me so much intelligence about Mr. Le Pelley's family and arms; the last of which is a full conviction that he was no relation to us...... I return you the impression of Mr. Le Pelley's arms with a great many thanks.* Letter XX. p. 74.

(4) Having disconnected her from France, or at any rate from Sark, there remains to attach her to some other part of the world. I think that any one looking at the engraving by Heath of her portrait done before her marriage would certainly say, That is a Teutonic face, and not a Celtic one. But, perhaps, that evidence is not worth much.

(5) She was certainly the daughter of General Nicholas Lepel and Mary Brooke, his wife, and there is good reason for attaching her father to Northern Europe.

Note 27.—*Continued*.

In 1683 were married the Princess Ann, afterwards Queen of England, and Prince George of Denmark. In 1684 Claus (Niclaus) Wedig Lepel was one of Prince George's pages. Luttrell's Diary (which I quote at second hand from Notes & Queries, 4th Ser. X. 197) thus mentions him: *Tuesday, 10 Jan. 1698/9. Mr. Lepell, for whom the Commons yesterday past a bill of naturalization, is page to the Prince of Denmark, and has lately married a lady worth £20,000.*

Among the London Marriage Licenses, 1521—1869, edited by Mr. Joseph Foster, is the following: *Lepell Nicholas, of St. Martin-in-the-Fields, Middlesex, gen: bachelor, 32, and Mary Brooke, of same, spinster, 25, her parents dead, alleged by John Adames, of St. Margaret, Westminster, gent.—at any time or place in England.* 10 *Aug.* 1698.

His being a foreigner, and his being in the train of the Prince of Denmark, give some reason for attaching him to Northern Europe.

(6) But still further reason may be found in a little pamphlet called, *Memoirs of the Life and Misfortunes of Mr. Pless, humbly dedicated to her Grace the Duchess Dowager of Marlborough. Written by a lady. London,* 1731. From this pamphlet I learn that the unfortunate Mr. Pless was nephew to the late Brigadier Lepel, *"whom your Grace favoured with your protection to his dying day"*; that he (Mr. Pless) was of a very ancient family settled for many hundred years in the Duchy of Mecklenburg; that a county or Lordship of Pless once belonged to them, but was mortgaged and given up to the Landgraves of Hessen; that a gentleman of this name and family, a native of Mecklenburg, had been Prime Minister at the Danish Court, but being ordered to make his choice between two masters, the King of Denmark and his brother, Prince George, he chose to follow the latter into England, to whom he was Privy-

Note 27.—*Continued.*

Purse, and was distinguished by Queen Anne after the Prince's death; that two of the said gentleman's sons are now of the King of Denmark's Privy Council; they have estates in Denmark and in Mecklenburg; that Frederick Gasper Pless, the subject of this pamphlet, was born at Vienna, his father having been sent there by the States of Mecklenburg to manage a law suit against their Prince before the Aulick Council; that his Godfather, Count Bothmer, then residing at the Hague, had him educated at school and at Leyden University; that in 1714 he accompanied Count Bothmer to England, being desirous both to see England and his uncle, the late Brigadier Lepel; that soon after the arrival in England of the Princess of Wales, now Queen, Miss Lepel, the Brigadier's daughter, told Mr. Pless of her desire to serve her Royal Highness as Maid of Honour; that Mr. Pless told Count Bothmer of it, whom with Monsieur Bernstorff, then Prime Minister at Hanover, he conducted to visit the young lady, who, through the joint interest of the Duchess Dowager of Marlborough and the above two German Ministers, soon after obtained her wish. "*Thus Miss Lepel was placed in a station, wherein the many endowments Providence has adorned her mind and person with could not but be very conspicuous, and shine out in their full lustre, and this lady's virtues have been crowned since with a just reward in the happy union she enjoys with her husband, the Lord Hervey, son and heir apparent to the Right Hon. the Earl of Bristol.*"

Then follows the tale of his hardships, including eleven months in Newgate gaol, with which we are not now concerned. I merely extract so much from the pamphlet, because it shows us a Dano-Germanish family named Pless, one of whom apparently married

Note 27.—*Continued.*

a sister of Nicholas Lepel, and therefore helps to detach the Lepels from Sark and to attach them to North Germany.

(7) In addition to this I have very good authority for saying that 20 years ago there was a Captain Ernst von Lepel living on his estate at Neuendorf, in the Island of Usedom, in the Baltic, which island formerly belonged to the Dukes of Pomerania. This estate is said to have been owned by the Von Lepels since the 13th century. A friend of the family has sent me an impression of the Von Lepel seal as used now, which is exactly the same as the escutcheon of pretence borne by Lord Hervey on his shield, as shown on his tombstone in Ickworth Church, and on Faber's engraving of his portrait by Van Loo.

(8) There is a town called Lepel, with a population of 6,000, in the Russian department of Vitebsk. My father sends me a reference to it that he has met with in General Mabot's Memoirs: "Lepel en Lithuaine," Vol. III, 162.

Now what is the story, a possible story, that may be deduced from these eight headings? It is that somewhere about the 12th or 13th century a family went forth from Lithuania, taking their name from the town from which they went forth; that they moved Westward along the coast of the Baltic, one branch settling down in the Pomeranian Island of Usedom, while another branch, perhaps taking Denmark in its way, moved on further Westward still, till it reached England in the person of Nicholas Lepel, page to Prince George of Denmark, and eventually Brigadier-General in the English army.

If that be so, then Lady Hervey in spite of her French sympathies was as little French as she well could be.

The date of General Lepel's death is not known. He was appointed Brigadier-General on Jan. 1, 1710. A novel called Maids of Honour, by Frank Ranelagh, was published in 3 volumes in 1845. Mary Lepel and John, Lord Hervey, play a prominent part in it. General Lepel is represented as living at Petersham, as being a very vain man and filling his house with portraits of himself, and as being an old lover of the Duchess of Marlborough's; and his daughter's marriage is represented as taking place in the house at Petersham. Whether these statements have any historical foundation or are pure inventions of the novelist I know not. I have never come across any of the numerous portraits of the General, and I do not think that he was alive at the time of his daughter's marriage. Where that marriage took place is not known, and is therefore one of the things that yet remain to be hunted out. In one statement the novelist is certainly quite wrong. He represents Mary Lepel as having lost her mother at a very early age, whereas Mrs. Lepel did not die till 1742. Her death is one of the last events recorded by Lord Bristol in his diary. I do not think that there is any allusion to General Lepel in either the Diary or Letter-books. Mrs. Lepell was Mary, daughter and heiress of John Brooke of Rendlesham, Co. Suffolk, five brothers and three sisters having died without children.

Note 28, p. 73. Lepel Hervey married in 1743 Constantine Phipps, 1st Baron Mulgrave of the Irish Peerage. Their eldest son, Constantine John, 1st Baron Mulgrave of the English Peerage, commanded an expedition to the North Pole in 1773 in the Racehorse, accompanied by the Carcass. He published his journal of this expedition in 1774. Lady Lepel Phipps died in 1780. Horace Walpole writing to Sir Horace Mann from London, Jan. 7, 1741/2, thus alludes to her : "*I forgot to tell you all our beauties ; there was Miss Hervey, my lord's daughter, a fine black girl, but as masculine as her father should be.*" Hor. Walpole's Corr : I. 113.

Note 29, p. 74. Augustus John entered the navy as midshipman in 1736 ; married Miss Elizabeth Chudleigh in 1774, from whom he was afterwards divorced ; member for Saltash in Cornwall in 1763, member for Bury St. Edmunds at different times between 1757 and 1775, when he succeeded his brother George as 3rd Earl of Bristol. He died at St. James' Square in Dec. 1779.

Note 30, p. 74. Charles Hervey's University career puzzles me a little by reason of its great length. He went up to Queen's College, Cambridge, in October 1724, and did not leave till Michaelmas 1732. According to the Graduati Cantabrigienses, 1823, he took his M.A. degree in 1728 ; so what he went on struggling after for 4 years more, I don't know. In 1726 there was an idea of taking him away from Cambridge and sending him to Oxford. (See Letter 866.) He was decidedly dull, I should imagine ; (see letters 866, 924, 926.) He was apparently ordained by the Bishop of Lincoln in 1732, two livings in Lincolnshire being ready for him ; (see letters 951, 952.) In 1736 he succeeded Dr. Butts as Rector of Ickworth and Chedburgh ; in 1748 he resigned these, and succeeded his madcap brother, Harry, at Shotley. He also held the living of Sproughton. He married Martha Maria Howard on the last day of 1740, (see letters 1139, 1142, 1143, 1148,) and died without issue in 1783. Thanks to his father's old friend Dr· Butts, Bishop of Ely and formerly Rector of Ickworth, he obtained his only preferment in the Church, being Prebendary of Ely. His will, like everything else that one knows about him, gives one the idea of a man without a friend. Only two people are named in it ; his servant, Sarah Marshall, to whom he leaves everything and whom he appoints sole executrix, and a parishioner, Thomas Woodward of Sproughton Hall, whom he appoints overseer. He was buried at Ickworth, but no one has ever taken the trouble to cut his name upon a stone. I do not see any mention of any portrait of him. Of all his father's many sons he was almost the only one who never gave any trouble or anxiety, except by his slowness in learning at College ; but for all that there is, or at least seems to be, an absence of anything like affection in the mention of him in the Diary and Letter-books. When Lord Bristol felt much affection, he was not the man to hide it, but was most vehement in his expression of it. Charles was not sent to Eton or Westminster like his other brothers, but educated at smaller schools. Mr. Louis Valet or Vaslet, of Hampstead, had the educating of him from 1714 to 1717, and then Mr. Arthur Kinsman had him for the next three years. (See Expenses, p. 104—106.) I am not sure, but I think Mr. Kinsman was Master of the Bury School. Since writing the above note I have come across the following notice of him in Bentham's History of Ely Cathedral, published in 1771, during his life-time. *Prebendaries of the fifth stall, 12. The Hon. Charles Hervey M.A. and since D.D., 4th son of the late Earl, and uncle to the present Earl of Bristol. He was educated at the School of Bury St. Edmunds in Suffolk ; thence admitted as Nobleman of Queen's College in Cambridge, Oct. 28, 1724, where he took his degree of M.A. in right of his family, continued his residence in College for several years after, and then entering into Holy Orders was not long after collated to this*

Prebend on June 10, *and installed June* 12, 1742; *he was afterwards presented by his father to the Rectories of Sproughton and Shotley in Suffolk, and is the present possessor of this Prebendall stall, June* 21, 1770.

The 2nd edition, published in 1812, adds the following note. *He died at Ely,* 1783, *and was buried at Ixworth (sic).*

The following information extracted from Collins' Peerage, 5th ed. 1784, shows the connection between Mrs. Charles Hervey and Lord Warrington, a connection which Lord Bristol tells Lord Warrington "was an ingredient which induced him to make several concessions towards the attainment of the alliance." Letter No. 1139. Collins says that Philip, seventh son of Thomas, 1st Earl of Berkshire, was baptized in 1629, and died in 1717. He had two sons, James and Charles, and two daughters, viz. Mary Lucy, who died unmarried in May 1744, and was buried at Bury St. Edmunds, and Henrietta who died unmarried in 1750, and was buried at Windsor. James, the eldest of the two sons, born in St. James' Palace March 1, 1679, was seated at Boughton, near Chester, died June 1722, and was buried in the Booth family vault in St. Werbergh's, Chester. His wife was Katherine, daughter of George Booth, of Woodford, Essex, by whom he had two sons who died infants, and two daughters, one of which, Martha Maria, married in 1740 the Hon. and Rev. Charles Hervey.

Note 31. p. 75. Mary married George Fitzgerald of Turlough, Co. Mayo, a Captain in the Austrian service. They had two sons, George Robert, who was hung for murder, and Charles Lionel, whose descendants are still living at Maperton, in Somersetshire.

Note 32, p. 76. Fanny was a dog. Kickaninny was another dog, whose death is lamented at p. 86, and Chance at p. 85.

PP

Note 33, p. 78.   Elizabeth, wife of Hon. Bussy Mansel, died without children. Her death was a painfully lingering one. (See Letters 874, 876, 877, 878.) The lines on her tombstone in Ickworth Church, written by her brother, Lord Hervey, will be found printed in the volume containing the Ickworth Registers, p. 74.

Note 34, p. 80.   This daughter, Elizabeth, motherless from the day of her birth, is said in Collins' Peerage (Brydges' edition) to have been living single in London in 1800.   She is occasionally mentioned in Lord Bristol's Letters.

Note 35, p. 80.   Frederick was educated at Westminster School and St. Benet alias Corpus Christi College, Cambridge : in 1767 Bishop of Cloyne; in 1768 translated to Derry; died in Italy 1803.   In 1752 he married Elizabeth, daughter of Sir Jermyn Davers and sister and heiress of Sir Charles Davers of Rushbrooke, who (Lady B.) died in 1800.   Some letters to Frederick at College from his grandfather will be found in the Letter-books. (Nos. 1227, 1282, 1301, 1330, 1354, 1359.)

Note 36, p. 82.   William, familiarly called Gwog, a General in the army, died unmarried in 1815, aged 82 years. He had a house on Putney Heath, which he left to his nephew, Lord Bristol, and a house in Lincolnshire.   He has left a diary behind him.

Note 37, p. 83.   Emily died unmarried June 1814, aged 80 years; buried at Preston near Brighton.

Note 38, p. 84.   Caroline died unmarried at Brighton, March 1819, aged 83 years.   In the volume containing the Ickworth Registers I gave the inscription on the tombstone at Preston relating to Lady Emily, copied from the Cullum notes, (p. 82.) Evidently Sir Thomas Cullum copied it between 1814 and 1819, as he does not give the inscription on the same stone relating to Lady Caroline. I now give the whole inscription, a copy of which has been sent me.

IN MEMORIAM.

Lady Emily Caroline Nassau Hervey, daughter of John Lord Hervey of Ickworth, eldest son of John Earl of Bristol, who was called from the lower House of Peers (sic.) during the life-time of his father and appointed Lord Privy Seal to George II. Her Ladyship died the 4th June 1814 in the 80th year of her age.

Also are deposited in this tomb the remains of Lady Caroline, sister of Lady Emily Hervey, whose pedigree is engraved on the contraside of this monument. Her Ladyship died 1st March 1819, in the 83rd year of her age.

ADDITIONAL NOTES.

I. Lord Bristol's Sons-in-Law and Daughters-in-Law.

1.—Hon. Bussy Mansel. He was younger son of Sir Thomas Mansel, 4th Bart., who was created Baron Mansel of Margam, Co. Glamorgan, on Jan. 1, 1712. Lord Mansel dying in 1723 was succeeded by his grandson Thomas (son of his eldest son Robert); who dying unmarried in 1743 was succeeded by his uncle Christopher, 2nd son of the first Baron; who dying unmarried in 1744 was succeeded by his brother Bussy; upon whose death in 1750 the title became extinct. Lady Elizabeth Mansel, his wife, eldest daughter of John, Lord Bristol, died in 1727. The lines on her tombstone in Ickworth Church were written by her brother, John, Lord Hervey.

2.—Sir Robert Smith or Smyth. Sir James Smyth, knighted by Charles II, was Lord Mayor of London in the first year of James II, and died Dec. 1706, æt. 73. His only son, James, was made a Baronet in the first year of George I. He married Mirabella, daughter of Sir Robert Legard, and died in Feb. 1717, being buried at West Ham in Essex.

His only son, Robert, 2nd Bart., married Lady Louisa Carolina Isabella Hervey in 1731, and had one son and one daughter. The son, Hervey, born in 1734, was page of honour to George II, aid-de-camp to General Wolfe at the siege of Quebec, and a Colonel in the foot-guards. I am told that he figures in West's picture of the death of General Wolfe.

The Daughter, Anne Mirabella Henrietta, born in 1738, married in 1761 William Beale Brand of Polstead Hall, Suffolk. (Kimber and Johnson's Baronetage.)

For the inscription on Lady Louisa Smyth's tombstone in West Ham Church, see Ickworth Registers, p. 82.

3.—Mary, Lady Hervey, I have already dealt with.

4.—Ann, wife of Thomas Hervey, whom she married in or about 1744, was daughter of Francis Coghlan, Counsellor of law in Ireland. In his will Thomas Hervey denied the marriage; and some time before he had published the following advertisement in the papers : *Whereas Mrs. Hervey has been three times from home last year and at least as often the year before without either my leave or privity, and has encouraged her son to persist in the like rebellious practices, I hereby declare that I neither am nor will be accountable for any future debts of hers whatever. She is now keeping forcible possession of my house, to which I never did invite or thought of inviting her in all my life. Tho : Hervey.* Horace Walpole says that before his death he sent for her and acknowledged her. (Corr : VI. 182.) There seems to have been an only son by this marriage, viz. William, who is mentioned among the remainder-men in the first and second Lord Bristol's wills, and who died without issue in 1791; at least so says a private Act of Parliament passed in 1807 to enable Lord Bristol to sell certain lands. The Dictionary of National Biography says that this son was aide-de-camp to General Shirley, and killed at Ticonderoga. But that son, whose death is mentioned by his father in his letter to the Duke of Newcastle, must have been a natural son.

5.—Elizabeth, wife of William Hervey, whom she married in 1729, was daughter of Thomas Ridge of Portsmouth. She died just after giving birth to her only child, Elizabeth, in 1730. Brydges edition of Collins' Peerage says that Elizabeth Hervey was living single in London in 1800.

6.—Catherine, wife of Henry Hervey, whom she married in 1730, was daughter of Sir Thomas Aston, Bart. of Aston Hall, Co. Cheshire. Sir Thomas dying in 1725 was succeeded by his son Thomas, who died abroad in Feb. 1744 s.p., when the Baronetcy reverted to a collateral line, and the estate passed under his will to his sister, Catherine. Henry Hervey, who thereupon took the name of Aston, died in 1748, and was succeeded by his son Henry Hervey Aston, who died in 1785, æt. 45. Two generations more, and then the male line came to an end; the present owner of Aston Hall, Mr. Hervey Talbot, is a descendant in the female line. (Ormerod's History of Cheshire.)

7.—Martha Maria, wife of Charles Hervey, whom she married in 1740, is called in the pedigrees the daughter of Colonel Howard of Bury St. Edmunds. According to Collins' Peerage, he was James, son of Philip, seventh son of Thomas, 1st Earl of Berkshire; and was seated at Boughton near Chester, and married Katherine Booth, and died in 1722, and was buried in the Booth family vault in St. Werbergh's, Chester. Possibly after his death his widow came to live at Bury, where a maiden sister of his, Mary Lucy, was buried in 1744. (Collins.)—There were no children by this marriage.

8.—Dorothy, wife of Felton Hervey, whom she married in 1740, was daughter of Solomon Ashley, of Westminster, and widow of Charles Pitfield,

of Hoxton. Besides daughters, there was a son, Lionel Felton
Hervey, Remembrancer of the Court of Exchequer, who shot
himself in a gunsmith's shop in the Strand on Sept. 9, 1785. By
his wife Selina Mary, daughter and co-heiress of Sir John Elwell,
Lionel had three sons, and two daughters. The eldest of these
three sons was Felton Elwell Hervey, A.D.C. to the Duke of
Wellington at Waterloo, created a Baronet, and died s.p. 1819.
The second son was Sir Frederick Ann Hervey, who succeeded his
brother in the Baronetcy, and took the name of Bathurst, and from
whom the present Sir Frederick Hervey Bathurst is descended.
The third son was Lionel Charles Hervey.

II. LORD BRISTOL'S STAFFORDSHIRE OR SHROPSHIRE ESTATE.

The following extract refers to the Staffordshire or Shropshire
estate, to which frequent allusion will be found in Lord Bristol's
Letters.

*Not far from Bromley, being in the same parish, is the Hore cross,
where is a fair gentleman's seat and a park, some time the house of
Humphry Wells, and now a nephew of his of the same surname is
owner thereof.*

*Hore cross is in the parish of Yoxall... It passed from the Wells
family to Winifred Cassey married to Robert Howard, son of Sir Robert
Howard, younger son of Thomas Howard, Earl of Suffolk. His
daughter and heiress Winifred married Peter Giffard of Chillington
Esq., and having no issue it passed to her heirs the Earl of Bristol and
Lord Griffin of Braybrook, who sold it about 1734 to Webb, who in
1748 sold it to Hon. Charles Talbot, whose son and heir Charles, Earl*

of Shrewsbury, took down the ancient house and sold the estate to Hugo Meynell Esq., whose son is the present proprietor. Erdeswick's Survey of Staffordshire, new ed. by Harwood, 1844, page 270.

PEDIGREE I, SHOWING THE DESCENT OF THOMAS HERVEY

FROM THE HERVEYS OF THURLEIGH.*

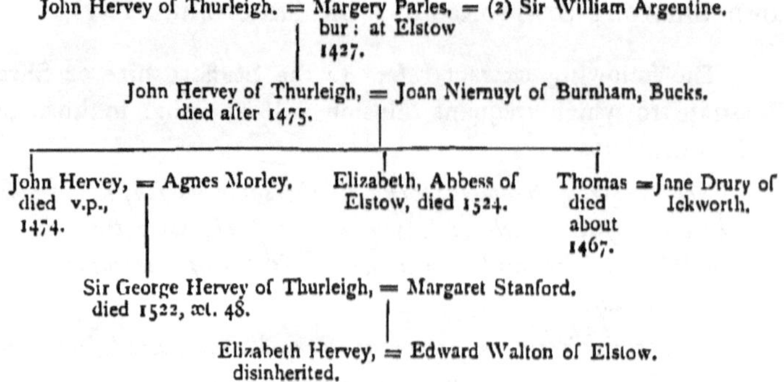

* For these pedigrees I am chiefly indebted to Lord Arthur Hervey's History of the Hervey Family, and for Hervey's Visitation of Suffolk with Mr. J. J. Howard's additions. I have not put in all the children of each marriage, but only so many as were neccessary for my purpose.

PEDIGREE II, SHOWING THE DESCENT OF JOHN LORD BRISTOL FROM THOMAS HERVEY.

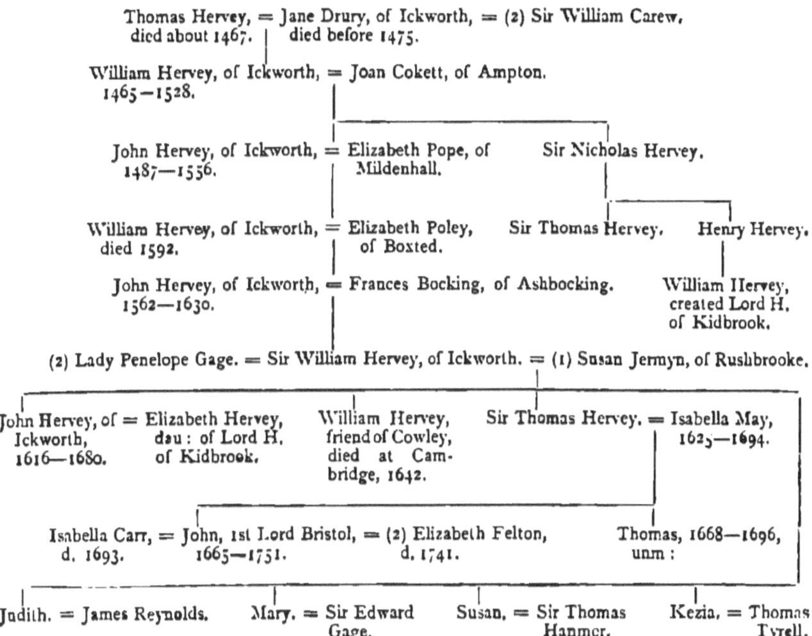

22

PEDIGREE III, SHEWING THE DESCENT OF ISABELLA CARR, FIRST WIFE OF JOHN, LORD BRISTOL.

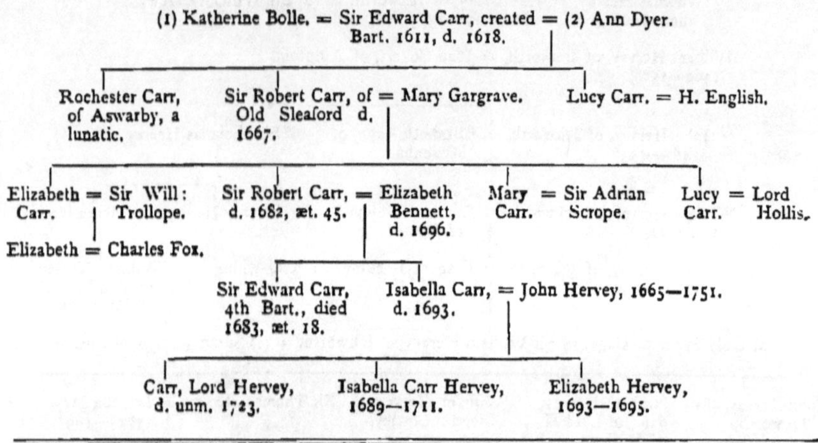

PEDIGREE IV, SHEWING THE DESCENT OF ELIZABETH FELTON, SECOND WIFE OF JOHN LORD BRISTOL.

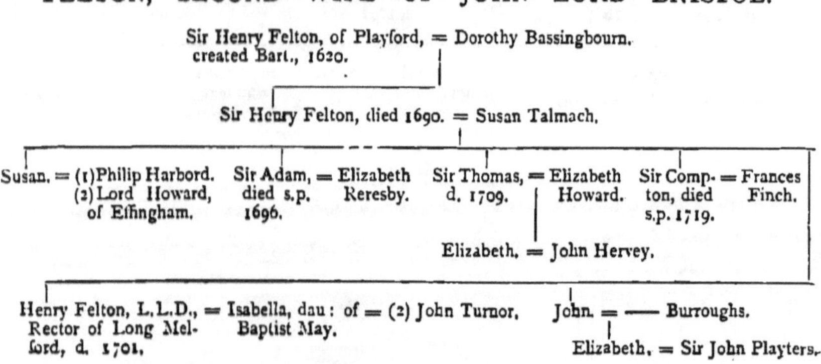

PEDIGREE V, SHOWING THE DESCENT OF LADY ELIZABETH FELTON, MOTHER OF LADY BRISTOL.

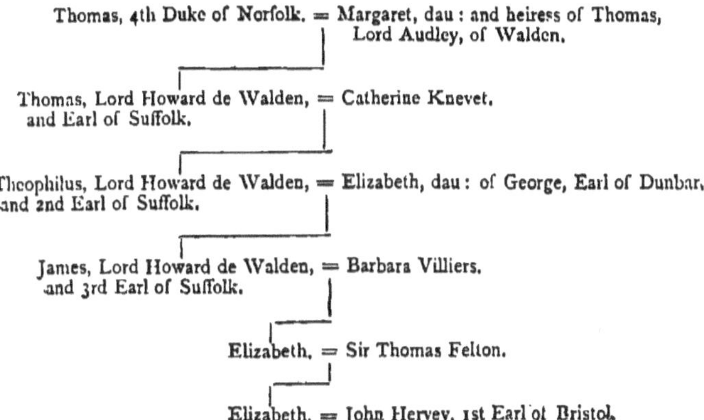

PEDIGREE VI, SHOWING THE DESCENDANTS OF JOHN, FIRST LORD BRISTOL.

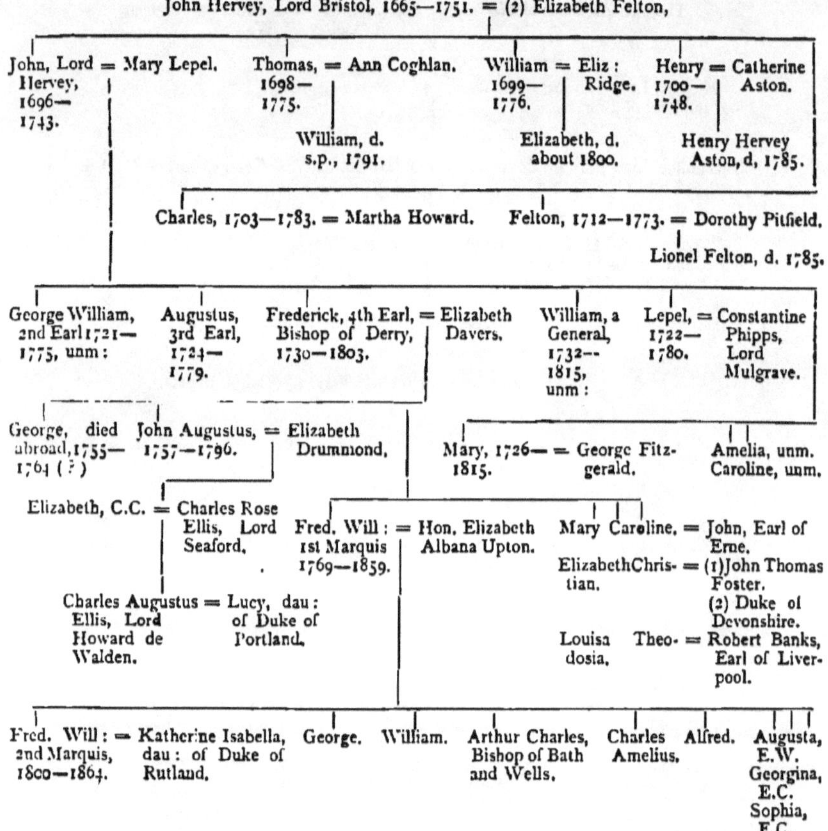

INDEX OF BIRTHS.

INDEX OF MARRIAGES.

* This entry is probably an error of Lord Bristol's. See Jan. 1735.—S.H.A.H.

INDEX OF DEATHS.

ALEXANDER Rev. Joseph, May 1719.
ALEXANDER 8, Pope, Jan. 1691.
ANN Queen, Aug. 1714.
ASHTON John, Jan. 1691.

BATTELY Samuel, July 1714.
BOND Mrs., Dec. 1698.
— Sir Henry, Aug. 1721.
BRISTOL Lady, May 1741.
BURSLEM John, June 1711.

CAROLINE Queen, Nov. 1737.
CARR Lady, Aug. 1696.
CHICKLEY Sir John, May 1691.
COELL Thomas, Oct. 1698.
CORNARO Captain General Oct. 1690.
CORNWALLIS Lord, April 1698.
COVELL William, April 1707.
CROFTS William, Jan. 1695.
CULLUM Thomas, Dec. 1700.

DE LORAIN Lady, Oct. 1720.
DENMARK Prince of, Oct. 1708.
DOVER Lord, April 1709.
DUNCOMBE Cousin Jenny, Nov. 1691.

ELWES Isabella, Oct. 1696, July 1714.
— Lady, Jan. 1698.
— Sir Gervase, April 1706.

FELTON Doctor, April 1701.
— Elizabeth, March 1724.
— Lady, June 1734.

FELTON Sir Adam, Feb. 1697.
— Sir Compton, Nov. 1719.
— Sir Thomas, March 1709.
FENWICK Sir John, Jan. 1697.
FOX Mrs., March 1704.

GAGE Sir Edward, Dec. 1707.
GEORGE I. King, June 1727.
GLOUCESTER Duke of, July 1700.
GODOLPHIN Lord, April 1712.
GRAFTON Duke of, Sept. Oct. 1690.
— Duchess of, Feb. 1723.

HAMILTON Sir David, Aug. 1721.
HANMER Lady, March 1741.
HERVEY Barbara, July 1727.
— Betty, Jan. 1695.
— Felton, July 1710.
— Henrietta, April 1712, July 1732.
— Humphry, June 1708.
— Isabella, March 1693.
— Isabella Carr, Oct. 1711.
— James, May 1713.
— James Porter, Aug. 1706.
— Lord (Carr) Nov. 1723.
— Mrs. William, July 1730.
— Thomas, Dec. 1695.
— Sir Thomas, May 1694.
  (See Bristol, Mansel.)
HOLLAND Col. Thomas, Dec. 1698.
— Sir John, Jan. 1701.
HOPES Mr., March 1704.
HOWARD of Effingham, Lady, Dec. 1726.
— Mary, May 1732.

INNOCENT XI. Pope, Aug. 1689.

INNOCENT XII. Pope, Sept. 1700.

JERMYN Thomas, Dec. 1692.

LEEDS Elward Nov. 1707.
LE PELL Mrs., Jan. 1742.
LE ROY Mr., Aug. 1698.
LORRAINE Duke of, April 1690.
LOUVOIS Mr. De, July 1691.
LUXEMBURGH Mareschall, Dec. 1694.

MANLEY Mrs. Elizabeth, May 1719.
MANSEL Lady Elizabeth, Sept. 1727.
MARLBOROUGH Duke of, June 1722.
MARY Queen, Dec. 1694.
MAY Uncle Baptist, March 1697.
— Uncle Sir Algernon, July 1704.
MEGGOTT Nephew, May 1718.

NEWCASTLE Duke of, July 1691.
NORTH Sir Henry, July 1695.
NORTON Major, Dec. 1708,

OSSULSTONE Lord, Feb. 1695.

POLEY Sir John, Sept. 1705.
— Lady, Nov. 1713.
POPE. (See Alexander, Innocent.)
PORTER Brother, April 1717
— Sister, June 1689.

PORTER Nephew Tom, Dec. 1705.
PRINCE George William, Feb. 1718.

REYNOLDS Uncle, April 1690.
RIDGE Thomas, Feb. 1730.

SCHOMBERG Duke, July 1690.
SMITH Marv, Nov. 1700.
SOLYMAN Sultan, June 1691.
SPAIN King of, Nov. 1700.
SUFFOLK Countess of, Oct. 1720.

TILLOTSON Doctor, Nov. 1694.

TRUMP Admiral, May 1691.
TURNOR La ly Isabella, April 1730.

WADKINS John, March 1690.
WEBSTER Roger, April 1701.
WILDMAN Robert, April 1721.
WILLIAM III. King, March 1702.

GENERAL INDEX.

This index does not pretend to contain everybody and everything that is mentioned in the Diary.